S0-BZO-972

CTLS, Inc.
5555 North Lamar
Suite L-115
Austin, TX 78751

## DATE DUE

|  |  |  |  |
|---|---|---|---|
|  |  |  |  |
|  |  |  |  |
|  |  |  |  |
|  |  |  |  |
|  |  |  |  |

# BLOOD PROMISE

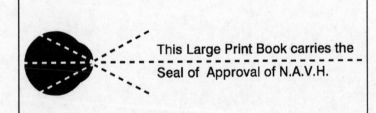

This Large Print Book carries the
Seal of Approval of N.A.V.H.

VAMPIRE ACADEMY, BOOK 4

# BLOOD PROMISE

## RICHELLE MEAD

**THORNDIKE PRESS**
*A part of Gale, Cengage Learning*

GALE
CENGAGE Learning®

Detroit • New York • San Francisco • New Haven, Conn • Waterville, Maine • London

GALE
CENGAGE Learning®

Recommended for Middle Readers.
Copyright © 2009 by Richelle Mead.
Thorndike Press, a part of Gale, Cengage Learning.

**ALL RIGHTS RESERVED**
The publisher does not have any control over and does not assume any responsibility for author or third-party websites or their content.
Thorndike Press® Large Print The Literacy Bridge.
The text of this Large Print edition is unabridged.
Other aspects of the book may vary from the original edition.
Set in 16 pt. Plantin.

**LIBRARY OF CONGRESS CATALOGING-IN-PUBLICATION DATA**

Mead, Richelle.
    Blood promise / by Richelle Mead. — Large print ed.
      p. cm. - (Thorndike press large print the literacy bridge)-
    (Vampire Academy)
    Summary: Just days before graduating from St. Vladimir's Academy, guardian-in-training Rose travels to Siberia to drive a stake into the heart of the boy she loves, the monstrous vampire Dimitri.
    ISBN 978-1-4104-4705-0 (hardcover) — ISBN 1-4104-4705-7 (hardcover)
    1. Large type books. [1. Vampires—Fiction. 2. Supernatural—Fiction. 3. High schools—Fiction. 4. Schools—Fiction. 5. Siberia (Russia)—Fiction. 6. Russia (Federation)—Fiction. 7. Large type books.] I. Title.
    PZ7.M478897Bl 2012
    [Fic]—dc23                          2011049354

Published in 2012 by arrangement with Razorbill, a division of Penguin Young Readers Group, a member of Penguin Group (USA) Inc.

Printed in the United States of America
1 2 3 4 5 6 7 16 15 14 13 12

*In memory of my grandmother,
a feisty southern lady and
the best cook I've ever known.*

# PROLOGUE

Once when I was in ninth grade, I had to write a paper on a poem. One of the lines was, "If your eyes weren't open, you wouldn't know the difference between dreaming and waking." It hadn't meant much to me at the time. After all, there'd been a guy in the class that I liked, so how could I be expected to pay attention to literary analysis? Now, three years later, I understood the poem perfectly.

Because lately, my life really did seem like it was on the precipice of being a dream. There were days I thought I'd wake up and discover that recent events in my life hadn't actually happened. Surely I must be a princess in an enchanted sleep. Any day now, this dream — no, nightmare — would end, and I'd get my prince and happy ending.

But there was no happy ending to be found, at least not in the foreseeable future.

And my prince? Well, that was a long story. My prince had been turned into a vampire — a Strigoi, to be specific. In my world, there are two kinds of vampires who exist in secrecy from humans. The Moroi are living vampires, good vampires who wield elemental magic and don't kill when seeking the blood they need to survive. Strigoi are undead vampires, immortal and twisted, who kill when they feed. Moroi are born. Strigoi are *made* — forcibly or by choice — through evil means.

And Dimitri, the guy I loved, had been made a Strigoi against his will. He'd been turned during a battle, an epic rescue mission that I'd been part of as well. Strigoi had kidnapped Moroi and dhampirs from the school I attended, and we'd set out with others to save them. Dhampirs are half-vampire and half-human — gifted with human strength and hardiness, and Moroi reflexes and senses. Dhampirs train to become guardians, the elite bodyguards who protect Moroi. That's what I am. That's what Dimitri had been.

After his conversion, the rest of the Moroi world had considered him dead. And to a certain extent, he was. Those who were turned Strigoi lost all sense of the goodness and life they'd had before. Even if they

8

hadn't turned by choice, it didn't matter. They would still become evil and cruel, just like all Strigoi. The person they'd been was gone, and honestly, it was easier to imagine them moving on to heaven or the next life than to picture them out stalking the night and taking victims. But I hadn't been able to forget Dimitri, or accept that he was essentially dead. He was the man I loved, the man with whom I'd been so perfectly in sync that it was hard to know where I ended and he began. My heart refused to let him go — even if he was technically a monster, he was still out there somewhere. I also hadn't forgotten a conversation he and I had once had. We'd both agreed that we'd rather be dead — truly dead — than walk the world as Strigoi.

And once I'd had my mourning time for the goodness he'd lost, I'd decided I had to honor his wishes. Even if he no longer believed in them. I had to find him. I had to kill him and free his soul from that dark, unnatural state. I knew it was what the Dimitri I had loved would have wanted. Killing Strigoi isn't easy, though. They're insanely fast and strong. They have no mercy. I'd killed a number of them already — pretty crazy for someone who was freshly eighteen. And I knew taking on Dimitri would be my greatest challenge, both physically and emotionally.

In fact, the emotional consequences had kicked in as soon as I made my decision. Going after Dimitri had meant doing a few life-altering things (and that wasn't even counting the fact that fighting him could very likely result in the loss of my life). I was still in school, only a handful of months away from graduating and becoming a full-fledged guardian. Every day I stuck around at St. Vladimir's Academy — a remote, protected school for Moroi and dhampirs — meant one more day was going by in which Dimitri was still out there, living in the state he'd never wanted. I loved him too much to allow that. So I'd had to leave school early and go out among humans, abandoning the world I'd lived in nearly my entire life.

Leaving had also meant abandoning one other thing — or rather, a person: my best friend, Lissa, also known as Vasilisa Dragomir. Lissa was Moroi, the last in a royal line. I'd been slated to be her guardian when we graduated, and my decision to hunt Dimitri had pretty much destroyed that future with her. I'd had no choice but to leave her.

Aside from our friendship, Lissa and I had a unique connection. Each Moroi specializes in a type of elemental magic — earth, air, water, or fire. Until recently, we'd believed there were only those four elements. Then we'd discovered a fifth: spirit.

That was Lissa's element, and with so few spirit users in the world, we hardly knew anything about it. For the most part, it seemed to be tied to psychic powers. Lissa wielded amazing compulsion — the ability to exert her will on almost anyone. She could also heal, and that's where things got a little strange between us. You see, I technically died in the car accident that killed her family. Lissa had brought me back from the world of the dead without realizing it, creating a psychic bond between us. Ever since then, I was always aware of her presence and thoughts. I could tell what she was thinking and feel when she was in trouble. We had also recently discovered I could see ghosts and spirits who hadn't yet left this world, something I found disconcerting and struggled to block out. The whole phenomenon was called being shadow-kissed.

Our shadow-kissed bond made me the ideal choice to protect Lissa, since I would instantly know if she was in trouble. I'd promised to protect her my whole life, but then Dimitri — tall, gorgeous, fierce Dimitri — had changed it all. I'd been faced with that horrible choice: continue to protect Lissa or free Dimitri's soul. Choosing between them had broken my heart, leaving an ache in my chest and tears in my eyes. My parting with Lissa had been agonizing. We'd been best friends since kindergarten, and my departure was a shock for both of us. To be fair, she'd never seen it coming. I'd kept my romance with Dimitri a secret. He was my instructor, seven years older than me, and had been assigned to be her guardian as well. As such, he and I had tried hard to fight our attraction, knowing we had to focus on Lissa more than anything else and that we'd also get in a fair amount of trouble for our student-teacher relationship.

But being kept from Dimitri — even though I'd agreed to it — had caused me to build up a lot of unspoken resentment toward Lissa. I probably should have talked to her about it and explained my frustration over having my entire life planned out. It didn't seem fair, somehow, that while Lissa was free to live and love however she wanted, I would always have to sacrifice my own happiness to ensure that she was protected. She was my best friend, though, and I couldn't bear the thought of upsetting her. Lissa was particularly vulnerable because using spirit had the nasty side effect of driving people insane. So I'd sat on my feelings until they finally exploded, and I left the Academy — and her — behind for good.

One of the ghosts I'd seen — Mason, a friend who had been killed by Strigoi — had told me Dimitri had returned to his homeland: Siberia. Mason's soul had found peace and left this world shortly thereafter, without giving me any other clues about *where* in Siberia Dimitri might have gone. So I'd had to set out there blindly, braving a world of humans and a language I didn't know in order to fulfill the promise I'd made to myself.

After a few weeks on my own, I had finally made it to Saint Petersburg. I was still looking, still floundering — but determined to find him, even though I dreaded it at the same time. Because if I really did pull this insane plan off, if I actually managed to kill the man I loved, it would mean Dimitri would truly be gone from the world. And I honestly wasn't sure I could go on in a world like that.

None of it seems real. Who knows? Maybe it isn't. Maybe it's actually happening to someone else. Maybe it's something I imagined. Maybe soon I'm going to wake up and find everything fixed with Lissa and Dimitri. We'll all be together, and he'll be there to smile and hold me and tell me everything's going to be okay. Maybe all of this really has been a dream.

But I don't think so.

# ONE

I as being followed.

It was kind of ironic, considering the way I'd been following others for the last few weeks. At least it wasn't a Strigoi. I would have already known. A recent effect of my being shadow-kissed was the ability to sense the undead — through bouts of nausea, unfortunately. Still, I appreciated my body's early warning system and was relieved my stalker tonight wasn't an insanely fast, insanely vicious vampire. I'd fought enough of those recently and kind of wanted a night off.

I had to guess my follower was a dhampir like me, probably one from the club. Admittedly, this person was moving a little less stealthily than I would have expected of a dhampir. Footsteps were clearly audible against the pavement of the dark side streets I was traveling on, and once, I'd caught a brief glimpse of a shadowy figure. Still, considering my rash actions tonight, a dhampir was the most likely culprit.

It had all started earlier at the Nightingale. That wasn't the club's true name, only a translation. Its real name was something Russian that was beyond my ability to pronounce. Back in the U.S., the Nightingale was well known among rich Moroi who traveled abroad, and now I could understand why. No matter what time of the day it was, people at the Nightingale dressed like they were at an imperial ball. And, well, the whole place actually kind of looked like something from the old, royal days of Russia, with ivory walls covered in gold scrollwork and molding. It reminded me a lot of the Winter Palace, a royal residence left over from when Russia had still been ruled by czars. I'd toured it upon first arriving in Saint Petersburg.

At the Nightingale, elaborate chandeliers filled with real candles glittered in the air, lighting up the gold décor so that even in dim lighting, the whole establishment sparkled. There was a large dining room filled with velvet-draped tables and booths, as well as a lounge and bar area where people could mingle. Late in the evening, a band would set up in there, and couples would hit the dance floor.

I hadn't bothered with the Nightingale when I arrived in the city a couple weeks ago. I'd been arrogant enough to think I could find Moroi right away who could direct me to Dimitri's hometown in Siberia. With no other clues about where Dimitri had gone in Siberia, heading to the town he'd grown up in had been my best chance of getting closer to him. Only, I didn't know where it was, which was why I was trying to find Moroi to help me. There were a number of dhampir towns and communes in Russia but hardly any in Siberia, which made me believe most local Moroi would be familiar with his birthplace. Unfortunately, it turned out that the Moroi who lived in human cities were very good at keeping themselves hidden. I checked what I thought were likely Moroi hangouts, only to come up empty. And without those Moroi, I had no answers.

So, I'd begun staking out the Nightingale, which wasn't easy. It was hard for an eighteen-year-old girl to blend into one of the city's most elite clubs. I'd soon found that expensive clothes and large enough tips went a long way toward helping me get by. The waitstaff had come to know me, and if they thought my presence was strange, they didn't say so and were happy to give me the corner table I always asked for. I think they thought I was the daughter of some tycoon or politician. Whatever my background, I had the money to be there, which was all they cared about.

Even so, my first few nights there had been discouraging. The Nightingale might have been an elite hangout for Moroi, but it was also frequented by humans. And at first, it had seemed those were the club's only patrons. Crowds grew larger as the night progressed, and in peering through the packed tables and people lingering at the bar, I'd seen no Moroi. The most notable thing I'd seen was a woman with long, platinum-blond hair walking into the lounge with a group of friends. For a moment, my heart had stopped. The woman had her back to me, but she had looked so much like Lissa that I'd felt certain I'd been tracked down. The weird thing was, I didn't know whether to feel excited or horrified. I missed Lissa so, so much — yet at the same time, I didn't want her involved in this dangerous trip of mine. Then the woman had turned around. It wasn't Lissa. She wasn't even a Moroi, just a human. Slowly, my breathing returned to normal.

Finally, a week or so ago, I'd had my first sighting. A group of Moroi women had come in for a late lunch, accompanied by two guardians, one male and one female, who sat dutifully and quietly at the table as their charges gossiped and laughed over afternoon champagne. Dodging those guardians had been the trickiest part. For those who knew what to look for, Moroi were easy to spot: taller than most humans, pale, and über-slim. They also had a certain funny way of smiling and holding their lips in order to hide their fangs. Dhampirs, with our human blood, appeared . . . well, human.

That was certainly how I looked to the untrained human eye. I was about five foot seven, and whereas Moroi tended to have unreal, runway-model bodies, mine was athletically built and curvy in the chest. Genetics from my unknown Turkish father and too much time in the sun had given me a light tan that paired well with long, nearly black hair and equally dark eyes. But those who had been raised in the Moroi world could spot me as a dhampir through close examination. I'm not sure what it was — maybe some instinct that drew us to our own kind and recognized the mix of Moroi blood.

Regardless, it was imperative that I appear human to those guardians, so I didn't raise their alarms. I sat across the room in my corner, picking over caviar and pretending to read my book. For the record, I thought caviar was disgusting, but it seemed to be everywhere in Russia, particularly in the nice places. That and borscht — a kind of beet soup. I almost never finished my food at the Nightingale and would ravenously hit McDonald's afterward, even though the Russian McDonald's restaurants were a bit different from what I'd grown up with in the U.S. Still, a girl had to eat.

So it became a test of my skill, studying the Moroi when their guardians weren't watching. Admittedly, the guardians had little to fear during the day, since there would be no Strigoi out in the sun. But it was in guardian nature to watch everything, and their eyes continually swept the room. I'd had the same training and knew their tricks, so I managed to spy without detection.

The women came back a lot, usually late in the afternoon. St. Vladimir's ran on a nocturnal schedule, but Moroi and dhampirs living out among humans either ran on a daylight schedule or something in between. For a while, I'd considered approaching them — or even their guardians. Something held me back. If anyone would know where a town of dhampirs lived, it would be *male* Moroi. Many of them visited dhampir towns in hopes of scoring easy dhampir girls. So I promised myself I'd wait another week to see if any guys came by. If not, I would see what kind of information the women could give me.

At last, a couple days ago, two Moroi guys had started showing up. They tended to come later in the evening, when the real partiers arrived. The men were about ten years older than me and strikingly handsome, wearing designer suits and silk ties. They carried themselves like powerful, important people, and I would have bet good money that they were royal — particularly since each one came with a guardian. The guardians were always the same, young men who wore suits to blend in but still carefully watched the room with that clever guardian nature.

And there were women — always women. The two Moroi were terrible flirts, continually scoping out and hitting on every woman in sight — even humans. But they never went home with any humans. That was a taboo still firmly ingrained in our world. Moroi had kept themselves separate from humans for centuries, fearing detection from a race that had grown so plentiful and powerful.

Still, that didn't mean the men went home alone. At some point in the evening, dhampir women usually showed up — different ones every night. They'd come in wearing low-cut dresses and lots of makeup, drinking heavily and laughing at everything the guys said — which probably wasn't even that funny. The women always wore their hair down, but every once in a while, they'd shift their heads in a way that showed their necks, which were heavily bruised. They were blood whores, dhampirs who let Moroi drink blood during sex. That was also a taboo — though it still happened in secret.

I kept wanting to get one of the Moroi men alone, away from the watchful eyes of his guardians so that I could question him. But it was impossible. The guardians never left their Moroi unattended. I even attempted to follow them, but each time the group left the club, they'd almost immediately hop into a limousine — making it impossible for me to track them on foot. It was frustrating.

I finally decided tonight that I'd have to approach the whole group and risk detection by the dhampirs. I didn't know if anyone from back home was actually looking for me, or if the group would even care who I was. Maybe I just had too high an opinion of myself. It was definitely possible that no one was actually concerned about a runaway dropout. But if anyone *was* looking for me, my description had undoubtedly been circulated amongst guardians worldwide. Even though I was now eighteen, I wouldn't have put it past some of the people I knew to haul me back to the U.S., and there was no way I could return until I'd found Dimitri.

Then, just as I was considering my move on the group of Moroi, one of the dhampir women left the table to walk up to the bar. The guardians watched her, of course, but seemed confident about her safety and were more fixated on the Moroi. All this time, I'd been thinking Moroi men would be the best way to go to get information about a village of dhampirs and blood whores — but what better way to locate this place than by asking an *actual* blood whore?

I strolled casually from my table and approached the bar, like I too was going to get a drink. I stood by as the woman waited for the bartender and studied her in my periphery. She was blond and wore a long dress covered in silver sequins. I couldn't decide if it made my black satin sheath dress appear tasteful or boring. All of her movements — even the way she stood — were graceful, like a dancer's. The bartender was helping others, and I knew it was now or never. I leaned toward her.

"Do you speak English?"

She jumped in surprise and looked over at me. She was older than I'd expected, her age cleverly concealed by makeup. Her blue eyes assessed me quickly, recognizing me as a dhampir. "Yes," she said warily. Even the one word carried a thick accent.

"I'm looking for a town . . . a town where lots of dhampirs live, out in Siberia. Do you know what I'm talking about? I need to find it."

Again she studied me, and I couldn't read her expression. She might as well have been a guardian for all that her face revealed. Maybe she'd trained at one time in her life.

"Don't," she said bluntly. "Let it go." She turned away, her gaze back on the bartender as he made someone a blue cocktail adorned with cherries.

I touched her arm. "I have to find it. There's a man . . ." I choked on the word. So much for my cool interrogation. Just thinking about Dimitri made my heart stick in my throat. How could I even explain it to this woman? That I was following a long-shot clue, seeking out the man I loved most in the world — a man who had been turned

24

into a Strigoi and who I now needed to kill? Even now, I could perfectly picture the warmth of his brown eyes and the way his hands used to touch me. How could I do what I had crossed an ocean to do?

*Focus, Rose. Focus.*

The dhampir woman looked back at me. "He's not worth it," she said, mistaking my meaning. No doubt she thought I was a lovesick girl, chasing some boyfriend — which, I supposed, I kind of was. "You're too young . . . it's not too late for you to avoid all that." Her face might have been impassive, but there was sadness in her voice. "Go do something else with your life. Stay away from that place."

"You know where it is!" I exclaimed, too worked up to explain that I wasn't going there to be a blood whore. "Please — you have to tell me. I have to get there!"

"Is there a problem?"

Both she and I turned and looked into the fierce face of one of the guardians. Damn. The dhampir woman might not be their top priority, but they would have noticed someone harassing her. The guardian was only a little older than me, and I gave him a sweet smile. I might not be spilling out of my dress like this other woman, but I knew my short skirt did great things for my legs. Surely even a guardian wasn't immune to that? Well, apparently he was. His hard expression showed that my charms weren't working. Still, I figured I might as well try my luck with him on getting intel.

"I'm trying to find a town in Siberia, a town where dhampirs live. Do you know it?"

He didn't blink. "No."

Wonderful. Both were playing difficult. "Yeah, well, maybe your boss does?" I asked demurely, hoping I sounded like an aspiring blood whore. If the dhampirs wouldn't talk, maybe one of the Moroi would. "Maybe he wants some company and would talk to me."

"He already has company," the guardian replied evenly. "He doesn't need any more."

I kept the smile on. "Are you sure?" I purred. "Maybe we should ask him."

"No," replied the guardian. In that one word, I heard the challenge and the command. *Back off.* He wouldn't hesitate to take on anyone he thought was a threat to his master — even a lowly dhampir girl. I considered pushing my case further but quickly decided to follow the warning and indeed back off.

I gave an unconcerned shrug. "His loss."

And with no other words, I walked casually back to my table, like the rejection was no big deal. All the while I held my breath, half-expecting the guardian to drag me out of the club by my hair. It didn't happen. Yet as I gathered my coat and set some cash on the table, I saw him watching me, eyes wary and calculating.

I left the Nightingale with that same nonchalant air, heading out toward the busy street. It was a Saturday night, and there were lots of other clubs and restaurants nearby. Partygoers filled the streets, some dressed as richly as the Nightingale's patrons; others were my age and dressed in casual wear. Lines spilled out of the clubs, dance music loud and heavy with bass. Glass-fronted restaurants showed elegant diners and richly set tables. As I walked through the crowds, surrounded by Russian conversation, I resisted the urge to look behind me. I didn't want to raise any further suspicion if that dhampir was watching.

Yet when I turned down a quiet street that was a shortcut back to my hotel, I could hear the soft sounds of footsteps. I apparently had raised enough alarm that the guardian had decided to follow me. Well, there was no way I was going to let him get the drop on me. I might have been smaller than him — and wearing a dress and heels

— but I had fought plenty of men, including Strigoi. I could handle this guy, especially if I used the element of surprise. After walking this neighborhood for so long, I knew it and its twists and turns well. I picked up my pace and darted around a few corners, one of which led me into a dark, deserted alley. Scary, yeah, but it made for a good ambush spot when I ducked into a doorway. I quietly stepped out of my high-heeled shoes. They were black with pretty leather straps but not ideal in a fight, unless I planned on gouging someone in the eye with a heel. Actually, not a bad idea. But I wasn't quite that desperate. Without them, the pavement was cold beneath my bare feet since it had rained earlier in the day.

I didn't have to wait long. A few moments later, I heard the footsteps and saw my pursuer's long shadow appear on the ground, cast in the flickering light of a street lamp on the adjacent road. My stalker came to a stop, no doubt searching for me. Really, I thought, this guy was careless. No guardian in pursuit would have been so obvious. He should have moved with more stealth and not revealed himself so easily. Maybe the guardian training here in Russia wasn't as good as what I'd grown up with. No, that couldn't be true. Not with the way Dimitri had dispatched his enemies. They'd called him a god at the Academy.

My pursuer took a few more steps, and that's when I made my move. I leapt out, fists ready. "Okay," I exclaimed. "I only wanted to ask a few questions, so just back off or else —"

I froze. The guardian from the club wasn't standing there.

A human was.

A girl, no older than me. She was about my height, with cropped dark blond hair and a navy blue trench coat that looked expensive. Underneath it, I could see nice dress pants and leather boots that looked as pricey as the coat. More startling still was that I recognized her. I'd seen her twice at the Nightingale, talking to the Moroi men. I'd assumed she was just another of the women they liked to flirt with and had promptly dismissed her. After all, what use was a human to me?

Her face was partly covered in shadow, but even in poor lighting, I could make out her annoyed expression. That wasn't quite what I'd expected. "It's you, isn't it?" she asked. Cue more shock. Her English was as American as my own. "You're the one who's been leaving the string of Strigoi bodies around the city. I saw you back in the club tonight and knew it had to be you."

"I . . ." No other words formed on my lips. I had no idea how to respond. A human talking casually about Strigoi? It was unheard of. This was almost more astonishing than actually running into a Strigoi out here. I'd never experienced anything like this in my life. She didn't seem to care about my stupefied state.

"Look, you can't just do that, okay? Do you know what a pain in the ass it is for me to deal with? This internship is bad enough without you making a mess of it. The police found the body you left in the park, you know. You *cannot* even imagine how many strings I had to pull to cover that up."

"Who . . . who are you?" I asked at last. It was true. I *had* left a body in the park, but seriously, what was I supposed to do? Drag him back to my hotel and tell the bellhop my friend had had too much to drink?

"Sydney," the girl said wearily. "My name's Sydney. I'm the Alchemist assigned here."

"The what?"

She sighed loudly, and I was pretty sure she rolled her eyes. "Of course. That explains everything."

"No, not really," I said, finally regaining my composure. "In fact, I think you're the one who has a lot of explaining to do."

"And attitude too. Are you some kind of test they sent here for me? Oh, man. That's it."

I was getting angry now. I didn't like being chastised. I certainly didn't like being chastised by a human who made it sound like me killing Strigoi was a bad thing.

"Look, I don't know who you are or how you know about any of this, but I'm not going to stand here and —"

Nausea rolled over me and I tensed, my hand immediately going for the silver stake I kept in my coat pocket. Sydney still wore that annoyed expression, but it was mingled with confusion now at the abrupt change in my posture. She was observant, I'd give her that.

"What's wrong?" she asked.

"You're going to have another body to deal with," I said, just as the Strigoi attacked her.

# TWO

Going for her instead of me was bad form on the Strigoi's part. I was the threat; he should have neutralized me first. Our positioning had put Sydney in his way, however, so he had to dispatch her before he could get to me. He grabbed her shoulder, jerking her to him. He was fast — they always were — but I was on my game tonight.

A swift kick knocked him into a neighboring building's wall and freed Sydney from his grasp. He grunted on impact and slumped to the ground, stunned and surprised. It wasn't easy to get the drop on a Strigoi, not with their lightning-fast reflexes. Abandoning Sydney, he focused his attention on me, red eyes angry and lips curled back to show his fangs. He sprang up from his fall with that preternatural speed and lunged for me. I dodged him and attempted a punch that he dodged in return. His next blow caught me on the arm, and I stumbled, just barely keeping my balance. My stake was still clutched in my right hand, but I needed an opening to hit his chest. A smart Strigoi would have angled himself in a way that ruined the line of sight to his heart. This guy was only doing a so-so job, and if I could stay alive long enough, I'd likely get an opening.

Just then, Sydney came up and hit him on the back. It wasn't a very strong blow, but it startled him. It was my opening. I sprinted as hard as I could, throwing my full weight at him. My stake pierced his heart as we slammed against the wall. It was as simple as that. The life — or undead life or whatever — faded away from him. He stopped moving. I jerked out my stake once I was certain he was dead and watched as his body crumpled to the ground.

Just like with every Strigoi I'd killed lately, I had a momentary surreal feeling. *What if this had been Dimitri?* I tried to imagine Dimitri's face on this Strigoi, tried to imagine him lying before me. My heart twisted in my chest. For a split second, the image was there. Then — gone. This was just some random Strigoi.

I promptly shook the disorientation off and reminded myself that I had important things to worry about here. I had to check on Sydney. Even with a human, my protective nature couldn't help but kick in. "Are you okay?"

She nodded, looking shaken but otherwise unharmed. "Nice work," she said. She sounded as though she were forcibly trying to sound confident. "I've never . . . I've never actually seen one of them killed. . . ."

I couldn't imagine how she would have, but then, I didn't get how she knew about any of this stuff in the first place. She looked like she was in shock, so I took her arm and started to lead her away. "Come on, let's get out to where there's more people." Strigoi lurking near the Nightingale wasn't that crazy of an idea, the more I thought about it. What better place to stalk Moroi than at one of their hangouts? Though, hopefully, most guardians would have enough sense to keep their charges out of alleys like this.

The suggestion of departure snapped Sydney out of her daze. "What?" she exclaimed. "You're just going to leave him too?"

I threw up my hands. "What do you expect me to do? I guess I can move him behind those trash cans and then let the sun incinerate him. That's what I usually do."

"Right. And what if someone shows up to

take out the trash? Or comes out of one of these back doors?"

"Well, I can hardly drag him off. Or set him on fire. A vampire barbecue would kind of attract some attention, don't you think?"

Sydney shook her head in exasperation and walked over to the body. She made a face as she looked down at the Strigoi and reached into her large leather purse. From it, she produced a small vial. With a deft motion, she sprinkled the vial's contents over the body and then quickly stepped back. Where the drops had hit his corpse, yellow smoke began to curl away. The smoke slowly moved outward, spreading horizontally rather than vertically until it cocooned the Strigoi entirely. Then it contracted and contracted until it was nothing but a fist-size ball. In a few seconds, the smoke drifted off entirely, leaving an innocuous pile of dust behind.

"You're welcome," said Sydney flatly, still giving me a disapproving look.

"What the hell was that?" I exclaimed.

"My job. Can you please call me the next time this happens?" She started to turn away.

"Wait! I can't call you — I have no idea who you are."

She glanced back at me and brushed

blond hair out of her face. "Really? You're serious, aren't you? I thought you were all taught about us when you graduated."

"Oh, well. Funny thing . . . I kind of, uh, didn't graduate."

Sydney's eyes widened. "You took down one of those . . . things . . . but never graduated?"

I shrugged, and she remained silent for several seconds.

Finally, she sighed again and said, "I guess we need to talk."

Did we ever. Meeting her had to be the strangest thing that had happened to me since coming to Russia. I wanted to know why she thought I should have been in contact with her and how she'd dissolved that Strigoi corpse. And, as we returned to the busy streets and walked toward a café she liked, it occurred to me that if she knew about the Moroi world, there might be a chance she also knew where Dimitri's village was.

Dimitri. There he was again, popping back into my mind. I had no clue if he really would be lurking near his hometown, but I had nothing else to go on at this point. Again, that weird feeling came over me. My mind blurred Dimitri's face with that of the Strigoi I'd just killed: pale skin, red-ringed eyes. . . .

*No,* I sternly told myself. *Don't focus on that yet. Don't panic.* Until I faced Dimitri the Strigoi, I would gain the most strength from remembering the Dimitri I loved, with his deep brown eyes, warm hands, fierce embrace. . . .

"Are you okay . . . um, whatever your name is?"

Sydney was staring at me strangely, and I realized we'd come to a halt in front of a restaurant. I didn't know what look I wore on my face, but it must have been enough to raise even her attention. Until now, my impression as we walked had been that she wanted to speak to me as little as possible.

"Yeah, yeah, fine," I said brusquely, putting on my guardian face. "And I'm Rose. Is this the place?"

It was. The restaurant was bright and cheery, albeit a far cry from the Nightingale's opulence. We slid into a black leather — by which I mean fake plastic leather — booth, and I was delighted to see the menu had both American and Russian food. The listings were translated into English, and I nearly drooled when I saw fried chicken. I was starving after not eating at the club, and the thought of deep-fried meat was luxurious after weeks of cabbage dishes and so-called McDonald's.

A waitress arrived, and Sydney ordered in fluent Russian, whereas I just pointed at the menu. Huh. Sydney was just full of surprises. Considering her harsh attitude, I expected her to interrogate me right away, but when the waitress left, Sydney remained quiet, simply playing with her napkin and avoiding eye contact. It was so strange. She was definitely uncomfortable around me. Even with the table between us, it was like she couldn't get far enough away. Yet her earlier outrage hadn't been faked, and she'd been adamant about me following whatever these rules of hers were.

Well, she might have been playing coy, but I had no such hesitation about busting into uncomfortable topics. In fact, it was kind of my trademark.

"So, are you ready to tell me who you are and what's going on?"

Sydney looked up. Now that we were in brighter light, I could see that her eyes were brown. I also noticed that she had an interesting tattoo on her lower left cheek. The ink looked like gold, something I'd never seen before. It was an elaborate design of flowers and leaves and was only really visible when she tilted her head certain ways so that the gold caught the light.

"I told you," she said. "I'm an Alchemist."

"And I told you, I don't know what that is. Is it some Russian word?" It didn't sound like one.

A half-smile played on her lips. "No. I take it you've never heard of alchemy either?"

I shook my head, and she propped her chin up with her hand, eyes staring down at the table again. She swallowed, like she was bracing herself, and then a rush of words came out. "Back in the Middle Ages, there were these people who were convinced that if they found the right formula or magic, they could turn lead into gold. Unsurprisingly, they couldn't. This didn't stop them from pursuing all sorts of other mystical and supernatural stuff, and eventually they did find something magical." She frowned. "Vampires."

I thought back to my Moroi history classes. The Middle Ages were when our kind really started pulling away from humans, hiding out and keeping to ourselves. That was the time when vampires truly became myth as far as the rest of the world was concerned, and even Moroi were regarded as monsters worth hunting.

Sydney verified my thoughts. "And that was when the Moroi began to stay away. They had their magic, but humans were

starting to outnumber them. We still do."
That almost brought a smile to her face.
Moroi sometimes had trouble conceiving,
whereas humans seemed to have too easy a
time. "And the Moroi made a deal with the
Alchemists. If the Alchemists would help
Moroi and dhampirs and their societies stay
secret from humans, the Moroi would give
us these." She touched the golden tattoo.

"What is that?" I asked. "I mean, aside
from the obvious."

She gently stroked it with her fingertips
and didn't bother hiding the sarcasm when
she spoke. "My guardian angel. It's actually
gold and" — she grimaced and dropped her
hand — "Moroi blood, charmed with water
and earth."

"What?" My voice came out too loud, and
some people in the restaurant turned to
look at me. Sydney continued speaking, her
tone much lower — and very bitter.

"I'm not thrilled about it, but it's our
'reward' for helping you guys. The water
and earth bind it to our skin and give us the
same traits Moroi have — well, a couple of
them. I almost never get sick. I'll live a long
life."

"I guess that sounds good," I said uncer-
tainly.

"Maybe for some. We don't have a choice.

This 'career' is a family thing — it gets passed down. We all have to learn about Moroi and dhampirs. We work connections among humans that let us cover up for you since we can move around more freely. We've got tricks and techniques to get rid of Strigoi bodies — like that potion you saw. In return, though, we want to stay apart from you as much as we can — which is why most dhampirs aren't told about us until they graduate. And Moroi hardly ever." She abruptly stopped. I guessed the lesson was over.

My head was reeling. I had never, never considered anything like this — wait. Had I? Most of my education had emphasized the physical aspects of being a guardian: watchfulness, combat, etc. Yet every so often I'd heard vague references to those out in the human world who would help hide Moroi or get them out of weird and dangerous situations. I'd never thought much about it or heard the term *Alchemist*. If I had stayed in school, maybe I would have.

This probably wasn't an idea I should have suggested, but my nature couldn't help it. "Why keep the charm to yourselves? Why not share it with the human world?"

"Because there's an extra part to its power. It stops us from speaking about your kind in a way that would endanger or expose them."

A charm that bound them from speaking . . . that sounded suspiciously like compulsion. All Moroi could use compulsion a little, and most could put some of their magic into objects to give them certain properties. Moroi magic had changed over the years, and compulsion was regarded as an immoral thing now. I was guessing this tattoo was an old, old spell that had come down through the centuries.

I replayed the rest of what Sydney had said, more questions spinning in my head. "Why . . . why do you want to stay away from us? I mean, not that I'm looking to become BFFs or anything. . . ."

"Because it's our duty to God to protect the rest of humanity from evil creatures of the night." Absentmindedly, her hand went to something at her neck. It was mostly covered by her jacket, but a parting of her collar briefly revealed a golden cross.

My initial reaction to that was unease, seeing as I wasn't very religious. In fact, I was never entirely comfortable around those who were hard-core believers. Thirty seconds later, the full impact of the rest of her words sank in.

"Wait a minute," I exclaimed indignantly.

"Are you talking about all of us — dhampirs and Moroi? We're *all* evil creatures of the night?"

Her hands dropped from the cross, and she didn't respond.

"We're not like Strigoi!" I snapped.

Her face stayed bland. "Moroi drink blood. Dhampirs are the unnatural offspring of them and humans."

No one had ever called me unnatural before, except for the time I put ketchup on a taco. But seriously, we'd been out of salsa, so what else was I supposed to do? "Moroi and dhampirs are *not* evil," I told Sydney. "Not like Strigoi."

"That's true," she conceded. "Strigoi are *more* evil."

"Hey, that's not what I —"

The food arrived just then, and the fried chicken was almost enough to distract me from the outrage of being compared to a Strigoi. Mostly all it did was delay me from responding immediately to her claims, and I bit into the golden crust and nearly melted then and there. Sydney had ordered a cheeseburger and fries and nibbled her food delicately.

After taking down an entire chicken leg, I was finally able to resume the argument. "We're not like Strigoi at all. Moroi don't

kill. You have no reason to be afraid of us."
Again, I wasn't keen on cozying up to
humans. None of my kind were, not with
the way humans tended to be trigger-happy
and ready to experiment on anything they
didn't understand.

"Any human who learns about you will
inevitably learn about Strigoi," she said. She
was playing with her fries but not actually
eating them.

"Knowing about Strigoi might enable
humans to protect themselves, though."
Why the hell was I playing devil's advocate
here?

She finished toying with a fry and dropped
it back on her plate. "Perhaps. But there are
a lot of people who would be tempted by
the thought of immortality — even at the
cost of serving Strigoi in exchange for being
turned into a creature from hell. You'd be
surprised at how a lot of humans respond
when they learn about vampires. Immortality's a big draw — despite the evil that goes
with it. A lot of humans who learn about
Strigoi will try to serve them, in the hopes
of eventually being turned."

"That's insane —" I stopped. Last year,
we'd discovered evidence of humans helping Strigoi. Strigoi couldn't touch silver
stakes, but humans could, and some had

used those stakes to shatter Moroi wards. Had those humans been promised immortality?

"And so," said Sydney, "that's why it's best if we just make sure no one knows about any of you. You're out there — all of you — and there's nothing to be done about it. You do your thing to get rid of Strigoi, and we'll do ours and save the rest of my kind."

I chewed on a chicken wing and restrained myself from the implied meaning that she was saving her kind from people like me, too. In some ways, what she was saying made sense. It wasn't possible that we could always move through the world invisibly, and yes, I could admit, it was necessary for someone to dispose of Strigoi bodies. Humans working with Moroi were an ideal choice. Such humans would be able to move around the world freely, particularly if they had the kinds of contacts and connections she kept implying.

I froze mid-chew, remembering my earlier thoughts when I'd first come along with Sydney. I forced myself to swallow and then took a long drink of water. "Here's a question. Do you have contacts all over Russia?"

"Unfortunately," she said. "When Alchemists turn eighteen, we're sent on an internship to get firsthand experience in the trade and make all sorts of connections. I would have rather stayed in Utah."

That was almost crazier than everything else she'd told me, but I didn't push it. "What kind of connections exactly?"

She shrugged. "We track the movements of a lot of Moroi and dhampirs. We also know a lot of high-ranking government officials — among humans and Moroi. If there's been a vampire sighting among humans, we can usually find someone important who can pay someone off or whatever. . . . It all gets swept under the rug."

*Track the movements of a lot of Moroi and dhampirs.* Jackpot. I leaned in close and lowered my voice. Everything seemed to hinge on this moment.

"I'm looking for a village . . . a village of dhampirs out in Siberia. I don't know its name." Dimitri had only ever mentioned its name once, and I'd forgotten. "It's kind of near . . . Om?"

"Omsk," she corrected.

I straightened up. "Do you know it?"

She didn't answer right away, but her eyes betrayed her. "Maybe."

"You do!" I exclaimed. "You have to tell me where it is. I have to get there."

She made a face. "Are you going to be . . . one of *those*?"

So Alchemists knew about blood whores. No surprise. If Sydney and her associates knew everything else about the vampire world, they'd know this too.

"No," I said haughtily. "I just have to find someone."

"Who?"

"Someone."

That almost made her smile. Her brown eyes were thoughtful as she munched on another fry. She'd only taken two bites out of her cheeseburger, and it was rapidly growing cold. I kind of wanted to eat it myself on principle.

"I'll be right back," she said abruptly. She stood up and strode across to a quiet corner of the café. Producing a cell phone from that magic purse of hers, she turned her back to the room and made a call.

I'd polished off my chicken by then and helped myself to some of her fries since it was looking less and less like she was going to do anything with them. As I ate, I pondered the possibilities before me, wondering if finding Dimitri's town would really be this simple. And once I was there . . . would it be simple then? Would he be there, living in the shadows and hunting prey? And when faced with him, could I really drive my stake into his heart? That unwanted image came to me again, Dimitri with red eyes and —

"Rose?"

I blinked. I'd totally spaced out, and Sydney was back. She slid back into her spot across from me. "So, it looks like —" She paused and looked down. "Did you eat some of my fries?"

I had no clue how she knew, seeing as it was such a huge stack. I'd barely made a dent. Figuring me stealing fries would count as further evidence of being an evil creature of the night, I said glibly, "No."

She frowned a moment, considering, and then said, "I do know where this town is. I've been there before."

I straightened up. Holy crap. This was actually going to happen, after all these weeks of searching. Sydney would tell me where this place was, and I could go and try to close this horrible chapter in my life.

"Thank you, thank you so much —"

She held up a hand to silence me, and I noticed then how miserable she looked.

"But I'm not going to tell you where it is."

My mouth gaped. "What?"

"I'm going to take you there myself."

# THREE

"Wait — what?" I exclaimed.

That wasn't in the plan. That wasn't in the plan at all. I was trying to move through Russia in as incognito a way as possible. Plus, I didn't really relish the thought of having a tagalong — particularly one who appeared to hate me. I didn't know how long it would take to get to Siberia — a couple days, I thought — and I couldn't imagine spending them listening to Sydney talk about what an unnatural, evil being I was.

Swallowing my outrage, I attempted reason. After all, I was asking a favor here. "That's not necessary," I said, forcing a smile. "It's nice of you to offer, but I don't want to inconvenience you."

"Well," she replied dryly, "there's no getting around *that*. And it's not me being nice. It's not even my choice. It's an order from my superiors."

"It still sounds like a pain in the ass for you. Why don't you just tell me where it is and blow them off?"

"You obviously don't know the people I work for."

"Don't need to. I ignore authority all the time. It's not hard once you get used to it."

"Yeah? How's that working out for you with finding this village?" she asked mockingly. "Look, if you want to get there, this is the only way."

Well — it was the only way I could get there if I used Sydney for information. I could always go back to staking out the Nightingale . . . but it had taken me this long to get a lead from there. Meanwhile, she was here right in front of me with the information I needed.

"Why?" I asked. "Why do you have to go too?"

"I can't tell you that. Bottom line: They told me to."

Lovely. I eyed her, trying to figure out what was going on here. Why on earth would anyone — let alone humans with their hands in the Moroi world — care where one teenage dhampir went? I didn't think Sydney had any ulterior motives — unless she was a very, very good actress. Yet, clearly the people she answered to had an agenda, and I didn't like playing into anyone's plan. At the same time, I was anxious to get on with this. Each day that passed was another in which I didn't find Dimitri.

"How soon can we leave?" I asked at last. Sydney, I decided, was a paper-pusher. She'd shown no real skill in tracking me earlier. Surely it wouldn't be that hard to ditch her once we were near enough to Dimitri's town.

She looked kind of disappointed at my response, almost as though she'd hoped I would decline and then she'd be off the hook. She didn't want to come with me any more than I wanted her to. Opening her purse, she took out her cell phone again, fiddled with it a couple of minutes, and finally produced some train times. She showed me the schedule for the next day.

"Does that work for you?"

I studied the screen and nodded. "I know where that station is. I can be there."

"Okay." She stood up and tossed some cash on the table. "I'll see you tomorrow." She started to walk away and then glanced back at me. "Oh, and you can have the rest of my fries."

When I first came to Russia, I stayed in youth hostels. I'd certainly had the money to stay elsewhere, but I wanted to remain under the radar. Besides, luxury hadn't really been the first thing on my mind. When I began going to the Nightingale, however, I found I could hardly return to a boarding house of backpacking students while wearing a designer dress.

So I was now staying at a posh hotel, complete with guys who always held the doors open and a marble-floored lobby. That lobby was so big that I think an entire hostel could have fit in it. Maybe two hostels. My room was large and overdone too, and I was grateful to reach it and change out of the heels and dress. I realized with only a small pang of regret that I'd have to leave the dresses I'd bought in Saint Petersburg behind. I wanted to keep my luggage light while jaunting around the country, and even if my backpack was large, there was only so much I could carry. Oh well. Those dresses would make some cleaning woman's day, no doubt. The only bit of ornamentation I really needed was my *nazar,* a pendant that looked like a blue eye. It had been a gift from my mother, which had in turn been a gift from my father. I always wore it around my neck.

Our train for Moscow left late in the morning, and we would then catch a cross-country train to Siberia. I wanted to be well rested and ready for it all. Once in my pajamas, I snuggled under the bed's heavy comforter and hoped sleep would come soon. Instead, my mind spun with all the things that had happened recently. The Sydney situation was a bizarre twist but one I could handle. As long as we stuck to public transportation, she could hardly lead me into the clutches of her mysterious superiors. And from what she'd said about our travel time, it would indeed only take a couple of days or so to reach the village. Two days seemed both impossibly long and impossibly short.

It meant I could very well be confronting Dimitri in a few days . . . and then what? Could I do it? Could I bring myself to kill him? And even if I decided I could, would I actually have the skill to overpower him? The same questions that I'd been asking myself for the last two weeks kept plaguing me over and over. Dimitri had taught me everything I knew, and with enhanced Strigoi reflexes, he would truly be the god I'd always joked he was. Death was a very real possibility for me.

But worrying wasn't helpful right now and, looking over at the clock in the room, I discovered I'd been lying awake for almost an hour. That was no good. I needed to be in peak condition. So I did something I knew I shouldn't do, but which always worked to get my mind off my worries — largely because it involved me being in someone else's mind.

Slipping inside Lissa's head required only a small amount of concentration on my part. I hadn't known if I could do it when we were far apart, but I'd discovered the process was no different than if I were standing right beside her.

It was late morning back in Montana, and Lissa had no classes today since it was Saturday. During my time away, I'd worked very hard to put up mental walls between us, almost completely blocking her and her feelings out. Now, inside her, all the barriers were down, and her emotions hit me like a tidal wave. She was pissed off. Really pissed off.

"Why does she think she can just snap her fingers and get me to go anywhere she wants, anytime she wants?" Lissa growled.

"Because she's the queen. And because you made a deal with the devil."

Lissa and her boyfriend, Christian, were lounging in the attic of the school's chapel. As soon as I recognized the surroundings, I nearly pulled out of her head. The two of them had had way too many "romantic" encounters up here, and I didn't want to stick around if clothes were going to be ripped off soon. Fortunately — or perhaps not — her annoyed feelings told me there'd be no sex today, not with her bad mood.

It was kind of ironic, actually. Their roles were reversed. Lissa was the raging one while Christian remained cool and collected, trying to appear calm for her sake. He sat on the floor, leaning up against the wall, while she sat in front of him, his legs apart and his arms holding her. She rested her head on his chest and sighed.

"For the last few weeks, I've done everything she's asked! 'Vasilisa, please show this stupid visiting royal around campus.' 'Vasilisa, please jump on a plane for the weekend so that I can introduce you to some boring officials here at Court.' 'Vasilisa, please put in some volunteer time with the younger students. It looks good.' " Despite Lissa's frustration, I couldn't help a little amusement. She had Queen Tatiana's voice down perfectly.

"You would have done that last one willingly," Christian pointed out.

"Yeah . . . the point being *willingly*. I hate her trying to dictate every part of my life lately."

Christian leaned over and kissed her cheek. "Like I said, you made a deal with the devil. You're her darling now. She wants to make sure you're making her look good."

Lissa scowled. Although Moroi lived inside human-run countries and were subject to those governments, they were also ruled by a king or queen who came from one of the twelve royal Moroi families. Queen Tatiana — an Ivashkov — was the current ruler, and she'd taken a particular interest in Lissa as the last living member of the Dragomir family. As such, Tatiana had cut Lissa a deal. If Lissa lived at Court after graduating from St. Vladimir's, the queen would arrange for her to attend Lehigh University in Pennsylvania. Lissa was a total brain and thought living in Tatiana's household would be worth it to attend a semi-big, prestigious university, as opposed to the tiny ones Moroi usually went to (for safety reasons).

As Lissa was finding out, though, the strings attached to that deal were already in place now. "And I just sit and take it," Lissa said. "I just smile and say 'Yes, your majesty. Anything you want, your majesty.' "

"Then tell her the deal's off. You'll be eighteen in a couple of months. Royal or not, you're under no obligations. You don't need her to go to a big school. We'll just take off, you and me. Go to whatever college you want. Or don't go to college at all. We can run off to Paris or something and work at a little café. Or sell bad art on the streets."

This actually made Lissa laugh, and she snuggled closer to Christian. "Right. I can totally see you having the patience to wait on people. You'd be fired your first day. Looks like the only way we'll survive is if I go to college and support us."

"There are other ways to get to college, you know."

"Yeah, but not to any that are this good," she said wistfully. "Not easily, at least. This is the only way. I just wish I could have all this and stand up to her a little. Rose would."

"Rose would have gotten herself arrested for treason the first time Tatiana asked her to do something."

Lissa smiled sadly. "Yeah. She would have." The smile turned into a sigh. "I miss her so much."

Christian kissed her again. "I know." This was a familiar conversation for them, one that never grew old because Lissa's feelings for me never faded. "She's okay, you know. Wherever she is, she's okay."

Lissa stared off into the attic's darkness. The only light came from a stained-glass window that made the whole place look like a fairyland. The space had been recently cleaned out — by Dimitri and me, actually. It had only been a couple of months ago, but already, dust and boxes were accumulating once more. The priest here was a nice guy but kind of a pack rat. Lissa noticed none of this, though. Her thoughts were too focused on me.

"I hope so. I wish I had some idea — any idea — where she is. I keep thinking that if anything happened to her, if she —" Lissa couldn't finish the thought. "Well, I keep thinking that I'd *know* somehow. That I'd feel it. I mean, I know the bond's one-way . . . that's never changed. But I'd have to know if something happened to her, right?"

"I don't know," said Christian. "Maybe. Maybe not." Any other guy would have said something overly sweet and comforting, assuring her that yes, yes, *of course* she'd know. But it was part of Christian's nature to be brutally honest. Lissa liked that about him. So did I. It didn't always make him a pleasant friend, but at least you knew he wasn't bullshitting you.

She sighed again. "Adrian says she's okay.

He visits her dreams. I'd give anything to be able to do that. My healing's getting better and better, and I've got the aura thing down. But no dreams yet."

Knowing Lissa missed me hurt almost more than if she'd completely written me off. I'd never wanted to hurt her. Even when I'd resented her for feeling like she was controlling my life, I'd never hated her. I loved her like a sister and couldn't stand the thought of her suffering now on my behalf. How had things gotten so screwed up between us?

She and Christian continued sitting there in comfortable silence, drawing strength and love from each other. They had what Dimitri and I had had, a sense of such oneness and familiarity that words often weren't needed. He ran his fingers through her hair, and while I couldn't see it so well through her own eyes, I could imagine the way that pale hair would gleam in the rainbow light of the stained-glass windows. He tucked several long locks behind her ear and then tipped her head back, bringing his lips down to hers. The kiss started off light and sweet and then slowly intensified, warmth spreading from his mouth to hers.

*Uh-oh,* I thought. It might be time to take

off after all. But she ended it before I had to.

"It's time," she said regretfully. "We've got to go."

The look in Christian's crystal-blue eyes said otherwise. "Maybe this is the perfect time for you to stand up to the queen. You should just stay here — it'd be a great way to build character."

Lissa lightly elbowed him and then planted a kiss on his forehead before standing up. "That is *not* why you want me to stay, so don't even try to play me."

They left the chapel, and Christian mumbled something about wanting to do more than play that earned him another elbow. They were heading toward the administration building, which was in the heart of the upper school's campus. Aside from the first blushes of spring, everything looked like it had when I'd left — at least on the outside. The stone buildings remained grand and imposing. The tall, ancient trees continued their watch. Yet, inside the hearts of the staff and students, things had changed. Everyone carried scars from the attack. Many of our people had been killed, and while classes were up and running again, everyone still grieved.

Lissa and Christian reached their destination: the administration building. She didn't know the reason for her summoning, only that Tatiana had wanted her to meet some royal guy who had just arrived at the Academy. Considering how many people Tatiana was always forcing her to meet lately, Lissa didn't think too much of it. She and Christian stepped inside the main office, where they found Headmistress Kirova sitting and chatting with an older Moroi and a girl about our age.

"Ah, Miss Dragomir. There you are."

I'd gotten in trouble with Kirova a lot while I'd been a student, yet seeing her now made me feel kind of nostalgic. Getting suspended for starting a fight in class seemed worlds better than traipsing through Siberia to find Dimitri. Kirova had the same birdlike appearance she'd always had, the same glasses balanced at the end of her nose. The man and girl stood up, and Kirova gestured to them.

"This is Eugene Lazar and his daughter Avery." Kirova turned back toward Lissa. "This is Vasilisa Dragomir and Christian Ozera."

A fair bit of sizing up went on then. Lazar was a royal name, but that was no surprise since Tatiana had initiated this meeting. Mr. Lazar gave Lissa a winning smile as he shook her hand. He seemed a bit surprised to meet Christian, but the smile stayed. Of course, that kind of reaction to Christian wasn't so unusual.

The two ways to become Strigoi were by choice or by force. A Strigoi could turn another person — human, Moroi, or dhampir — by drinking their blood and then feeding Strigoi blood back to them. That was what had happened to Dimitri. The other way to become Strigoi was unique to Moroi — and it was done by choice. Moroi who purposely chose to kill a person by drinking blood would also turn Strigoi. Usually, Moroi only drank small, nonlethal amounts from willing humans. But taking so much that it destroyed another's life force? Well, that turned Moroi to the dark side, taking away their elemental magic and transforming them into the twisted undead.

That was exactly what Christian's parents had done. They'd willingly killed and become Strigoi to gain eternal life. Christian had never shown any desire to become Strigoi, but everyone acted as though he were about to. (Admittedly, his snarky attitude didn't always help.) A lot of his close family — despite being royal — had been unfairly shunned as well. He and I had teamed up to kick a fair amount of Strigoi ass during the attack, though. Word of that was getting around and improving his reputation.

Kirova was never one to waste time with formalities, so she got straight to the point. "Mr. Lazar is going to be the new headmaster here."

Lissa had still been smiling at him politely, but her head immediately jerked toward Kirova. *"What?"*

"I'm going to be stepping down," explained Kirova, voice flat and emotionless enough to rival any guardian's. "Though I'll still be serving the school as a teacher."

*"You're* going to teach?" Christian asked incredulously.

She gave him a dry look. "Yes, Mr. Ozera. It was what I originally went to school for. I'm sure if I try hard enough, I can remember how to do it."

"But why?" asked Lissa. "You do a great job."

It was more or less true. Despite my disputes with Kirova — usually over me breaking rules — I still had a healthy respect for her. Lissa did too.

"It's something I've thought about returning to for some time," explained Kirova. "Now seemed as good a time as any, and Mr. Lazar is a very capable administrator."

Lissa was pretty good at reading people. I think it was part of spirit's side effects, along with how spirit made its users very, very charismatic. Lissa thought Kirova was lying, and so did I. If I'd been able to read Christian's mind, my guess would have been that he felt the same way. The attack on the Academy had sent a lot of people into a panic, royals in particular, even though the problem that had led to the attack had long since been fixed. I was guessing that Tatiana's hand was at work here, forcing Kirova to step down and have a royal take her place, thus making other royals feel better.

Lissa didn't let her thoughts show, and she turned back to Mr. Lazar. "Well, it's very nice to meet you. I'm sure you'll do a great job. Let me know if there's anything I can do for you." She was playing the proper princess role perfectly. Being polite and sweet was one of her many talents.

"Actually," said Mr. Lazar, "there is." He had a deep, booming voice, the kind that filled a room. He gestured toward his daughter. "I was wondering if you could show Avery around and help her find her way here. She graduated last year but will be assisting me in my duties. I'm sure she'd much rather be spending time with someone her own age, however."

Avery smiled, and for the first time, Lissa really paid attention to her. Avery was beautiful. Stunning. Lissa was beautiful too, between that gorgeous hair and the jade green eyes that ran in her family. I thought she was a hundred times prettier than Avery, but beside the older girl, Lissa felt kind of plain. Avery was tall and slim like most Moroi but had a few sexy curves thrown in. That kind of chest, like mine, was coveted among Moroi, and her long brown hair and blue-gray eyes completed the package.

"I promise not to be too much of a pain," said Avery. "And if you want, I'll give you some insider's tips on Court life. I hear you're going to be moving there."

Instantly, Lissa's defenses went up. She realized what was going on. Not only had Tatiana ousted Kirova, she'd sent a keeper for Lissa. A beautiful, perfect companion who could spy on Lissa and attempt to train her up to Tatiana's standards. Lissa's words were perfectly polite when she spoke, but there was a definite edge of frost in her voice.

"That'd be great," she said. "I'm pretty busy lately, but we can try to make the time."

Neither Avery's father nor Kirova seemed to notice the *back off* subtext, but something

65

flashed in Avery's eyes that told Lissa the message had come through.

"Thanks," said Avery. Unless I was mistaken, there was some legitimate hurt in her face. "I'm sure we'll figure something out."

"Good, good," said Mr. Lazar, totally oblivious to the girl drama. "Maybe you can show Avery to guest housing? She's staying in the east wing."

"Sure," said Lissa, wishing she could do anything but that.

She, Christian, and Avery started to leave, but just then, two guys entered the room. One was a Moroi, a little younger than us, and the other was a dhampir in his twenties — a guardian, from the look of his hard, serious features.

"Ah, there you are," said Mr. Lazar, beckoning the guys in. He rested his hand on the boy's shoulder. "This is my son Reed. He's a junior and will be attending classes here. He's very excited about it."

Actually, Reed looked extremely unexcited. He was pretty much the surliest guy I'd ever seen. If I ever needed to play the role of a disgruntled teen, I could have learned everything there was to know about it from Reed Lazar. He had the same good looks and features as Avery, but they were marred by a grimace that seemed permanently attached to his face. Mr. Lazar introduced the others to Reed. Reed's only response was a guttural, "Hey."

"And this is Simon, Avery's guardian," continued Mr. Lazar. "Of course, while on campus, he doesn't need to be with her all the time. You know how it goes. Still, I'm sure you'll see him around."

I hoped not. He didn't look as completely unpleasant as Reed, but he had a certain dour nature that seemed extreme even among guardians. Suddenly, I kind of felt sorry for Avery. If this was her only company, I'd want to befriend someone like Lissa pretty badly. Lissa, however, made it clear that she wouldn't be part of Tatiana's schemes. With little conversation, she and Christian escorted Avery to guest housing and promptly left. Normally, Lissa would have stayed to help Avery get settled and offered to eat with her later. Not this time. Not with ulterior motives afoot.

I came back to my own body, back in the hotel. I knew I shouldn't care about Academy life anymore and that I should even feel bad for Avery. Yet lying there and staring into the darkness, I couldn't help but take some smug — and yes, very selfish — satisfaction out of this encounter: Lissa wouldn't be shopping for a new best friend anytime soon.

# FOUR

At any other time in my life, I would have loved exploring Moscow. Sydney had planned our trip so that when our train arrived there, we'd have a few hours before we had to board the next one to Siberia. This gave us some time to wander around and grab dinner, though she wanted to make sure we were safely inside the station before it grew too dark out. Despite my badass claims or my *molnija* marks, she didn't want to take any chances.

It made no difference to me how we spent our downtime. So long as I was getting closer to Dimitri, that was all that mattered. So Sydney and I walked aimlessly, taking in the sights and saying very little. I had never been to Moscow. It was a beautiful city, thriving and full of people and commerce. I could have spent days there just shopping and trying out the restaurants. Places I'd heard about all my life — the Kremlin, Red

Square, the Bolshoi Theatre — were all at my fingertips. Despite how cool it all was, I actually tried to tune out the city's sights and sounds after a while because it reminded me of . . . well, Dimitri.

He used to talk to me about Russia all the time and had sworn up and down that I'd love it here.

"To you, it'd be like a fairy tale," he'd told me once. It was during a before-school practice late last autumn, just before the first snowfall. The air had been misty, and dew coated everything.

"Sorry, comrade," I'd replied, reaching back to tie my hair into a ponytail. Dimitri had always loved my hair down, but in combat practice? Long hair was a total liability. "Borg and out-of-date music aren't part of any happy ending I've ever imagined."

He'd given me one of his rare, easy grins then, the kind that just slightly crinkled up the corners of his eyes. "Borscht, not borg. And I've seen your appetite. If you were hungry enough, you'd eat it."

"So starvation's necessary for this fairy tale to work out?" There was nothing I loved more than teasing Dimitri. Well, aside from maybe kissing him.

"I'm talking about the land. The buildings. Go to one of the big cities — it's like nothing you've ever seen. Everyone in the U.S. tends to build the same — always in big, chunky blocks. They do what's fast and easy. But in Russia, there are buildings that are like pieces of art. They *are* art — even a lot of the ordinary, everyday buildings. And places like the Winter Palace and Troitsky Church in Saint Petersburg? Those will take your breath away."

His face had been aglow with the memory of sites he'd seen, that joy making his already handsome features divine. I think he could have named landmarks all day. My heart had burned within me, just from watching him. And then, just like I always did when I worried I might turn sappy or sentimental, I'd made a joke to shift the attention away and hide my emotions. It had switched him back into business mode, and we'd gotten to work.

Now, walking the city streets with Sydney, I wished I could take back that joke and listen to Dimitri talk more about his homeland. I would have given anything to have Dimitri with me here, the way he used to be. He'd been right about the buildings. Sure, most were blocky copies of anything you'd find in the U.S. or anywhere else in the world, but some were exquisite —

painted with bright colors, adorned with their strange yet beautiful onion-shaped domes. At times, it really did seem like something from another world. And all the while, I kept thinking that it should have been Dimitri here by my side, pointing things out and explaining them to me. We should have been having a romantic get-away. Dimitri and I could have eaten at exotic restaurants and then gone dancing at night. I could have worn one of the designer dresses I'd had to leave behind in the Saint Petersburg hotel. That's how it was supposed to be. It wasn't supposed to be me with a glowering human.

"Unreal, huh? Like something from a story."

Sydney's voice startled me, and I realized we'd come to a stop in front of our train station. There were a number of them in Moscow. Her echoing of my conversation with Dimitri sent chills down my spine — largely because she was right. The station didn't have the onion domes but still looked like something straight out of a storybook, like a cross between Cinderella's castle and a gingerbread house. It had a big arched roof and towers on either end. Its white walls were interspersed with patches of brown brick and green mosaic, almost making it look striped. In the U.S., some might have called it gaudy. To me, it was beautiful.

I felt tears start to spring to my eyes as I wondered what Dimitri would have said about this building. He probably would have loved it just as he loved everything else here. Realizing that Sydney was waiting for a response, I swallowed back my grief and played flippant teenager. "Maybe something from a story about a train station."

She arched an eyebrow, surprised at my indifference, but she didn't question it. Who could say? Maybe if I kept up the sarcasm, she'd eventually get annoyed and ditch me. Somehow, I doubted I'd be that lucky. I was pretty sure her fear of her superiors trumped any other feelings she might have in regard to me.

We had first-class train accommodations, which turned out to be a lot smaller than I expected. There was a combination bed/sitting bench on each side, a window, and a TV high on the wall. I supposed that would help pass the time, but I often had trouble following Russian television — not just because of the language but also because some of the shows were downright bizarre. Still, Sydney and I would each have our own space, even if the room was cozier than we would have liked.

The colors reminded me a lot of the same fanciful patterns I'd seen throughout the cities. Even the hall outside our cabin was brightly colored, with plush carpet in red and yellow designs and a teal and yellow runner going down the middle. Inside our room, the benches were covered in cushions with rich orange velvet, and the curtains matched in shades of gold and peach, made of thick heavy fabric embossed with a silky pattern. Between all that and the ornate table in the middle of the cabin, it was almost like traveling in a mini-palace.

It was dark out by the time the train left the station. For whatever reason, the Trans-Siberian always left Moscow at night. It wasn't that late yet, but Sydney said she wanted to sleep, and I didn't want to make her more irate than she already was. So we turned off all the lights, save for a tiny reading lamp by my bed. I'd bought a magazine at the train station, and even if I couldn't understand the language, the pictures of makeup and clothes transcended all cultural barriers. I flipped through the pages as quietly as I could, admiring summer tops and dresses and wondering when — if ever — I'd be able to start worrying about that kind of thing again.

I wasn't tired when I lay down, but sleep

took me nonetheless. I was dreaming about water-skiing when suddenly, the waves and sun around me dissolved into a room lined with shelves and shelves of books. Tables with state-of-the-art computers lined the rooms, and there was a calmness that permeated the place. I was in the library at St. Vladimir's Academy.

I groaned. "Oh, come *on*. Not today."

"Why not today? Why not every day?"

I turned and found myself looking into the handsome face of Adrian Ivashkov. Adrian was a Moroi, the queen's great-nephew, and someone I'd left behind in my old life when I took off on this suicide mission. He had beautiful emerald-green eyes that made most girls swoon, particularly since they were paired with stylishly messy brown hair. He was also kind of in love with me and the reason I had so much money on this trip. I'd sweet-talked him out of it.

"True," I admitted. "I suppose I should be grateful you only show up about once a week."

He grinned and sat down backward in one of the slatted wooden chairs. He was tall, like most Moroi, with a leanly muscled build. Moroi guys never got too bulky. "Absence makes the heart grow fonder, Rose. Don't want you to take me for granted."

"We're in no danger of that; don't worry."

"I don't suppose you're going to tell me where you are?"

"Nope."

Aside from Lissa, Adrian was the only other known living spirit user, and among his talents was the ability to show up in my dreams — often uninvited — and talk to me. I took it as a blessing that his powers never actually let him know where I was.

"You kill me, Rose," he said melodramatically. "Every day is agony without you. Empty. Alone. I pine for you, wondering if you're even still alive."

He spoke in an exaggerated, silly sort of way that was characteristic of him. Adrian rarely took things seriously and always had a flippant edge. Spirit also had a tendency to make people unstable, and while he fought it, he wasn't unaffected. Underneath that melodrama, though, I sensed a kernel of truth. No matter how shallow an appearance he gave off, he really did care about me.

I crossed my arms. "Well, I'm still alive, clearly. So I guess you can let me go back to sleep."

"How many times have I told you? You *are* asleep."

"And yet I inexplicably feel exhausted talking to you."

This made him laugh. "Oh, I do so miss you." That smile faded. "She misses you too."

I stiffened. *She.* He didn't even need to say her name. There was no question as to whom he was talking about.

*Lissa.*

Even saying her name in my mind caused me pain, particularly after seeing her last night. Choosing between Lissa and Dimitri had been the hardest decision of my life, and time passing hadn't made it any easier. I might have chosen him, but being away from her was like having an arm cut off, particularly because the bond ensured we were never truly apart.

Adrian gave me a canny look, like he could guess my thoughts. "Do you go see her?"

"No," I said, refusing to acknowledge that I'd just seen her last night. Let him think I was truly free of all that. "That's not my life anymore."

"Right. Your life is all about dangerous vigilante missions."

"You wouldn't understand anything that isn't drinking, smoking, or womanizing."

He shook his head. "You're the only one I want, Rose."

Unfortunately, I believed him. It would have been easier for both of us if he could find someone else. "Well, you can keep feeling that way, but you're going to have to keep waiting."

"Much longer?"

He asked me this all the time, and every time, I emphasized how long it would be and how he was wasting his time. Thinking of Sydney's possible lead, I hesitated tonight. "I don't know."

Hope blossomed on Adrian's face. "That's the most optimistic thing you've told me so far."

"Don't read too much into it. 'I don't know' could be one day or one year. Or never."

His mischievous grin returned, and even I had to admit it was cute. "I'm going to hope it's one day."

Thinking of Sydney brought a question to my mind. "Hey, have you ever heard of the Alchemists?"

"Sure," he said.

Typical. "Of course you have."

"Why? Did you run into them?"

"Kind of."

"What'd you do?"

"Why do you think I did anything?"

He laughed. "Alchemists only show up

when trouble happens, and you bring trouble wherever you go. Be careful, though. They're religious nuts."

"That's kind of extreme," I said. Sydney's faith didn't seem to be anything bad.

"Just don't let them convert you." He winked. "I like you being the sinner you are."

I started to tell him that Sydney probably thought I was beyond all salvation, but he ended the dream, sending me back to sleep.

Except, instead of returning to my own dreams, I woke up. Around me, the train hummed comfortingly as we sped through the Russian countryside. My reading lamp was still on, its light too bright for my sleepy eyes. I reached over to turn it off and noticed then that Sydney's bed was empty. *Probably in the bathroom,* I thought. Yet, I felt uneasy. She and her group of Alchemists were still mysteries, and I suddenly worried that she might have some sinister plan going on. Was she off meeting with some covert operative? I decided to find her.

Admittedly, I had no idea where she could be on a train of this size, but logic had never really deterred me before. No reason they should now. Thankfully, after slipping on my shoes and stepping out in the hall adjacent to our cabin, I discovered I didn't have to look very far.

The corridor was lined with windows, all draped in those rich curtains, and Sydney stood with her back to me, gazing outside, a blanket wrapped around her. Her hair was messy from sleep and looked less gold in the poor lighting.

"Hey . . ." I began hesitantly. "Are you okay?"

She turned slightly toward me. One hand held the blanket; the other played with the cross around her neck. I remembered Adrian's comments about religion.

"I can't sleep," she said bluntly.

"Is it . . . is it because of me?"

Her only answer was to turn back to the window.

"Look," I said, feeling helpless. "If there's anything I can do . . . I mean, aside from going back and canceling this trip . . ."

"I'll handle it," she said. "This is just, well, it's really strange for me. I deal with you guys all the time, but I don't actually *deal* with you, you know?"

"We could probably get you a room of your own, if that would help. We can find an attendant, and I've got the money."

She shook her head. "It's just a couple of days, if that."

I didn't know what else to say. Having

Sydney along was inconvenient in the grand scheme of my plans, but I didn't want her to suffer. Watching her play with the cross, I tried to think of something comforting to tell her. Bonding over our views of God might have been a way to get closer, but somehow, I didn't think telling her how I had daily battles with God and doubted His existence lately would really help me out with the whole evil-creature-of-the-night reputation.

"Okay," I said at last. "Let me know if you change your mind."

I returned to my bed and fell asleep surprisingly fast, despite worrying that Sydney would be standing in the hall all night. Yet, when I woke in the morning, she was curled up on her bed, fast asleep. Apparently, her exhaustion had been so strong that even fear of me had driven her to rest. I got up quietly and changed out of the T-shirt and sweatpants I'd gone to bed in. I was hungry for breakfast and figured Sydney might sleep longer if I wasn't around.

The restaurant was in the next car over and looked like something out of an old movie. Elegant burgundy linens draped the tables, and brass and dark wood, along with bits of bright-colored stained glass art, gave the whole place an antique feel. It looked more like a restaurant I'd find on the streets of Saint Petersburg than a train dining car. I ordered something that reminded me vaguely of french toast, except that it had cheese on it. It came with sausage, which thus far seemed to be the same everywhere I went.

I was just about finished when Sydney wandered in. When I'd met her that first night, I'd assumed her dress pants and blouse had been for the sake of the Nightingale. I was discovering, however, that that was her normal style. She struck me as one of those people who didn't own jeans or T-shirts. She'd been mussed while standing in the hall last night, but now she was in neat black slacks and a dark green sweater. I was in jeans and a long-sleeved gray thermal shirt and felt kind of sloppy beside her. Her hair was brushed and styled but had a slightly messy look that I suspected never went away, no matter how hard she tried. At least I had my sleek ponytail going for me today.

She slid across from me and ordered an omelet when the server came by, again speaking in Russian.

"How do you know that?" I asked.

"What, Russian?" She shrugged. "I had to learn it growing up. And a few other languages."

"Wow." I had taken intros to a couple of languages too and performed miserably in all of them. I hadn't thought much of it at the time, but now, because of this trip and because of Dimitri, I really wished I'd learned Russian. I supposed it wasn't too late, and I had picked up a few phrases in my time here, but still . . . it was a daunting task.

"You must have to learn a lot of stuff for this job," I mused, pondering what it must mean to be part of a secret group that crossed international lines and interacted with all sorts of governments. Something else crossed my mind. "And what about that stuff you used on the Strigoi? That disintegrated the body?"

She smiled. Almost. "Well, I told you the Alchemists started off as a group of people trying to make potions, right? That's a chemical we developed to get rid of Strigoi bodies fast."

"Could you use it to actually kill one?" I asked. Dousing a Strigoi in some dissolving liquid would be a lot easier than the usual ways: decapitation, staking, or burning.

"Afraid not. Only works on corpses."

"Bummer," I said. I wondered if she had other potions up her sleeve but figured I should ration my amount of Sydney questions for the day. "What are we going to do when we get to Omsh?"

"Omsk," she corrected. "We'll get a car and drive the rest of the way."

"Have you been there? To this village?"

She nodded. "Once."

"What's it like?" I asked, surprised to hear a wistful note in my own voice. Aside from my quest to find Dimitri, there was a piece of me that just wanted to cling to everything I could of him. I wanted to know everything about him that I hadn't known before. If the school had given me his possessions, I would have slept with them each night. His room had been cleared out pretty quickly, though. Now I could only gather what pieces of him I could, as though hoarding these bits of information would keep him with me somehow.

"It's like any other dhampir town, I guess."

"I've never been to one."

The server set Sydney's omelet down, and she paused with her fork in the air. "Really? I thought all of you . . . well, I don't know."

I shook my head. "I've been at the Academy my whole life. More or less." My two-year stint among humans wasn't really relevant.

Sydney chewed thoughtfully. I was willing

84

to wager she wouldn't finish the omelet. From what I'd seen that first night and while waiting for trains yesterday, she hardly seemed to eat anything. It was like she subsisted on air alone. Maybe it was another Alchemist thing. Most likely it was just a Sydney thing.

"The town is half-human and half-dhampir, but the dhampirs blend in. They have a whole underground society that the humans are completely oblivious to."

I'd always figured there was a whole subculture going on, but I'd had no idea how it would fit into the rest of the town. "And?" I asked. "What's that subculture like?"

She set her fork down. "Let's just say you'd better brace yourself."

# FIVE

The rest of the trip passed uneventfully. Sydney never entirely lost that discomfort she seemed to have around me, but sometimes, while I was trying to figure out Russian television, she'd take the time to explain what was going on. There were some cultural differences between these shows and the ones we'd both grown up with, so we had that in common. Every once in a while, she'd crack a smile over something we both found funny, and I'd sense there was someone in there I could possibly be friends with. I knew there was no way I'd ever find a replacement for Lissa, but I think some part of me still longed to fill the void of friendship that had been opened up when I left her behind.

Sydney napped throughout the day, and I began to think she was just an insomniac with bizarre sleep patterns. She also continued her equally odd treatment of food, hardly touching her meals. She always let me have the leftovers and was a bit more adventurous with Russian cuisine. I'd had to experiment when I first arrived, and it was nice to have the guidance of someone who, though not a local, knew a lot more about this country than me.

On the third day of our trip, we arrived in Omsk. Omsk was a larger and prettier city than I'd expected of Siberia. Dimitri had always teased me that my images of Siberia looking like Antarctica were wrong, and I could tell that he was right — at least as far as the southern part of the region was concerned. The weather wasn't much different from what I'd have found in Montana this time of year, cool spring air occasionally warmed by sunshine.

Sydney had told me when we got there, she'd get us a ride from some Moroi she knew. Several lived in the city, blending in with the large population. Yet as the day went on, we discovered a problem. No Moroi would take us to the village. Apparently, the road was dangerous. Strigoi often hung out near it at night, hoping to catch traveling Moroi or dhampirs. The more Sydney explained it, the more worried I became about my plan. Apparently, there weren't many Strigoi *in* Dimitri's town itself. According to her, they lurked on the town's periphery, but few lived out there permanently. If that was the case, my odds of finding Dimitri had dropped. Things got even worse as Sydney continued describing the situation.

"A lot of Strigoi travel the country looking for victims, and the village is just an area they pass through," she explained. "The road is kind of remote, so some Strigoi will stay for a while and try to get easy prey. Then they move on."

"In the U.S., Strigoi often hide in large cities," I said uneasily.

"They do that here too. It's easier for them to take victims without being noticed."

Yes, this definitely threw a wrench into my plans. If Dimitri wasn't residing in this town, I was going to have some serious problems. I'd known Strigoi liked big cities, but somehow, I'd convinced myself Dimitri would return to the place where he grew up.

But if Dimitri wasn't there . . . well, suddenly, the enormity of Siberia hit me. I'd learned Omsk wasn't even the biggest city in the region, and finding even one Strigoi here could be hard. Looking for him in any number of cities that might be larger? Things could get very, very ugly if my hunch proved wrong.

Since setting out to find Dimitri, I'd occasionally had weak moments in which I half-hoped I'd never find him. The idea of him as a Strigoi still tormented me. I was also visited by other images . . . images of the way he'd been and memories of the time we'd spent together.

I think my most precious memory was of just before he was turned. It was one of those times when I'd sucked up a lot of the spirit-induced darkness from Lissa. I'd been out of control, unable to get a grip. I was afraid of becoming a monster, afraid of killing myself like another shadow-kissed guardian had.

Dimitri had brought me back to myself, lending me his strength. I'd realized then just how strong our connection was, how perfectly we understood each other. I'd been skeptical about people being soul mates in the past, but at that moment, I knew it was true. And with that emotional connection had come a physical one. Dimitri and I had finally given in to the attraction. We'd sworn we never would, but . . . well, our feelings were just too strong. Staying away from each other had turned out to be impossible. We'd had sex, and it had been my first time ever. Sometimes I felt certain it would be my only time.

The act itself had been amazing, and I'd been unable to separate the physical joy from the emotional. Afterward, we'd lain together in that small cabin for as long as we dared, and that had been amazing too. It had been one of the few moments where I'd felt he was truly mine.

"Do you remember Victor's lust charm?" I had asked, snuggling closer against him.

Dimitri looked at me like I was crazy. "Of course."

Victor Dashkov was a royal Moroi, one who had been friends with Lissa and her family. Little did we know that he'd secretly studied spirit for years and had identified Lissa as a spirit user before she even knew. He'd tortured her with all sorts of mind games that truly made her think she was going crazy. His schemes had fully culminated in his kidnapping and torturing her until she healed the disease that was killing him.

Victor was now in prison for life, both for what he'd done to Lissa and because of his treasonous plans for rebellion against the Moroi government. He had been one of the few to know about my relationship with Dimitri, something that had worried me to no end. He'd even furthered our relationship by creating a lust charm — a necklace infused with earth and compulsion. The charm was full of dangerous magic that had made Dimitri and me give into our most basic instincts. We had pulled back at the last moment, and until our night in the cabin, I had believed our charm-induced encounter to be the ultimate physical high.

"I didn't realize it could get better," I had told Dimitri after we'd actually slept together. I felt a little shy talking about it. "I thought about it all the time . . . what happened between us."

He turned to me, tugging the covers up. The cabin was cold, but its bed had warm blankets. I suppose we could have put clothes on, but that was the last thing I wanted to do. Being pressed skin-to-skin felt too good.

"I did too."

"You did?" I asked, surprised. "I thought . . . I don't know. I thought you were too disciplined for that. I thought you'd try to forget it."

Dimitri laughed and kissed my neck. "Rose, how could I forget being naked with someone as beautiful as you? I stayed awake so many nights, replaying every detail. I told myself over and over that it was wrong, but you're impossible to forget." His lips moved to my collarbone, and his hand stroked my hip. "You're burned into my mind forever. There is nothing, nothing in this world that will ever change that."

And it was memories like that that made it so hard to comprehend this quest to kill him, even if he was a Strigoi. Yet . . . at the same time, it was exactly because of memories like that that I had to destroy him. I needed to remember him as the man who'd loved me and held me in bed. I needed to remember that that man would not want to stay a monster.

I wasn't very excited when Sydney showed me the car she'd bought, particularly since I'd given her the money for it.

"We're going in that?" I exclaimed. "Can it even make it that far?" The trip was apparently seven hours.

She gave me a shocked look. "Are you serious? Do you know what this is? It's a 1972 Citroën. These things are amazing. Do you have any idea how hard it would have been to get this into the country back in the Soviet days? I can't believe that guy actually sold it. He's clueless."

I knew little about the Soviet era and even less about classic cars, but Sydney stroked the shiny red hood like she was in love. Who would have guessed? She was a car geek. Maybe it was valuable, and I just couldn't appreciate it. I was more into sleek, brand-new sports cars. To be fair, this car didn't have any dents or rust, and aside from an outdated look, it appeared clean and well cared for.

"Will it run?" I asked.

If possible, her expression grew even more incredulous. "Of course!"

And it did. The engine sprang to life with a steady hum, and with the way it accelerated, I started to understand her fascination. She wanted to drive, and I was about to argue that it had been my money that bought it. Seeing the adoring look on her face, though, I finally decided not to come between her and the car.

I was just glad we were leaving right away. It was already late afternoon. If the road was as dangerous as everyone claimed, we wouldn't want to be out there while it was dark. Sydney agreed but said we could get most of the trip in before sundown and then stay overnight at a place she knew. We'd arrive at our destination in the morning.

The farther we drove from Omsk, the more remote the terrain became. As I studied it, I began to understand Dimitri's love of this land. It had a scrubby, barren look, true, but spring was turning the plains green, and there was something hauntingly beautiful about seeing all this untouched wilderness. It reminded me of Montana in some ways yet had a certain quality that was all its own.

I couldn't help but use Sydney's crush on the car as a means of conversation. "Do you know a lot about cars?" I asked.

"Some," she said. "My dad's the Alchemist in our family, but my mom's a mechanic."

"Really?" I asked, surprised. "That's kind of . . . unusual." Of course, I was hardly one to talk about gender roles. Considering my life was dedicated to fighting and killing, I couldn't really claim to have a traditionally feminine job either.

"She's really good and taught me a lot. I wouldn't have minded doing that for a living. Wouldn't have minded going to college, either." There was a bitter note in her voice. "I guess there are a lot of other things I wish I could do."

"Why can't you?"

"I had to be the next family Alchemist. My sister . . . well, she's older, and usually it's the oldest kid who has to do the job. But, she's kind of . . . worthless."

"That's harsh."

"Yeah, maybe. But she just couldn't handle this kind of thing. When it comes to organizing her lip gloss collection, she's unstoppable. But managing the kinds of networks and people we do? No, she'd never be able to do it. Dad said I was the only one capable of it."

"That's a compliment, at least."

"I guess."

Sydney looked so sad now that I felt bad for bringing it up. "If you could go to college, what would you study?"

"Greek and Roman architecture."

I decided then it was a good thing I wasn't behind the wheel, because I probably would have driven off the road. "Seriously?"

"You know anything about it?"

"Um, no."

"It's amazing." The sad expression was replaced by one of wonder — she looked nearly as enamored as she'd been of the car. I understood then why she'd liked the train station. "The ingenuity it took for some of that . . . well, it's just unreal. If the Alchemists won't send me back to the U.S. after this, I'm hoping I'll get assigned to Greece or Italy."

"That would be cool."

"Yeah." Her smile faded. "But there are no guarantees you'll get what you want with this job."

She fell silent after that, and I decided that coaxing her into this small conversation had been victory enough. I left her to her own thoughts of classic cars and architecture while my mind wandered to topics of my own. Strigoi. Duty. Dimitri. Always Dimitri . . .

Well, Dimitri and Lissa. It was always a toss-up over who would cause me more pain. Today, as the car lulled me into a daze, it was Lissa I went to, thanks largely to Adrian's recent visit in my dream.

Early evening in Russia meant early morning in Montana. Of course, since the school ran on a nocturnal schedule, it was technically night for them too in spite of the sunshine. It was nearly curfew, and everyone would have to return to their own dorms soon.

Lissa was with Adrian, over in his room in guest housing. Adrian, like Avery, had graduated, but as the only other known spirit user, he'd come to stay indefinitely at the school and work with Lissa. They'd just spent a long, exhausting evening working on dream walking and sat on the floor facing each other. With a sigh, Lissa collapsed back and lay down, stretching her arms over her head.

"This is useless," she groaned. "I'm never going to learn it."

"Never took you for a quitter, cousin." Adrian's voice was as flippant as usual, but I could tell he was weary too. They weren't really cousins; that was just a term royals sometimes used with each other.

"I just don't understand how you do it."

"I don't know how to explain it. I just think about it, and . . . well, it happens." He shrugged and pulled out the cigarettes he always carried. "Do you mind?"

"Yes," she said. To my surprise, he put them away. What the hell? He'd never asked me if I minded if he smoked — which I did. In fact, half the time, I swore he did it to annoy me, which made no sense. Adrian was way past the age when guys tried to attract girls they liked by picking on them.

He tried to explain the process. "I just think about who I want and sort of . . . I don't know. Expand my mind toward them."

Lissa sat up and crossed her legs. "Sounds a lot like how Rose described reading me."

"Probably the same principle. Look, it took you a while to learn auras. This is no different. And you're not the only one with a learning curve. I'm only now finally moving past healing scratches, and you can bring back the dead, which — call me crazy

97

— is kind of hard-core." He paused. "Of course, some would argue that I *am* actually crazy."

At the mention of auras, she studied him and summoned the ability to see the field of light that shone around every living thing. His aura came into focus, surrounding him in a golden glow. According to Adrian, her aura was the same. No other Moroi had that kind of pure gold. Lissa and Adrian figured it was unique to spirit users.

He smiled, guessing what she was doing. "How's it look?"

"The same."

"See how good you are at it now? Just be patient with the dreams."

Lissa wanted so badly to walk dreams the same way he could. Despite her disappointment, I was glad she couldn't. Adrian's dream visits were hard enough on me. Seeing her would . . . well, I wasn't entirely sure, but it would make this cool, hard attitude I was trying to maintain in Russia a lot harder.

"I just want to know how she is," said Lissa in a small voice. "I can't stand not knowing." It was the conversation with Christian all over again.

"I saw her the other day. She's fine. And I'll go again soon."

Lissa nodded. "Do you think she'll do it? Do you think she can kill Dimitri?"

Adrian took a long time in answering. "I think she can. The question will be if it kills her in the process."

Lissa flinched, and I was a bit surprised. The answer was as blunt as one Christian might give. "God, I wish she hadn't decided to go after him."

"Wishing's useless now. Rose has got to do this. It's the only way we can get her back." He paused. "It's the only way she'll be able to move on."

Adrian surprised me sometimes, but this took the prize. Lissa thought it was foolish and suicidal to go after Dimitri. I knew Sydney would agree if I told her the truth about this trip. But Adrian . . . silly, shallow, party-boy Adrian understood? Studying him through Lissa's eyes, I realized he actually did. He didn't like it, and I could hear the hurt in his words. He cared about me. My having such strong feelings for someone else caused him pain. And yet . . . he truly believed that I was doing the right thing — the only thing I *could* do.

Lissa looked at the clock. "I've got to go before curfew. I should probably study for my history test, too."

Adrian grinned. "Studying's overrated.

Just find someone smart to copy off."

She stood up. "Are you saying I'm not smart?"

"Hell no." He rose also and went to pour himself a drink from the fully stocked bar he kept on hand. Self-medicating was his irresponsible way of keeping spirit's effects at bay, and if he'd been using spirit all night, he would want the numbness of his vices. "You're the smartest person I know. But that doesn't mean you have to do unnecessary work."

"You can't succeed in life if you don't work. Copying from others won't get you anywhere."

"Whatever," he said with a grin. "I copied all through school, and look how well I'm doing today."

With an eye roll, Lissa gave him a quick hug goodbye and left. Once out of his sight, her smile faded a bit. In fact, her thoughts took a decidedly dark turn. Mentioning me had stirred up all sorts of feelings within. She was worried about me — desperately worried. She'd told Christian that she felt bad about what had happened between us, but the full force of that didn't hit me until now. She was racked by guilt and confusion, continually berating herself for what she should have done. And above all, she missed me. She had that same feeling I did — like a part of her had been cut out.

Adrian lived on the fourth floor, and Lissa opted for the stairs rather than the elevator. All the while, her mind spun with worry. Worries about whether she'd ever master spirit. Worry for me. Worry that she wasn't currently feeling spirit's dark side effects, which made her wonder if I was absorbing them, just as a guardian named Anna had. She'd lived centuries ago and was bonded to St. Vladimir, the school's namesake. She'd absorbed spirit's nasty effects from him — and had been driven insane.

On the second floor, Lissa could make out the sounds of shouting, even through the door that separated the stairwell from the hallway. Despite knowing it had nothing to do with her, she hesitated, curiosity getting the best of her. A moment later, she quietly pushed the door open and stepped into the hall. The voices were coming from around the corner. She carefully peered around it — not that she needed to. She recognized the voices.

Avery Lazar stood in the hallway, hands on her hips as she stared at her father. He stood in the doorway to what must have been his suite. Their stances were rigid and hostile, and anger crackled between them.

"I'll do what I want," she yelled. "I'm not your slave."

"You're my daughter," he said in a voice both calm and condescending. "Though at times I wish you weren't."

*Ouch.* Both Lissa and I were shocked.

"Then why are you making me stay in this hellhole? Let me go back to Court!"

"And embarrass me further? We barely got out without damaging this family's reputation — much. No way am I going to send you there alone and let you do God knows what."

"Then send me to Mom! Switzerland's got to be better than this place."

There was a pause. "Your mother is . . . busy."

"Oh, nice," said Avery, voice heavy with sarcasm. "That's a polite way of saying she doesn't want me. No surprise. I'd just interfere with her and that guy she's sleeping with."

"Avery!" His voice rang out loud and angry. Lissa flinched and stepped back. "This conversation is done. Get back to your room and sober up before someone sees you. I expect you at breakfast tomorrow, and I expect you to be respectable. We have some important visitors."

"Yeah, and God knows we've got to keep

up appearances."

"Go to your room," he repeated. "Before I call Simon and make him drag you there."

"Yes, sir," she simpered. "Right away, sir. Anything you say, sir."

And with that, he slammed the door. Lissa, ducking back behind the corner, could hardly believe he'd said those things to his own daughter. For a few moments, there was silence. Then, Lissa heard the sound of footsteps — coming toward her. Avery suddenly rounded the corner and stopped in front of Lissa, giving us our first good look of her.

Avery was wearing a tight, short dress made of some kind of blue fabric that shone silvery in the light. Her hair hung long and wild, and the tears pouring from her blue-gray eyes had destroyed the heavy makeup she wore. The scent of alcohol came through loud and clear. She hastily ran a hand over her eyes, obviously embarrassed at being seen like this.

"Well," she said flatly. "I guess you overheard our family drama."

Lissa felt equally embarrassed at being caught spying. "I — I'm sorry. I didn't mean to. I was just passing by . . ."

Avery gave a harsh laugh. "Well, I don't think it matters. Probably everyone in the building heard us."

"I'm sorry," Lissa repeated.

"Don't be. You didn't do anything wrong."

"No . . . I mean, I'm sorry he . . . you know, said those things to you."

"It's part of being a 'good' family. Everyone's got skeletons in their closet." Avery crossed her arms and leaned against the wall. Even upset and messy, she was beautiful. "God, I hate him sometimes. No offense, but this place is so fucking boring. I found some sophomore guys to hang with tonight, but . . . they were pretty boring too. The only thing they had going for them was their beer."

"Why . . . why did your dad bring you here?" Lissa asked. "Why aren't you . . . I don't know, in college?"

Avery gave a harsh laugh. "He doesn't trust me enough. When we were at Court, I got involved with this cute guy who worked there — total non-royal, of course. Dad freaked out and was afraid people would find out. So when he got the job here, he brought me along to keep an eye on me — and torture me. I think he's afraid I'll run off with a human if I go to college." She sighed. "I swear to God, if Reed wasn't here, I'd just run away, period."

Lissa didn't say anything for a long time.

She'd gone out of her way to avoid Avery diligently. With all the orders the queen was giving Lissa lately, this seemed the only way Lissa could fight back and stop herself from being controlled. But now, she wondered if she'd been wrong about Avery. Avery didn't seem like a spy for Tatiana. She didn't seem like someone who wanted to mold Lissa into a perfect royal. Mostly, Avery seemed like a sad, hurting girl, whose life was spinning out of control. Someone who was being ordered around as much as Lissa was lately.

With a deep breath, Lissa rushed forward with her next words. "Do you want to eat lunch with Christian and me tomorrow? No one would mind if you came to our lunch period. I can't promise it'll be, um, as exciting as you want."

Avery smiled again, but this time, it was less bitter. "Well, my other plans were to get drunk by myself in my room." She lifted a bottle of what looked like whiskey out of her purse. "Scored some stuff of my own."

Lissa wasn't entirely sure what kind of an answer that was. "So . . . I'll see you at lunch?"

Now Avery hesitated. But slowly, a faint gleam of hope and interest appeared on her face. Concentrating, Lissa tried to bring up her aura. She had a little difficulty at first, probably worn out from all the practice with Adrian tonight. But when she was finally able to get a grip on Avery's aura, she saw it was a mix of colors: green, blue, and gold. Not uncommon. It was currently ringed in red, as often happened when people were upset. But right before Lissa's eyes, that redness faded.

"Yeah," Avery said at last. "That would be great."

"I think this is as far as we can go today."

On the other side of the world, Sydney's voice startled me out of Lissa's thoughts. I didn't know how long I'd been daydreaming, but Sydney had turned off the main highway and was driving us into a small town that fit perfectly with my backwoods images of Siberia. In fact, "town" was a total exaggeration. There were a few scattered houses, a store, and a gas station. Farmland stretched beyond the buildings, and I saw more horses than cars. The few people who were out stared at our car in amazement. The sky had turned deep orange, and the sun was sinking farther and farther into the horizon. Sydney was right. It was nearly nightfall, and we needed to be off the road.

"We're only a couple hours away at most,"

she continued. "We made really good time and should get there pretty quickly in the morning." She drove to the other side of the village — which took, like, a minute — and pulled up in front of a plain white house with a barn beside it. "Here's where we're staying."

We got out of the car and approached the house. "Are these friends of yours?"

"Nope. Never met them. But they're expecting us."

More mysterious Alchemist connections. The door was answered by a friendly looking human in her twenties who urged us to come inside. She only spoke a few words of English, but Sydney's translation skills carried us through. Sydney was more outgoing and charming than I'd seen her thus far, probably because our hosts weren't despicable vampiric offspring.

You wouldn't think riding in a car all day would be tiring, but I felt exhausted and was anxious to get an early start in the morning. So after dinner and a little TV, Sydney and I went to the room that had been prepared for us. It was small and plain but had two twin beds covered in thick, fluffy blankets. I snuggled into mine, grateful for the softness and the warmth, and wondered if I'd dream of Lissa or Adrian.

I didn't. I did, however, wake up to a slight wave of nausea rolling through me — the nausea that told me there was a Strigoi nearby.

# SIX

I bolted upright, every part of me awake and alert. There were no city lights to shine through the window, and it took me several seconds to make out anything in the darkened room. Sydney was curled up in her own bed, her face unusually at peace as she slept.

Where was the Strigoi? Definitely not in our room. Was it in the house? Everyone had said the road to Dimitri's town was dangerous. Still, I would have thought Strigoi would be going after Moroi and dhampirs — though humans were a big part of their diet too. Thinking of the nice couple who'd welcomed us into their home, I felt something tight clench in my chest. No way would I let anything happen to them.

Slipping quietly out of the bed, I grabbed a hold of my stake and crept from the room without disturbing Sydney. No one else was awake, and as soon as I was in the living room, the nausea went away. Okay. The Strigoi wasn't inside, which was a good thing. It was outdoors, apparently on the side of the house near my room. Still moving silently, I went out the house's front door and walked around the corner, as quiet as the night around me.

The nausea grew stronger as I approached the barn, and I couldn't help but feel smug. I was going to surprise this Strigoi who'd thought it could sneak into a tiny human village for dinner. There. Right near the barn's entrance, I could see a long shadow moving. *Gotcha,* I thought. I readied the stake and started to spring forward —

— And then something struck me on the shoulder.

I stumbled, astonished, and looked into the face of a Strigoi. Out of the corner of my eye, I saw the shadow by the barn materialize into *another* Strigoi striding forward. Panic shot through me. There were two, and my secret detection system hadn't been able to tell the difference. Worse, they'd gotten the drop on me.

A thought immediately flashed into my mind: *What if one's Dimitri?*

It wasn't. At least, this close one wasn't. It was a woman. I had yet to get a feel for the second one. That one was approaching from my other side, moving fast. I had to deal with this immediate threat, though, and swiped at the woman with my stake, hoping to wound her, but she dodged so quickly, I hardly saw her move. She struck out toward me in an almost casual way. I wasn't fast enough to react and went flying toward the other Strigoi — a guy who was *not* Dimitri.

I responded quickly, leaping up and kicking him. I held the stake out, creating distance between us, but it did little good when the woman came up from behind and grabbed me, jerking my body against hers. I gave a muffled cry and felt her hands on my throat. She was probably going to break my neck, I realized. It was a fast, easy technique for Strigoi that then let them drag off a victim for feeding.

I struggled, jostling her hands slightly, but as the other Strigoi leaned over us, I knew it was useless. They'd surprised me. There were two of them. They were strong.

Panic surged in me again, an overwhelming sense of fear and desperation. I was afraid every time I fought Strigoi, but this fear was reaching a breaking point. It was unfocused and out of control, and I suspected it was touched by a bit of the madness and darkness I'd absorbed from Lissa. The feelings exploded within me, and I

111

wondered if they'd destroy me before the Strigoi did. I was in very real danger of dying here — of letting Sydney and the others get killed. The rage and distress of that thought were smothering.

Then, suddenly, it was like the earth burst open. Translucent forms, glowing softly in the darkness, sprang up everywhere. Some looked like normal people. Others were horrible, their faces gaunt and skull-like. Ghosts. Spirits. They surrounded us, their presence making my hair stand on end and sending a splitting headache through my skull.

The ghosts turned toward me. I'd had this happen before, on a plane, when apparitions had swarmed and threatened to consume me. I braced myself, trying desperately to summon up the strength to build barriers that would shut me off from the spirit world. It was a skill I'd had to learn, one I usually kept in place without any effort. The desperation and panic of this situation had cracked my control. In that horrible, blood-curdling moment, I again selfishly wished Mason hadn't found peace and left this world. I would have felt better if his ghost were here.

Then I realized I wasn't their target.

The ghosts were mobbing the two Strigoi.

The spirits didn't have solid forms, but every place they touched and passed through me felt like ice. The female Strigoi immediately began waving her arms to fend the apparitions off, snarling in rage and something almost like fear. The ghosts didn't appear to be able to hurt the Strigoi, but they were apparently pretty annoying — and distracting.

I staked the male Strigoi before he ever saw me coming. Immediately, the ghosts around him moved to the woman. She was good, I'd give her that. Despite struggling to fend the spirits off, she was still able to dodge my attacks fairly well. A lucky punch from her made stars burst before my eyes and sent me into the barn wall. I still had that ghost-induced splitting headache, and my head slamming into the barn didn't help. Staggering up, dizzy, I made my way back to her and continued my efforts to get a shot in at her heart. She managed to keep her chest out of my range — at least until one particularly terrifying ghost caught her off guard. Her momentary distraction gave me my chance, and I staked her, too. She fell to the ground — leaving me alone with the spirits.

With the Strigoi, the ghosts had clearly wanted to attack them. With me, it was a lot like on the plane. They seemed fascinated by me, desperate to get my attention. Only, with dozens of phantoms swarming, it might as well have been an attack.

Desperately, I tried again to summon my walls, to block the ghosts off from me as I'd done long ago. The effort was excruciating. Somehow, my out-of-control emotions had brought the spirits, and while I was calmer now, that control was harder to bring about. My head continued throbbing. Gritting my teeth, I focused every ounce of my strength into blocking out the ghosts.

"Go away," I hissed. "I don't need you anymore."

For a moment, it looked like my efforts were going to be useless. Then, slowly, one by one, the spirits began to fade. I felt the control I'd learned before gradually slip into place. Soon, there was nothing there but me, the darkness, and the barn — and Sydney.

I noticed her just as I collapsed to the ground. She was running out of the house in her pajamas, face pale. Kneeling at my side, she helped me sit up, legitimate fear all over her. "Rose! Are you okay?"

I felt like every scrap of energy in my brain and body had been sucked out. I couldn't move. I couldn't think.

"No," I told her.

And then I passed out.

I dreamed of Dimitri again, his arms around me and beautiful face leaning over me to care for me as he'd done so often when I was sick. Memories of things past came to me, the two of us laughing over some joke. Sometimes, in these dreams, he'd carry me away. Sometimes, we'd be riding in a car. Occasionally, his face would start to take on that fearsome Strigoi image that always tormented me. Then I'd quickly order my mind to brush such thoughts away.

Dimitri had taken care of me so many times and had always been there when I needed him. It had gone both ways, though. Admittedly, he had not seemed to end up in the infirmary as much as me. That was just my luck. Even when he was injured, he wouldn't acknowledge it. And as I dreamed and hallucinated, images came to me of one of the few times I'd been able to take care of him.

Just before the school had been attacked, Dimitri had been involved in a number of tests with me and my fellow novices to see how well we reacted to surprise assaults. Dimitri was so tough that he was almost impossible to beat, though he still got bruised up a number of times. I'd run into him in the gym once during these tests, surprised to see a cut on his cheek. It was hardly fatal, but there was a fair amount of blood showing.

"Do you realize you're bleeding to death?" I'd exclaimed. It was kind of an exaggeration, but still.

He touched his cheek absentmindedly and seemed to notice the injury for the first time. "I wouldn't quite go that far. It's nothing."

"It's nothing until you get an infection!"

"You know that's not likely," he said obstinately. That was true. Moroi — aside from contracting the occasional rare disease, as Victor had — hardly ever got sick. We dhampirs had inherited that from them, just as Sydney's tattoo gave her some protection. Nonetheless, I wasn't about to let Dimitri bleed all over.

"Come *on*," I said, pointing to the small bathroom in the gym. My voice had been fierce, and to my surprise, he'd actually obeyed.

After wetting a washcloth, I gently cleaned his face. He continued protesting at first but finally fell quiet. The bathroom was small, and we were just a few inches from each other. I could smell his clean, intoxicating scent and studied every detail of his face and strong body. My heart raced in my chest, but we were supposed to be on good behavior, so I tried to appear cool and collected. He was eerily calm too, but when I brushed his hair back behind his ears to clean the rest of his face, he flinched. My fingertips touching his skin had sent shock waves through me, and he'd felt them too. He caught hold of my hand and pulled it away.

"Enough," he said, voice husky. "I'm fine."

"Are you sure?" I asked. He hadn't released my hand. We were so, so close. The small bathroom seemed ready to burst with the electricity building between us. I knew this couldn't last but hated to let go of him. God, it was hard being responsible sometimes.

"Yes," he said. His voice was soft, and I knew he wasn't mad at me. He was afraid, afraid of how little it would take to ignite a fire between us. As it was, I was warm all over, just from the feel of his hand. Touching him made me feel complete, like the person I was always meant to be. "Thank you, Roza."

He released my hand, and we left, both off to do our own things that day. But the feel of his skin and hair stayed with me for hours afterward. . . .

I don't know why I dreamed that memory after being attacked near the barn. It seemed weird that I'd dream of taking care of Dimitri when *I* was the one who needed care. I guess it didn't really matter what the memory was, so long as it involved him. Dimitri always made me feel better, even in my dreams, giving me strength and resolve.

But as I lay in that delirium and moved in and out of consciousness, his comforting face would occasionally take on those terrible red eyes and fangs. I'd whimper, fighting hard to push that sight away. Other times, he didn't look like Dimitri at all. He'd turn into a man I didn't know, an older Moroi with dark hair and cunning eyes, gold jewelry glinting on his neck and ears. I'd cry out for Dimitri again, and eventually, his face would return, safe and wonderful.

At one point, though, the image shifted again, this time into a woman's. Clearly, she wasn't Dimitri, but there was something about her brown eyes that reminded me of him. She was older, in her forties maybe, and a dhampir. She laid a cool cloth across my forehead, and I realized I wasn't dreaming anymore. My body ached, and I was in an unfamiliar bed, in an unfamiliar room.

No sign of the Strigoi. Had I dreamed them, too?

"Don't try to move," the woman said with the faintest trace of a Russian accent. "You took some bad hits."

My eyes widened as the events by the barn came back to me, the ghosts I'd summoned up. It hadn't been a dream. "Where's Sydney? Is she okay?"

"She's fine. Don't worry." Something in the woman's voice told me I could believe her.

"Where am I?"

"In Baia."

Baia, Baia. Somewhere, in the back of my head, that name was familiar. All of a sudden, it clicked. Long, long ago, Dimitri had said it. He'd only ever mentioned his town's name once and, even though I'd tried, I had never been able to remember it. Sydney would never tell me the name. But now we were here. Dimitri's home.

"Who are you?" I asked.

"Olena," she said. "Olena Belikova."

# SEVEN

It was like Christmas morning.

I wasn't usually big on God or fate, but now I was seriously reconsidering. After I'd passed out, Sydney had apparently made some frantic calls, and someone she knew in Baia had driven to us — risking the darkness — to rescue us and take us back where I could be treated. That was no doubt why I'd had vague sensations of being in a car during my delirium; it hadn't all been part of the dream.

And then, somehow, out of all the dhampirs in Baia, I had been taken to Dimitri's mother. That was enough to make me seriously consider that there might truly be forces greater than me at work in the universe. No one told me exactly how it happened, but I soon learned Olena Belikova had a reputation among her peers for healing — and not even any sort of magical healing. She'd had medical training and was the person other dhampirs — and even some Moroi — went to in this region when they wanted to avoid human attention. Still. The coincidence was eerie, and I couldn't help but think there was something going on that I didn't understand.

For now, I didn't worry too much about the hows and whys of my current situation. I was too busy staring wide-eyed at my surroundings and its inhabitants. Olena didn't live alone. All of Dimitri's sisters — three of them — lived in the house too, along with their kids. The family resemblance was startling. None of them looked exactly like Dimitri, but in every face, I could see him. The eyes. The smile. Even the sense of humor. Seeing them fed the Dimitri withdrawal I'd had since he'd disappeared — and made it worse at the same time. Whenever I looked at any of them out of my peripheral vision, I'd think I was seeing Dimitri. It was like a house of mirrors, with distorted reflections of him everywhere.

Even the house gave me a thrill. There were no obvious signs that Dimitri had ever lived there, but I kept thinking, *This is where he grew up. He walked these floors, touched these walls. . . .* As I walked from room to room, I'd touch the walls too, trying to draw his energy from them. I'd envision him lounging on the couch, home on break from school. I wondered if he'd slid down the banisters when he was little. The images were so real that I had to keep reminding myself that he hadn't been here in ages.

"You've made an amazing recovery," Olena noted the next morning after I'd been brought to her. She watched with approval as I inhaled a plate of blini. They were ultra-thin pancakes stacked and layered with butter and jam. My body always required a lot of food to keep its strength up, and I figured as long as I wasn't chewing with my mouth open or anything, I had no reason to feel bad about eating so much. "I thought you were dead when Abe and Sydney brought you in."

"Who?" I asked between bites of food.

Sydney sat at the table with the rest of the family, hardly touching her food as usual. She seemed clearly uneasy at being in a dhampir household, but when I'd first come downstairs this morning, I'd definitely seen some relief in her eyes.

"Abe Mazur," said Sydney. Unless I was mistaken, some of the other people at the table exchanged knowing glances. "He's a Moroi. I . . . I didn't know how badly you were injured last night, so I called him. He drove down with his guardians. He was the one who brought you here."

Guardians. Plural. "Is he royal?" Mazur wasn't a royal name, but that wasn't always a sure sign of someone's lineage. And while I was beginning to trust Sydney's social networking and connections to powerful people, I couldn't imagine why a royal would go out of his way for me. Maybe he owed the Alchemists a favor.

"No," she said bluntly. I frowned. A non-royal Moroi with more than one guardian? Very odd. It was clear she wasn't going to say anything else on the matter — at least not for now.

I swallowed another mouthful of blini and turned my attention back to Olena. "Thanks for taking me in."

Dimitri's older sister, Karolina, sat at the table too, along with her baby girl and son Paul. Paul was about ten and seemed fascinated by me. Dimitri's teenage sister, Viktoria, was also there. She appeared to be a little younger than me. The third Belikov sister was named Sonya and had left for work before I woke up. I'd have to wait to meet her.

"Did you really kill two Strigoi all by yourself?" Paul asked me.

"Paul," chastised Karolina. "That's not a nice question to ask."

"But it's an exciting one," said Viktoria with a grin. Her brown hair was streaked with gold, but her dark eyes sparkled so much like Dimitri's when he was excited that it tugged at my heart. Again, I had that taunting sensation of Dimitri being here but not here.

"She did," said Sydney. "I saw the bodies. Like always."

She wore that comically tormented expression of hers, and I laughed. "At least I left them where you could find them this time." My humor suddenly dimmed. "Did anyone . . . any other humans notice or hear?"

"I got rid of the bodies before anyone saw," she said. "If people heard anything . . . Well, backwoods places like that are always filled with superstitions and ghost stories. They don't have factual evidence of vampires, per se, but there's always sort of this belief that the supernatural and dangerous are out there. Little do they know."

She said "ghost stories" without any change of expression. I wondered if she'd seen any of the spirits last night but finally decided she probably hadn't. She'd come outside near the tail end of the fight, and if past evidence was any indication, nobody else could see the spirits I saw — except Strigoi, as it turned out.

"You must have had some good training then," said Karolina, shifting so the baby leaned against her shoulder. "You look like you should still be in school."

"Just got out," I said, earning another scrutinizing look from Sydney.

"You're American," said Olena matter-of-factly. "What in the world could bring you out here?"

"I . . . I'm looking for someone," I said after a few moments' hesitation.

I was afraid they were going to press for details or that she too would have blood whore suspicions, but just then, the kitchen door opened and Dimitri's grandmother, Yeva, walked in. She had poked her head in earlier and scared the hell out of me. Dimitri had told me that she was a witch of sorts, and I could believe it. She looked like she was a gazillion years old and was so thin, it was a wonder the wind didn't blow her away. She barely stood five feet tall, and her hair covered her head in patchy gray wisps. But it was her eyes that truly frightened me. The rest of her might be frail, but those dark eyes were sharp and alert and seemed to bore into my soul. Even without Dimitri's explanation, I would have taken her for a witch. She was also the only one in the household who didn't speak English.

She sat down at one of the empty chairs, and Olena hastily jumped up to get some more blini. Yeva muttered something in Russian that made the others look uncomfortable. Sydney's lips twitched into a small smile. Yeva's eyes were on me as she spoke, and I glanced around for translation. "What?" I asked.

"Grandmother says you're not telling us the whole truth about why you're here. She says the longer you delay, the worse it will be," Viktoria explained. She then gave Sydney an apologetic look. "And she wants to know when the Alchemist is leaving."

"As soon as possible," said Sydney dryly.

"Well, why I'm here . . . it's kind of a long story." Could I be any vaguer?

Yeva said something else, and Olena retorted with what sounded like a chastisement. To me, she spoke gently: "Ignore her, Rose. She's in one of her moods. Why you're here is your own business — although I'm sure Abe would like to talk to you at some point." She frowned slightly, and I was reminded of the earlier looks at the table. "You should make sure you thank him. He seemed very concerned about you."

"I'd kind of like to see him too," I mumbled, still curious about this well-protected, non-royal Moroi who had given me a ride and seemed to make everyone uneasy. Eager to avoid more talk of why I was here, I hastily changed the subject. "I'd also love to look around Baia. I've never been in a place like this before — where so many dhampirs live, I mean."

Viktoria brightened. "I can definitely give you a tour — if you're sure you're feeling okay. Or if you don't have to leave right away."

She believed I was passing through, which was just as well. Honestly, I wasn't sure what I was doing anymore, now that it seemed likely Dimitri wasn't in the area. I glanced at Sydney questioningly.

She shrugged. "Do whatever you want. I'm not going anywhere." I found that a little disconcerting too. She'd brought me here as her superiors had told her to do — but now what? Well, that was a concern for later.

As soon as I finished my food, Viktoria practically dragged me out the door, as if I was the most exciting thing that had happened around here in a while. Yeva hadn't taken her eyes off me for the rest of the meal, and even though she'd never said anything else, her suspicious look clearly told me she didn't believe a word I'd said. I invited Sydney along on the outing, but she declined, choosing instead to lock herself away in a bedroom to read about Greek temples or make world-controlling phone calls or do whatever it was she did.

Viktoria said downtown wasn't far from where they lived and was easy to walk to. The day was clear and cool, with enough sun to make being outside pretty pleasant.

"We don't get a lot of visitors," she explained. "Except for Moroi men, but most don't stay long."

She added no more, but I wondered about her implications. Were these Moroi men off to find some action with dhampir women? I'd grown up thinking of these women, dhampirs who chose not to become guardians, as disgraceful and dirty. The ones in the Nightingale had certainly met the blood whore stereotype, but Dimitri had assured me that not all dhampir women were like that. After meeting the Belikovs, I believed him.

As we approached the center of town, I soon discovered another myth shattered. People always talked about blood whores living in camps or communes, but that wasn't the case here. Baia wasn't huge, not like Saint Petersburg or even Omsk, but it was a real town with a large human population. Hardly a rural camp or farm settlement. The whole setting was astonishingly normal, and when we reached downtown, lined with small shops and restaurants, it too seemed like any other place in the world people might live. Modern and ordinary, just with a slight village feel.

"Where are all the dhampirs?" I wondered aloud. Sydney had said there was a secret dhampir subculture, but I saw no signs of it.

Viktoria smiled. "Oh, they're here. We have a lot of businesses and other places that humans don't know about." While I could understand dhampirs going unnoticed in big cities, it seemed remarkable to pull that off here. "And lots of us just live and work with humans." She nodded over toward what looked like a drugstore. "That's where Sonya works now."

"Now?"

"Now that she's pregnant." Viktoria rolled her eyes. "I'd take you to meet her, but she's grumpy all the time lately. I hope the baby's early."

She left it at that, and I again wondered about the dynamics of dhampirs and Moroi here. We didn't mention it again, and our conversation stayed light and even teasing. Viktoria was easy to like, and in only an hour, we'd clicked as though we'd known each other forever. Maybe my connection to Dimitri bound me to his family, too.

My thoughts were cut off when someone called Viktoria's name. We turned to see a very cute dhampir guy crossing the street. He had bronze hair and dark eyes, his age falling somewhere between mine and Viktoria's.

He said something chatty and conversational to her. She grinned at him and then gestured to me, giving my introduction in Russian. "This is Nikolai," she told me in English.

"Nice to meet you," he said, also switching languages. He gave me a quick assessment in the way guys often do, but when he turned back to Viktoria, it was clear who the object of his affections was. "You should bring Rose to Marina's party. It's Sunday night." He hesitated, turning a bit shy. "You're going, aren't you?"

Viktoria turned thoughtful, and I realized she was completely oblivious to his crush. "I'll be there, but . . ." She turned to me. "Will you still be around?"

"I don't know," I said honestly. "But I'll go if I'm still here. What kind of party is it?"

"Marina's a friend from school," explained Viktoria. "We're just going to get together and celebrate before we go back."

"To school?" I asked stupidly. Somehow, it had never occurred to me that the dhampirs out here would be in school.

"We're on break right now," said Nikolai. "For Easter."

"Oh." It was late April, but I had no clue what day Easter fell on this year. I'd lost track of the days. It hadn't happened yet, so their school must have their break the week before Easter. St. Vladimir's took its vacation afterward. "Where is your school?"

"It's about three hours away. Even more remote than here." Viktoria made a face.

"Baia's not so bad," teased Nikolai.

"Easy for you to say. You'll eventually leave and go see new and exciting places."

"Can't you?" I asked her.

She frowned, suddenly uncomfortable. "Well, I *could* . . . but that's not how we do it here — at least not in my family. Grandmother has some . . . strong opinions about men and women. Nikolai will be a guardian, but I'll stay here with my family."

Nikolai suddenly gave me a new appraisal. "Are you a guardian?"

"Ah, well." Now I was the uncomfortable one.

Viktoria spoke before I could come up with anything to say. "She killed two Strigoi

131

outside of town. By herself."

He looked impressed. "You *are* a guardian."

"Well, no . . . I've killed before, but I'm not actually sworn." Turning around, I lifted up my hair to show them my neck. In addition to all my regular *molnija* marks, I also had the little star-shaped tattoo that meant I'd been in a battle. They both gasped, and Nikolai said something in Russian. I let my hair drop and looked back. "What?"

"You're . . ." Viktoria bit her lip, eyes contemplative as she groped for what she wanted to say. "Unpromised? I don't know the English word."

"Unpromised?" I said. "I guess . . . but technically, aren't all the women here?"

"Even if we aren't guardians, we still get marks showing we completed our training. No promise mark, though. For you to have killed so many Strigoi and have no loyalties to a school or the guardians . . ." Viktoria shrugged. "We call it being unpromised — it's a strange thing."

"It's strange where I come from too," I admitted. Unheard of, really. So much so, that we didn't have a term for it. It just wasn't done.

"I should let you two go," said Nikolai, his lovesick eyes back on Viktoria. "But I'll see you at Marina's for sure? Maybe sooner?"

"Yes," she agreed. They said their farewells in Russian, and then he loped off across the street with the kind of easy, athletic grace guardians often acquired with training. It reminded me a bit of Dimitri's.

"I must have scared him off," I said.

"No, he thinks you're exciting."

"Not as exciting as he thinks you are."

Her eyebrows rose. "What?"

"He likes you . . . I mean, *really* likes. Can't you tell?"

"Oh. We're just friends."

I could tell from her attitude that she meant it. She was completely indifferent to him, which was too bad. He was cute and nice. Letting poor Nikolai go, I brought up the guardians again. I was intrigued by the different attitudes around here. "You said you can't . . . but do you *want* to be a guardian?"

She hesitated. "I've never really considered it. I get all the same training at school, and I like being able to defend myself. But I'd rather use it in defense of my family than Moroi. I guess it sounds . . ." She paused again to think of the right word. ". . . Sexist? But, the men become guardians, and women stay at home. Only my brother left."

I nearly tripped. "Your brother?" I asked, keeping my voice as steady as possible.

"Dimitri," she said. "He's older than me and has been a guardian for a while. He's over in the United States, actually. We haven't seen him in a long time."

"Huh."

I felt horrible and guilty. Guilty because I was keeping the truth from Viktoria and the others. Horrible because apparently no one from back home had bothered to pass the news on to his family yet. Smiling at her own memories, she didn't notice my change in mood.

"Paul actually looks exactly like he did at that age. I should show you pictures of him — and some recent ones, too. Dimitri's pretty cute. For my brother, I mean."

I was sure seeing pictures of Dimitri as a little boy would rip my heart out. As it was, the more Viktoria began to talk about him, the sicker I felt. She had no clue about what had happened, and even though it had been a couple of years since she'd seen him, it was clear she and the rest of the family loved him like crazy. Not that that should be a surprise. (And really, who couldn't love Dimitri?) Being around them just one morning had shown me how close they all were. I knew from Dimitri's stories that he was crazy about all of them, too.

"Rose? Are you okay?" Viktoria was peering at me with concern, probably because I hadn't said anything in the last ten minutes.

We had circled around and were almost back at her house. Looking at her, at her open, friendly face and eyes that were so much like Dimitri's, I realized I had another task ahead of me before I could go after Dimitri, wherever he was. I swallowed.

"I . . . yeah. I think . . . I think I need to sit down with you and the rest of your family."

"Okay," she said, the worry still in her voice.

Inside the house, Olena was bustling around the kitchen with Karolina. I thought they were making plans for tonight's dinner, which was startling considering we'd just finished a huge breakfast. I could definitely get used to the way they ate around here. In the living room, Paul was building an elaborate racetrack out of Legos. Yeva sat in a rocking chair and appeared to be the world's most stereotypical grandmother as she knit a pair of socks. Except most grandmothers didn't look like they could incinerate you with a single glance.

Olena was talking to Karolina in Russian

but switched to English when she saw me. "You two are back earlier than I expected."

"We saw the town," said Viktoria. "And . . . Rose wanted to talk to you. To all of us."

Olena gave me a look as puzzled and concerned as Viktoria's. "What's going on?"

The weight of all those Belikov eyes on me made my heart start thumping in my chest. How was I going to do this? How could I explain something I hadn't spoken about in weeks? I couldn't stand to put them — or myself — through it. When Yeva scuttled in, it made things that much worse. Maybe she'd had some mystical sense that something big was about to go down.

"We should sit," I said.

Paul stayed in the living room, for which I was grateful. I was pretty sure I couldn't handle saying what I had to with a little kid — one who looked like Dimitri, apparently — watching me.

"Rose, what's wrong?" asked Olena. She looked so sweet and, well . . . motherly, that I nearly cried. Whenever I'd been angry with my own mother for not being around or doing a good job, I'd always compared her to some idealized image of a mom — a mom who seemed a lot like Dimitri's, I realized. Dimitri's sisters looked equally worried, like I was someone they'd known forever. That acceptance and concern made my eyes burn even more, seeing as they'd just met me this morning. Yeva wore a very strange expression, however — almost like she'd been expecting something like this all along.

"Well . . . the thing is, the reason I came here, to Baia, was to find you guys."

That wasn't entirely true. I'd come to search for Dimitri. I'd never thought much about finding his family, but now, I realized that it was a good thing I had.

"You see, Viktoria was talking about Dimitri earlier." Olena's face brightened when I said her son's name. "And . . . I knew — er, know him. He used to be a guardian at my school. My teacher, actually."

Karolina and Viktoria lit up as well. "How is he?" asked Karolina. "It's been ages since we've seen him. Do you know when he's going to visit?"

I couldn't even think about answering her question, so I pushed forward with my story before I lost my courage in front of all those loving faces. As the words came out of my mouth, it was almost like someone else was saying them and I was simply watching from a distance. "A month ago . . . our school was attacked by Strigoi. A really bad attack . . . a huge group of Strigoi. We lost a lot of people — Moroi and dhampirs, both."

Olena exclaimed in Russia. Viktoria leaned toward me. "St. Vladimir's?"

I halted in my story, surprised. "You've heard of it?"

"Everyone's heard of it," said Karolina. "We all know what happened. That was your school? You were there that night?"

I nodded.

"No wonder you have so many *molnija* marks," breathed Viktoria in wonder.

"And that's where Dimitri's at now?" asked Olena. "We lost track of his latest assignment."

"Um, yeah . . ." My tongue felt thick in my throat. I couldn't breathe. "I was at the school the night of the attack," I reaffirmed. "And so was Dimitri. He was one of the leaders in the battle . . . and the way he fought . . . he was . . . he was so brave . . . and . . ."

My words were breaking up, but by this point, the others were catching on. Olena gasped and again murmured in Russian. I picked out the word for "God." Karolina sat frozen, but Viktoria leaned toward me. Those eyes that were so like her brother's stared at me intently, as intently as he would if pushing me to tell the truth, no matter how awful.

"What happened?" she demanded. "What

138

happened to Dimitri?"

I looked away from their faces, my eyes drifting to the living room. On the far wall, I caught sight of a bookcase filled with old, leather-covered books. They had gold-embossed lettering on the spines. It was totally random, but I suddenly remembered Dimitri mentioning those. *They were these old adventure novels my mother collected,* he'd told me once. *The covers were so beautiful, and I loved them. If I was careful, she'd let me read them sometimes.* The thought of a young Dimitri sitting in front of that bookcase, carefully turning the pages — and oh, he would have been careful — almost made me lose it. Had that been where he'd developed his love of western novels?

I was losing it. I was getting distracted. I wasn't going to be able to tell them the truth. My emotions were growing too powerful, my memories flooding me as I fought to think about something — anything — that didn't involve that horrible battle.

Then I glanced at Yeva again, and something about her eerie, knowing expression inexplicably spurred me on. I had to do this. I turned back to the others. "He fought really bravely in the battle, and afterward, he helped lead a rescue mission to save some people that the Strigoi had captured. He was really amazing there, too, only . . . he . . ."

I stopped again and realized tears were running down my cheeks. In my mind, I was replaying that awful scene in the cave, with Dimitri so close to freedom and taken by a Strigoi at the last minute. Shaking that thought away, I took another deep breath. I had to finish this. I owed it to his family.

There was no gentle way to say it. "One of the Strigoi there . . . well, he overpowered Dimitri."

Karolina buried her face in her mother's shoulder, and Olena made no effort to hide her own tears. Viktoria wasn't crying, but her face had gone perfectly still. She was working hard to keep her emotions in check, just as Dimitri would have. She searched my face, needing to know for sure.

"Dimitri is dead," she said.

It was a statement, not a question, but she was looking to me for confirmation. I wondered if I'd given away something, some hint that there was still more to the story. Or maybe she just needed the certainty of those words. And for a moment, I considered telling them that Dimitri was dead. It was what the Academy would tell them, what the guardians would tell them. It would be easier on them . . . but somehow, I couldn't stand to lie to them — even if it was a comforting lie. Dimitri would have wanted the whole truth, and his family would too.

"No," I said, and for a heartbeat, hope sprang up in everyone's faces — at least until I spoke again. "Dimitri's a Strigoi."

# EIGHT

The reactions were mixed among Dimitri's family members. Some cried. Some were stunned. And some — mainly Yeva and Viktoria — simply took it in and kept their emotions from their faces, just as Dimitri would have done. That upset me almost as much as the tears; it reminded me too much of him. Out of all of them, pregnant Sonya — who came home shortly after the news broke — had the most intense physical reaction. She ran sobbing to her room and wouldn't come out.

It didn't take long, however, for Yeva and Olena to spring into action. They spoke rapidly in Russian, clearly planning something. Phone calls were made, and Viktoria was dispatched to run an errand. No one seemed to need me, so I mostly wandered the house and tried to stay out of the way.

I found myself studying the shelves I'd seen earlier, running my hands along the leather-bound books. The titles were in Cyrillic, but it didn't matter. Touching them and imagining Dimitri having held and read them somehow made me feel closer to him.

"Looking for a little light reading?" Sydney walked up and stood beside me. She hadn't been around earlier but had heard the news.

"Very light, seeing as I don't understand any of them," I replied. I gestured to the scurrying family members. "What's going on here?"

"They're planning Dimitri's funeral," Sydney explained. "Or, well, his memorial service."

I frowned. "But he's not dead —"

"Shh." She cut me off with a sharp gesture and glanced warily at the others as they hustled around. "Don't say that."

"But it's true," I hissed back.

She shook her head. "Not to them. Out here . . . out in these villages . . . there's no in-between state. You're alive or you're dead. They aren't going to acknowledge him being one of . . . *those*." She couldn't keep the disgust out of her voice. "For all intents and purposes, he is dead to them. They'll mourn him and move on. So should you." I didn't take offense at her blunt attitude because I knew she hadn't meant to give any. It was just her way.

The problem was, that in-between state was very real to me, and there was no way I could move on. Not yet.

"Rose . . ." began Sydney after several seconds of silence. She wouldn't meet my eyes. "I'm sorry."

"You mean, for Dimitri?"

"Yeah . . . I had no idea. I haven't really been that nice to you. I mean, I'm not going to act like I feel any better about hanging out with your kind, but you guys are still . . . well, not human, obviously. But . . . I don't know. You still have feelings; you still love and hurt. And while we were coming here, you had all this horrible news in you, and I didn't make it any easier for you. So I'm sorry for that. And I'm sorry for thinking the worst of you."

At first, I thought she was talking about thinking I was evil, but then I got it. She'd thought this whole time that I really was coming to be a blood whore and now believed delivering the news to Dimitri's family had been my only purpose. I didn't bother to correct her.

"Thanks, but you couldn't have known. And honestly, if I were in your place . . . I don't know. I'd probably act the same way."

"No," she said. "You wouldn't. You're

144

always nice to people."

I gave her an incredulous look. "Have you been traveling with someone else these last few days? Back home, I've got a reputation for not always being so nice. I've got attitude, and I know it."

She smiled. "Yeah, you do. But you also say the right things to people when you have to. Telling the Belikovs what you did . . . well, that was hard. And no matter what you say, you *can* be polite and go out of your way to make people feel good. Most of the time."

I was a bit startled. Was that how I appeared? I often thought of myself as a trigger-happy queen bitch and tried to think about my behavior with her these last few days. I had sparred with her a lot, but among the others we'd met, I supposed I had been friendly.

"Well, thanks," I said, not knowing what else to say.

"Did you see Abe yet? When you walked around town?"

"No," I said, realizing I'd forgotten about my mysterious rescuer. "Should I have?"

"I just figured he'd find you."

"Who is he? Why did he come get us when you told him I was hurt?"

Sydney hesitated, and I thought I was going to get some more of the Alchemist silent treatment. Then, after glancing around uneasily, she said in a low voice, "Abe's not royal, but he's a really important guy. He's not Russian either, but he's in the country a lot, always on business — both illegal and legal, I think. He's friends with all the important Moroi, and half the time, it seems like he controls the Alchemists, too. I know he's involved in the process of making our tattoos . . . but his business goes far beyond that. We have a name for him behind his back . . . *Zmey*."

"Zma what?" I had barely heard the word. It sounded like *zz-may*. It was certainly nothing I'd ever heard before.

She gave a small smile at my confusion. "*Zmey* is Russian for 'snake.' But not just any snake." Her eyes narrowed as she pondered a better explanation. "It's a term used in lots of myths. Sometimes for giant snakes heroes have to battle. There are also a few stories about wizards with snake blood who get called that. The snake in the Garden of Eden? Who made Eve fall? He was called a *zmey* too."

I shivered. Okay, that was pretty freaky, but it made something click into place. The Alchemists allegedly had ties to leaders and authorities, and Abe apparently wielded a lot of influence with them. "Is Abe the one who wanted you to come with me to Baia? The reason the Alchemists made you come here?"

Again, she paused, then nodded. "Yeah . . . when I called that night in Saint Petersburg, I was told there was a search going on for you. Abe gave orders through the Alchemists for me to stay with you until he could meet up with us here. He's apparently been searching for you on someone's behalf."

I went cold. My fears were being realized. People *had* been looking for me. But who? If Lissa had initiated a manhunt, I would have sensed it when I visited her mind. I didn't think it was Adrian either, not from the way he seemed so desperate and clueless about my whereabouts. Plus, he seemed to accept my need for this quest.

So who was looking for me? And for what reason? This Abe sounded like a high-ranking person — albeit someone involved in shady business — someone who might very well be connected to the queen or others almost as important. Had he been ordered to find me and bring me back? Or — considering how much the queen hated me — had he perhaps been ordered to make sure I *didn't* come back? Was I dealing with an assassin? Sydney certainly seemed to regard him with a weird mix of fear and respect.

"Maybe I don't want to meet him," I said.

"I don't think he'll hurt you. I mean, if he wanted to, he already would have. But be careful. He's always playing several games at once, and he deals in enough secrets to rival the Alchemists."

"So you don't trust him?"

She gave me a rueful grin as she turned to walk away. "You forget: I don't trust any of you."

When she was gone, I decided to go outside, away from the sorrow and business indoors. I sat down on the top step of the backyard porch, watching Paul play. He was building a fort for some of his action figures. While sensitive to the grief in his family, it was hard for him to be too affected by the "death" of an uncle he'd only met a couple of times. The news didn't mean as much to him as it did to the rest of us.

With so much time on my hands for the rest of the day, I decided to do a quick check-in with Lissa. In spite of myself, I was kind of curious about how things had panned out with Avery Lazar.

While Lissa's intentions were good, she'd still had some misgivings about bringing Avery along to lunch. And yet, she was pleasantly surprised to see Avery fitting in perfectly, charming both Adrian and Christian. Admittedly, Adrian was impressed by pretty much anything female. Christian was harder to crack, but even he seemed to be growing fond of her — probably because she kept teasing Adrian. Anyone who could make a joke at Adrian's expense ranked high on Christian's list.

"So, explain this," Avery said, winding linguine around her fork. "You just, what, hang around the Academy all day? Are you trying to redo your high school experience?"

"Nothing to redo," said Adrian loftily. "I totally ruled my high school. I was worshipped and adored — not that that should come as a shock." Beside him, Christian nearly choked on his food.

"So . . . you're trying to relive your glory days. It's all gone downhill since then, huh?"

"No way," said Adrian. "I'm like a fine wine. I get better with age. The best is yet to come."

"Seems like it'd get old after a while," said Avery, apparently not convinced by the compelling wine simile. "I'm certainly bored, and I even spend part of the day helping my dad."

"Adrian sleeps most of the day," noted Lissa, trying to keep a straight face. "So he doesn't actually have to worry about finding things to do."

"Hey, I spend a good portion of my time helping *you* unravel the mysteries of spirit," Adrian reminded her.

Avery leaned forward, curiosity all over her pretty face. "So it's actually real? I heard stories about spirit . . . about how you can heal people?"

It took Lissa a moment to respond. She wasn't sure she'd ever get used to her magic being out in the open now. "Among other things. We're still figuring it out."

Adrian was more eager than she was to discuss it — probably in the hopes of impressing Avery — and provided a quick rundown of some of spirit's abilities, like auras and compulsion. "And," he added, "I can visit people in their dreams."

Christian held up a hand. "Stop. I can feel there's a comment coming on about how women already dream about you. I just ate, you know."

"I wasn't going to go there," said Adrian. But he kind of looked like he wished he'd thought of the joke first. I couldn't help being a little amused. Adrian was so brash and flippant in public . . . and then, in my dreams, he'd show that serious and concerned side. He was more complex than anyone gave him credit for.

Avery looked floored. "Man. I used to think using air was cool. I guess not." A small breeze suddenly blew her hair back, making her look as though she were posing for a swimsuit photo shoot. She gave the group a dazzling smile. All that was missing was a photographer.

The sound of the bell made them all stand up. Christian realized he'd left homework in another class and hurried off to get it — after kissing Lissa goodbye, of course.

Adrian departed equally as fast. "The teachers start giving me dirty looks if I hang around once classes start." He gave Lissa and Avery a small half-bow. "Until next time, ladies."

Avery, who couldn't care less about what teachers thought, walked with Lissa to her next class. The older girl's face was thoughtful. "So . . . you really are *with* Christian, right?" Was she ever. If Avery'd seen half the things I'd seen Christian and Lissa do through the bond, there'd be no question.

Lissa laughed. "Yes, why?"

Avery hesitated, piquing Lissa's curiosity. "Well . . . I heard that you were involved with Adrian."

Lissa nearly stopped walking. "Where did you hear that?"

"At Court. The queen was saying how happy she is about you guys being a couple and how you're always together."

Lissa groaned. "That's because whenever I go to Court, she invites him too and then sends us both off to do things for her. It's not by choice . . . well, I mean, don't get me wrong. I don't mind spending time with him, but the reason we're always together there is because Tatiana makes us."

"She seems to like you, though. She talks about you all the time, about how much potential you have and how proud she is of you."

"I think she's proud to manipulate me. Going there is such a pain. She either completely ignores the fact that I'm dating Christian or takes whatever chance she can get to slip in insults about him." Queen Tatiana, like so many other people, could never forgive Christian's parents for willingly turning Strigoi.

"Sorry," said Avery, looking like she felt really bad. "I didn't mean to bring up a bad subject. I just kind of wanted to know if Adrian was available, that's all."

Lissa wasn't mad at Avery. Her fury was turned toward the queen, at how she assumed everyone would behave the way she wanted and dance when she commanded it.

The Moroi world had been ruled by a king or a queen since the beginning of time, and sometimes, Lissa thought it was time for a change. They needed a system where everyone had an equal say — royal and non-royal alike. Even the dhampirs.

The more she thought about it, the more she felt her temper spike, anger and frustration flaring up in a way more common to me than her. It made her want to scream sometimes, to walk right up to Tatiana and tell her their deal was off. No college was worth this. Maybe she'd even tell Tatiana that it was time for a revolution, time to overturn the Moroi's backward —

Lissa blinked, astonished to find she was shaking. Where had that emotion come from? It was one thing to be upset with Tatiana, but this . . . ? She hadn't had such out-of-control rages since she first began using spirit. With a deep breath, she tried to use some of the calming techniques she'd acquired so that Avery wouldn't know what a nutcase she'd nearly turned into.

"I just hate people talking about me, that's all," Lissa said at last.

Avery hadn't seemed to notice Lissa's lapse into anger. "Well, if it makes you feel better, not everyone thinks that about you. I met a girl . . . Mia? Yeah, that was her name.

Some non-royal." Avery's dismissive tone suggested she held the view a lot of royals had toward "common" Moroi. "She just laughed about you and Adrian being together. Said it was ridiculous."

Lissa almost smiled at that. Mia had once been Lissa's rival and a self-centered brat. But after Strigoi killed her mother, Mia had taken on a fierce, determined attitude, one both Lissa and I liked immensely. Mia lived at Court with her father, secretly training to fight so that she would be able to battle Strigoi some day.

"Oh," said Avery suddenly. "There's Simon. I should go."

Lissa looked across the hall and saw Avery's stern guardian. Simon might not be as grim as Avery's brother Reed, but he still had that same stiff and dour look he'd had when Lissa first met him. Avery seemed to get along with him fine, though.

"Okay," said Lissa. "I'll see you later."

"You bet," said Avery, starting to turn.

"Oh, and Avery?"

Avery glanced at Lissa. "Yeah?"

"Adrian *is* available."

Avery's only answer was a quick grin before she headed off to join Simon.

Back with the Belikovs in Baia, the memorial service was going forward. Neighbors and friends, all dhampirs, slowly arrived, many bringing food. It was my first glimpse of the dhampir community, though it still didn't seem as mysterious as Sydney had implied. The kitchen turned into a banquet hall, with every counter and table surface covered in dishes. Some were foods I knew, and there were lots of desserts — cookies and pastries covered in nuts and icing that smelled freshly baked. Some of the dishes I'd never seen before and wasn't sure I wanted to ever again. There was a slimy bowl of cabbage in particular that I went out of my way to avoid.

But before we ate, everyone went outside and gathered in a semicircle in the backyard. It was the only place that could accomodate so many people. A priest appeared just then, a human one. That surprised me a little, but I supposed when living in a human town, dhampirs would attend a human church. And to most humans, dhampirs looked just like them, so the priest no doubt thought he was making an ordinary house call. A handful of Moroi who had been in town were also present, but they, too, could more or less pass for humans — pale ones — if they were discreet with the fangs. Humans didn't expect to see the supernatural, so their minds rarely considered it an option, even when it was right in front of them.

Everyone grew silent. It was sunset now, with orange fire burning in the western sky, and shadows falling across all of us. The priest performed a funeral service in Russian, chanting in a voice that sounded unearthly in the darkening yard.

All the church services I'd ever attended were in English, but I could see how this had the same feel. Every so often, those gathered would cross themselves. I didn't know the cues, so I simply watched and waited, letting the priest's mournful voice fill my soul. My feelings for Dimitri churned within me like a growing storm, and I worked to keep them in, locked up in my heart. When the service finally finished, the eerie tension that had engulfed the group dispersed. People moved again, hugging the Belikovs and shaking hands with the priest. He left shortly thereafter.

Food followed. Plates were loaded up, and everyone sat wherever they could find space, be it inside the house or in the backyard. None of the guests really knew me, and Dimitri's family was far too busy to pay much attention to me as they ran around and tried to make everyone feel welcome. Sydney stayed with me a lot of the time, and while conversation was light between us, I took comfort in her presence. We sat on the living room floor, leaning against the wall near the bookcase. She picked over her food, like always, which made me smile. There was something soothing about that familiar habit.

When dinner was over, people continued chatting in small groups. I couldn't understand any of it, but I kept hearing his name mentioned: *Dimitri, Dimitri.* It reminded me of the incomprehensible hissing that the ghosts made during their visits. It was oppressive and smothering, the force of his name pressing on my heart. *Dimitri, Dimitri.* After a while, it grew to be too much. Sydney had stepped away for a bit, so I went outside to get some air. Some people had built a bonfire in the back and were sitting around it, still talking about Dimitri, so I headed off toward the front yard.

I walked down the street, not intending to go far. The night was warm and clear, with the moon and stars burning brightly in the blackness above me. My feelings were tangled up, and now that I was away from the others, I allowed a bit of that pent-up emotion to burst forth, coming out as silent tears on my cheeks. When I was a couple of houses away, I sat down on the curb, resting and enjoying the stillness around me. My peace was short-lived, however — my sharp ears picked up the sound of voices coming from the Belikov house. Three figures appeared. One, tall and slim, was Moroi, and the others were dhampirs. I stared as they came to a stop in front of me. Not bothering with formalities, I remained where I was, looking up into the Moroi's dark eyes. I didn't recognize this group from the service — but I did recognize the Moroi from somewhere else. I gave him a wry half-smile.

"Abe Mazur, I presume."

# NINE

"I thought you were a dream," I said.

They all remained standing, the dhampirs fanning out around the Moroi in a sort of protective formation. Abe's was the strange face I'd seen while I'd been going in and out of consciousness after the fight by the barn. He was older than me, close to Olena's age. He had black hair and a goatee, and about as tan a complexion as Moroi ever had. If you've ever seen tan or dark-skinned people who are sick and grow pale, it's a lot like that. There was some pigment in his skin, but it was underscored by an intense pallor. Most astonishing of all was his clothing. He wore a long dark coat that screamed money, paired with a cashmere crimson scarf. Below it, I could see a bit of gold, a chain to match the gold hoop earring he wore in one of his ears. My initial impression of that flamboyance would have been pirate or pimp. A moment later, I changed my mind. Something about him said he was the kind of guy who broke kneecaps to get his way.

"Dream, eh? That," the Moroi said, with the very slightest hint of a smile, "is not something I hear very often. Well, no." He reconsidered. "I do occasionally show up in people's nightmares." He was neither American nor Russian; I couldn't identify the accent.

Was he trying to impress me or intimidate me with his big, bad reputation? Sydney hadn't been afraid of him, exactly, but she'd certainly possessed a healthy amount of wariness.

"Well, I assume you already know who I am," I said. "So, the question now is, what are you doing here?"

"No," he said, the smile turning harder. "The question is, what are *you* doing here?"

I gestured back to the house, trying to play it cool. "I'm going to a funeral."

"That's not why you came to Russia."

"I came to Russia to tell the Belikovs that Dimitri was dead, seeing as no one else bothered to." That was turning into a handy explanation for me being here, but as Abe studied me, a chill ran down my spine, kind of like when Yeva looked at me. Like that crazy old woman, he didn't believe me, and again I felt the dangerous edge to his otherwise jovial personality.

Abe shook his head, and now the smile was gone altogether. "That's not the reason either. Don't lie to me, little girl."

I felt my hackles going up. "And don't interrogate me, old man. Not unless you're ready to tell me why you and your sidekicks risked driving that road to pick up Sydney and me." Abe's dhampirs stiffened at the words *old man,* but to my surprise, he actually smiled again — though the smile didn't reach his eyes.

"Maybe I was just helping out."

"Not from what I hear. You're the one who had the Alchemists send Sydney with me here."

"Oh?" He arched an eyebrow. "Did she tell you that? Mmm . . . that was bad behavior on her part. Her superiors aren't going to like that. Not at all."

Oh, damn. I'd spoken without thinking. I didn't want Sydney to get in trouble. If Abe really was some kind of Moroi Godfather type — what had she called him? *Zmey?* The snake? — I didn't doubt he could talk to other Alchemists to make her life even more miserable.

"I forced it out of her," I lied. "I . . . I threatened her on the train. It wasn't hard.

She's already scared to death of me."

"I don't doubt she is. They're all scared of us, bound by centuries of tradition and hiding behind their crosses to protect them — despite the gifts they get from their tattoos. In a lot of ways, they get the same traits as you dhampirs — just no reproductive issues." He gazed up at the stars as he spoke, like some sort of philosopher musing on the mysteries of the universe. Somehow, that made me angrier. He was treating this like a joke, when clearly he had some agenda regarding me. I didn't like being part of anyone's plans — particularly when I didn't know what those plans were.

"Yeah, yeah, I'm sure we could talk about the Alchemists and how you control them all night," I snapped. "But I still want to know what you want with me."

"Nothing," he said simply.

"Nothing? You've gone to a lot of trouble to set me up with Sydney and follow me here for nothing."

He looked back down from the sky, and there was a dangerous glint in his eyes. "You're of no interest to me. I have my own business to run. I come on behalf of *others* who are interested in you."

I stiffened, and at last, true fear ran through me. Shit. There *was* a manhunt out for me. But who? Lissa? Adrian? Tatiana? Again, that last one made me nervous. The others would seek me out because they cared. But Tatiana . . . Tatiana feared I'd run off with Adrian. Once more I thought that if she wanted me found, it might be because she wanted to ensure I didn't come back. Abe struck me as the kind of person who could make people disappear.

"And what do the others want? Do they want me home?" I asked, trying to appear unafraid. "Did you think you could just come here and drag me back to the U.S.?"

That secretive smile of Abe's returned. "Do *you* think I could just drag you back?"

"Well," I scoffed, again without thinking, "*you* couldn't. Your guys here could. Well, maybe. I might be able to take them."

Abe laughed out loud for the first time, a rich, deep sound filled with sincere amusement. "You live up to your brash reputation. Delightful." Great. Abe probably had a whole file on me somewhere. He probably knew what I liked for breakfast. "I'll make a trade with you. Tell me why you're here, and I'll tell you why I'm here."

"I already told you."

In a flash, the laughter was gone. He took a step closer to where I sat, and I saw his guardians tense. "And I told you not to lie to me. You've got a reason for being here. I need to know what it is."

"Rose? Can you come in here?"

Back toward the Belikov house, Viktoria's clear voice rang out in the night. Glancing behind me, I saw her standing in the doorway. Suddenly, I wanted to get away from Abe. There was something lethal underneath that gaudy, jovial façade, and I didn't want to spend another minute with him. Leaping up, I began backing toward the house, half-expecting his guardians to come kidnap me, despite his words. The two guys stayed where they were, but their eyes watched me carefully. Abe's quirky smile returned to his face.

"Sorry I can't stay and chat," I said.

"That's all right," he said grandly. "We'll find time later."

"Not likely," I said. He laughed, and I hastily followed Viktoria into the house, not feeling safe until I shut the door. "I do *not* like that guy."

"Abe?" she asked. "I thought he was your friend."

"Hardly. He's some kind of mobster, right?"

"I suppose," she said, like it was no big deal. "But he's the reason you're here."

"Yeah, I know about him coming to get us."

Viktoria shook her head. "No, I mean *here.* I guess while you were in the car, you kept saying, 'Belikov, Belikov.' Abe figured you knew us. That's why he took you to our house."

That was startling. I'd been dreaming of Dimitri, so of course I would have said his last name. But I'd had no idea that was how I'd ended up here. I'd figured it was because Olena had medical training.

Then Viktoria added the most astonishing thing of all. "When he realized we didn't know you, he was going to take you somewhere else — but grandmother said we had to keep you. I guess she'd had some dream that you'd come to us."

"What?" Crazy, creepy Yeva who hated me? "Yeva dreamed about me?"

Viktoria nodded. "It's this gift she has. Are you sure you don't know Abe? He's too big-time to be here without a reason."

Olena hurried over to us before I could respond. She caught hold of my arm. "We've been looking for you. What took so long?" This question was directed to Viktoria.

"Abe was —"

Olena shook her head. "Never mind. Come on. Everyone's waiting."

"For what?" I asked, letting her drag me through the house to the backyard.

"I was supposed to tell you," explained Viktoria, scurrying along. "This is the part where everyone sits and remembers Dimitri by telling stories."

"Nobody's seen him in so long; we don't know what's happened to him recently," said Olena. "We need you to tell us."

I flinched. Me? I balked at that, particularly when we emerged outside and I saw all those faces around the campfire. I didn't know any of them. How could I talk about Dimitri? How could I reveal what was closest to my heart? Everyone seemed to blur together, and I thought I might faint. For the moment, none of them noticed me. Karolina was speaking, her baby in her arms. Every so often she'd pause, and the others would laugh. Viktoria sat down on a blanket-covered spot on the ground and pulled me down beside her. Sydney joined us a little while later.

"What's she saying?" I whispered.

Viktoria listened to her sister for a few moments and then leaned closer to me. "She's talking about when Dimitri was very young, how he used to always beg her and her friends to let him play with them. He was about six and they were eight and didn't

166

want him around." Viktoria paused again to take in the next part of the story. "Finally, Karolina told him he could if he agreed to be married off to their dolls. So Karolina and her friends dressed him and the dolls up over and over and kept having weddings. Dimitri was married at least ten times."

I couldn't help but laugh as I tried to picture tough, sexy Dimitri letting his big sister dress him up. He probably would have treated his wedding ceremony with a doll as seriously and stoically as he did his guardian duties.

Other people spoke, and I tried to keep up with the translations. All the stories were about Dimitri's kindness and strength of character. Even when not out battling the undead, Dimitri had always been there to help those who needed it. Almost everyone could recall sometime that Dimitri had stepped up to help others, going out of his way to do what was right, even in situations that could put him at risk. That was no surprise to me. Dimitri always did the right thing.

And it was that attitude that had made me love him so much. I had a similar nature. I too rushed in when others needed me, sometimes when I shouldn't have. Others called me crazy for it, but Dimitri had understood. He'd always understood me, and part of what we'd worked on was how to temper that impulsive need to run into danger with reason and calculation. I had a feeling no one else in this world would ever understand me like he did.

I didn't notice how strongly the tears were running down my cheeks until I saw everyone looking at me. At first, I thought they considered me crazy for crying, but then I realized someone had asked me a question.

"They want you to talk about Dimitri's last days," Viktoria said. "Tell us something. What he did. What he was like."

I used my sleeve to clean my face and looked away, focusing on the bonfire. I'd spoken in front of others before without hesitation, but this was different. "I . . . I can't," I told Viktoria, my voice strained and soft. "I can't talk about him."

She squeezed my hand. "Please. They need to hear about him. They need to know. Just tell us anything. What was he like?"

"He . . . he was your brother. You know."

"Yes," she said gently. "But we want to know what you think he was like."

My eyes were still on the fire, watching the way the flames danced and shifted from orange to blue. "He . . . he was the best man I've ever met." I stopped to gather myself, and Viktoria used the opportunity to translate my words into Russian. "And he was one of the best guardians. I mean, he was young compared to a lot of them, but everyone knew who he was. They all knew his reputation, and lots of people relied on him for advice. They called him a god. And whenever there was a fight . . . or danger . . . he was always the first one to put himself out there. He never flinched. And a couple months ago, when our school was attacked . . ."

I choked up here a bit. The Belikovs had said they knew of the attack — that *everyone* knew about it — and from the faces here, it was true. I didn't need to elaborate on that night, on the horrors I'd seen.

"That night," I continued, "Dimitri rushed out to face the Strigoi. He and I were together when we realized they were attacking. I wanted to stay and help him, but he wouldn't let me. He just told me to go, to run off and alert others. And he stayed behind — not knowing how many Strigoi he'd have to take on while I went for help. I still don't know how many he fought — but there were a bunch. And he took them all down alone."

I dared to look up at the faces around me. Everyone was so quiet and still that I wondered if they were breathing. "It was so hard," I told them. Without realizing it, my voice had dropped to a whisper. I had to repeat myself more loudly. "It was so hard. I didn't want to leave him, but I knew I had to. He taught me so much, but one of the biggest things was that we have to protect others. It was my duty to warn everyone else, even though I just wanted to stay with him. The whole time, my heart kept saying, 'Turn around, turn around. Go to him!' But I knew what I had to do — and I also knew part of him was trying to keep me safe. And if the roles had been reversed . . . well, I would have made him run too."

I sighed, surprised I'd revealed so much of my heart. I switched back to business. "Even when the other guardians joined him, Dimitri never backed down. He took down more Strigoi than almost anyone." Christian and I had actually killed the most. "He . . . he was amazing."

I told them the rest of the story that I'd told the Belikovs. Only I actually forced a little detail this time, telling them vividly just how brave and fierce he had been. The words hurt me as I spoke, and yet . . . it was almost a relief to get them out. I'd kept the memories of that night too close to me. But eventually, I had to tell them about the cave. And that . . . that was the worst.

"We'd trapped the escaping Strigoi in a cave. It had two entrances, and we came at them from both sides. Some of our people got trapped, though, and there were more Strigoi than we'd expected. We lost people . . . but we would have lost a lot more if Dimitri hadn't been there. He wouldn't leave until everyone was out. He didn't care about the risk to himself. He only knew he had to save others. . . ."

I'd seen it in his eyes, that determination. Our plan had finally been to retreat as soon as we were all out, but I'd had the feeling he would have stayed and killed every Strigoi he could find. But he'd followed orders too, finally beginning his retreat when the others were safe. And in those last moments, just before the Strigoi had bitten him, Dimitri had met my eyes with a look so full of love that it was like that whole cave filled with light. His expression had said what we'd talked about earlier: *We can be together, Rose. Soon. We're almost there. And nothing will ever keep us apart again.* . . .

I didn't mention that part, though. When I finished the rest of the tale, the faces of those gathered were grim but filled with awe and respect. Near the back of the crowd, I noticed Abe and his guardians listening as well. His expression was unreadable. Hard, but not angry or scary. Small cups began circulating through the group, and someone handed me one. A dhampir I didn't know, one of the few men present, stood up and raised his cup in the air. He spoke loudly and reverently, and I heard Dimitri's name mentioned several times. When he finished, he drank from the cup. Everyone else did too, so I followed suit.

And nearly choked to death.

It was like fire in liquid form. It took every ounce of strength I had to swallow it and not spray it on those around me. "Wh . . . what is this?" I asked, coughing.

Viktoria grinned. "Vodka."

I peered at the glass. "No, it isn't. I've had vodka before."

"Not Russian vodka."

Apparently not. I forced the rest of the cup down out of respect to Dimitri, even though I had a feeling that if he were here, he'd be shaking his head at me. I thought I was done being in the spotlight after my story, but apparently not. Everyone kept asking me questions. They wanted to know more about Dimitri, more about what his life had been like recently. They also wanted to know about me and Dimitri as a couple. They all seemed to have figured out that

172

Dimitri and I had been in love — and they were okay with it. I was asked about how we'd met, how long we'd been together . . .

And the whole time, people kept refilling my cup. Determined not to look like an idiot again, I kept drinking until I could finally take the vodka down without coughing or spitting. The more I drank, the louder and more animated my stories became. My limbs started to tingle, and part of me knew this was all probably a bad idea. Okay, all of me knew it.

Finally, people began to clear out. I had no idea what time it was, but I think it was the middle of the night. Maybe later. I stood as well, finding it much harder to do than I'd expected. The world wobbled, and my stomach wasn't very happy with me. Someone caught a hold of my arm and steadied me.

"Easy," said Sydney. "Don't push it." Slowly, carefully, she led me toward the house.

"God," I moaned. "Do they use that stuff as rocket fuel?"

"No one made you keep drinking it."

"Hey, don't get preachy. Besides, I had to be polite."

"Sure," she said.

We made it inside and then had the impossible task of getting up the stairs to the room Olena had given me. Each step was agony.

"They all knew about me and Dimitri," I said, wondering if I'd be saying any of this sober. "But I never told them we were together."

"You didn't have to. It's written all over your face."

"They acted like I was his widow or something."

"You might as well be." We reached my room, and she helped me sit down on the bed. "Not a lot of people get married around here. If you're with someone long enough, they figure it's almost the same."

I sighed and stared off without any particular focus. "I miss him so much."

"I'm sorry," she said.

"Will it ever get better?"

The question seemed to catch her by surprise. "I . . . I don't know."

"Have you ever been in love?"

She shook her head. "No."

I wasn't sure if that made her lucky or not. I wasn't sure if all the bright days I'd had with Dimitri were worth the hurt I felt now. A moment later, I knew the truth. "Of course they were."

"Huh?" asked Sydney.

I realized I'd spoken my thoughts out

loud. "Nothing. Just talking to myself. I should get some sleep."

"Do you need anything else? Are you going to be sick?"

I assessed my queasy stomach. "No, but thanks."

"Okay." And in her typically brusque way, she left, turning off the lights and shutting the door.

I would have thought I'd pass out right away. Honestly, I *wanted* to. My heart had been opened up to too much of Dimitri tonight, and I wanted that pain to go away. I wanted blackness and oblivion. Instead, maybe because I was a glutton for punishment, my heart decided to finish the job and rip itself completely open.

I went to visit Lissa.

## TEN

Everyone had hit it off so well at lunch with Avery that the group had gotten together again that evening and had kind of a wild time. Lissa was thinking about that as she sat in her first-period English class the next morning. They'd stayed up late last night, sneaking out past curfew. The memory brought a smile to Lissa's face, even as she stifled a yawn. I couldn't help but feel a tiny bit of jealousy. I knew Avery was responsible for Lissa's happiness, and that bothered me on a petty level. Yet . . . Avery's new friendship was also making me feel less guilty about leaving Lissa.

Lissa yawned again. It was hard to concentrate on *The Scarlet Letter* while fighting a slight hangover. Avery seemed to have a never-ending supply of liquor. Adrian had taken to this right away, but Lissa had been a little more hesitant. She'd abandoned her partying days a long time ago, but she'd finally succumbed last night and drunk more glasses of wine than she really should have. It wasn't unlike my situation with the vodka, ironically enough. Both of us overindulging, despite being miles and miles apart.

Suddenly, a high-pitched wail pierced the air. Lissa's head shot up, along with everyone else's in the class. In a corner of the room, a small fire alarm flashed and shrieked its warning. Naturally, some students started cheering while some pretended to be scared. The rest just looked surprised and waited.

Lissa's instructor also looked a little caught off guard, and after a quick examination, Lissa decided this wasn't a planned alarm. Teachers usually had a heads-up when there were drills, and Ms. Malloy didn't wear the usual weary expression teachers had when trying to figure out how much time the drill would cut from their lessons.

"Up and at 'em," said Ms. Malloy in annoyance, grabbing a clipboard. "You know where to go." Fire drill procedure was pretty standard.

Lissa followed the others and fell in step with Christian. "Did you set this up?" she teased.

"Nope. Wish I had, though. This class is

killing me."

"You? I have the worst headache ever."

He gave her a knowing grin. "Let that be a lesson to you, Little Miss Lush."

She made a face in return and gave him a light punch. They reached their class's meeting spot out on the quad and joined in the semblance of a line the others were trying to form. Ms. Malloy arrived and checked everyone off on her clipboard, satisfied no one had been left behind.

"I don't think this was planned," said Lissa.

"Agreed," said Christian. "Which means even if there's no fire, it might take a while."

"Well, then. No use waiting around, huh?"

Christian and Lissa turned around in surprise at the voice behind them and saw Avery. She wore a purple sweaterdress and black heels that seemed totally out of place on the wet grass.

"What are you doing here?" asked Lissa. "Figured you'd be in your room."

"Whatever. It's *so* boring there. I had to come liberate you guys."

"You did this?" asked Christian, slightly impressed.

Avery shrugged. "I told you, I was bored. Now, come on while it's still chaotic."

Christian and Lissa exchanged glances.

"Well," said Lissa slowly, "I suppose they *did* already take attendance . . ."

"Hurry!" said Avery. Her excitement was contagious, and, feeling bold, Lissa hurried after her, Christian in tow. With all the milling students, no one noticed them cutting across the campus — until they reached the outside of guest housing. Simon stood leaning against the door, and Lissa stiffened. They were busted.

"Everything set?" Avery asked him.

Simon, definitely the strong-and-silent type, gave a swift nod as his only answer before straightening up. He stuffed his hands into his coat pockets and walked off. Lissa stared in amazement.

"He just . . . he just let us go? And is he in on it?" Simon wasn't on campus as a teacher, but still . . . that didn't necessarily mean he'd let students skip out on class because of a faked fire drill.

Avery grinned mischievously, watching him go. "We've been together for a while. He's got better things to do than babysit us."

She led them inside, but instead of going to her room, they cut off to a different section of the building and went somewhere I knew well: Adrian's room.

Avery beat on the door. "Hey, Ivashkov!

179

Open up."

Lissa slapped a hand over her mouth to smother her giggles. "So much for stealth. Everyone's going to hear you."

"I need *him* to hear me," Avery argued.

She kept pounding on the door and yelling, and finally, Adrian answered. His hair stuck up at odd angles, and he had dark circles under his eyes. He'd drunk twice as much as Lissa last night.

"What . . . ?" He blinked. "Shouldn't you guys be in class? Oh God. I didn't sleep that much, did I?"

"Let us in," said Avery, pushing past. "We've got refugees from a fire here."

She flounced onto his couch, making herself at home while he continued staring. Lissa and Christian joined her.

"Avery sprang the fire alarm," explained Lissa.

"Nice work," said Adrian, collapsing into a fluffy chair. "But why'd you have to come *here?* Is this the only place that's not burning down?"

Avery batted her eyelashes at him. "Aren't you happy to see us?"

He eyed her speculatively for a moment. "Always happy to see you."

Lissa was normally pretty straitlaced about this kind of thing, but something about it amused her. It was so wild, so silly . . . it was a break from all her recent worries. "It's not going to take them that long to figure it out, you know. They could be letting everyone in right now."

"They could be," agreed Avery, putting her feet up on the coffee table. "But I have it on good authority that *another* alarm is going to go off in the school once they open the doors."

"How the hell did you manage that?" asked Christian.

"Top secret."

Adrian rubbed his eyes and was clearly amused by this, despite the abrupt wake-up. "You can't pull fire alarms all day, Lazar."

"Actually, I have it on good authority that once they give the all-clear on a second alarm, a third's going to go off."

Lissa laughed out loud, though a lot of it was due more to the guys' reactions and less to Avery's announcement. Christian, in fits of antisocial rebellion, had set people on fire. Adrian spent most of his days drunk and chain-smoking. For a cute society girl like Avery to astonish them, something truly remarkable had to happen. Avery looked very pleased at having outdone them.

"If the interrogation's over now," she said,

181

"aren't you going to offer your guests any refreshments?"

Adrian stood up and yawned. "Fine, fine, you insolent girl. I'll make coffee."

"With a kick?" She inclined her head toward Adrian's liquor cabinet.

"You have got to be kidding," said Christian. "Do you even have a liver left?"

Avery wandered over to the cabinet and picked up a bottle of something. She held it out to Lissa. "You game?"

Even Lissa's morning rebelliousness had limits. The wine headache still throbbed in her skull. "Ugh, no."

"Cowards," said Avery. She turned back to Adrian. "Well then, Mr. Ivashkov, you'd best put on the pot. I always like a little coffee with my brandy."

Not long after that, I faded away from Lissa's head and drifted back into my own, returning to the blackness of sleep and ordinary dreams. It was short-lived, however, seeing as a loud pounding soon jerked me into consciousness.

My eyes flew open, and a deep, searing pain shot through the back of my skull — the aftereffects of that toxic vodka, no doubt. Lissa's hangover had nothing on mine. I started to close my eyes, wanting to sink back under and let sleep heal the worst of my pain. Then, I heard the pounding again — and worse, my whole bed shook violently. Someone was kicking it.

Opening my eyes again, I turned and found myself staring into Yeva's shrewd dark eyes. If Sydney had met many dhampirs like Yeva, I could understand why she thought our race were minions of hell. Pursing her lips, Yeva kicked the bed again.

"Hey," I cried. "I'm awake, okay?"

Yeva muttered something in Russian, and Paul peered around from behind her, translating. "She says you're not awake until you're actually out of bed and standing up."

And with no more warning, that sadistic old woman continued kicking the bed. I jerked upright, and the world spun around me. I'd said this before, but this time, I really meant it: I was never going to drink again. No good *ever* came from it. The covers looked awfully tempting to my agonized body, but a few more kicks from Yeva's pointy-toed boots made me shoot up off the bed.

"Okay, okay. Are you happy now? I'm up." Yeva's expression didn't change, but at least she stopped with the kicking. I turned to Paul. "What's going on?"

"Grandmother says you have to go with her."

"Where?"

"She says you don't need to know."

I started to say that I wasn't following that crazy old wench anywhere, but after one look at her scary face, I thought better of it. I didn't put it past her to be able to turn people into toads.

"Fine," I said. "I'll be ready to go once I shower and change."

Paul translated my words, but Yeva shook her head and spoke again. "She says there's no time," he explained. "We have to go now."

"Can I at least brush my teeth?"

She allowed that small concession, but a change of clothes was apparently out of the question. It was just as well. Each step I took made me feel woozy, and I probably would have passed out doing something as complicated as dressing and undressing. The clothes didn't smell or anything either; they were mostly just wrinkled from where I'd fallen asleep in them.

When I got downstairs, I saw that no one else was awake except Olena. She was washing leftover dishes from last night and seemed surprised to see me up. That made two of us.

"It's early for you, isn't it?" she asked.

I turned and caught sight of the kitchen clock. I gasped. It was only about four hours after I'd gone to bed. "Good God. Is the sun even up?"

Amazingly, it was. Olena offered to make me breakfast, but again, Yeva reiterated our time crunch. My stomach seemed to simultaneously want and loathe food, so I couldn't say if abstaining was a good thing or not.

"Whatever," I said. "Let's just go and get this over with."

Yeva walked into the living room and returned a few moments later with a large satchel. She handed it to me expectantly. I shrugged and took it, hanging it over one shoulder. It clearly had stuff in it, but it wasn't that heavy. She went back out to the other room and returned with another tote bag. I took this one too and hung it over the same shoulder, balancing both of them. This one was heavier, but my back didn't complain too much.

When she left for a third time and returned with a giant box, I started to get irate. "What is this?" I demanded, taking it from her. It felt like it had bricks in it.

"Grandmother needs you to carry some things," Paul told me.

"Yes," I said through gritted teeth. "I sort of figured that out fifty pounds ago."

Yeva gave me one more box, stacking it on top of the other. It wasn't as heavy, but by this point, it honestly didn't matter. Olena shot me a sympathetic look, shook her head, and returned silently to her dishes, apparently not about to argue with Yeva.

Yeva set off after that, and I followed obediently, trying to both hold the boxes and not let the bags fall off my shoulder. It was a heavy load, one my hungover body really didn't want, but I was strong enough that I figured it wouldn't be a problem to get into town or wherever she was leading me. Paul ran along at my side, apparently there to let me know if Yeva found anything along the road she wanted me to carry too.

It seemed like spring was charging into Siberia far faster than it ever did into Montana. The sky was clear, and the morning sun was heating things up surprisingly fast. It was hardly summer weather, but it was definitely enough to notice. It would have made very uncomfortable walking weather for a Moroi.

"Do *you* know where we're going?" I asked Paul.

"No," he said cheerfully.

For someone so old, Yeva could move at a pretty good pace, and I found myself having to hurry to keep up with her with my load. At one point, she glanced back and said something that Paul translated as, "She's kind of surprised that you can't move faster."

"Yeah, well, I'm kind of surprised that no one else can carry any of this."

He translated again: "She says if you're really such a famous Strigoi killer, then this shouldn't be a problem."

I was filled with great relief when downtown came into sight . . . only we kept walking past it.

"Oh, come *on,*" I said. "Where the hell are we going?"

Without giving me a backward glance, Yeva rattled off something. "Grandmother says Uncle Dimka never would have complained so much," Paul said.

None of this was Paul's fault; he was just the messenger. Yet, every time he spoke, I kind of wanted to kick him. Nonetheless, I kept carrying my burden and didn't say anything else for the rest of the walk. Yeva was right to a certain extent. I was a Strigoi hunter, and it was true that Dimitri would have never complained about some old lady's crazy whims. He would have done his duty patiently.

I tried to summon him up in my mind and draw strength from him. I thought about that time in the cabin again, thought about the way his lips had felt on mine and the wonderful scent of his skin when I'd pressed closer to him. I could hear his voice once more, murmuring in my ear that he loved me, that I was beautiful, that I was the only one . . . Thinking of him didn't take away the discomfort of my journey with Yeva, but it made it a little more bearable.

We walked for almost an hour more before reaching a small house, and I was ready to fall over in relief, soaked in sweat. The house was one floor, made of plain, weatherworn brown boards. The windows, however, were surrounded on three sides by exquisite, highly stylized blue shutters overlaid with a white design. It was that same sort of flashy use of color I'd seen on the buildings in Moscow and Saint Petersburg. Yeva knocked on the door. At first there was only silence, and I panicked, thinking we'd have to turn right around and head back.

Finally, a woman answered the door — a Moroi woman. She was maybe thirty, very pretty, with high cheekbones and strawberry-blond hair. She exclaimed in surprise at seeing Yeva, smiling and greeting her in Russian. Glancing over at Paul and me, the woman quickly stepped aside and gestured us in.

She switched to English as soon as she realized I was American. All these bilingual people were kind of amazing. It wasn't something I saw very often in the U.S. She pointed to a table and told me to set everything there, which I did with relief.

"My name's Oksana," she said, shaking my hand. "My husband, Mark, is in the garden and should be in soon."

"I'm Rose," I told her.

Oksana offered us chairs. Mine was wooden and straight-backed, but at that moment, it felt like a down-filled bed. I sighed happily and wiped the sweat off my brow. Meanwhile, Oksana unpacked the things I'd carried.

The bags were filled with leftovers from the funeral. The top box contained some dishes and pots, which Paul explained had been borrowed from Oksana some time ago. Oksana finally reached the bottom box, and so help me, it was filled with *garden bricks*.

"You have got to be kidding," I said. Across the living room, Yeva looked very smug.

Oksana was delighted by the gifts. "Oh, Mark will be happy to have these." She smiled at me. "It was very sweet of you to carry these that whole way."

"Happy to help," I said stiffly.

The back door opened, and a man walked in — Mark, presumably. He was tall and stockily built, his graying hair indicating an age greater than Oksana's. He washed his hands in the kitchen sink and then turned to join us. I nearly gasped when I saw his face and discovered something stranger than the age difference. He was a dhampir. For a moment, I wondered if this was someone else and not her husband, Mark. But that was the name Oksana introduced him with, and the truth hit me: a Moroi and dhampir married couple. Sure, our two races hooked up all the time. But marriage? It was very scandalous in the Moroi world.

I tried to keep the surprise off my face and behave as politely as I could. Oksana and Mark seemed very interested in me, though she did most of the talking. Mark simply watched, curiosity all over his face. My hair was down, so my tattoos couldn't have given away my unpromised status. Maybe he was just wondering how an American girl had found her way out to the middle of nowhere. Maybe he thought I was a new blood whore recruit.

By my third glass of water, I began to feel

better. It was around that time that Oksana said we should eat, and by then, my stomach was ready for it. Oksana and Mark prepared the food together, dismissing any offers of help.

Watching the couple work was fascinating. I had never seen such an efficient team. They never got in each other's way and never needed to talk about what needed doing next. They just knew. Despite the remote location, the kitchen's contents were modern, and Oksana placed a dish of some sort of potato casserole in the microwave. Mark's back was to her while he rummaged in the refrigerator, but as soon as she hit start, he said, "No, it doesn't need to be that long."

I blinked in surprise, glancing back and forth between them. He hadn't even seen what time she'd selected. Then I got it. "You're bonded," I exclaimed.

Both looked at me in equal surprise. "Yes. Didn't Yeva tell you?" Oksana asked.

I shot a quick look at Yeva, who was again wearing that annoyingly self-satisfied look on her face. "No. Yeva hasn't been very forthcoming this morning."

"Most everyone around here knows," Oksana said, returning to her work.

"Then . . . then you're a spirit user."

That made her pause again. She and Mark

exchanged startled looks. "That," she said, "is *not* something that's widely known."

"Most people think you haven't specialized, right?"

"How did you know?"

Because it was exactly how it had been for Lissa and me. Stories of bonds had always existed in Moroi folklore, but how bonds formed had always been a mystery. It was generally believed they "just happened." Like Oksana, Lissa had generally been regarded as a non-specializing Moroi — one who didn't have any special ability with one element. We realized now, of course, that bonding only occurred with spirit users, when they saved the lives of others.

Something in Oksana's voice told me she wasn't really all that surprised I knew. I couldn't figure out how she'd realized that, however, and I was too stunned by my discovery to say anything else. Lissa and I had never, ever met another bonded pair. The only such two we knew about were the legendary Vladimir and Anna. And those stories were shrouded by centuries of incomplete history, making it difficult to know fact from fiction. The only other leads we had to the world of spirit were Ms. Karp — a former teacher who went insane — and Adrian. Until now, he had been our biggest discovery, a spirit user who was more or less stable — depending on how you looked at it.

When the meal was ready, spirit never came up. Oksana led the conversation, keeping to light topics and jumping between languages. I studied her and Mark as I ate, looking for any signs of instability. I saw none. They seemed like perfectly pleasant, perfectly ordinary people. If I hadn't known what I did, I would have had no reason to suspect anything. Oksana didn't seem depressed or unhinged. Mark hadn't inherited that vile darkness that sometimes seeped into me.

My stomach welcomed the food, and the last of my headache faded away. At one point, though, a strange sensation swept through me. It was disorienting, like a fluttering in my head, and a wave of heat and then ice coursing through me. The feeling disappeared as quickly as it came on, and I hoped it'd be the last of that demon vodka's ill effects.

We finished eating, and I jumped up to help. Oksana shook her head. "No, there's no need. You should go with Mark."

"Huh?" I asked.

He dabbed at his face with a napkin and then stood up. "Yes. Let's go out to the garden."

I started to follow, then paused to glance back at Yeva. I expected her to chastise me for abandoning the dishes. Instead, I found no smug or disapproving looks. Her expression was . . . knowing. Almost expectant. Something about it sent a shiver down my back, and I recalled Viktoria's words: Yeva had dreamed of my arrival.

The garden Mark led me to was much bigger than I expected, enclosed in a thick fence and lined with trees. New leaves hung on them, blocking the worst of the heat. Lots of bushes and flowers were already in bloom, and here and there, young shoots were well on their way to adulthood. It was beautiful, and I wondered if Oksana had had a hand in it. Lissa was able to make plants grow with spirit. Mark gestured me over to a stone bench. We sat down side by side, and silence fell.

"So," he said. "What would you like to know?"

"Wow. You don't waste time."

"I don't see any point in it. You must have lots of questions. I'll do my best to answer."

"How did you know?" I asked. "That I'm shadow-kissed too. You did, right?"

He nodded. "Yeva told us."

Okay, *that* was a surprise. "Yeva?"

"She can sense things . . . things the rest of us can't. She doesn't always know what she's sensing, however. She only knew there was a strange feel to you, and she'd only ever felt that around one other person. So she brought you to me."

"Seems like she could have done that without me having to carry a household's worth of stuff."

This made him laugh. "Don't take it personally. She was testing you. She wanted to see if you're a worthy match for her grandson."

"What's the point? He's dead now." I nearly choked on the words.

"True, but for her, it's still important. And, by the way, she does think you're worthy."

"She has a funny way of showing it. I mean, aside from bringing me to meet you, I guess."

He laughed again. "Even without her, Oksana would have known what you are as soon as she met you. Being shadow-kissed has an effect on the aura."

"So she can see auras too," I murmured. "What else can she do? She must be able to heal, or you wouldn't be shadow-kissed. Does she have super-compulsion? Can she walk dreams?"

That caught him off guard. "Her compulsion is strong, yes . . . but what do you mean, walk dreams?"

"Like . . . she'd be able to enter someone else's mind when they're asleep. Anyone's mind — not just yours. Then they could have conversations, just as if they were together. My friend can do it."

Mark's expression told me that was news to him. "Your friend? Your bondmate?"

Bondmate? I'd never heard that term. It was weird-sounding, but it made sense. "No . . . another spirit user."

"Another? How many do you know?"

"Three, technically. Well, four now, counting Oksana."

Mark turned away, staring absentmindedly at a cluster of pink flowers. "That many . . . that's incredible. I've only met one other spirit user, and that was years ago. He too was bonded to his guardian. That guardian died, and it ripped him apart. He still helped us when Oksana and I were trying to figure things out."

I braced myself for my own death all the time, and I feared for Lissa's. Yet it had never occurred to me just what it would be like with a bond. How would it affect the other person? What would it be like to have a gaping hole, where once you'd been intimately linked to someone else?

"He never mentioned walking dreams either," Mark continued. He chuckled again, friendly lines crinkling up around his blue eyes. "I thought I would be helping you, but maybe you're here to help me."

"I don't know," I said doubtfully. "I think you guys have more experience at this than we do."

"Where's your bondmate?"

"Back in the U.S." I didn't have to elaborate, but somehow, I needed to tell him the whole truth. "I . . . I left her."

He frowned. "Left as in . . . you simply traveled? Or left as in you abandoned her?"

*Abandoned.* The word was like a slap in the face, and suddenly, all I could envision was that last day I'd seen her, when I'd left her crying.

"I had things to do," I said evasively.

"Yes, I know. Oksana told me."

"Told you what?"

Now he hesitated. "She shouldn't have done it. . . . She tries not to."

"Done what?" I exclaimed, uneasy for reasons I couldn't explain.

"She, well . . . she brushed your mind. During brunch."

I thought back and suddenly recalled the tickling in my head, the heat rolling over

197

me. "What does that mean exactly?"

"An aura can tell a spirit user about someone's personality. But Oksana can also dig further, reaching in and actually reading more specific information about a person. Sometimes she can tie that ability into compulsion . . . but the results are very, very powerful. And wrong. It's not right to do that to someone you have no bond with."

It took me a moment to process that. Neither Lissa nor Adrian could read the thoughts of others. The closest Adrian could come to someone's mind was the dream walking. Lissa couldn't do that, not even for me. I could feel her, but the opposite wasn't true.

"Oksana could feel . . . oh, I don't know how to explain it. There's a recklessness in you. You're on some sort of quest. There's vengeance written all over your soul." He suddenly reached over and lifted my hair up, peering at my neck. "Just as I thought. You're unpromised."

I jerked my head back. "Why is that such a big deal? That whole town back there is filled with dhampirs who aren't guardians." I still thought Mark was a nice guy, but being preached to always irritated me.

"Yes, but they've chosen to settle down. You . . . and others like you . . . you become vigilantes of sorts. You're obsessed with hunting Strigoi on your own, with personally setting out to right the wrongs that whole race has brought down upon us. That can only lead to trouble. I see it all the time."

"All the time?" I asked, startled.

"Why do you think guardian numbers are dwindling? They're leaving to have homes and families. Or they're going off like you, still fighting but answering to no one — unless they're hired to be bodyguards or Strigoi hunters."

"Dhampirs for hire . . ." I suddenly began to understand how a non-royal like Abe had gotten his bodyguards. Money could make anything happen, I supposed. "I've never heard of anything like that."

"Of course not. You think the Moroi and other guardians want that widely known? Want to dangle that in front of you as an option?"

"I don't see what's so wrong with Strigoi hunting. We're always defensive, not offensive, when it comes to Strigoi. Maybe if more dhampirs set out after them, they wouldn't be such a problem."

"Perhaps, but there are different ways of going about that, some better than others. And when you're going out like you are —

with a heart filled with sorrow and revenge? That's not one of the better ways. It'll make you sloppy. And the shadow-kissed darkness will just complicate things."

I crossed my arms over my chest and stared stonily ahead. "Yeah, well, it's not like I can do much about that."

He turned to me, expression surprised once more. "Why don't you just have your bondmate heal the darkness out of you?"

# ELEVEN

I stared at Mark for several long seconds. Finally, stupidly, I asked, "Did you say . . . heal?"

Mark stared at me in equal surprise. "Yes, of course. She can heal other things, right? Why not this?"

"Because . . ." I frowned. "That doesn't make any sense. The darkness . . . all the bad side effects . . . those come from Lissa. If she could just heal it, why wouldn't she heal it out of herself?"

"Because when it's in her, it's too ingrained. Too tied into her being. She can't heal it the way she can other things. But once your bond has pulled it into *you*, it's like any other sickness."

My heart was pounding in my chest. What he was suggesting was too ridiculously easy. No, it was just ridiculous, period. There was no way after all that we'd been through that Lissa could heal that rage and depression the way she could a cold or a broken leg. Victor Dashkov, despite his wicked schemes, had known an astonishing amount about spirit and had explained it to us. The other four elements were more physical in nature, but spirit came from the mind and soul. To use that much mental energy — to be able to do such powerful things — couldn't be done without devastating side effects. We'd been fighting those side effects from the beginning, first in Lissa and then in me. They couldn't just go away.

"If that were possible," I said quietly, "then everyone would have done it. Ms. Karp wouldn't have lost her mind. Anna wouldn't have committed suicide. What you're saying is too easy." Mark didn't know who I was talking about, but clearly it didn't matter for what he wanted to express.

"You're right. It's not easy at all. It requires a careful balance, a circle of trust and strength between two people. It took Oksana and me a long time to learn . . . many hard years . . ."

His face darkened, and I could only imagine what those years had been like. My short time with Lissa had been bad enough. They'd had to live with this a lot longer than we had. It had to have been unbearable at times. Slowly, wonderingly, I dared to give credence to his words.

"But now you guys are okay?"

"Hmm." There was a flicker of a wry smile on his lips. "I'd hardly say we're *perfectly* okay. There's only so much she can do, but it makes life manageable. She spaces out the healings as long as we can handle it, since it takes a lot out of her. It's draining, and it limits her overall power."

"What do you mean?"

He shrugged. "She can still do the other things . . . healing, compulsion . . . but not to the levels she would if she wasn't always healing me."

My hope faltered. "Oh. Then . . . I couldn't. I couldn't do that to Lissa."

"Compared to what she's doing to you? Rose. I have a feeling she'd think it was a fair trade."

I thought back to our last meeting. I thought about how I'd left her there, despite her begging. I thought about the lows she'd been experiencing in my absence. I thought about how she'd refused to heal Dimitri when I'd thought there might still be hope for him. We'd both been bad friends.

I shook my head. "I don't know," I said in a small voice. "I don't know if she would."

Mark gave me a long, level look, but he didn't push me on the matter. He glanced up at the sun, almost as if he could tell the time from it. He probably could. He had that surviving-in-the-wilderness kind of feel to him. "The others will wonder what happened to us. Before we go . . ." He reached into his pocket and pulled out a small, plain silver ring. "Learning to heal will take time. What worries me the most right now is this vigilante mood you're in. The darkness is only going to make it worse. Take this."

He extended the ring to me. I hesitated and then reached for it. "What is it?"

"Oksana infused it with spirit. It's a healing charm."

Once again, shock ran through me. Moroi charmed objects with elements all the time. Stakes were charmed with all four of the physical elements, making them lethal to Strigoi. Victor had charmed a necklace with earth magic, using the base nature of earth to turn the necklace into a lust charm. Even Sydney's tattoo was a charm of sorts. I supposed there was no reason that spirit couldn't charm objects too, but it had never occurred to me, probably because Lissa's powers were still too new and too foreign.

"What's it do? I mean, what kind of healing?"

"It'll help with your moods. It can't get rid of them, but it'll lessen them — help you think more clearly. Might keep you out of trouble. Oksana makes these for me to help between healings." I started to slip it on, but he shook his head. "Save it for when you really feel out of control. The magic won't last forever. It fades just like any other charm."

I stared at the ring, my mind suddenly open to all sorts of new possibilities. A few moments later, I slipped it into my coat pocket.

Paul stuck his head out the back door.

"Grandmother wants to leave now," he told me. "She wants to know why you're taking so long and said to ask why you'd make someone as old as her keep waiting and suffering with her back."

I recalled how fast Yeva had been walking while I struggled to keep up with my load. Her back hadn't seemed all that bad to me, but again, I remembered that Paul was only the messenger and spared him my commentary.

"Okay. I'll be right there." When he was gone, I shook my head. "It's hard being worthy." I moved toward the door, then gave Mark a backward glance, as a random thought occurred to me. "You're telling me that going off on your own is bad . . . but you aren't a guardian either."

He smiled at me again, one of those sad, wry smiles. "I used to be. Then Oksana saved my life. We bonded and eventually fell in love. I couldn't stand to be separated from her after that, and the guardians would have assigned me elsewhere. I had to go."

"Was it hard to leave them?"

"Very. Our age difference made it even more scandalous." A strange chill ran through me. Mark and Oksana were the embodiment of the two halves of my life. They fought against a shadow-kissed bond as Lissa and I did and also faced the same condemnation for their relationship that Dimitri and I had. Mark continued, "But sometimes, we have to listen to our hearts. And even though I left, I'm not out there recklessly going after Strigoi. I'm an old man living with the woman he loves and tending his garden. There's a difference — don't forget that."

My mind was reeling when I returned to the Belikov house. Without the bricks, the walk back had been a lot easier. It had given me a chance to ponder Mark's words. I felt like I'd received a lifetime of information in a one-hour conversation.

Olena was going about the house, doing her normal tasks of cooking and cleaning.

While I would personally never want to spend my days doing those sorts of domestic duties, I had to admit there was something comforting about always having someone who was around, ready to cook and worry about me on a daily basis. I knew it was a purely selfish desire, just as I knew my own mom was doing important things with her life. I shouldn't judge her. Still, it made me feel warm and cared for to have Olena treat me like a daughter when she hardly knew me.

"Are you hungry?" she asked automatically. I think one of the greatest fears in her life was that someone might go hungry in her home. Sydney's perpetual lack of appetite had been a nonstop worry for Olena.

I hid a smile. "No, we ate at Mark and Oksana's."

"Ah, that's where you were? They're good people."

"Where is everyone?" I asked. The house was unusually quiet.

"Sonya and Karolina are at work. Viktoria's out at a friend's, but she'll be glad you're back."

"What about Sydney?"

"She left a little while ago. She said she was going back to Saint Petersburg."

"What?" I exclaimed. "Left for good? Just

like that?" Sydney had a blunt nature, but this was abrupt even for her.

"The Alchemists . . . well, they're always on the move." Olena handed me a piece of paper. "She left this for you."

I took the note and immediately opened it. Sydney's handwriting was neat and precise. Somehow this didn't surprise me.

Rose,

I'm sorry I had to leave so quickly, but when the Alchemists tell me to jump . . . well, I jump. I've hitched a ride back to that farm town we stayed in so that I can pick up the Red Hurricane, and then I'm off to Saint Petersburg. Apparently, now that you've been delivered to Baia, they don't need me to stick around anymore.

I wish I could tell you more about Abe and what he wants from you. Even if I was allowed to, there isn't much to say. In some ways, he's as much a mystery to me as he is to you. Like I said, a lot of the business he deals in is illegal — both among humans and Moroi. The only time he gets directly involved with people is when something relates to that business — or if it's a very, very special case. I think you're one of those cases, and even if he doesn't intend you harm, he might want to use you for his own purposes. It could be as simple as him wanting to contract you as a bodyguard, seeing as you're rogue. Maybe he wants to use you to get to others. Maybe this is all part of someone else's plan, someone who's even more mysterious than him. Maybe he's doing someone a favor. Zmey can be dangerous or kind, all depending on what he needs to accomplish.

I never thought I'd care enough to say this to a dhampir, but be careful. I don't know what your plans are now, but I have a feeling trouble follows you around. Call me if there's anything I can help with, but if you go back to the big cities to hunt Strigoi, don't leave any more bodies unattended!

All the best,<br>Sydney

P.S. "The Red Hurricane" is what I named the car.

P.P.S. Just because I like you, it doesn't mean I still don't think you're an evil creature of the night. You are.

Her cell phone number was added at the bottom, and I couldn't help but smile. Since we'd ridden to Baia with Abe and his guardians, Sydney had had to leave the car behind, which had traumatized her almost as much as the Strigoi. I hoped the Alchemists would let her keep it. I shook my head, amused in spite of her warnings about Abe. The Red Hurricane.

As I headed upstairs to my room, my smile faded. Despite her abrasive attitude, I was going to miss Sydney. She might not exactly be a friend — or was she? — but in this brief time, I'd come to regard her as a constant in my life. I didn't have many of those left anymore. I felt adrift, unsure what to do now. I'd come here to bring peace to Dimitri and had only ended up bringing grief to his family. And if what everyone said was true, I wasn't going to find many Strigoi here in Baia. Somehow, I couldn't picture Dimitri, wandering the road and farms for the occasional prey. Even as a Strigoi — and it killed me to think those words — Dimitri would have a purpose. If he wasn't returning to the familiar sights of his hometown, then he would be doing something else meaningful — inasmuch as a Strigoi could. Sydney's comment in the note had verified what I kept hearing over and over: Strigoi were in the cities. But which one? Where would Dimitri go?

Now *I* was the one without a purpose. On top of it all, I couldn't help but replay Mark's words. Was I really on an insane vigilante mission? Was I foolishly rushing to my death? Or was I foolishly rushing into . . . nothing? Was I doomed to spend the rest of my days wandering? Alone?

Sitting on my bed, I felt my mood plummet and knew I had to distract myself. I was too susceptible to dark emotions as long as Lissa used spirit; I didn't need to further encourage them. I slipped on the ring that Mark had given me, hoping it would bring some sort of clarity and tranquility. I felt no noticeable difference, though, and decided to seek peace from that same place I always did: Lissa's mind.

She was with Adrian, and the two were practicing spirit again. After some initial bumps in the road, Adrian was proving a quick study at healing. That had been the first of Lissa's powers to manifest, and it always irked her that he made more progress on what she had to teach him than vice versa.

"I'm running out of things for you to heal," she said, setting some tiny potted plants onto a table. "Unless we start cutting off limbs or something."

Adrian smiled. "I used to tease Rose about

that, how I was going to impress her by healing amputees or something equally absurd."

"Oh, and I'm sure she had a smartass response for you each time."

"Yes, yes, she did." His face was fond as he recalled the memory. There was a part of me that was always insanely curious to hear them talk about me . . . yet at the same time, I always felt bad at the grief my name seemed to invoke.

Lissa groaned and stretched out on the carpeted floor. They were in a dorm lounge, and curfew was swiftly approaching. "I want to talk to her, Adrian."

"You can't," he said. There was an unusual seriousness in his voice. "I know she still checks in on you — that's the closest you'll get to talking to her. And honestly? That's not so bad. You can tell her exactly how you feel."

"Yeah, but I want to hear her talk back like you do in your dreams."

This made him smile again. "She does plenty of talking back, believe me."

Lissa sat up straight. "Do it now."

"Do what now?"

"Go visit her dreams. You always try to explain it to me, but I've never actually seen it. Let me watch."

He stared, at a loss for words. "That's kind of voyeuristic."

"Adrian! I want to learn this, and we've tried everything else. I can feel the magic around you sometimes. Just do it, okay?"

He started to protest again but then bit off his comment after studying her face for a moment. Her words had been sharp and demanding — very uncharacteristic for her. "Okay. I'll try."

The whole idea of Adrian trying to get into my head while I was watching him through Lissa's head was surreal, to say the least. I didn't quite know what to expect from him. I'd always wondered if he had to be asleep or at least have his eyes closed. Apparently not. He instead stared off at nothing, his eyes going vacant as his mind left the world around him. Through Lissa's eyes, I could see some of the magic radiating off him and his aura, and she tried to analyze each strand. Then, without warning, all the magic faded. He blinked and shook his head.

"Sorry. I can't do it."

"Why not?"

"Proobably because she's awake. Did you learn anything by watching?"

"A little. Probably would've been more useful if you'd actually made the connection." Again, Lissa had that petulant tone.

"She could be anywhere in the world, you know, on any schedule." His words were smothered by a yawn. "Maybe we can try at different times of the day. I've been getting her . . . actually, close to this time. Or sometimes I catch her really early in the day."

"She could be closeby then," said Lissa.

"Or on a human daylight schedule in some other part of the world."

Her enthusiasm dropped. "Right. That too."

"How come you guys never look like you're working?"

Christian strolled into the room, looking amused at Lissa sitting on the floor and Adrian sprawling on the couch. Standing behind Christian was someone I hadn't thought I'd see anytime soon. Adrian, who could detect women a mile away, also immediately noticed the newcomer.

"Where'd you get the jailbait?" he asked.

Christian shot Adrian a warning look. "This is Jill." Jill Mastrano allowed herself to be nudged forward, her light green eyes impossibly wide as she looked around. "Jill, this is Lissa and Adrian."

Jill was one of the last people I'd expected to see here. I'd met her a little over a month ago. She was in ninth grade, which meant she'd be here on the upper campus in the fall. She had the same super-slim build that most Moroi had, but it was paired with height that was impressive even by vampiric standards. It made her look rail-thin. Her hair fell in light brown curls to the middle of her back and would be beautiful — when she learned how to style it properly. For now, it was kind of messy, and her overall impression — while cute — was kind of awkward.

"H-hi," she said, looking from face to face. As far as she was concerned, these were Moroi gold star celebrities. She'd nearly passed out when she first met me and Dimitri, thanks to our reputations. From her expression, she was in a similar state now.

"Jill wants to learn how to use her power for good instead of evil," said Christian with an exaggerated wink. That was his coy way of saying Jill wanted to learn how to fight with her magic. She'd expressed the interest to me, and I'd told her to find Christian. I was glad she'd had the courage to take me up on my advice. Christian was a campus celebrity too, albeit an infamous one.

"Another recruit?" asked Lissa, shaking her head. "Think you'll keep this one around?"

Jill gave Christian a startled look. "What's that mean?"

"After the attack, lots of people said they wanted to learn to fight with magic," Christian explained. "So they found me, and we worked together . . . once or twice. Then everyone faded away once it got hard, and they realized they had to keep practicing."

"It doesn't help that you're a mean teacher," pointed out Lissa.

"And so now you've got to recruit among children," said Adrian solemnly.

"Hey," said Jill indignantly. "I'm fourteen." Immediately, she flushed at having spoken so boldly to him. He found it amusing, as he did so many other things.

"My mistake," he said. "What's your element?"

"Water."

"Fire and water, huh?" Adrian reached into his pocket and pulled out a one-hundred-dollar bill. He snapped it out straight. "Sweetheart, I'll make you a deal. If you can make a bucket of water appear and dump over Christian's head, I'll give you this."

"I'll add in ten," laughed Lissa.

Jill looked stunned, but I suspected it was because Adrian had called her "sweetheart." I took Adrian for granted so often that it was easy to forget he really was a hot guy. Christian pushed Jill toward the door.

"Ignore them. They're just jealous because spirit users can't go charging into battle like we can." He knelt down to Lissa's height on the floor and gave her a quick kiss. "We were practicing in the lounge upstairs, but I've got to walk her back now. I'll see you tomorrow."

"You don't have to," said Jill. "I can get back there fine. I don't want to be any trouble."

Adrian stood up. "You aren't. If anyone's going to step up and be the knight in shining armor here, it might as well be me. I'll take you back and leave the lovebirds to their lovebirding." He gave Jill a grand bow. "Shall we?"

"Adrian —" said Lissa, a sharp note in her voice.

"Oh, come on," he said, rolling his eyes. "I've got to head back anyway — you guys are of no use once curfew comes. And honestly, give me some credit here. Even I have boundaries."

He gave Lissa a meaningful look, one that told her she was an idiot for thinking he was going to hit on Jill. Lissa held his gaze for a few moments and realized he was right. Adrian was a scoundrel at times and had never made his interest in me a secret, but walking Jill home wasn't part of some grand seduction. He really was just being nice.

"All right," said Lissa. "I'll see you later. Nice meeting you, Jill."

"You too," said Jill. She dared a smile at Christian. "Thanks again."

"You better show up for our next practice," he warned.

Adrian and Jill started to step out the door, just as Avery stepped through it.

"Hey, Adrian." Avery gave Jill a once-over. "Who's your jailbait?"

"Will you guys stop calling me that?" exclaimed Jill.

Adrian pointed at Avery chastisingly. "Hush. I'll deal with you later, Lazar."

"I certainly hope so," she said in a sing-song voice. "I'll leave the door unlocked."

Jill and Adrian left, and Avery sat down next to Lissa. She seemed animated enough to be drunk, but Lissa smelled no liquor on her. Lissa was rapidly learning that some part of Avery was always just vivacious and carefree, regardless of intoxication.

"Did you really just invite Adrian to your room later?" asked Lissa. She spoke teasingly but had been secretly wondering if something was going on between them. And yeah, that made two of us who wondered.

Avery shrugged. "I don't know. Maybe. Sometimes we hang out once you guys are all tucked into bed. You aren't going to get jealous, are you?"

"No," laughed Lissa. "Just curious. Adrian's a good guy."

"Oh?" asked Christian. "Define 'good.'"

Avery held up her hand and began ticking items off with each finger. "He's devastatingly handsome, funny, rich, related to the queen . . ."

"You got your wedding colors picked out?" asked Lissa, still laughing.

"Not yet," said Avery. "I'm still testing the waters. I figured he'd be an easy notch on the Avery Lazar belt, but he's kind of hard to read."

"I really don't want to be hearing this," Christian said.

"Sometimes he acts like a love 'em and leave 'em type. Other times, he mopes like some heartbroken romantic." Lissa exchanged a knowing glance with Christian that Avery didn't catch while talking. "Anyway, I'm not here to talk about him. I'm here to talk about you and me busting out of here." Avery threw her arm around Lissa, who nearly fell over.

"Out of where? The dorm?"

"No. This school. We're going off on a wild weekend to the Royal Court."

"What, this weekend?" Lissa felt like she was three steps behind, and I didn't blame her. "Why?"

"Because it's Easter. And her royal majesty thought it would be 'lovely' if you could join her for the holiday." Avery's tone was grand and high-pitched. "And, since I've been hanging out with you, Dad's decided I'm on good behavior now."

"Poor oblivious bastard," murmured Christian.

"So he said I can go with you." Avery glanced at Christian. "You can too, I guess. The queen said Lissa could bring a guest — in addition to me, of course."

Lissa looked into Avery's radiant face and didn't share her enthusiasm. "I *hate* going to Court. Tatiana just goes on and on, giving what she thinks is useful advice for me. It's always boring and miserable now." Lissa didn't add that she'd once found Court fun — when I'd gone with her.

"That's because you haven't gone with me yet. It'll be a blast! I know where all the good stuff is. And I bet Adrian'll come too. He can push his way into anything. It'll be like a double date."

Slowly, Lissa began to acknowledge that

this might be fun. She and I had managed to find a little of the "good stuff" that hid underneath the polished surface of Court life. Every other visit since had been just as she described — stuffy and businesslike. But now, going with Christian and wild, spontaneous Avery? That had potential.

Until Christian ruined it. "Well, don't count me in," he said. "If you can only bring one person, bring Jill."

"Who?" asked Avery.

"Jailbait," explained Lissa. She looked at Christian in astonishment. "Why on earth would I bring Jill? I just met her."

"Because she's actually serious about learning to defend herself. You should introduce her to Mia. They're both water users."

"Right," said Lissa knowingly. "And the fact that you hate it at Court has nothing to do with it?"

"Well . . ."

"Christian!" Lissa was suddenly getting upset. "Why can't you do this for me?"

"Because I hate the way Queen Bitch looks at me," he said.

Lissa didn't find this convincing. "Yeah, but when we graduate, I'll be living there. You'll have to go then."

"Yeah, well, then give me this small vacation first."

Lissa's irritation grew. "Oh, I see how it is. I have to put up with your crap all the time, but you can't go out of your way for me."

Avery glanced between them and then stood up. "I'll leave you kids to work this out on your own. I don't care whether Christian or Jailbait goes, as long as *you're* there." She peered down at Lissa. "You are going, right?"

"Yeah. I'll go." If anything, Christian's refusal had suddenly spurred Lissa more.

Avery grinned. "Awesome. I'm going to head out of here, but you two had better kiss and make up when I'm gone."

Avery's brother Reed suddenly appeared in the doorway. "Are you ready?" he asked her. Every time he spoke, it always came out as sort of a grunt. Avery flashed the others a triumphant look.

"See? My gallant brother, coming to walk me back before those dorm matrons start yelling at me to leave. Now Adrian'll have to find a new and exciting way to prove his chivalry."

Reed didn't look very gallant or chivalrous, but I supposed it was nice of him to come walk her back to her room. His timing had been eerily perfect. Maybe she was right about him not being as bad as people always thought.

As soon as Avery was gone, Lissa turned on Christian. "Are you really serious about me bringing Jill instead of you?"

"Yep," said Christian. He tried to lie back into her lap, but she pushed him away. "But I'll count the seconds until you return."

"I can't believe you think this is a joke."

"I don't," he said. "Look, I didn't mean to get you all worked up, okay? But really . . . I just don't want to deal with all that Court drama. And it would be good for Jill." He frowned. "You don't have anything against her, do you?"

"I don't even know her," said Lissa. She was still upset — more so than I would have expected, which was odd.

Christian caught hold of Lissa's hands, face serious. Those blue eyes she loved softened her anger a little. "Please, I'm not trying to upset you. If it's really that important . . ."

Like that, Lissa's anger diffused. It was abrupt, like a switch. "No, no. I'm fine bringing Jill — though I'm not sure she should be hanging out with us and doing whatever Avery has in mind."

"Give Jill to Mia. She'll look after her for the weekend."

Lissa nodded, wondering why he was so interested in Jill. "Okay. But you're not doing this because you don't like Avery, are you?"

"No, I like Avery. She makes you smile more."

"You make me smile."

"That's why I added on the 'more.' " Christian gently kissed Lissa's hand. "You've been so sad since Rose left. I'm glad you're hanging out with someone else — I mean, not that you can't get everything you need from me."

"Avery's not a Rose replacement," said Lissa quickly.

"I know. But she reminds me of her."

"What? They have nothing in common."

Christian straightened up and sat beside her, resting his face against her shoulder. "Avery's like how Rose used to be, back before you guys left."

Both Lissa and I paused to ponder that. Was he right? Before Lissa's spirit powers had begun showing, she and I had lived a party girl lifestyle. And yes, half the time I was the one coming up with the crazy ideas to find a good time and get us into trouble. But had I been as out there as Avery seemed sometimes?

"There'll never be another Rose," said

Lissa sadly.

"No," agreed Christian. He gave her a brief, soft kiss on the mouth. "But there will be other friends."

I knew he was right, but I couldn't help but feel a small stab of jealousy. I also couldn't help feel a small amount of worry. Lissa's brief spurt of irritation had been kind of out of the blue. I could understand her wishing Christian could go, but her attitude had been a little bitchy — and her almost jealous worry over Jill was weird too. Lissa had no reason to doubt Christian's feelings, certainly not over someone like Jill. Lissa's moodiness reminded me too much of the old days.

Most likely she was overtired, but some instinct — maybe it was part of the bonding — told me something was wrong. It was a fleeting sensation, one I couldn't quite get a hold of, like water slipping through my fingers. Still, my instincts had been right before, and I decided I'd be checking in on Lissa more frequently.

# TWELVE

Being with Lissa left me with more questions than answers, and so without a course of action, I simply continued to stay with the Belikovs for the next few days. I fell into their normal routine, again surprised by how easy it was. I tried hard to make myself useful, doing any chores they'd let me do and even going so far as watching the baby (something I wasn't entirely comfortable with, seeing as guardian training hadn't left much time for after school jobs like babysitting). Yeva eyed me the whole time, never saying anything but always looking like she disapproved. I wasn't sure if she wanted me to go or if that was simply the way she always looked. The others, however, didn't question me at all. They were delighted to have me around and made it obvious in every action. Viktoria was especially happy.

"I wish you could come back to school

with us," Viktoria said wistfully one evening. She and I had been spending a lot of time together.

"When do you go back?"

"Monday, right after Easter."

I felt a little sadness stir in me. Whether I was still here or not, I would miss her. "Oh, man. I didn't realize it was so soon."

A small silence fell between us; then she gave me a sidelong look. "Have you thought . . . well, have you maybe thought about coming back to St. Basil's with us?"

I stared. "St. Basil's? Your school is named after a saint too?" Not all of them were. Adrian had attended an East Coast school called Alder.

"Ours is a human saint," she said with a grin. "You could enroll there. You could finish your last year — I'm sure they'd take you."

Of all the crazy options I'd considered on this trip — and believe me, I'd considered a lot of crazy things — that was one that had never crossed my mind. I'd written school off. I was pretty sure there was nothing else I could learn — well, after meeting Sydney and Mark, it had become obvious there were still a *few* more things. Considering what I wanted to do with my life, however, I didn't think another semester of math and science would do much for me. And as far as guardian training went, mostly all I had left to do was prepare for the end-of-year trials. I somehow doubted those tests and challenges would even come remotely close to what I'd experienced with Strigoi already.

I shook my head. "I don't think so. I think I'm pretty much done with school. Besides, it'd all be in Russian."

"They'd translate for you." A mischievous grin lit her face. "Besides, kicking and punching transcend language." Her smile faded to a more thoughtful expression. "But seriously. If you aren't going to finish school, and you aren't going to be a guardian . . . well, why don't you stay here? I mean, just in Baia. You could live with us."

"I'm not going to be a blood whore," I said immediately.

An odd look crossed her face. "That's not what I meant."

"I shouldn't have said that. Sorry." I felt bad about the comment. While I kept hearing rumors about blood whores in town, I'd only seen one or two, and certainly the Belikov women weren't among them. Sonya's pregnancy was something of a mystery, but working in a drugstore didn't seem that sordid. I'd learned a little bit more about Karolina's situation. The father of her children was a Moroi she apparently had a genuine connection with. She hadn't cheapened herself to be with him, and he hadn't used her. After the baby was born, the two of them had decided to part ways, but it had been friendly. Karolina was now apparently dating a guardian who visited whenever he had leave.

The few blood whores I had seen around town very much fit my stereotype. Their clothing and makeup screamed easy sex. The bruises on their necks clearly showed that they had no problem with letting their partners drink blood during sex, which was pretty much the sleaziest thing a dhampir could do. Only humans gave blood to Moroi. My race didn't. To allow it — particularly during sexual activities — well, like I said, it was sleazy. The dirtiest of the dirty.

"Mother would love it if you stayed. You could get a job too. Just be part of our family."

"I can't take Dimitri's place, Viktoria," I said softly.

She reached out and gave my hand a reassuring squeeze. "I know. No one expects you to. We like you for you, Rose. You being here just feels right — there's a reason Dimka chose to be with you. You fit in here."

229

I tried to imagine the life she described. It sounded . . . easy. Comfortable. No worries. Just living with a loving family, laughing and hanging out together each night. I could go about my own life, not having to trail someone else all day. I would have sisters. There'd be no fighting — unless it was to defend. I could give up this plan to kill Dimitri — which I knew would kill me too, either physically or spiritually. I could choose the rational path, let him go and accept him as dead. And, yet . . . if I did that, why not just go back to Montana? Back to Lissa and the Academy?

"I don't know," I told Viktoria at last. "I don't know what I'm going to do."

It was just after dinner, and she glanced hesitantly at the clock. "I don't want to leave you since we don't have much time together, but . . . I was supposed to meet someone soon. . . ."

"Nikolai?" I teased.

She shook her head, and I tried to hide my disappointment. I'd seen him a few times, and he'd grown more and more likeable. It was too bad Viktoria couldn't kindle any feelings for him. Now, though, I wondered if there might be something holding her back — or rather, someone.

"Oh, spill," I said with a grin. "Who is he?"

She kept her face blank in a fair imitation of Dimitri's. "A friend," she said evasively. But I thought I saw a smile in her eyes.

"Someone at school?"

"No." She sighed. "And that's the problem. I'm going to miss him so much."

My smile faded. "I can imagine."

"Oh." She looked embarrassed. "That's stupid of me. My problems . . . well, they're nothing compared to yours. I mean, I may not see him for a while . . . but I *will* see him. But Dimitri's gone. You won't see him ever again."

Well, that might not be *entirely* true. I didn't tell her that, though. Instead, I just said, "Yeah."

To my surprise, she gave me a hug. "I know what love's like. To lose that . . . I don't know. I don't know what to say. All I can tell you is that we're here for you. All of us, okay? You can't replace Dimitri, but you do feel like a sister."

Her calling me a sister both stunned and warmed me at the same time. She had to go get ready for her date after that. She hurriedly changed clothes and put on makeup — definitely more than a friend, I decided — and headed out the door. I was kind of glad because I didn't want her to see the tears that her words had brought to my eyes. I'd spent my life as an only child. Lissa had been the closest I had to a sister. I'd always thought of Lissa as one; one I'd now lost. To hear Viktoria call me a sister now . . . well, it stirred something in me. Something that told me I really did have friends and wasn't alone.

I headed down to the kitchen after that, and Olena soon joined me. I was rummaging for food.

"Was that Viktoria I heard leave?" she asked.

"Yeah, she went off to see a friend." To my credit, I kept my expression neutral. No way would I sell Viktoria out.

Olena sighed. "I'd wanted her to run an errand for me in town."

"I'll do it," I said eagerly. "After I grab something to eat."

She gave me a kind smile and patted my cheek. "You have a good heart, Rose. I can see why Dimka loved you."

It was so amazing, I thought, how accepted my relationship with Dimitri was around here. No one brought up age or teacher-student relationships. As I'd told Sydney, it was like I was his widow or something, and Viktoria's words about me staying replayed in my head. The way Olena looked at me made me feel like I really was her daughter, and once more, I experienced those traitorous feelings about my own mom. She probably would have scoffed at me and Dimitri. She would have called it inappropriate and said I was too young. Or would she have? Maybe I was being too harsh.

Seeing me in front of the open cupboard, Olena shook her head reproachfully. "But you need to eat first."

"Just a snack," I assured her. "Don't go to any trouble."

She ended up slicing me off big pieces of black bread she'd baked earlier that day and put out a tub of butter because she knew I loved to slather up my slices. Karolina had teased me that Americans might be shocked to know what was in this bread, so I never asked any questions. It was somehow sweet and tangy at the same time, and I loved it.

Olena sat down across from me and watched me eat. "This was his favorite when he was little."

"Dimitri's?"

She nodded. "Whenever he was on break from school, the first thing he'd do is ask for that bread. I practically had to make him his own loaf each time with the way he ate.

The girls never ate that much."

"Guys always seem to eat more." Admittedly, I could keep up with most of them. "And he's bigger and taller than most."

"True," she mused. "But I eventually reached a point where I made him start making it himself. I told him if he was going to eat all my food, he'd best know how much work went into it."

I laughed. "I can't imagine Dimitri baking bread."

And yet, as soon as the words came out, I reconsidered. My immediate associations with Dimitri were always intense and fierce; it was his sexy, battle-god persona that came to mind. Yet, it had been Dimitri's gentleness and thoughtfulness mixed with that deadliness that made him so wonderful. The same hands that wielded stakes with such precision would carefully brush the hair out of my face. The eyes that could astutely spot any danger in the area would regard me wonderingly and worshipfully, like I was the most beautiful and amazing woman in the world.

I sighed, consumed by that bittersweet ache in my chest that had become so familiar now. What a stupid thing, getting worked up over a loaf of bread of all things. But that was how it was. I got emotional whenever I thought about Dimitri.

Olena's eyes were on me, sweet and compassionate. "I know," she said, guessing my thoughts. "I know exactly how you feel."

"Does it get easier?" I asked.

Unlike Sydney, Olena had an answer. "Yes. But you'll never be the same."

I didn't know whether to take comfort from those words or not. After I finished eating, she gave me a brief grocery list, and I set off toward downtown, happy to be outside and moving. Inactivity didn't suit me.

While in the grocery store, I was surprised to run into Mark. I'd gotten the impression he and Oksana didn't come to town that often. I wouldn't have put it past them to grow their own food and live off the land. He gave me a warm smile. "I wondered if you were still around."

"Yeah." I held up my basket. "Just doing some shopping for Olena."

"I'm glad you're still here," he said. "You seem more . . . at peace."

"Your ring is helping, I think. At least with the peace. It hasn't done much as far as any decision making goes."

He frowned, shifting the milk he held in one arm to the other. "What decisions?"

"What to do now. Where to go."

"Why not stay here?"

It was eerie, so similar to the conversation I'd had with Viktoria. And my response was equally similar. "I don't know what I'd do if I stayed here."

"Get a job. Live with the Belikovs. They love you, you know. You fit right in with their family."

That warm, loved feeling came back, and I again tried to imagine myself just settling down with them, working in a store like this or waiting tables. "I don't know," I said. I was a broken record. "I just don't know if that's right for me."

"Better than the alternative," he warned. "Better than running off with no real purpose, throwing yourself in the face of danger. That's no choice at all."

And yet, it was the reason I'd come to Siberia in the first place. My inner voice scolded me. *Dimitri, Rose. Have you forgotten Dimitri? Have you forgotten how you came here to free him, like he would have wanted?* Or was that really what he would have wanted? Maybe he would have wanted me to stay safe. I just didn't know, and with no more help from Mason, my choices were even more muddled. Thinking of Mason suddenly reminded me of something I'd totally forgotten.

"When we talked before . . . well, we talked about what Lissa and Oksana could do. But what about *you?*"

Mark narrowed his eyes. "What do you mean?"

"Have you ever . . . have you ever run into, um, ghosts?"

Several moments passed, and then he exhaled. "I'd hoped that wouldn't happen to you."

It astonished me then how much relief I felt to know I wasn't alone in my ghostly experiences. Even though I now understood that having died and been to the world of the dead made me a target for spirits, it was still one of the freakiest things about being shadow-kissed.

"Did it happen without you wanting it?" I asked.

"At first. Then I learned to control it."

"Me too." I suddenly recalled the barn. "Actually, that's not entirely true."

Lowering my voice further, I hastily re-capped what had happened on my trip here with Sydney. I'd never spoken of it to any-one.

"You must never, ever do that again," he said sternly.

"But I didn't mean to! It just happened."

"You panicked. You needed help, and

237

some part of you called out to the spirits around you. Don't do it. It's not right, and it's easy to lose control."

"I don't even know how I did it."

"Like I said, lapse of control. Don't ever let your panic get the best of you."

An older woman passed us, a scarf over her head and a basket of vegetables in her arms. I waited until she was gone before asking Mark, "Why did they fight for me?"

"Because the dead hate Strigoi. The Strigoi are unnatural, neither living nor dead — just existing in some state in between. Just as we sense that evil, so do the ghosts."

"Seems like they could be a good weapon."

That face, normally easy and open, frowned. "It's dangerous. People like you and me already walk the edge of darkness and insanity. Openly calling upon the dead only brings us closer to falling over that edge and losing our minds." He glanced at his watch and sighed. "Look, I have to go, but I'm serious, Rose. Stay here. Stay out of trouble. Fight Strigoi if they come to you, but don't go seeking them blindly. And definitely leave the ghosts alone."

It was a lot of advice to get in a grocery store, a lot of advice I wasn't sure I could follow. But I thanked him and sent my

238

regards to Oksana before paying and leaving as well. I was heading back toward Olena's neighborhood when I rounded a corner and nearly walked right into Abe.

He was dressed in his usual flashy way, wearing that expensive coat and a yellow-gold scarf that matched the gold in his jewelry. His guardians hovered nearby, and he leaned casually against a building's brick wall.

"So this is why you came to Russia. To go to the market like some peasant."

"No," I said. "Of course not."

"Just sightseeing then?"

"No. I'm just being helpful. Stop trying to get information out of me. You're not as smart as you think you are."

"That's not true," he said.

"Look, I told you already. I came here to tell the Belikovs the news. So go back and tell whoever you're working for that that's that."

"And *I* told you before not to lie to me," he said. Again, I saw that odd mix of danger and humor. "You have no idea how patient I've been with you. From anyone else, I would have gotten the information I needed that first night."

"Lucky me," I snapped back. "What now? Are you going to take me down an alley and beat me up until I tell you why I'm here? I'm losing interest in this whole scary-mob-boss routine, you know."

"And I'm losing patience with you," he said. There went the humor, and as he stood over me, I couldn't help but uneasily note that he was better built than most Moroi. A lot of Moroi avoided fights, but I wouldn't have been surprised if Abe had roughed up as many people as his bodyguards had. "And honestly? I don't care why you're here anymore. You just need to leave. Now."

"Don't threaten me, old man. I'll leave whenever the hell I want." It was funny, I'd just sworn to Mark that I didn't know if I could stay in Baia, but when pressured by Abe, I just wanted to dig my feet in. "I don't know what you're trying to keep me from, but I'm not scared of you." That also wasn't entirely true.

"You should be," he returned pleasantly. "I can be a very good friend or a very bad enemy. I can make it worth your while if you leave. We can strike a bargain."

There was an almost excited gleam in his eyes as he spoke. I recalled Sydney describing him manipulating others, and I got the feeling this was what he lived for — negotiating, striking trades to get what he wanted.

"No," I said. "I'll leave when I'm ready.

And there's nothing you or whoever you're working for can do about it."

Hoping I appeared bold, I turned around. He reached out and grabbed my shoulder, jerking me back, nearly causing me to lose the groceries. I started to lunge forward in attack mode, but his guardians were right there in a flash. I knew I wouldn't get far.

"Your time is up here," hissed Abe. "In Baia. In Russia. Go back to the U.S. I'll give you what you need — money, first-class tickets, whatever."

I stepped out of his reach, backing carefully away. "I don't need your help or your money — God only knows where it comes from." A group of people turned the corner across the street, laughing and talking, and I stepped back further, certain Abe wouldn't start a scene with witnesses present. It made me feel braver, which was probably stupid on my part. "And I already told you: I'll go back whenever the hell I want."

Abe's eyes lifted to the other pedestrians, and he too retreated back with his guardians. That chilling smile was on his face. "And I told you. I can be a very good friend or a very bad enemy. Get out of Baia before you find out which."

He turned around and left, much to my relief. I didn't want him to see just how much fear his words had left on my face.

I went to bed early that night, suddenly feeling antisocial. I lay there for a while, flipping through another magazine I couldn't read, and amazingly found myself growing more and more tired. I think the encounters with Mark and Abe had exhausted me. Mark's words about staying had hit too close to home after my earlier conversation with Viktoria. Abe's thinly veiled threats had raised all my defenses, putting me on guard against whoever was working with him to make me leave Russia. At what point, I wondered, would he truly lose patience and stop trying to bargain?

I drifted off to sleep and the familiar sense of an Adrian-dream settled around me. It had been a long time since this had happened, and I'd actually thought he'd listened to me when I'd told him to stay away before. Of course, I always told him that. This had been the longest time span to go by without a visit, and as much as I hated to admit it, I'd kind of missed him.

The setting he'd chosen this time was a piece of the Academy's property, a woodsy area near a pond. Everything was green and in bloom, and sunlight shone down on us. I suspected Adrian's creation didn't match what Montana's weather was really like right now, but then, he was in control. He could do whatever he wanted.

"Little dhampir," he said, smiling. "Long time no see."

"I thought you were done with me," I said, sitting down on a large, smooth rock.

"Never done with you," he said, stuffing his hands in his pockets and strolling over to me. "Although . . . to tell the truth, I *did* intend to stay away this time. But, well, I had to make sure you were still alive."

"Alive and well."

He smiled down at me. The sun glinted off his brown hair, giving it golden-chestnut highlights. "Good. You seem very well, actually. Your aura's better than I've ever seen it." His eyes drifted from my face down to where my hands lay in my lap. Frowning, he knelt down and picked up my right hand. "What's this?"

Oksana's ring was on it. Despite the ring's lack of ornamentation, the metal gleamed brightly in the light. The dreams were so strange. Even though Adrian and I weren't together, exactly, the ring had followed me in and kept its power enough that he could sense it.

"A charm. It's infused with spirit."

Like me, this was apparently something

he'd never considered. His expression grew eager. "And it heals, right? It's what's keeping some of the darkness from your aura."

"Some," I said, uneasy about his fixation on it. I took it off and slipped it into my pocket. "It's temporary. I met another spirit user — and a shadow-kissed dhampir."

More surprise registered on his face. "What? Where?"

I bit my lip and shook my head.

"Damn it, Rose! This is big. You know how Lissa and I have been looking for other spirit users. Tell me where they are."

"No. Maybe later. I don't want you guys coming after me." For all I knew, they were already after me, using Abe as their agent.

His green eyes flashed angrily. "Look, pretend for a moment the world doesn't revolve around you, okay? This is about Lissa and me, about understanding this crazy magic inside of us. If you've got people who can help us, we need to know."

"Maybe later," I repeated stonily. "I'm moving on soon — then I'll tell you."

"Why are you always so difficult?"

"Because you like me that way."

"At the moment? Not so much."

It was the kind of joking comment Adrian usually made, but just then, something about it bothered me. For some reason, I got the tiniest, *tiniest* feeling that I suddenly wasn't as endearing to him as usual.

"Just try being patient," I told him. "I'm sure you guys have other stuff to work on. And Lissa seems pretty busy with Avery." The words slipped out before I could help it, and some of the bitterness and envy I'd felt watching them the other night laced my tone.

Adrian raised an eyebrow. "Ladies and gentlemen, she admits it. You have been spying on Lissa — I knew it."

I looked away. "I just like to know she's alive too." As if I could go anywhere in the world and not know that.

"She is. Alive and well, like you. Er . . . mostly well." Adrian frowned. "Sometimes I get this strange vibe off of her. She doesn't seem quite right or her aura will flicker a little. Never lasts long, but I still worry." Something in Adrian's voice softened. "Avery worries about her too, so Lissa's in good hands. Avery's pretty amazing."

I gave him a scathing look. "*Amazing?* Do you like her or something?" I hadn't forgotten Avery's comment about leaving the door unlocked for him.

"Of course I like her. She's a great person."

"No, I mean *like*. Not like."

"Oh, I see," he said, rolling his eyes. "We're dealing with elementary school definitions of 'like.' "

"You're not answering the question."

"Well, like I said, she's a great person. Smart. Outgoing. Beautiful."

Something in the way he said "beautiful" bugged me. I averted my eyes again, playing with the blue *nazar* around my neck as I tried to parse my feelings. Adrian figured things out first.

"Are you jealous, little dhampir?"

I looked back up at him. "No. If I was going to be jealous over you, I would have gone crazy a long time ago, considering all the girls you mess around with."

"Avery's not the kind of girl you mess around with."

Again, I heard that affection in his voice, that dreaminess. It shouldn't have bothered me. I should have been glad he was interested in another girl. After all, I'd been trying to convince him to leave me alone for a very long time. Part of the conditions of him giving me money for this trip had involved me promising to give him a fair shot at dating when — and if — I returned to Montana. If he got together with Avery, it would be one less thing for me to worry about.

And honestly, if it had been any other girl except Avery, I probably wouldn't have minded. But somehow, the idea of her enchanting him was just too much. Wasn't it bad enough that I was losing Lissa to her? How was it possible that one girl could so easily take my place? She'd stolen my best friend, and now the guy who'd sworn up and down that I was the one he wanted was seriously considering replacing me.

*You're being a hypocrite,* a stern voice inside of me said. *Why should you feel so wronged about someone else coming into their lives? You abandoned them. Lissa and Adrian both. They have every right to move on.*

I stood up angrily. "Look, I'm done talking to you tonight. Will you let me out of this dream? I'm not telling you where I am. And I'm not interested in hearing about how wonderful Avery is and how much better than me she is."

"Avery would never act like a little brat," he said. "She wouldn't get so offended that someone actually cares enough to check on her. She wouldn't deny me the chance to learn more about my magic because she was paranoid someone would ruin her crazy attempt to get over her boyfriend's death."

"Don't talk to me about being a brat," I

shot back. "You're as selfish and self-centered as usual. It's always about you — even this dream is. You hold me against my will, whether I want it or not, because it amuses you."

"Fine," he said, voice cold. "I'll end this. And I'll end everything between us. I won't be coming back."

"Good. I hope you mean it this time."

His green eyes were the last thing I saw before I woke up in my own bed.

I sat up, gasping. My heart felt like it was breaking, and I almost thought I might cry. Adrian was right — I had been a brat. I'd lashed out at him when it wasn't really deserved. And yet . . . I hadn't been able to help it. I missed Lissa. I even kind of missed Adrian. And now someone else was taking my place, someone who wouldn't just walk away like I had.

*I won't be coming back.*

And for the first time ever, I had a feeling he really wouldn't be.

# THIRTEEN

The next day was Easter. Everyone was up and around, getting ready to go to church. The whole house smelled delicious, filled with the scents of Olena's baking. My stomach rumbled, and I wondered if I could wait until this afternoon for the huge dinner she'd prepared. Even though I wasn't always sure about God, I'd gone to church a lot in my life. Mostly, it was a courtesy to others, a way of being polite and social. Dimitri had gone because he found peace there, and I wondered if going today might offer me some insight on what I should do.

I felt a little shabby accompanying the others. They'd dressed up, but I didn't have anything other than jeans and casual shirts. Viktoria, noticing my dismay, lent me a lacy white blouse that was a little tight but still looked good. Once I was settled with the family into a pew, I looked around, wondering how Dimitri could have taken solace in the Academy's tiny chapel when he'd grown up with this place.

It was huge. It could have held four chapels. The ceilings were higher and more elaborate, and gold decorations and icons of saints seemed to cover every surface. It was overwhelming, dazzling to the eye. Sweet incense hung heavy in the air, so much so that I could actually see the smoke.

There were a lot of people there, human and dhampir, and I was surprised to even spot some Moroi. Apparently, the Moroi visiting town were pious enough to come to church, despite whatever sordid activities they might be engaging in. And speaking of Moroi . . .

"Abe isn't here," I said to Viktoria, glancing around. She was on my left; Olena sat on my right. While he hadn't struck me as the religious type, I'd kind of expected him to follow me here. I hoped that maybe his absence meant he'd left Baia. I was still unnerved by our last encounter. "Did he leave town?"

"I think he's Muslim," Viktoria explained. "But last I knew, he's still around. Karolina saw him this morning."

Damn Zmey. He hadn't left. What was it he'd said? *A good friend or a bad enemy.*

When I said nothing, Viktoria gave me a

concerned look. "He's never really done anything bad when he's around. He usually has meetings and then disappears. I meant it before when I said I didn't think he'd hurt you, but now you're worrying me. Are you in some kind of trouble?"

Excellent question. "I don't know. He just seems interested in me, that's all. I can't figure out why."

Her frown deepened. "We won't let anything happen to you," she said fiercely.

I smiled, both at her concern and because of her resemblance to Dimitri in that moment. "Thanks. There are some people back home who might be looking for me, and I think that Abe is just . . . checking up on me." That was a nice way of describing someone who was either going to drag me back to the U.S. kicking and screaming — or just make me vanish for good.

Viktoria seemed to sense I was softening the truth. "Well, I mean it. I won't let him hurt you."

The service started, cutting off our conversation. While the priest's chanting was beautiful, it meant even less to me than church services usually did. It was all in Russian, like at the funeral, and no one was going to bother translating it for me today. It didn't matter. Still taking in the beauty of my surroundings, I found my mind wandering. To the left of the altar, a golden-haired angel looked at me from a four-foot-tall icon.

An unexpected memory came to me. Dimitri had once gotten permission for me to accompany him on a quick weekend trip to Idaho to meet with some other guardians. Idaho wasn't any place I was keen on going, but I welcomed the time with him, and he'd convinced school officials that it was a "learning experience." That had been shortly after Mason's death, and after the shock wave that tragedy had sent through the school, I think they would have allowed me anything, to be honest.

Unfortunately, there was little that was leisurely or romantic about the trip. Dimitri had a job to do, and he had to do it quickly. So we made the best time we could, stopping only when absolutely necessary. Considering our last road trip had involved us stumbling onto a Moroi massacre, this one being uneventful was probably for the best. As usual, he wouldn't let me drive, despite my claims that I could get us there in half the time. Or maybe that was *why* he wouldn't let me drive.

We stopped at one point to get gas and scrounge some food from the station's store.

We were up in the mountains somewhere, in a tiny town that rivaled St. Vladimir's for remote location. I could see mountains on clear days at school, but it was a totally different experience being in them. They surrounded us and were so close it seemed like you could just jump over and land on one. Dimitri was finishing up with the car. Holding my sub sandwich, I walked around to the back of the gas station to get a better view.

Whatever civilization the gas station offered disappeared as soon as I cleared it. Endless snowy pines stretched out before me, and all was still and quiet, save for the distant sound of the highway behind me. My heart ached over what had happened to Mason, and I was still having nightmares about the Strigoi who'd held us captive. That pain was a long way from disappearing, but something about this peaceful setting soothed me for a moment.

Looking down at the unbroken, foot-high snow, a crazy thought suddenly came to me. I let myself go, falling back-first to the ground. The thick snow embraced me, and I rested there a moment, taking comfort in lying down. Then I moved my legs and arms back and forth, carving out new hollows in the snow. When I finished, I didn't get up right away. I simply continued lounging, staring up at the blue, blue sky.

"What," asked Dimitri, "are you doing? Aside from getting your sandwich cold."

His shadow fell over me, and I looked up at his tall form. In spite of the cold, the sun was out, and its rays backlit his hair. He could have been an angel himself, I thought.

"I'm making a snow angel," I replied. "Don't you know what that is?"

"Yes, I know. But why? You must be freezing."

I had on a heavy winter coat, hat, gloves, and all the other requisite cold-weather accessories. He was right about the sandwich. "Not so much, actually. My face is a little, I guess."

He shook his head and gave me a wry smile. "You'll be cold when you're in the car and all that snow starts melting."

"I think you're more worried about the car than about me."

He laughed. "I'm more worried about you getting hypothermia."

"In this? This is nothing." I patted the ground beside me. "Come on. You make one too, and then we can go."

He continued looking down at me. "So I can freeze too?"

"So you can have fun. So you can leave

your mark on Idaho. Besides, it shouldn't bother you at all, right? Don't you have some sort of super cold resistance from Siberia?"

He sighed, a smile still on his lips. It was enough to warm me even in this weather. "There you go again, convinced Siberia is like Antarctica. I'm from the *southern* part. The weather's almost the same as here."

"You're making excuses," I told him. "Unless you want to drag me back to the car, you're going to have to make an angel too."

Dimitri studied me for several heavy moments, and I thought he might actually haul me away. His face was still light and open, though, and his expression was filled with a fondness that made my heart race. Then, without warning, he flopped into the snow beside me, lying there quietly.

"Okay," I said when he did nothing more. "Now you have to move your arms and legs."

"I know how to make a snow angel."

"Then do it! Otherwise, you're more like a chalk outline at a police crime scene."

He laughed again, and the sound was rich and warm in the still air. Finally, after a little more coaxing on my part, he moved his arms and legs too, making an angel of his own. When he finished, I expected him to jump up and demand we get back on the road, but instead, he stayed there too, watching the sky and the mountains.

"Pretty, huh?" I asked. My breath made frosty clouds in the air. "I guess in some ways, it's not that different from the ski resort's view . . . but I don't know. I feel different about it all today."

"Life's like that," he said. "As we grow and change, sometimes things we've experienced before take on new meaning. It'll happen for the rest of your life."

I started to tease him about his tendency to always deliver these profound life lessons, but it occurred to me then that he was right. When I'd first begun falling for Dimitri, the feelings had been all-consuming. I'd never felt anything like it before. I'd been convinced there was no possible way I could love him more. But now, after what I'd witnessed with Mason and the Strigoi, things were different. I did love Dimitri more intensely. I loved him in a different way, in a deeper way. Something about seeing how fragile life was made me appreciate him more. It had made me realize how much he meant to me and how sad I'd be if I ever lost him.

"You think it'd be nice to have a cabin up there?" I asked, pointing to a nearby peak.

"Out in the woods where no one could find you?"

"*I* would think it was nice. I think you'd be bored."

I tried to imagine being stuck in the wilderness with him. Small room, fireplace, bed . . . I didn't think it'd be *that* boring. "It wouldn't be so bad if we had cable. And Internet." And body heat.

"Oh, Rose." He didn't laugh, but I could tell he was smiling again. "I don't think you'd ever be happy someplace quiet. You always need something to do."

"Are you saying I have a short attention span?"

"Not at all. I'm saying there's a fire in you that drives everything you do, that makes you *need* to better the world and those you love. To stand up for those you can't. It's one of the wonderful things about you."

"Only one, huh?" I spoke lightly, but his words had thrilled me. He'd meant what he said about thinking those were wonderful traits, and feeling his pride in me meant more than anything just then.

"One of many," he said. He sat up and looked down at me. "So, no peaceful cabin for you. Not until you're an old, old woman."

"What, like forty?"

He shook his head in exasperation and stood up, not gracing my joke with a response. Still, he regarded me with the same affection I'd heard in his voice. There was admiration too, and I thought I could never be unhappy as long as Dimitri thought I was wonderful and beautiful. Leaning down, he extended his hand. "Time to go."

I took it, letting him help pull me up. Once standing, we held hands for a heartbeat longer than necessary. Then we let go and surveyed our work. Two perfect snow angels — one much, much taller than the other. Careful to step inside each outline, I leaned down and hacked out a horizontal line above each head.

"What's that?" he asked, when I stood beside him again.

"Halos," I said with a grin. "For heavenly creatures like us."

"That might be a stretch."

We studied our angels for a few moments more, looking at where we had lain side by side in that sweet, quiet moment. I wished what I'd said was true, that we had truly left our mark on the mountain. But I knew that after the next snowfall, our angels would disappear into the whiteness and be nothing more than a memory.

Dimitri touched my arm gently, and

without another word, we turned around and headed back to the car.

Compared to that memory of him and the way he'd looked at me out there on the mountain, I thought the angel looking back at me in church seemed pale and boring in comparison. No offense to her.

The congregation was filing back to their seats after taking bread and wine. I'd stayed seated for that, but I did understand a few of the priest's words. *Life. Death. Destroy. Eternal.* I knew enough about all this to string together the meaning. I would have bet good money "resurrection" was in there too. I sighed, wishing it were truly that easy to vanquish death and bring back those we loved.

Church ended, and I left with the Belikovs, feeling melancholy. As people passed each other near the entrance, I saw some eggs being exchanged. Viktoria had explained that it was a big tradition around here. A few people I didn't know gave some to me, and I felt a little bad that I had nothing to give in return. I also wondered how I was going to eat them all. They were decorated in various ways. Some were simply colored; others were elaborately designed.

Everyone seemed chatty after church, and

we all stood around outside it. Friends and family hugged and caught up on gossip. I stood near Viktoria, smiling and trying to follow the conversation that often took place in both English and Russian.

"Viktoria!"

We turned and saw Nikolai striding toward us. He gave us — by which I mean, he gave her — a brilliant smile. He'd dressed up for the holiday and looked amazing in a sage shirt and dark green tie. I eyed Viktoria, wondering if it had any effect on her. Nope. Her smile was polite, genuinely happy to see him, but there was nothing romantic there. Again, I wondered about her mystery "friend."

He had a couple of guys with him whom I'd met before. They greeted me too. Like the Belikovs, they seemed to think I was a permanent fixture around here.

"Are you still going to Marina's party?" asked Nikolai.

I'd nearly forgotten. That was the party he'd invited us to the first day I'd met him. Viktoria had accepted then, but to my surprise, she now shook her head. "We can't. We have family plans."

That was news to me. There was a possibility something had come up that I didn't know about yet, but I doubted it. I had a feeling she was lying, and being a loyal friend, I said nothing to contradict her. It was hard watching Nikolai's face fall, though.

"Really? We're going to miss you."

She shrugged. "We'll all see each other at school."

He didn't seem pacified by that. "Yeah, but —"

Nikolai's eyes suddenly lifted from her face and focused on something behind us. He frowned. Viktoria and I both glanced back, and I felt her mood shift too.

Three guys were strolling toward my group. They were dhampirs as well. I didn't notice anything unusual about them — smirks aside — but other dhampirs and Moroi gathered outside the church took on expressions similar to those of my companions. Troubled. Worried. Uncomfortable. The three guys came to a stop by us, pushing their way into our circle.

"I thought you might be here, Kolya," said one. He spoke in perfect English, and it took me a moment to realize he was talking to Nikolai. I would never understand Russian nicknames.

"I didn't know you were back," replied Nikolai stiffly. Studying the two of them, I could see a distinct resemblance. They had the same bronze hair and lean build. Brothers, apparently.

Nikolai's brother's gaze fell on me. He brightened. "And you must be the unpromised American girl." It didn't surprise me that he knew who I was. After the memorial, most of the local dhampirs had left telling tales about the American girl who had fought battles against Strigoi but carried neither a promise mark nor a graduation mark.

"I'm Rose," I said. I didn't know what was up with these guys, but I certainly wasn't going to show any fear in front of them. The guy seemed to appreciate my confidence and shook my hand.

"I'm Denis." He gestured to his friends. "Artur and Lev."

"When did you come to town?" asked Nikolai, still not looking happy about this reunion.

"Just this morning." Denis turned to Viktoria. "I heard about your brother. I'm sorry."

Viktoria's expression was hard, but she nodded politely. "Thank you."

"Is it true he fell defending Moroi?"

I didn't like the sneer in Denis's voice, but it was Karolina who voiced my angry thoughts. I hadn't noticed her approaching our group. She didn't look happy to see Denis at all.

"He fell fighting Strigoi. He died a hero."

Denis shrugged, unaffected by the angry tone of her voice. "Still makes him dead. I'm sure the Moroi will sing his name for years to come."

"They will," I replied. "He saved a whole group of them. And dhampirs too."

Denis's gaze fell back on me, his eyes thoughtful as he studied my face for a few seconds. "I heard you were there too. That both of you were sent into an impossible battle."

"It wasn't impossible. We won."

"Would Dimitri say that if he were alive?"

Karolina crossed her arms over her chest. "If you're only here to start something, then you should leave. This is a church." It was funny. Upon meeting her, I'd thought she seemed so gentle and kind, just an ordinary young mother working to support her family. But in this moment, she seemed more like Dimitri than ever. I could see that same strength within her, that fierceness that drove her to protect loved ones and stand up to her enemies. Not that these guys were her enemies, exactly. I honestly didn't yet understand who they were.

"We're just talking," said Denis. "I just

want to understand what happened to your brother. Believe me, I think his death was a tragedy."

"He wouldn't have regretted it," I told them. "He died fighting for what he believed in."

"Defending others who took him for granted."

"That's not true."

"Oh?" Denis gave me a lopsided smile. "Then why don't you work for the guardians? You've killed Strigoi but have no promise mark. Not even a graduation mark, I heard. Why aren't you out there throwing yourself in front of Moroi?"

"Denis," said Nikolai uneasily, "please just leave."

"I'm not talking to you, Kolya." Denis's eyes were still on me. "I'm just trying to figure Rose out. She kills Strigoi but doesn't work for the guardians. She's clearly not like the rest of you soft people in this town. Maybe she's more like us."

"She's nothing like you," Viktoria snapped back.

I got it then, and a chill ran down my spine. These were the kind of dhampirs that Mark had been talking about. The true unpromised ones. The vigilantes who sought out Strigoi on their own, the ones who neither settled down nor answered to any guardians. They shouldn't have unnerved me, not really. In some ways, Denis was right. In the simplest terms, I really was like them. And yet . . . there was an air about these guys that just rubbed me the wrong way.

"Then why are you in Russia?" asked one of Denis's friends. I already couldn't remember his name. "This is a long trip for you. You wouldn't have come here without a good reason."

Viktoria was picking up her sister's anger. "She came to tell us about Dimka."

Denis eyed me. "I think she's here to hunt Strigoi. There are more in Russia to choose from than there are in the States."

"She wouldn't be in Baia if she was hunting Strigoi, you idiot," returned Viktoria evenly. "She'd be in Vladivostok or Novosibirsk or somewhere like that."

*Novosibirsk.* The name was familiar. But where had I heard it? A moment later, the answer came to me. Sydney had mentioned it. Novosibirsk was the largest city in Siberia.

Denis continued. "Maybe she's just passing through. Maybe she'll want to join us when we go to Novosibirsk tomorrow."

"For God's sake," I exclaimed. "I'm right

here. Stop talking about me like I'm not. And why would I want to go with you?"

Denis's eyes gleamed with an intense, feverish light. "Good hunting there. Lots of Strigoi. Come with us, and you can help us go after them."

"And how many of you will come back from this?" Karolina asked in a hard voice. "Where's Timosha? Where's Vasiliy? Your hunting party keeps getting smaller each time you return here. Which one of you will be next? Whose family will be the next to mourn?"

"Easy for you to talk," retorted the friend. Lev, I think his name was. "You stay here and do nothing while *we* go out and keep you safe."

Karolina gave him a disgusted look, and I recalled how she was dating a guardian. "You go out and rush into situations without thinking. If you want to keep us safe, then stay here and defend your families when they need it. If you want to go after Strigoi, go join the guardians and work with those who have some sense."

"The guardians don't hunt Strigoi!" cried Denis. "They sit and wait and cower before the Moroi."

The unfortunate part was, he had a point. But not entirely.

"That's changing," I said. "There's a movement to start taking the offensive against the Strigoi. There's also talk of the Moroi learning to fight with us. You could help be a part of that."

"Like you are?" he laughed. "You still haven't told us why you're here and not with them. You can say what you want to the rest of this group, but *I* know why you're here. I can see it in you." The crazy, eerie look he gave me almost made me think that he could. "You know the only way to rid the world of evil is to do it on our own. To seek out the Strigoi ourselves and kill them, one by one."

"Without a plan," finished Karolina. "Without any thought of the consequences."

"We're strong and we know how to fight. That's all we need to know when it comes to killing Strigoi."

And that was when I understood. I finally got what Mark had been trying to tell me. Denis was saying exactly what I had been thinking since I left St. Vladimir's. I'd run off without a plan, wanting to throw myself into danger because I felt I had a mission that only I could carry out. Only I could kill Dimitri. Only I could destroy the evil within him. I'd been giving no thought to how I'd pull it off — seeing as Dimitri had beat me more often than not in fights when he was still a dhampir. With a Strigoi's strength and speed now? The odds were definitely against me. Still, I hadn't cared. I'd been obsessed, convinced I had to do this.

In my own head, what I had to do made sense, but now . . . hearing those sentiments from Denis, it sounded crazy. Just as reckless as Mark had warned. Their motives might be good — just as mine were — but they were also suicidal. Without Dimitri, I honestly hadn't cared much about my own life. I'd never been afraid to risk it before, but now I realized there was a big difference between dying uselessly and dying for a reason. If I died trying to kill Dimitri because I had no strategy, then my life would have meant nothing.

Just then, the priest walked over and said something to us in Russian. From his tone and expression, I think he was asking if everything was okay. He'd mingled with the rest of the congregation after the service. Being human, he probably didn't know all the dhampir politics afoot, but he could undoubtedly sense trouble.

Denis offered him a simpering smile and gave what sounded like a polite explanation. The priest smiled in return, nodded, and wandered off when someone else called to him.

"Enough," said Karolina harshly, once the priest was out of earshot. "You need to go. Now."

Denis's body tensed, and mine responded, ready for a fight. I thought he might start something then and there. A few seconds later, he relaxed and turned to me.

"Show them to me first."

"Show you what?" I asked.

"The marks. Show me how many Strigoi you've killed."

I didn't respond right away, wondering if this was a trick. Everyone's eyes were on me. Turning slightly, I lifted the hair off the back of my neck and showed my tattoos. Little lightning-shaped *molnija* marks were there, along with the mark I'd gotten for the battle. From the sound of Denis's gasp, I was guessing he'd never seen that many kills before. I let my hair go and met his gaze levelly.

"Anything else?" I asked.

"You're wasting your time," he said at last, gesturing to the people behind me. "With them. With this place. You should come with us to Novosibirsk. We'll help make your life worthwhile."

"I'm the only one who can make anything

of my life." I pointed down the street. "You were asked to leave. Now go."

I held my breath, still bracing for a fight. After several tense moments, the group retreated. Before turning around, Denis gave me one last piercing look.

"This isn't what you want and you know it. When you change your mind, come find us at 83 Kasakova. We leave at sunrise tomorrow."

"You'll be leaving without me," I said.

Denis's smile sent another chill down my spine. "We'll see."

# FOURTEEN

The encounter with Denis left me even more confused than before. It was a shocking illustration of Mark's warning, an omen of what I too might become if I wasn't careful. I wasn't really the same as Denis, was I? I wasn't *aimlessly* seeking danger. I was seeking danger . . . well, for a reason. I had to fulfill the promise I'd made to find Dimitri. Maybe it was suicidal and I was only deluding myself into thinking it was noble.

Viktoria left me little opportunity to ruminate. Later that evening, as the family was settling down in the living room after way too much food, she glibly asked Olena, "Can I go over to Marina's? She's having a party before we go back to school."

Wow. It looked like Abe and the Alchemists weren't the only ones keeping secrets around here. I glanced between Olena and Viktoria's faces, curious as to how this would play out. Olena and Yeva were both

271

knitting, but Yeva didn't look up. Viktoria had spoken in English. Olena's face turned thoughtful.

"You have to leave early tomorrow to go back to school."

"I know. But I can sleep on the bus. Everyone else will be there tonight."

" 'Everyone else' isn't a convincing argument," scoffed Olena.

"They'll all be tired tomorrow too," replied Viktoria, grinning.

"You'll miss your last night with Rose."

"I'll hang out with her after I get back."

"Great. And stay up even later."

"Not that late. I'll be back by two."

"Absolutely not. You'll be back by midnight." Olena returned to her knitting. But that had been permission if I'd ever heard it.

Viktoria looked at the clock. It was almost eight thirty. Her face told me she wasn't happy about the curfew, but she apparently decided to take what she could get. Karolina gave us an odd look as we left the room but remained silent. Sonya and Paul, engrossed in TV, barely noticed our departure. I had to find out what was going on.

"Okay," I said once we were heading upstairs, "what gives? I thought you weren't going to Marina's."

Viktoria grinned and beckoned me into her bedroom. I'd recently learned her bedroom used to be Dimitri's, and every time I was in here, I had to resist the urge to go bury myself in the bed, even though I knew the sheets had been washed countless times since those days. Somehow, I could imagine them smelling like Dimitri and feeling warm as though we were both lying there together.

"I'm not." Viktoria began rifling through her closet and pulled out a short, sleeveless red dress with lace around the straps. The fabric was stretchy — the kind that looked like it'd show *everything.* I was shocked when she began putting it on. It was pretty trashy.

"Is this a joke?"

Nope. Viktoria took off her shirt and jeans and pulled the dress on. She had no trouble with it, but it was every bit as clingy as it had appeared. She wasn't as filled out as I was on top, but in a dress like that, it didn't matter.

"Okay," I said, catching on at last. "What's his name?"

"Rolan," she said. "Oh, Rose. He's amazing. And this is the last night I'll get to see him before school."

I didn't know whether to feel happy for

her or sad for Nikolai. This Rolan guy must have been the reason she couldn't give Nikolai the time of day. She was totally in love with someone else. Still, that dress . . .

"You must really like him," I observed dryly.

Her eyes widened. "Do you want to meet him?"

"Er, well, I don't want to interfere with your date. . . ."

"You won't. Just stop by and say hi, okay?"

It felt pretty intrusive, yet at the same time . . . well, I was kind of curious about a guy who could get her to leave the house in that kind of outfit, particularly when she started applying really heavy makeup: extra-dark eyeliner and bright red lipstick. So I agreed to meet Rolan, and we left the house as quietly as we could. Despite wearing a coat over her dress, Viktoria still didn't want to run into her mother.

We headed downtown, following a few twists and turns until we ended up behind what looked like an ordinary warehouse in an abandoned part of town. All was quiet, but a tall, tough-looking dhampir stood by a door leading into the building, his arms crossed in front of him. Viktoria brought us to a halt nearby, saying we had to wait there. A minute later, a group of Moroi men of mixed ages wandered up, chatting and laughing. The dhampir gave them a once-over and then opened the door for them. Light and music spilled out until the door shut — and all went silent again.

"So this is Baia's secret dhampir world," I murmured. She didn't hear me because suddenly, her face lit up.

"There he is!"

She pointed to two approaching guys. Both were Moroi. Well, who knew? Viktoria's secret boyfriend wasn't a dhampir. I guessed that wasn't too shocking, really, though the way she'd dressed tonight still bothered me. She gave him a fierce hug and introduced us. His friend was named Sergey, and he smiled politely before hurrying inside where he was apparently meeting a girl too.

I had to give Viktoria credit: Rolan was hot. His hair was dark auburn, soft and wavy. The green of his eyes reminded me — painfully — of Adrian's. And when he smiled at Viktoria, it was dazzling. The look on her face was exactly like Nikolai's whenever he was around her.

Rolan took a hold of Viktoria's hands and brought them to his lips, kissing each one. Those green, green eyes gazed at hers, and he murmured something I couldn't hear.

She blushed and replied in Russian. I didn't need any translation to know the content was sexy and flirty. Still smiling, he glanced over at me, and although she'd introduced us, it was like he was noticing me for the first time — and was interested.

"You're new here, aren't you?" he asked.

Viktoria wrapped her arms around him and rested her head on his chest. "Rose is visiting. She's a friend of the family."

"Ah," he said. "Now I remember hearing about you. I had no idea such a fierce Strigoi killer would be so beautiful."

"It's part of the job description," I said dryly.

"Will you be returning to school with Viktoria?" he asked.

"No. I'll be staying here a little longer." I still had no clue, though, if "a little longer" was one hour or one year.

"Hmm," he said thoughtfully. He looked back down at Viktoria and pressed a kiss to her hair, running his fingers along her throat. His next words were to her. "I'm glad you were able to come here before you left. I don't know how I'll get by with you so far away."

She beamed. "There was no way I could leave without seeing you one more time. . . ." She trailed off, too overcome with emotion, and as he leaned down, hand still on her throat, I thought for an awful moment that they were going to start making out then and there.

Fortunately, the appearance of an approaching dhampir girl interrupted them. Viktoria broke from Rolan and embraced the other girl. They apparently hadn't seen each other in a while and chatted rapidly in Russian, ignoring Rolan and me. Free of her for a moment, he leaned toward me.

"Once Viktoria has returned to school, you'll be all alone here. Maybe I could show you around then?"

"Thanks, but I've already seen everything."

He kept that big smile on. "Of course. Well, then, perhaps we could simply get together and . . . talk?"

I couldn't believe it. This guy had had his hands all over Viktoria thirty seconds ago and was now trying to score plans with me the instant she left town. I was disgusted and had to restrain myself from doing something stupid.

"Sorry, but I don't think I'll be around long enough."

I got the impression that women didn't refuse him very often. He frowned and started to protest, but Viktoria returned and wrapped herself around him again. He studied me for several more puzzled seconds and then shifted his attention to her, smiling and turning on the charm. She ate it all up, and while the two tried to include me in their conversation, it was clear they were totally absorbed in each other. Rolan might be interested in me, but for now, she was an easier target — and one that wouldn't be available much longer. I felt that disgust roil up in me again. The longer we stood out there, the more I realized what was going on. All the people going inside were Moroi guys or dhampir girls. And the girls were all dressed like Viktoria. This was a blood whore den. Suddenly, Baia's secret dhampir world held no appeal.

I hated it. I wanted nothing more than to get out of here. No, wait. I wanted nothing more than to get out of here *and* drag Viktoria away, even kicking and screaming. Rolan was sleazy, no question, and I didn't want her anywhere near him. Yet it soon became clear they weren't going to stand out in the alley all night. They wanted to go inside and do God only knew what.

"Viktoria," I said, trying to be reasonable, "are you sure you don't want to come back home and hang out? I mean, I won't get to see you tomorrow."

She hesitated, then shook her head. "I won't get to see Rolan either. But I promise I'll come see you as soon as I get home later. We'll stay up all night. Mom won't care."

I didn't know what other protests to make. Rolan's impatience, now that I'd refused him, was starting to show. He wanted to go inside. I wondered what was there . . . a dance floor? Bedrooms? I probably could have gone with them to see for myself, despite being underdressed — or, well, overdressed as far as amounts of clothing went. Yet I couldn't bring myself to do it. All my life, I'd been taught about blood whores and why their lifestyle was wrong. I didn't know if Viktoria was becoming one — and I hoped she wasn't — but there was no way I could set foot in there. It was a matter of principle.

I watched them go with a heavy heart, wondering what I'd just let my friend walk into. Seeing her in that ultra-tight dress, plastered all over him, suddenly made me reevaluate everything. How much of this peaceful life in Baia was a sham? Was Viktoria — the girl who'd called me a sister — really not the person I thought she was? Confused, I turned away to head back home —

— And almost walked into Abe. Again.

"What the hell?" I exclaimed. He wore a tuxedo tonight, complete with tails and a silvery silk scarf. "Are you stalking me?" Stupid question. Of course he was. I hoped his formal wear meant he wouldn't be dragging me off this evening. His guardians were equally well dressed. Idly, I wondered if a place like this had something to do with his illegal business dealings. Was he trafficking blood whores? Like some kind of pimp? Unlikely, seeing as most of these girls didn't require much urging.

Abe gave me that annoying knowing smile of his. "I see your friend is off to an interesting night. I had no idea Viktoria had such lovely legs. Now everyone knows, thanks to that dress."

I clenched my fists and leaned toward him. "Don't you *dare* talk about her like that, old man."

"I'm not saying anything that isn't obvious to everybody else. It'll certainly be obvious to young Rolan soon."

"You don't know anything about them!" Yet I didn't believe my own words, not after seeing them walk off together. Abe, I could tell, knew what I was thinking.

"These girls all say it won't happen to them. But it always does. It's what'll happen to you if you stay."

"Oh, here we are," I said mockingly. "I knew a threat had to be coming. The part where you order me again to leave the country or else bad, bad things will happen."

He gestured toward the door, where more Moroi and dhampirs were going. "I don't even need to make anything bad happen. You'll do it on your own by staying here. You'll waste your life away, running errands for Olena Belikova. Potlucks will become the most exciting thing in your world."

"They're good people," I growled. "Don't mock them."

"Oh, I'm not denying that." He straightened his silk scarf. "They *are* good people. But they aren't your people. This is a fantasy. You're deluding yourself." He was all sternness now. "Your grief has sent you here. Your man was ripped away from you, and you've ripped yourself away from your old friends. You're trying to make up for it by convincing yourself that this is your family, that this is your home. They're not. This isn't."

"I could make this my home." I still wasn't sure of that, but my stubborn nature made me want to contradict him.

"You aren't meant for Baia," he said, dark eyes blazing. "You're meant for better things. You need to go back home, back to your school and the Dragomir princess."

"How the hell do you know about her? Who *are* you? When are you going to tell me who you work for? What do you want with me?" I had a feeling I was on the verge of hysterics. Hearing him refer to Lissa snapped something inside of me.

"I'm merely an observer who can tell you're wasting your time here. This is no life for you, Rose. Your life is back in the States. They say you were on track to be a great guardian. Do you know what an honor it is to be assigned to the last Dragomir? You could spend your life in elite, powerful circles. The reputation you've already gained will raise you in status and regard. You have a stunning career ahead of you, and it's not too late to go back to it. Not yet."

"Who are you to talk about how I should live my life? I've heard that your hands are bloody — *Zmey.* You're not exactly a good role model. What is it you're involved in, anyway?"

"My own affairs. And it's exactly *because* of the life I lead that you should listen to me when I say abandon this path and go back home."

His words were urgent and authoritative, and I couldn't believe he had the audacity to talk to me like that. "That's not my life anymore," I said icily.

He gave a harsh laugh and gestured around us once more. "What, and this is? You want to go off and be a blood whore like your friend in there?"

"Don't call her that!" I shouted. "I don't care if you've got bodyguards or not. I *will* hurt you, old man, if you say anything else about Viktoria."

He didn't flinch at my explosion. "That was harsh, I admit. She's not a blood whore. Not yet. But she's one step away from it. As I said, it always happens in the end. Even if you aren't used by someone like Rolan Kislyak — and believe me, he *will* use her, just like he did her sister — you'll still end up alone with a baby you're way too young for."

"Her . . . wait." I froze. "Are you saying he's the guy who got Sonya pregnant? Why would Viktoria be involved with him after he did that and left her sister?"

"Because she doesn't know. Sonya doesn't talk about it, and Mr. Kislyak thinks it's a game, getting two sisters into bed. Too bad for him that Karolina's smarter than the others or he could have had them all. Who knows?" He gave me a sardonic smile. "Maybe he'll consider you part of the family enough to go after you next."

"Like hell. I'd never get involved with anyone like that. I'm never going to be involved with anyone again. Not after Dimitri."

Abe's sternness gave way to momentary amusement. "Oh, Rose. You *are* young. You've barely lived. Everyone thinks their first love is the only one they'll ever have."

This guy was *really* pissing me off, but I gained enough control to decide I wasn't going to punch him. At least, I didn't think so. I backed up a little, toward the building. "I'm not going to play your game here. And you can tell whoever you're working for that I'm not playing theirs either — and that I'm not going back." One way or another, whether it was to hunt Dimitri or live with his family, I was staying in Russia. "You're going to have to box me up and ship me there."

Not that I wanted to give Abe any ideas. I suspected he could do it if he wanted. Damn it. Who was behind this? Who would want to find me badly enough to send this guy after me? Weirder still, whoever it was was someone who cared enough about me to attempt reason. If Abe had actually wanted to abduct me, he already would have. He could have done it the night he brought me to Baia. All he would have had to do was keep driving to the nearest airport. I eventually needed to figure this out, but first I needed to get away from Abe.

I backed up further. "I'm leaving, and you can't stop me. And don't spy on me anymore. This ends now."

Abe studied me for several seconds, his dark eyes narrowed thoughtfully. I could practically see the wheels of plots and world domination spinning in his head. At last he said, so quietly I could hardly hear him, "It won't end with *them*, though."

"Who?"

He pointed at the door. "Viktoria and Rolan."

"What are you getting at?"

"You know what I'm getting at. She thinks she's in love with him. He knows she'll be back in school tomorrow. Tonight's his last chance with her, and he won't waste it. There are lots of bedrooms in there. They're probably in one right now."

I tried to control my breathing. "Then I'll go tell her mother."

"It'll be too late. She'd never find them in time, and tomorrow, Viktoria will be on her way to school — and he'll have no interest anymore. What can her mother do after the fact? Ground her?"

I was getting angry, largely because I had a feeling he was right. "Fine. Then I'll drag her off myself."

"That'll never happen. She *wants* to do this. She won't leave with you. Even if she did, she'd just find him again."

I eyed him. "Enough. You're obviously hinting at something, so just get on with it."

He smiled, apparently pleased at my astuteness — or maybe my bluntness. "If you want to save her, you've got to go through him. Through Rolan."

I scoffed. "Not likely. The only way he'd leave her alone is if I offered to take her place." And hey, friendship only went so far.

"Not if I talk to him."

"What are you going to do, give him a talk on morality and sway him with reason?"

"Oh, I'll sway him, all right. But believe me, I won't do it with reason — well, at least not the kind you're thinking of. If I tell him to leave her alone, he'll leave her alone. For good."

I stepped backward without realizing it and hit the wall. Abe looked scary as hell. Zmey. I didn't doubt his words at all. He could get Rolan to leave Viktoria alone. In fact, he probably wouldn't even use his dhampirs. Abe could deliver enough terror

— and probably a good punch — to make it happen.

"Why would you do that for me?" I asked.

"As a sign of good faith. Promise to leave Baia, and I'll deal with him." His eyes gleamed. Both of us could feel the net closing around me.

"That's your tactic now? You're offering me a trade? My leaving isn't really worth you scaring some Moroi asshole."

The net grew tighter. "Isn't it, Rose?"

Frantically, I thought about what to do. Some part of me thought Viktoria was free to make her own choices, to love whom she wanted . . . but I knew for a fact that Rolan didn't love her. She was a conquest for him, as shown by his willingness to go after me — and Sonya, apparently. What would happen to Viktoria? Would she become like the rest of the women here? Would she be the next Belikov to have a baby? Even if she had no intentions of becoming a guardian, this wasn't the right path for her. Karolina had declined to join the guardians and now lived a respectable life with her kids and a job that — if not exciting — was steady and allowed her to keep her dignity. I couldn't let Viktoria turn down a road that could ruin the rest of her life. I couldn't let that happen to Dimitri's sister.

Dimitri . . .

I knew him. I knew his protective nature. He would *never* let anything happen to those he cared about. I hated the thought of that blood whore den, but I still would have run in to get her — because that was what Dimitri would have done. But I didn't know if I'd find her there in time. I knew, however, that Abe could — and that he could keep Rolan away forever. And so, I spoke without fully understanding the consequences of my words.

"I'll leave Baia."

# FIFTEEN

Abe glanced over at one of his guardians and gave a swift nod. The man instantly walked away. "It's done," Abe said.

"Just like that?" I asked in disbelief.

His lips quirked into a smile. "Rolan knows who I am. He knows who works for me. Once Pavel makes my . . . ah, wishes known, that will be the end of it."

I shivered, knowing Abe spoke the truth. Considering what a smartass I'd been to Abe this whole time, it really was a wonder I hadn't had my feet set in cement and been tossed into the ocean. "So why *aren't* you forcefully dragging me out of here?"

"I never like to make anyone do anything they don't want to. Even Rolan. It's much easier if people simply see reason and do what I ask them to, without the use of force."

"And by 'see reason,' you mean, 'blackmail,'" I said, thinking of what I'd just agreed to.

"We made a trade," he said. "That's all. Don't forget your end of the bargain. You promised to leave here, and you don't seem like the type to go back on your word."

"I don't."

"Rose!"

Viktoria suddenly appeared at the door. Wow, that was fast. Pavel was calmly dragging her by her arm. Her hair was mussed, and a dress strap was slipping from her shoulder. Her face was a mixture of incredulity and anger. "What did you do? That guy came and told Rolan to get out of here and never see me again! And then . . . Rolan agreed. He just left."

I found it slightly funny that Viktoria immediately blamed me for this. True, I was responsible, but Abe was standing right there. It wasn't a secret who his employees were. Nonetheless, I defended my actions.

"He was using you," I said.

There were tears in Viktoria's brown eyes. "He loves me."

"If he loves you, then why did he hit on me as soon as your back was turned?"

"He did not!"

"He's the one who got Sonya pregnant."

Even in the alley's dim lighting, I saw her face pale. "That's a lie."

I threw up my hands. "Why would I make that up? He wanted to make plans with me as soon as you were out of town!"

"If he did," she said, voice shaking, "it was because you led him on."

I gaped. Beside me, Abe listened quietly, a smug look on his face. He was so self-satisfied and probably thought he was being proven right. I wanted to punch him, but Viktoria was my concern.

"How can you think that? I'm your friend!" I told her.

"If you were my friend, you wouldn't be acting like this. You wouldn't try to stand in my way. You act like you loved my brother, but there's no way you could have — no way you really understand love!"

Didn't understand love? Was she crazy? If she only knew what I'd sacrificed for Dimitri, what I'd done to be where I was now . . . all for love. *She* was the one who couldn't understand. Love wasn't a fling in a back room at a party. It was something you lived and died for. My emotions surged, that darkness welling up within me that made me want to lash out in return for her horrible accusation. It was only through the strongest of efforts that I remembered she was already hurting, that she only said the things she did because she was confused

291

and upset.

"Viktoria, I do understand, and I'm sorry. I'm only doing this because you're my friend. I care about you."

"You aren't my friend," she hissed. "You aren't part of this family. You don't understand anything about us or how we live! I wish you'd never come here." She turned and stormed away, pushing back inside through the long line of partygoers. My heart ached as I watched her.

I turned to Abe. "She's going to go try to find him."

He still wore that damnably knowing expression. "It won't matter. He'll have nothing to do with her anymore. Not if he values that pretty face of his." I was worried for Viktoria but kind of had a feeling Abe was right about Rolan. Rolan would no longer be an issue. As for Viktoria's next guy . . . well, that was a worry for another day.

"Fine. Then we're done here. Do not follow me anymore," I growled.

"Keep your promise to leave Baia, and I won't have to."

I narrowed my eyes. "I told you: I always keep my promises."

And as I hurried back to the Belikov house, I suddenly wondered if that was true.

The blowout with Abe and Viktoria was like cold water on my face. What was I doing here? To a certain extent, Abe had been right . . . I had been deluding myself, pretending Dimitri's family was my own in order to soothe my grief over him. But they weren't. This wasn't home. The Academy wasn't my home either, not anymore. The only thing I had left was my promise — my promise to Dimitri. The promise I'd somehow lost sight of since coming here.

Some of the Belikov family was in bed when I got home, but others were still in the living room. I slipped upstairs to my room, waiting anxiously for Viktoria to get home. A half hour later, I heard footsteps on the stairs and the sound of her door closing. I knocked gently on it.

"Viktoria," I said in a loud whisper. "It's me. Please talk to me."

"No!" came the response. "I don't ever want to talk to you again."

"Viktoria —"

"Go away!"

"I'm just worried about you."

"You aren't my brother! You aren't even my sister. You have no place here!"

Ouch. Her voice was muffled by the door, but I didn't want to risk a fight in the hall and let the others hear. Going to my room, my heart breaking, I stopped and stood in front of the mirror. It was then that I knew she was right. Even Abe was right. Baia wasn't my place.

In a flash, my meager belongings were packed, but I hesitated before going downstairs. Viktoria's closed door stared at me, and I had to fight the urge to knock again. If I did, it would only trigger another fight. Or, maybe even worse, she would forgive me — and then I would want to stay forever, lost in the comfort of Dimitri's family and their simple life.

Taking a deep breath, I headed downstairs and walked out the front door. I wanted to tell the others goodbye but worried the same thing would happen, that I'd look at their faces and change my mind. I needed to go, I realized. I was angry at both Viktoria and Abe. Their words had hurt me, but there'd been truth in them. This wasn't my world. I had other things to do with my life. And I had a lot of promises to keep.

When I was about eight blocks away, I slowed down, not because I was tired but because I wasn't sure where I was going. Leaving that house had been the biggest step. I sank down on the curb in front of a neighbor's silent, dark yard. I wanted to cry without knowing why. I wanted my old life back. I wanted Dimitri and Lissa. Oh, God, I wanted them.

But Dimitri was gone, and the only way I'd see him was if I truly set out to kill him. And as for Lissa . . . she was more or less gone to me too. Even if I survived this, I didn't think she could forgive me. Sitting there, feeling lost and alone, I tried reaching out to her one more time. I knew it was foolish, considering what I'd seen before, but I had to try one more time. I had to know if I really could have my old place back there. I slipped inside her mind instantly, my runaway emotions making the transition easy. She was on a private jet.

If Jill had been stunned by meeting St. Vladimir's A-list students, going on a trip with them made her downright comatose. She stared at everything wide-eyed and barely said a word during the whole flight to the Royal Court. When Avery offered her a glass of champagne, Jill could barely stammer out, "N-no thanks." After that, the others seemed to forget about her and got carried away by their own conversation. Lissa noticed Jill's uneasiness but didn't do much to remedy it. That was a shock. The Lissa I had known would have gone out of her way to make Jill comfortable and be included. Fortunately, the younger girl seemed perfectly entertained by watching the others' antics.

I also took comfort in knowing Jill would be okay once she met up with Mia. Lissa had sent word ahead to Mia to come pick up Jill when they landed, seeing as Lissa and the others had to attend to one of Tatiana's functions right away. Mia had said she'd take Jill under her wing for the weekend and show her some of the innovative things she'd learned to do with her water magic. Lissa was glad for this, happy she wouldn't be babysitting a freshman all weekend.

Even if Jill was totally off of Lissa's radar, one person wasn't: Avery's brother Reed. Their father had decided it would be a good idea for Reed to go with them, and seeing as Mr. — excuse me — *Headmaster* Lazar had played a key role in working with Tatiana to arrange this trip, there was little argument. Avery had rolled her eyes and spoken to Lissa about it covertly, just before boarding.

"We're all riding your reputation," Avery said. "Part of the reason Dad let me come was because you're in good with the queen, and he wants it to rub off on me. He's then hoping *I'll* get in good with her, and then that'll rub off on Reed — and the rest of the family."

Lissa tried not to overthink the logic too much. Mostly, she was bothered because Reed Lazar was still as unpleasant as he'd been the first day they met. He wasn't really mean or anything; it just made her uncomfortable being around him. Really, he was the polar opposite of Avery. Whereas she was animated and could always strike up conversation, he stayed tight-lipped and spoke only when spoken to. Lissa couldn't really tell if it was shyness or disdain.

When Lissa had tried asking him if he was excited to go to Court, Reed had simply shrugged. "Whatever. I don't care." His tone had been almost hostile, like he resented her for asking, so she'd given up all other attempts at conversation. The only person, other than his sister, that Lissa saw Reed ever speak to was Avery's guardian Simon. He had also come along.

When the flight landed, Mia was as good as her word. She waved enthusiastically when Lissa stepped off the plane, her blond curls whipping around in the wind. Lissa grinned back, and they gave each other quick half-hugs, something that never failed to amuse me given their former enemy status.

Lissa made introductions for those who

needed them as an escort of guardians led them away from the landing strip and toward the inner portion of Court. Mia welcomed Jill so warmly that the younger girl's uneasiness faded, and excitement glowed in her green eyes. Smiling fondly, Mia glanced away from Jill and over to Lissa.

"Where's Rose?"

Silence fell, followed by uncomfortable glances.

"What?" demanded Mia. "What did I say?"

"Rose is gone," said Lissa. "Sorry . . . I thought you knew. She dropped out and left after the attack because there were some things . . . some personal things . . . she needed to take care of."

Lissa feared Mia would ask about the personal things. Only a few people knew about my search for Dimitri, and Lissa wanted to keep it that way. Most thought I'd just disappeared from post-battle trauma. Mia's next question completely shocked Lissa.

"Why didn't you go with her?"

"What?" Lissa stammered. "Why would I do that? Rose dropped out. No way am I going to."

"Yeah, I suppose." Mia turned speculative. "You guys are just so close — even without the bond. I assumed you'd follow each other to the ends of the earth and figure out the details later." Mia's own life had gone through so much upheaval that she took that kind of thing in stride.

That weird, fluctuating anger I'd been feeling pop up in Lissa every so often suddenly reared its head and turned on Mia. "Yeah, well, if we were so close, then it seems like she wouldn't have left in the first place. She's the selfish one, not me."

The words stung me and clearly shocked Mia. Mia had a temper of her own, but she sat on it and simply held up her hands in an apologetic way. She really had changed. "Sorry. Wasn't trying to accuse you of anything."

Lissa said nothing else. Since my departure, she'd beat herself up about a lot of things. She'd gone over and over things she could have done for me before or after the attack, things that might have made me stay. But it had never occurred to her to go with me, and the revelation hit her like a smack to the face. Mia's words made her feel guilty and angry all at the same time — and she wasn't sure who she was the maddest at: me or herself.

"I know what you're thinking," said

Adrian a few minutes later, once Mia had led Jill away and promised to meet up later.

"What, you read minds now?" asked Lissa.

"Don't have to. It's written all over your face. And Rose never would have let you go with her, so stop agonizing over it."

They entered the royal guest housing, which was just as lush and opulent as it had been when I'd stayed there. "You don't know that. I could have talked her into it."

"No," said Adrian sharply. "You couldn't have. I'm serious — don't give yourself one more thing to be depressed about."

"Hey, who said I'm depressed? Like I said, she abandoned *me*."

Adrian was surprised. Since my departure, Lissa had been more sad than anything. She'd occasionally been angry at my decision, but neither Adrian nor I had seen such vehemence from her. Dark feelings boiled within her heart.

"I thought you understood," said Adrian, with a small, puzzled frown. "I thought you said you'd —"

Avery suddenly interrupted, giving Adrian a sharp look. "Hey, hey. Leave her alone, okay? We'll see you at the reception."

They were at a point where the groups had to split, girls going to one part of the lodging and guys to the other. Adrian looked like he wanted to say more, but instead he nodded and headed off with Reed and a couple of guardians. Avery put a gentle arm around Lissa as she glared at Adrian's retreating figure.

"You okay?" Avery's normally laughing face was filled with concern. It startled Lissa in the same way Adrian's moments of seriousness always startled me.

"I guess. I don't know."

"Don't beat yourself up over what you could have or should have done. The past is gone. Move on to the future."

Lissa's heart was still heavy, her mood blacker than it had been in quite a while. She managed a tight smile. "I think that's the wisest thing you've ever said."

"I know! Can you believe it? Do you think it'll impress Adrian?"

They dissolved into laughter, yet despite her cheery exterior, Lissa was still struck by Mia's offhand comments. They plagued Lissa in a way she hadn't thought possible. What really bothered her the most wasn't the thought that if she'd come with me, she could have kept me out of trouble. No. Her biggest issue was that she hadn't thought of coming with me in the first place. I was her best friend. As far as she was concerned, that should have been her immediate reaction to my departure. It hadn't been, and now Lissa was racked with even more guilt than usual. The guilt was all-consuming, and she would occasionally transform it to anger to ease the pain. It didn't help much.

Her mood didn't improve as the evening progressed, either. Not long after the group's arrival, the queen hosted a small reception for the most elite of all visitors who had come to the Court. Lissa was quickly discovering that the queen always seemed to be hosting some party or another. At one point in her life, Lissa would have considered that fun. She no longer did, at least not when it came to these kinds of parties.

But keeping her dark feelings locked up, Lissa stayed good at playing the role of nice royal girl. The queen seemed happy that Lissa had a "suitable" royal friend and was equally pleased when Lissa impressed other royals and dignitaries she was introduced to. At one point, though, Lissa's resolve nearly faltered.

"Before you leave," said Tatiana, "we should see about your guardians."

She and Lissa stood together with a group of admirers and hangers-on who were keeping respectful distances. Lissa had been staring vacantly at the bubbles in her untouched champagne and looked up with a start.

"Guardians, your majesty?"

"Well, there's no delicate way to put this, but now, for better or for worse, you're without any protection." The queen paused respectfully. "Belikov was a good man."

My name naturally didn't come to her lips. I might as well have never existed. She'd never liked me, particularly since she thought I was going to run off with Adrian. As it was, Lissa had noticed Tatiana watching with some consideration while Avery and Adrian flirted. It was hard to say if the queen disapproved. Her partying aside, Avery seemed a model girl — save that Tatiana had wanted Lissa and Adrian to eventually get together.

"I don't need any protection right now," said Lissa politely, her heart clenching.

"No, but you'll be out of school soon enough. We think we've found some excellent candidates for you. One of them's a woman — a lucky find."

"Janine Hathaway offered to be my guardian," said Lissa suddenly. I hadn't known that, but as she spoke, I read the story in her mind. My mom had approached her not long after I left. I was a little shocked. My mom was very loyal to her current assignment. This would have been a big move for her.

"Janine Hathaway?" Tatiana's eyebrows rose nearly to her hairline. "I'm sure she has other commitments. No, we've got much better choices. This young lady's only a few years older than you."

A better choice than Janine Hathaway? Not likely. Before Dimitri, my mother had been the gold standard by which I measured all badassedness. Tatiana's "young lady" was undoubtedly someone under the queen's control — and more importantly, not a Hathaway. The queen didn't like my mom any more than she liked me. Once, when Tatiana had been bitching me out for something, she'd made a reference to a man my mother had been involved with — someone whom I suspected might be my father, a guy named Ibrahim. The funny thing was, the queen had almost sounded like *she* had once had an interest in the guy too, and I had to wonder if that was part of her dislike for my family.

Lissa put on a tight, polite smile for the queen and thanked her for the consideration. Lissa and I both understood what was going on. This was Tatiana's game. Everyone was part of her plan, and there was no way to go against her. For a brief moment, Lissa had that strange thought again, of something Victor Dashkov had once said to her. Aside from his crazy killing and kidnapping schemes, Victor had also wanted to start a revolution among the Moroi. He thought the power distribution was off — something Lissa occasionally believed too — and that it was wielded unfairly by those with too much control. The moment was gone almost as soon as it came. Victor Dashkov was a crazy villain whose ideas deserved no acknowledgment.

Then, as soon as courtesy allowed, Lissa excused herself from the queen and headed across the room, feeling like she was going to explode with grief and anger. She nearly ran into Avery as she did.

"God," said Avery. "Do you think Reed could embarrass me any more? Two people have tried to make conversation with him, and he keeps scaring them off. He actually just told Robin Badica to shut up. I mean, yeah, she was going on and on, but still. That is not cool." Avery's dramatic look of exasperation faded as she took in Lissa's face. "Hey, what's wrong?"

Lissa glanced at Tatiana and then turned back to Avery, taking comfort in her friend's blue-gray eyes. "I need to get out of here." Lissa took a deep, calming breath. "Remember all that good stuff you said you knew about? When is that going to happen?"

Avery smiled. "As soon as you want."

I returned to myself, sitting there on the curb. My emotions were still going crazy, and my eyes were fighting off tears. My earlier doubts were confirmed: Lissa didn't need me anymore . . . and yet, I still had that feeling that there was something odd going on that I couldn't quite put a finger on. I supposed her guilt over Mia's comment or spirit side effects could be affecting her, but still . . . she wasn't the same Lissa.

Footsteps on the pavement made me look up. Of all the people who might have found me, I would have expected Abe or maybe Viktoria. But it wasn't.

It was Yeva.

The old woman stood there, a shawl draped over her narrow shoulders, and her sharp, cunning eyes looking down at me disapprovingly. I sighed.

"What happened? Did a house fall on your sister?" I asked. Maybe there was a benefit to our language barrier. She pursed her lips.

"You can't stay here any longer," she said.

My mouth dropped open.

"You . . . you speak English?"

She snorted. "Of course."

I shot up. "All this time you've been pretending not to? You've been making Paul play translator?"

"It's easier," she said simply. "You avoid a lot of annoying conversation when you don't speak the language. And I've found that Americans make the most annoying conversation of all."

I was still aghast. "You don't even know me! But from the first day, you've been giving me hell. Why? Why do you hate me?"

"I don't hate you. But I am disappointed."

"Disappointed? How?"

"I dreamed you would come."

"I heard that. You dream a lot?"

"Sometimes," she said. The moonlight glinted in her eyes, enhancing her otherworldly appearance. A chill ran down my spine. "Sometimes my dreams are true. Sometimes not. I dreamed Dimka was dead, but I didn't want to believe it, not until I had proof. You were my proof."

"And that's why you were disappointed?"

Yeva drew the shawl more tightly around her. "No. In my dreams, you shone. You burned like a star, and I saw you as a warrior, someone who could do great deeds. Instead? You've sat around and moped. You've done nothing. You haven't done what you came to do."

307

I studied her, wondering if she really knew what she was talking about. "And what is that exactly?"

"You know what it is. I dreamed that, too."

I waited for more. When it didn't come, I laughed. "Nice vague answer. You're as bad as any scam fortune-teller."

Even in the darkness, I could see the anger kindle in her eyes. "You've come to search for Dimka. To try to kill him. You must find him."

"What do you mean 'try'?" I didn't want to believe her, didn't want to believe she might actually know my future. Nonetheless, I found myself getting hooked in. "Have you seen what happens? Do I kill him?"

"I can't see everything."

"Oh. Fantastic."

"I only saw that you must find him."

"But that's all you've got? I already knew that!"

"It's what I saw."

I groaned. "Damn it, I don't have time for these cryptic clues. If you can't help me, then don't say anything."

She stayed quiet.

I slung my bag over my shoulder. "Fine. I'm leaving then." And like that, I knew where I would go. "Tell the others . . . well, tell them thank you for everything. And that I'm sorry."

"You're doing the right thing," she said. "This isn't where you should be."

"So I've heard," I muttered, walking away.

I wondered if she'd say anything else: chastise me, curse me, give me more mysterious words of "wisdom." But she stayed silent, and I didn't look back.

I had no home, not here and not in America. The only thing left for me was to do what I'd come to do. I had told Abe I kept my promises. I would. I'd leave Baia like I told him. And I'd kill Dimitri, as I'd promised myself I would.

I knew where to go now. The address had never left my mind: 83 Kasakova. I didn't know where it was, but once I reached the town's center, I found a guy walking down the street who gave me directions. The address was close by, only about a mile, and I headed out at a brisk pace.

When I reached the house, I was glad to see that the lights were still on. Even as pissed off and raging as I was, I didn't want to wake anyone up. I also didn't want to speak to Nikolai and was relieved when Denis opened the door.

His expression was all astonishment when he saw me. Despite his bold words back at the church earlier, I don't think he'd really believed I'd join him and the other unpromised ones. He was speechless, so I did the talking.

"I changed my mind. I'm coming with you." I took a deep breath, bracing myself for what came next. I'd promised Abe I'd leave Baia — but I hadn't promised to return to the U.S. "Take me to Novosibirsk."

# SIXTEEN

Denis and his two unpromised friends, Artur and Lev, were ecstatic that I was going to be part of their posse. But if they expected me to share their crazy enthusiasm for reckless Strigoi hunting, they were about to be sorely disappointed. In fact, it didn't take long after I joined them before they realized that I was approaching the hunt very differently than they were. Denis's friend Lev had a car, and we took turns driving to Novosibirsk. The drive was about fifteen hours, and even though we stopped at a hotel for the night, it was still a lot of continuous time to be cooped up in a small space with three guys who couldn't stop talking about all the Strigoi they were going to kill.

In particular, they kept trying to draw me out. They wanted to know about how many Strigoi I'd slain. They wanted to know what the battle at the Academy had been like.

They wanted to know my methods. Anytime my mind turned to those topics, though, all I could think of was blood and grief. It was nothing I wanted to brag about, and it took about six hours on the road for them to finally figure out that they weren't going to get much information from me.

Instead, they regaled me with tales of their own adventures. To be fair, they'd slain several Strigoi — but they'd lost a number of their friends, all of whom had been in their teens, like these guys. My experiences weren't that dissimilar; I'd lost friends too. My losses had been a result of being outnumbered, though. Denis's group's casualties seemed to have been more due to rushing in to without thinking. Indeed, their plan once we got to Novosibirsk wasn't really that solid. They reiterated that Strigoi liked to hunt at places that were crowded at night, like dance clubs, or in remote places like alleys, that made for easy pickings. No one noticed as much when people disappeared from those kinds of places. So Denis's plans mostly involved trolling those hot spots in the hopes that we'd run into Strigoi.

My initial thought was to immediately ditch this group and strike out on my own. After all, my main goal had been to simply get to Novosibirsk. With everything I'd learned now, it seemed logical that Siberia's largest city would be the next best place to look. Then, the more I thought about it, the more I realized that jumping into the Strigoi scene alone would be as stupid as one of the unpromised gang's plans. I could use their backup. Plus, since I didn't actually know where Dimitri was yet, I had to come up with a method of getting some information. I'd need help for that.

We made it to Novosibirsk at the end of the second day of driving. Despite hearing about its size, I hadn't imagined it would be anything like Moscow or Saint Petersburg. And true, it turned out to be not quite as large as they were, but it was still just as much a city, complete with skyscrapers, theaters, commuters, and the same beautiful architecture.

We crashed with a friend of theirs who had an apartment downtown, a dhampir named Tamara. Her English wasn't very good, but from the sounds of it, she was another unpromised one and just as excited as everyone else to rid the world of Strigoi. She was a little older than the rest of us, which was why she had her own place, and was a cute brunette with freckles. It sounded as though she waited until whenever the guys came to town to hunt, which I took as a small blessing. At least she didn't go out alone. She seemed particularly excited to have another girl around, but like the others, she quickly picked up that I didn't share their enthusiasm.

When our first night of Strigoi hunting came around, I finally stepped up into a leadership position. The sudden change in behavior startled them at first, but they soon listened with rapt attention, still caught up in my superstar reputation.

"Okay," I said, looking from face to face. We were in Tamara's tiny living room, sitting in a circle. "Here's how it's going to work. We're going to hit the nightclub scene as a group, patrolling it and the alleys behind it for —"

"Wait," interrupted Denis. "We usually split up."

"Which is why you get killed," I snapped. "We're going as a group."

"Haven't you killed Strigoi by yourself, though?" asked Lev. He was the tallest of the group, with a long and lanky figure that was almost Moroi-like.

"Yes, but I got lucky." That, and I also just thought I was a better fighter than any of them. Call me arrogant, but I was a damned good guardian. Or near-guardian.

"We'll do better with all five of us. When we find Strigoi, we've got to make sure we take care of them in an isolated place." I hadn't forgotten Sydney's warnings. "But before we kill them, I need to talk to them. It'll be your job to restrain them."

"Why?" asked Denis. "What do you have to say to them?"

"Actually, it's what *they* have to say to *me*. Look, it won't take long. And you'll get to make your kill in the end, so don't worry about it. But . . ." This next part went against my grand plans, but I knew I had to say it. I wouldn't get them killed for the sake of my own quest. "If we get ourselves in a situation where you're trapped or in *immediate* danger, forget the talking and restraining. Kill. Save yourself."

Apparently, I seemed confident and bad-ass enough that they decided to go along with whatever I said. Part of our plan involved going "undercover," so to speak. Any Strigoi who was close or got a good enough look would immediately recognize us as dhampirs. It was important that we not attract any attention. We needed a Strigoi scanning for victims to pass right over us. We needed to look like other human club-goers.

So we dressed the part, and I was a bit

astonished at how well the guys cleaned up. Denis, crazy or not, was particularly good-looking, sharing the same dark gold hair and brown eyes that his brother Nikolai had. My few changes of clothes weren't quite up to partying standards, so Tamara delved into her wardrobe for me. She seemed to take a lot of delight in finding things for me to wear. We were actually similar in size, which was kind of amazing. With her tall, super-slim build, Lissa and I had never been able to share clothes. Tamara was my height and had a similar body type.

She first offered me a short, tight dress that was so similar to the one Viktoria had worn that I just shook my head and handed it back. The memories of our argument still hurt, and I wasn't going to relive that night or in any way play blood whore dress-up. Instead, Tamara settled for dressing me in black jeans and a black tank top. I consented to hair and makeup too, and studying myself in the mirror, I had to admit she did a good job. As vain as it was, I liked looking good. I especially liked that the guys looked at me in a way that was admiring and respectful — but not like I was some piece of meat. Tamara offered me jewelry too, but the only thing I'd wear was the *nazar* around my neck. My stake required a jacket, but she found a sexy leather one that didn't take away from the rest of the outfit's appeal.

Setting out around midnight, I couldn't help shaking my head. "We're the god-damned hottest vampire hunters ever," I muttered.

Denis led us to a club where they'd found Strigoi before. It was also apparently where one of their unpromised friends had been killed. It was in a seedy part of town, which I guess added to its appeal for Strigoi. A lot of the people there were middle- and upper-class young people, apparently drawn in by the "dangerous" aspect. If only they'd known just how dangerous it was. I'd made a lot of jokes to Dimitri about Russia and Eastern Europe being ten years behind in music, but when we entered, I discovered the ground-thumping techno song playing was something I'd heard in the U.S. just before leaving.

The place was crowded and dark, with flashing lights that were actually a little an-noying to dhampir eyes. Our night vision would adapt to the darkness and then be blasted when a strobe light kicked on. In this case, I didn't need my sight. My shadow-kissed senses didn't feel any Strigoi in the area.

"Come on," I said to the others. "Let's

dance for a while and wait. There are no Strigoi nearby."

"How do you know?" asked Denis, staring at me in wonder.

"I just do. Stay together."

Our little circle moved to the dance floor. It had been so long since I'd danced, and I was a bit surprised at how quickly I found myself getting into the rhythm. Part of me said I should have stayed ever vigilant, but my Strigoi alarm system would immediately snap me awake if any danger came. That nausea was kind of hard to ignore.

But after an hour of dancing, no Strigoi had appeared. We left the dance floor and started circling the club's edges, then moved outside to sweep that area too. Nothing.

"Is there another club nearby?" I asked.

"Sure," said Artur. He was stocky, with close-shaved hair and a ready smile. "A couple blocks over."

We followed him and found a similar scene: another secret club hidden in a run-down building. More flashing lights. More crowds. More pounding music. Disturbingly, what started to bother me first was the smell. That many people generated a lot of sweat. I had no doubt even the humans could smell it. To us, it was cloying. Tamara and I exchanged looks and wrinkled our noses, needing no words to convey our disgust.

We moved to the dance floor again, and Lev started to leave to get a drink. I punched him in the arm.

He exclaimed something in Russian that I recognized as a swear word. "What was that for?" he asked.

"For being stupid! How do you expect to kill something that's twice as fast as you while *drunk?*"

He shrugged, unconcerned, and I resisted the urge to hit him in the face this time. "One won't hurt. Besides, there aren't even any —"

"Be quiet!"

It was creeping over me, that weird stirring in my stomach. Forgetting my cover, I stopped dancing, scanning the crowd for the source. While I was relying on my senses to feel Strigoi, spotting them in the crowd was a bit harder. I took a few steps toward the entrance, and my nausea lessened. I moved toward the bar, and the feeling increased.

"This way," I told them. "Act like you're still into the music."

My tension was contagious, and I saw the anticipation sweep them — as well as a little fear. Good. Maybe they'd take this seriously.

As we headed in the bar's direction, I tried to keep my body language oriented toward it, like I was seeking a drink. All the while, my eyes swept the crowd's periphery.

There. I had him. A male Strigoi was standing off in a corner, his arm around a girl close to my age. In the dim lighting, he almost seemed attractive. I knew closer examination would reveal the deathly pale skin and red eyes that all Strigoi had. The girl might not have been able to see them in the darkened club, or the Strigoi might have been using compulsion on her. Probably both, judging from the smile on her face. Strigoi were able to compel others just as well as a spirit user like Lissa could. Better, even. Before our eyes, I saw the Strigoi lead the girl down a small, unnoticed hallway. At the end, I could just make out a glowing exit sign. At least, I presumed it was an exit sign. The letters were Cyrillic.

"Any idea where that door goes?" I asked the others.

The guys shrugged, and Denis repeated my question to Tamara. She answered back, and he translated. "There's a small alley out back where they keep trash. It's between this building and a factory. No one's usually there."

"Can we get to it by going around the club?"

Denis waited for Tamara's response. "Yes. It's open on both sides."

"Perfect."

We hurried out of the club by the front door, and I divided our group into two. The plan was to come at the Strigoi from both sides and trap him in the middle — provided he and his victim were still out back. It was possible he could have led her elsewhere, but I thought it more likely he'd want to subdue her and get his blood right there, particularly if it was as deserted as Tamara said it usually was.

I was right. Once my group had split off and peered around behind the club, I saw the Strigoi and the girl lurking in the shadow of a trash can. He was leaning over her, mouth near her neck, and I silently swore. They didn't waste any time. Hoping she was still alive, I came charging down the alley, the others on my heels. From the alley's other side, Denis and Lev also came running. As soon as he heard the first footfall, the Strigoi reacted instantly, his staggeringly fast reflexes kicking in. He immediately dropped the girl, and in the space of a heartbeat, he chose Denis and Lev over Artur, Tamara, and me. Not a bad strategy, really. There were only two of them. Because he was so fast, he probably hoped to incapacitate them quickly and then turn on us before we could flank him.

And it almost worked. A powerful hit sent Lev flying. To my relief, a couple of trash cans blocked him from the building's wall. Hitting them wouldn't feel good, but if I had the choice, I'd rather hit metal cans than solid bricks. The Strigoi pounced on Denis next, but Denis proved remarkably fast. Unfairly, I'd assumed none of these unpromised had any real fighting skills. I should have known better. They'd had the same training as me; they just lacked discipline.

Denis dodged the blow and struck out low, aiming for the Strigoi's legs. The hit landed, though it wasn't strong enough to knock him over. A flash of silver showed in Denis's hands, and he managed to partially swipe the Strigoi's cheek just before a backhanded slap knocked the dhampir into me. A cut like that wouldn't be lethal to the Strigoi, but the silver would hurt, and I heard him snarl. His fangs gleamed with saliva.

I sidestepped Denis quickly enough that he didn't knock me over. Tamara grabbed his arm, holding him so that he wouldn't fall either. She was fast too and had barely steadied him before leaping up at the Strigoi. He swatted her away but didn't manage to hit her hard enough to push her far. Artur and I were on him by that point, our combined force knocking him against the wall. Still, he was stronger and the pinning was brief before he broke free. A responsible voice in my head — that sounded suspiciously like Dimitri's — warned me that that had been my window to kill him. It would have been the smart and safe thing to do. I'd had the opening, and my stake was in my hand. If my crazy interrogation plan failed, the others' deaths would be on my head.

As one, Artur and I leapt out again. "Help us!" I yelled.

Tamara threw herself against the Strigoi, landing a swift kick to the stomach as well. I could feel him starting to shake us off, but then Denis joined in too. Between the four of us, we wrestled the Strigoi down so that he lay back-first on the pavement. But the worst wasn't over. Keeping him down wasn't easy. He thrashed around with incredible strength, limbs twisting everywhere. I heaved myself up, trying to throw my body's weight across his torso while the others restrained his legs. Another set of hands joined us, and I looked up to see Lev lending his strength too. His lip was bleeding, but his face was determined.

The Strigoi hadn't stopped moving, but I felt satisfied he wouldn't break away anytime soon, not with all five of us holding him. Shifting forward, I placed the point of my stake at his neck. It gave him pause, but he soon resumed his struggle. I leaned over his face.

"Do you know Dimitri Belikov?" I demanded.

He shouted something incomprehensible at me that didn't sound very friendly. I pressed the stake in harder and drew a long gash against his throat. He screamed in pain, pure evil and malice shining out from his eyes as he continued swearing in Russian.

"Translate," I demanded, not caring who did it. "What I said."

A moment later, Denis said something in Russian, presumably my question since I heard Dimitri's name in there. The Strigoi growled back a response, and Denis shook his head. "He says he isn't going to play games with us."

I took the stake and slashed at the Strigoi's face, widening the gash Denis had made earlier. Again, the Strigoi cried out, and I prayed club security wouldn't hear any of this. I gave him a smile filled with enough malice to match his own.

"Tell him we're going to keep playing games with him until he talks. One way or another, he dies tonight. It's up to him whether it happens slowly or quickly."

I honestly couldn't believe those words had come out of my mouth. They were so harsh . . . so, well, cruel. I'd never in my entire life expected to be torturing anyone, even a Strigoi. The Strigoi gave Denis's translation another defiant response, and so I kept on with the stake, making gashes and cuts that would have killed any human, Moroi, or dhampir.

Finally, he shot off a string of words that didn't sound like his usual insults. Denis immediately translated. "He said he's never heard of anyone named that and that if Dimitri's a friend of yours, he'll be sure to kill him slowly and painfully."

I almost smiled at the Strigoi's last effort at defiance. The problem with my strategy here was that the Strigoi could be lying. I'd have no way of knowing. Something in his response made me think he wasn't. He'd sounded like he thought I was referring to a human or a dhampir, not a Strigoi.

"He's useless then," I said. I leaned back

and glanced at Denis. "Go ahead and kill him."

It was what Denis had been dying to do. He didn't hesitate, his stake striking hard and swift through the Strigoi's heart. The frantic struggling stilled a moment later. The evil light faded from the red eyes. We stood up, and I saw my companions' faces watching me with apprehension and fear.

"Rose," asked Denis at last. "What are you hoping to —"

"Never mind that," I interrupted, moving over to the unconscious human girl's side. Kneeling down, I examined her neck. He'd bitten her, but not much blood had been taken. The wound was relatively small and bled only a little. She stirred slightly and moaned when I touched her, which I took as a good sign. Carefully, I dragged her away from the trash can and out into the light where she'd be most noticeable. The Strigoi, however, I dragged into as dark a place as I could, almost completely obscuring him. After that, I asked to borrow Denis's cell phone and dialed the number I'd kept crumpled in my pocket for the last week.

After a couple of rings, Sydney answered in Russian. She sounded sleepy.

"Sydney? This is Rose."

There was a slight pause. "Rose? What's

going on?"

"Are you back in Saint Petersburg?"

"Yes . . . where are you?"

"Novosibirsk. Do you guys have agents here?"

"Of course," she said warily. "Why?"

"Mmm . . . I've got something for you to clean up."

"Oh dear."

"Hey, at least I'm calling. And it's not like me ridding the world of another Strigoi is a bad thing. Besides, didn't you want me to let you know?"

"Yes, yes. Where are you?"

I put Denis on the phone briefly so that he could explain our specific location. He handed the phone back to me when he finished, and I told Sydney about the girl.

"Is she seriously injured?"

"Doesn't look like it," I said. "What should we do?"

"Leave her. The guy who's coming will make sure she's okay and doesn't go telling stories. He'll explain it when he gets there."

"Whoa, hey. I'm not going to be here when he arrives."

"Rose —"

"I'm out of here," I told her. "And I'd really appreciate it if you didn't tell anyone else that I called — say, like, Abe."

"Rose —"

"Please, Sydney. Just don't tell. Or else . . ." I hesitated. "If you do, I'll stop calling when this happens. We're going to be taking down a few more." God, what next? First torture, now threats. Worse, I was threatening someone I liked. Of course, I was lying. I understood why Sydney's group did what they did, and I wouldn't risk the exposure. She didn't know that, though, and I prayed she'd think I was just unstable enough to risk revealing us to the world.

"Rose —" she tried yet again. I didn't give her the chance.

"Thanks, Sydney. We'll be in touch." I disconnected and handed Denis the phone. "Come on, guys. We're not done tonight."

It was clear they thought I was crazy to be interrogating Strigoi, but considering how reckless they were sometimes, my behavior wasn't quite weird enough for them to lose their faith in me. Soon they grew enthusiastic again, high on the idea of our first kill on this trip. My uncanny ability to sense Strigoi made me even cooler in their eyes, and I grew confident they'd pretty much follow me anywhere.

We caught two more Strigoi that night and managed to repeat the procedure. The results were the same. Lots of insults in Russian. No new information. Once I was convinced a Strigoi had nothing to offer us, I'd let the unpromised go in for the kill. They loved it, but after that third one, I found myself growing weary both mentally and physically. I told the group we were going to go home — and then, while cutting around the back of a factory, I sensed a fourth Strigoi.

We jumped him. Another scuffle occurred, but we eventually managed to pin him as we had the others. "Go ahead," I told Denis. "You know what to —"

"I'm going to rip your throat out!" the Strigoi snarled.

Whoa. This one spoke English. Denis opened his mouth to begin the interrogation, but I shook my head. "I'll take over." Like the other Strigoi, he swore and struggled, even with the stake against his neck, making it hard for me to talk.

"Look," I said growing impatient and tired, "just tell us what we need to know. We're looking for a dhampir named Dimitri Belikov."

"I know him." The Strigoi's voice was smug. "And he's no dhampir."

Without realizing it, I'd called Dimitri a dhampir. I was tired and had slipped up.

No wonder this Strigoi was so pleased to talk. He assumed we didn't know about Dimitri turning. And like any arrogant Strigoi, he was happy to tell us more, clearly in the hopes of causing us pain.

"Your friend has been awakened. He stalks the night with us now, drinking the blood of foolish girls like you."

In a split second, a thousand thoughts raced through my head. Holy crap. I'd come to Russia thinking it would be easy to find Dimitri. I'd had those hopes dashed in his hometown, nearly causing me to give up, and I'd swung the other way, resigning myself to the near impossibility of my task. The thought that I might be close to something here was staggering.

"You're lying," I said. "You've never seen him."

"I see him all the time. I've killed with him."

My stomach twisted, and it had nothing to do with the Strigoi's proximity. *Don't think about Dimitri killing people. Don't think about Dimitri killing people.* I said the words over and over in my head, forcing myself to stay calm.

"If that's true," I hissed back, "then I've got a message for you to deliver to him. Tell him Rose Hathaway is looking for him."

"I'm not your errand boy," he said, glowering.

My stake slashed out, drawing blood, and he grimaced in pain. "You're anything I want you to be. Now go tell Dimitri what I told you. Rose Hathaway. Rose Hathaway is looking for him. Say it." I pressed the point to his neck. "Say my name so I know you'll remember."

"I'll remember it so I can kill you."

The stake pressed harder, spilling blood.

"Rose Hathaway," he said. He spit at me but missed.

Satisfied, I leaned back. Denis watched me expectantly, stake poised and ready.

"Now we kill him?"

I shook my head. "Now we let him go."

# SEVENTEEN

Convincing them to release a Strigoi — particularly when we had him trapped — wasn't easy. My questioning hadn't made sense to them either, but they'd gone along with it. Letting a Strigoi go? That was *really* crazy — even for the unpromised. They exchanged uneasy glances with one another, and I wondered if they'd disobey. In the end, my harshness and authority won out. They wanted me as their leader and put their faith in my actions — no matter how insane they seemed.

Of course, once we *did* let the Strigoi go, we had the new problem of making sure he actually went. At first, he started to attack again, and then, realizing he'd probably get overwhelmed, he finally skulked off. He gave us one last menacing look as he disappeared into the darkness. I didn't think being taken down by a group of teenagers had done a lot for his self-esteem. He gave me in particular a look of hatred, and I shuddered at the idea of him knowing my name. There was nothing to be done about it now; I could only hope my plan had a chance of working.

Denis and the others got over me letting the Strigoi go once we made a few other kills that week. We fell into a routine, investigating clubs and dangerous parts of town, relying on my senses to tell us when danger was near. It was funny to me how much the group soon began to rely on my leadership. They claimed they wanted no part of the guardians' rules and authority, but they responded surprisingly well to me telling them what to do.

Well, more or less. Every once in a while, I'd see a bit of that unhinged recklessness. One of them would try to play hero, under-estimate a Strigoi, or go in without the rest of us. Artur nearly ended up with a concussion that way. As the largest of all of us, he'd gotten a bit cocky and was therefore caught off guard when a Strigoi threw him into a wall. It had been a sobering moment for all of us. For a few agonizing moments, I'd feared Artur was dead — and that it was my fault as their leader. One of Sydney's Alchemists had come — though I'd made sure not to be around, lest Abe find me —

and had treated Artur. The guy said Artur would be fine with some bed rest, meaning he had to stop hunting for a while. It was hard for him to do — and I had to yell at him when he tried to follow us one night, reminding him of all their friends who had died before because of such stupidity.

Out in the human world, dhampirs tended to run on human schedules. Now I put myself on a nocturnal schedule, just like I'd been on at the Academy. The others followed suit, except for Tamara, since she had a day job. I didn't want to be asleep during the time Strigoi prowled the streets. I had called Sydney each time we left a kill, and word had to be getting around in the Strigoi community that someone was doing a lot of damage. And if the Strigoi we'd released had carried my message, some of those Strigoi could specifically come looking for me.

As days passed, our kills dropped a little, making me think the Strigoi were indeed being cautious now. I couldn't decide if that was a good or bad thing, but I urged the others to be extra careful. They were beginning to revere me as a goddess, but I took no satisfaction in their adoration. My heart still ached from all that had happened with Lissa and Dimitri. I wrapped myself up in my task, trying only to think of working the Strigoi community to get closer to Dimitri. But when we weren't out hunting Strigoi, I had a lot of downtime with nothing to do.

And so I kept visiting Lissa.

I'd known there were a lot of kids — like Mia — who lived at the Royal Court because their parents had jobs there. I didn't quite realize how many there were, though. Avery naturally knew them all, and to no one's surprise (at least not mine), most of them were spoiled and rich.

The rest of Lissa's visit had been a series of other functions and formal parties. The more she listened to royal Moroi talk business, the more it irritated her. She saw the same abuses of power she'd noted before, the same unfair way of distributing guardians like they were property. The controversial issue of whether Moroi should learn to fight alongside the guardians was also still a hot topic. Most of the people Lissa ran into at Court were of the old-school mentality: Let guardians fight and Moroi stay protected. After seeing the results of that policy — and the successes that had happened when people like Christian and I tried to change it — hearing the selfishness among the Moroi elite enraged Lissa.

She welcomed her escapes from these

events whenever she could, anxious to run wild with Avery. Avery was always able to find people to hang out with and attend parties of a much different nature than Tatiana's. Stifling Court politics never came up at these parties, but there were still plenty of other things to drag Lissa's mood down.

In particular, Lissa felt her guilt, anger, and depression over me spiraling deeper and deeper. She'd seen enough of spirit's effects on her moods to recognize potential warning signs, though she hadn't been actively using spirit while on this trip. Regardless of the moods' cause, she still continued to do her best to seek distraction and drown her depression.

"Watch it," warned Avery one evening. She and Lissa were at a party the night before they had to fly back to the Academy. A lot of those who lived at Court had permanent housing, and this party was at the town house of some Szelsky who served as an aide on a committee Lissa didn't know. Lissa didn't really know their host either, but that didn't matter, save that his parents were out of town.

"Watch what?" asked Lissa, staring around the sights. The town house had a courtyard out back, lit up by tiki torches and strings of twinkling lights. There were drinks and food in full force, and some Moroi guy had a guitar out and was trying to impress girls with his musical skills — which were non-existent. In fact, his music was so awful that he might have discovered a new way to kill Strigoi. He was cute enough, though, that his admirers didn't seem to care what he played.

"This," said Avery, pointing at Lissa's martini. "Are you keeping track of how many of those you're taking down?"

"Not from what I can tell," said Adrian. He was sprawled on a lounge chair nearby, a drink in his own hand.

Lissa felt a bit amateur compared to them. While Avery was still her wild and flirtatious self, she didn't have the crazed or stupid air of someone completely trashed. Lissa didn't know how much the other girl had been drinking, but it was presumably a lot since Avery always had a drink in hand. Likewise, Adrian never seemed to be without a beverage, the effects of which mostly mellowed him out. Lissa supposed they had a lot more experience than her. She'd gone soft over the years.

"I'm fine," lied Lissa, who was watching her surroundings spin a little and seriously contemplating joining some girls dancing on a table across the courtyard.

Avery's lips quirked into a smile, though her eyes showed a bit of worry. "Sure. Just don't get sick or anything. That kind of thing gets around, and the last thing we need is everyone knowing that the Dragomir girl can't hold her liquor. Your family has a fierce reputation to maintain."

Lissa downed the drink. "Somehow, I doubt alcohol consumption is part of my family's illustrious ancestry."

Avery pushed Adrian over and lay down next to him on the lounge chair. "Hey, you'd be surprised. In ten years, this group will be your peers on the council. And you'll be trying to pass some resolution, and they'll be like, 'Remember that time she got trashed and threw up at that party?' "

Lissa and Adrian both laughed at that. Lissa didn't *think* she was going to get sick, but like everything else, she would worry about it later. The bright point of all this was that drinking was helping numb the memories of what had happened earlier in the day. Tatiana had introduced her to her future guardians: a seasoned guy named Grant and the "young lady," who was named Serena. They had been nice enough, but their parallels to Dimitri and me had been overwhelming. Taking them on had seemed like a betrayal to us, yet Lissa had simply nodded and thanked Tatiana.

Later, Lissa had learned that Serena had originally been lined up to be the guardian for a girl she'd known her entire life. The girl wasn't royal, but sometimes, depending on guardian numbers, even non-royals got assigned guardians — though never more than one. When positions for Lissa's protection opened up, however, Tatiana had pulled Serena from the job with her friend. Serena had smiled and told Lissa it didn't matter. Duty came first, she said, and she was happy to serve her. Yet Lissa felt bad, knowing it had to have been hard on both girls — and terribly unfair. But there it was again: an unfair balance of power with no one to really keep it in line.

Leaving that encounter, Lissa had cursed her own meekness. If she hadn't had the courage to follow me, she thought, she should have at least put her foot down and demanded that Tatiana give her my mother instead. Then Serena could have gone back to her friend, and there'd be one friendship still left intact in the world.

The martini simultaneously seemed to numb the pain and make her feel worse, which honestly made no sense to Lissa. *Whatever,* she thought. And when she caught a glimpse of a server passing by, she waved him over to order more.

"Hey, can I — Ambrose?"

She stared in surprise at the guy standing before her. If there'd been a swimsuit calendar for hottest dhampir guys, this one would have been the cover model (aside from Dimitri — but then, I was biased). This guy's name was Ambrose, and she and I had met him on our trip there together. He had deeply tanned skin and well-formed muscles underneath his gray button-down shirt. He was a particular oddity at Court, a dhampir who'd rejected guardian service and performed all sorts of tasks here, like giving massages and — if rumor was true — having "romantic encounters" with the queen. That one still made me cringe, and I'd run into some pretty disgusting things in my life.

"Princess Dragomir," he said, flashing her one of his perfect white grins. "An unexpected surprise."

"How have you been?" she asked, genuinely happy to see him.

"Good, good. I have the best job in the world, after all. And you?"

"Great," she replied.

Ambrose paused, eyeing her. He didn't drop that gorgeous grin, but Lissa could tell he didn't agree with her. She could see the disapproval in his face. Avery accusing her of drinking too much was one thing. But some pretty dhampir servant? Unacceptable. Lissa's demeanor grew cold, and she held out her glass.

"I need another martini," she said, her voice as haughty as that of any perfect royal.

He sensed the change in her, and his friendly smile turned to one of polite indifference. "Right away." He gave her a small bow and headed off to the bar.

"Jeez," said Avery, watching admiringly as he walked away. "Why didn't you introduce us to your friend?"

"He's not my friend," snapped Lissa. "He's nobody."

"Agreed," said Adrian, putting an arm around Avery. "Why look elsewhere when you've got the best right here?" If I hadn't known any better, I'd have sworn there was a hint of legitimate jealousy underneath his jovial tone. "Didn't I go out of my way to bring you to breakfast with my aunt?"

Avery gave him a lazy smile. "That's a good start. You've still got a ways to go to impress me, Ivashkov." Her gaze drifted over Lissa's head and turned surprised. "Hey, Jailbait's here."

Mia, with Jill in tow, came striding through the garden, indifferent to the shocked looks she received. The two of them were clearly out of place.

"Hey," said Mia when she reached Lissa's group. "My dad just got called away, and I have to go with him. I've got to give Jill back."

"No problem," said Lissa automatically, though she clearly wasn't happy about Jill being there. Lissa still kept wondering if Christian had some special interest in her. "Everything okay?"

"Yeah, just business."

Mia made her farewells to everyone and left the party as quickly as she'd come, rolling her eyes at the other royals' sneers and shock as she passed.

Lissa turned her attention to Jill, who had sat gingerly in a nearby chair and was staring around her in wonder. "How's it been? Did you have fun with Mia?"

Jill turned back to Lissa, face brightening. "Oh yeah. She's really great. She's done so much work with water. It's crazy! And she taught me a few fighting moves, too. I can throw a right hook . . . although not very hard."

Ambrose returned then with Lissa's drink. He gave it to her wordlessly and softened a bit when he saw Jill. "You want anything?"

She shook her head. "No, thanks."

Adrian was watching Jill carefully. "You okay here? Do you want me to take you back to guest housing?" Like before, his intentions weren't romantic in the least. He seemed to regard her as a little sister, which I thought was cute. I hadn't thought him capable of that kind of protective behavior.

She shook her head again. "It's okay. I don't want you to have to leave . . . unless . . ." Her expression grew worried. "Do you want me to go?"

"Nah," said Adrian. "It's nice to have someone responsible around in the midst of all this madness. You should get yourself some food, if you're hungry."

"You're so motherly," teased Avery, echoing my thoughts.

For whatever reason, Lissa took Adrian's "responsible" comment personally, like he was directly slamming her. I didn't think that was the case at all, but she wasn't really thinking all that clearly. Deciding she wanted some food herself, she got up and wandered over to the table in the court-yard's garden that had trays of appetizers on it. Well, it had earlier. Now the table was being used by the dancing girls Lissa had noticed before. Someone had cleared space by moving all the trays of food to the ground. Lissa leaned over and picked up a mini sandwich, watching the girls and wondering how they could find any sort of beat in that royal guy's horrible music.

One of the girls spotted Lissa and grinned. She extended a hand. "Hey, come on up."

Lissa had met her once but couldn't recall her name. Dancing suddenly seemed like a great idea. Lissa finished the sandwich and, drink in hand, allowed herself to be pulled up. This got a few cheers from people gathered around. Lissa discovered that the crappy music was irrelevant and found herself getting into it. Her and the other girls' moves varied from overtly sexual to mockeries of disco. It was all fun, and Lissa wondered if Avery would claim this would haunt her in ten years too.

After a while, she and the others actually attempted some synchronized moves. They started by swaying their arms in the air and then moved on to some chorus line kicks. Those kicks proved disastrous. A misstep — Lissa was wearing heels — suddenly sent her over the table's edge. She lost the drink and nearly collapsed before a pair of arms caught her and kept her upright. "My hero," she muttered. Then she got a good look at her savior's face. "Aaron?"

Lissa's ex-boyfriend — and the first guy she'd ever slept with — looked down at her with a smile and released her once he seemed certain she could stand. Blond-haired and blue-eyed, Aaron was handsome in a surfer kind of way. I couldn't help but wonder what would have happened if Mia had seen him. She, Aaron, and Lissa had once been involved in a triangle worthy of any soap opera.

"What are you doing here? We thought you disappeared," Lissa said. Aaron had left the Academy a few months ago.

"I'm going to school out in New Hampshire," he replied. "We're here visiting family."

"Well, it's great to see you," said Lissa. Things hadn't ended well between them, but in her current state, she meant her words. She'd had enough booze to think it was great to see everyone at the party.

"You too," he said. "You look amazing."

His words struck her more than she would have expected, probably because everyone else here had implied that she looked trashed and irresponsible. And breakup or no, she couldn't help but recall how attractive she'd once found him. Honestly, she still found him attractive. She just didn't love him anymore.

"You should stay in touch," she said. "Let us know what's going on." For a moment, she wondered if she should have said that, in light of having a boyfriend. Then she dismissed her worries. There was nothing wrong with hanging out with other guys — particularly since Christian hadn't cared enough to come with her on this trip.

"I'd like that," Aaron said. There was something in his eyes she found pleasurably disconcerting. "I don't suppose, though, that I could get a goodbye kiss, seeing as I rescued you and all?"

The idea was preposterous — then, after a moment, Lissa laughed. What did it matter? Christian was the one she loved, and a kiss between friends would mean nothing. Looking up, she let Aaron lean down and cup her face. Their lips met, and there was no denying it: The kiss lasted a *bit* longer than a friendly one. When it ended, Lissa found herself smiling like a dazed schoolgirl — which, technically, she was.

"See you around," she said, heading back toward her friends.

Avery wore a chastising look, but it wasn't over Aaron and the kiss. "Are you crazy? You nearly broke your leg. You can't do that kind of thing."

"You're supposed to be the fun one," pointed out Lissa. "It wasn't a big deal."

"Fun isn't the same as stupid," Avery

retorted, face serious. "You can't go do stupid shit like that. I think we should get you home."

"I'm fine," said Lissa. She stubbornly looked away from Avery and instead focused on some guys who were doing shots of tequila. They were having some sort of competition — and half of them looked ready to pass out.

"Define 'fine,' " said Adrian wryly. Yet he looked concerned too.

"I'm fine," Lissa repeated. Her gaze snapped back to Avery. "I didn't get hurt at all." She'd expected grief about Aaron and was surprised they hadn't given it to her — which made it even more surprising when it came from another source.

"You kissed that guy!" exclaimed Jill, leaning forward. Her face was aghast, and she displayed none of her usual reticence.

"It was nothing," said Lissa, who was irked to have Jill reprimanding her of all people. "Certainly none of *your* business."

"But you're with Christian! How could you do that to him?"

"Relax, Jailbait," said Avery. "A drunken kiss is nothing compared to a drunken fall. God knows I've kissed plenty of guys drunk."

"And yet, I remain unkissed tonight,"

mused Adrian, with a shake of his head.

"It doesn't matter." Jill was really worked up. She'd grown to like and respect Christian. "You cheated on him."

With those words, Jill might as well have practiced her right hook on Lissa. "I did not!" Lissa exclaimed. "Don't drag your crush on him into this and imagine things that aren't there."

"I didn't imagine that kiss," said Jill, flushing.

"That kiss is the least of our worries," sighed Avery. "I'm serious — just let it go for now, you guys. We'll talk in the morning."

"But —" began Jill.

"You heard her. Let it go," a new voice growled. Reed Lazar had appeared out of nowhere and was looming over Jill, face as hard and scary as ever.

Jill's eyes went wide. "I'm just telling the truth. . . ." I had to admire her courage here, considering her normally timid nature.

"You're pissing everyone off," said Reed, leaning closer and clenching his fists. "And you're pissing me off." I was pretty sure this was the most I'd ever heard him say. I tended to kind of think of him as a caveman, stringing three-word sentences together.

"Whoa." Adrian leapt up and rushed to Jill's side. "*You* need to let this go. What, are you going to start a fight with some girl?"

Reed turned his glare on Adrian. "Stay out of this."

"The hell I will! You're crazy."

If anyone had asked me to make up a list of people most likely to risk a fight in defense of a lady's honor, Adrian Ivashkov would have been low on that list. Yet there he stood, face hard and hand sitting protectively on Jill's shoulder. I was in awe. And impressed.

"Reed," cried Avery. She too had risen and now stood on Jill's other side. "She didn't mean anything. Back off."

The two siblings stood there, eyes locked in some kind of silent showdown. Avery wore the harshest look I'd ever seen on her, and at last, he glowered and stepped back. "Fine. Whatever."

The group stared in amazement as he walked abruptly away. The music was so loud that only a few of the partygoers had overhead the argument. They stopped and stared, and Avery looked embarrassed as she sank back in her chair. Adrian still stood by Jill. "What the hell was that?" Adrian demanded.

"I don't know," Avery admitted. "He gets

weird and overprotective sometimes." She gave Jill an apologetic smile. "I'm really sorry."

Adrian shook his head. "I think it's time for us to go."

Even in her drunken state, Lissa had to agree. The confrontation with Reed had shocked her into soberness, and she was suddenly uneasily evaluating her actions tonight. The glittering lights and fancy cocktails of the party had lost their charm. The drunken antics of the other royals seemed clumsy and stupid. She had a feeling she might regret this party tomorrow.

Once back in my own head, I felt fear set in. Okay. Something was very wrong with Lissa, and no one else seemed to notice it — well, not to the extent they should have. Adrian and Avery did seem concerned, but I had the feeling they were blaming her behavior on the drinking. Lissa was still reminding me a lot of how she'd been when we'd first returned to St. Vladimir's, when spirit had been seizing her and messing with her mind. Except . . . I knew enough about myself now to realize that my anger and fixation on punishing Strigoi was being influenced by spirit's dark side too. That meant *I* was draining it away from her. It

should have been leaving Lissa, not building up. So what was wrong with her? Where
was this short-tempered, crazy, and jealous
persona coming from? Was spirit's darkness
simply growing in intensity so that it spread
to both of us? Were we splitting it?

"Rose?"

"Huh?" I glanced up from where I'd been
staring blankly at the TV. Denis was looking
down at me, his cell phone in his hand.

"Tamara had to work late. She's ready to
go now, but . . ."

He nodded toward the window. The sun
was almost down, the sky purple, with only
a little orange on the horizon. Tamara
worked within walking distance, and while
there probably wasn't any real danger, I
didn't want her out alone after sunset. I
stood up. "Come on, we'll go get her." To
Lev and Artur I said, "You guys can stay
here."

Denis and I walked the half-mile to the
small office where Tamara worked. She did
assorted clerical tasks, like filing and copying, and there'd apparently been some
project that kept her there late tonight. We
met her at the door and walked back to the
apartment without incident, talking animat-
edly about our hunting plans for the
evening. When we reached Tamara's build-

ing, I heard a strange wailing across the street. We all turned, and Denis chuckled.

"Good God, it's that crazy woman again," I muttered.

Tamara didn't live in a bad part of town but, as in any city, there were homeless people and panhandlers. The woman we watched was almost as ancient as Yeva, and she regularly walked up and down the street, muttering to herself. Today, she lay on her back on the sidewalk, making strange noises while waving her limbs like a turtle.

"Is she hurt?" I asked.

"Nope. Just crazy," said Denis. He and Tamara turned to go inside, but some soft part of me couldn't abandon her. I sighed.

"I'll be right in."

The street was quiet (aside from the old lady) and I cut across without fear of traffic. Reaching the woman, I held out my hand to help her out, trying not to think about how dirty hers was. Like Denis had said, she merely appeared to be in crazy mode today. She wasn't hurt; she'd apparently just decided to lie down. I shuddered. I tossed the word *crazy* around a lot when it came to Lissa and me, but *this* was truly crazy. I really, really hoped spirit never took us this far. The homeless lady looked surprised at the help but took my hand and began talking excitedly in Russian. When she tried to hug me in gratitude, I stepped back and held up my hands in the international "back off" signal.

She did indeed back off but continued chatting happily. She grabbed the sides of her long coat and held them out like a ballroom skirt and began spinning around and singing. I laughed, surprised that in my grim world, this would cheer me up. I started to cross back over to Tamara's place. The old woman stopped dancing and began talking happily to me again.

"Sorry, I have to go," I told her. It didn't seem to register.

Then she froze mid-sentence. Her expression gave me warning only half a millisecond before my nausea did. In one fluid motion, I spun around to face what was behind me, pulling my stake out as I moved. There was a Strigoi there, tall and imposing, having sneaked up while I was distracted. Stupid, stupid. I'd refused to let Tamara walk home alone, but I'd never even considered danger right outside my —

"No . . ."

I wasn't sure if I said the word or thought it. It didn't matter. The only thing that mattered just then was what my eyes saw before me. Or, rather, what my eyes *thought* they saw. Because surely, surely, I had to be imagining this. It couldn't be real. Not after all this time.

Dimitri.

I knew him instantly, even though he'd . . . changed. I think in a crowd of a million people, I would have recognized him. The connection between us would allow nothing else. And after being deprived of him for so long, I drank in every feature. The dark, chin-length hair, worn loose tonight and curling slightly around his face. The familiar set of lips, quirked now in an amused yet chilling smile. He even wore the duster he always wore, the long leather coat that could have come straight out of a cowboy movie.

And then . . . there were the Strigoi features. His dark eyes — the eyes I loved — ringed in red. The pale, pale, death-white skin. In life, his complexion had been as tanned as mine, thanks to so much time outdoors. If he opened his mouth, I knew I'd see fangs.

My whole assessment took place in the blink of an eye. I'd reacted fast when I'd felt him — faster than he'd probably expected. I still had the element of surprise, my stake poised and ready. It was perfectly lined up with his heart. I could tell, then and there, that I could make the hit faster than he could defend. But . . .

The eyes. Oh God, the eyes.

Even with that sickening red ring around his pupils, his eyes still reminded me of the Dimitri I'd known. The look in his eyes — the soulless, malicious gleam — that was nothing like him. But there was just enough resemblance to stir my heart, to overwhelm my senses and feelings. My stake was ready. All I had to do was keep swinging to make the kill. I had momentum on my side. . . .

But I couldn't. I just needed a few more seconds, a few more seconds to drink him in before I killed him. And that's when he spoke.

"Roza." His voice had that same wonderful lowness, the same accent . . . it was all just colder. "You forgot my first lesson: Don't hesitate."

I just barely saw his fist striking out toward my head . . . and then I saw nothing at all.

# Eighteen

Unsurprisingly, I woke up with a headache.

For a few addled seconds, I had no idea what had happened or where I was. As drowsiness wore off, the events on the street came slamming back to me. I sat upright, all of my defenses kicking into action, despite the slight wooziness in my head. Time to figure out where I was now.

I sat up on an enormous bed in a darkened room. No — not just a room. More like a suite or a studio. I'd thought the hotel in Saint Petersburg was opulent, but this blew it away. The half of the studio I sat in contained the bed and usual bedroom accessories: a dresser, nightstands, etc. The other half looked like a living room area, with a couch and a television. Shelves were built into the walls, all of them filled with books. Off to my right was a short hall with a door at the end. Probably a bathroom. On my other side was a large picture window, tinted, as Moroi windows often were. This one had more tint than any I'd ever seen. It was almost solid black, nearly impossible to see through. Only the fact that I could differentiate the sky from the horizon — after a fair amount of squinting — let me know it was daytime out there.

I slid off the bed, my senses on high alert as I tried to assess my danger. My stomach felt fine; there were no Strigoi in the area. That didn't necessarily rule out some other person, however. I couldn't take anything for granted — doing so was what had gotten me in trouble on the street. There was no time to ponder that, though. Not quite yet. If I did, my resolve here was going to falter.

Sliding off the bed, I reached into my coat pocket for the stake. Gone, of course. I saw nothing else nearby that would pass as a weapon, meaning I'd have to rely on my own body to do my fighting. Out of the corner of my eye, I caught sight of a light switch on the wall. I flipped it on and froze, waiting to see what — or who — the overhead lights would unveil.

Nothing unusual. No one else. Immediately, I did the first obvious thing and checked the door. It was locked, as I'd expected, and the only way of opening it was a numeric keypad. Plus, it was heavy and made of what looked like steel. It reminded me of a fire door. There was no getting past it, so I turned back around to continue my exploration. It was actually kind of ironic. A lot of my classes had gone over detailed ways of checking out a place. I'd always hated those; I'd wanted to learn about fighting. Now it appeared those lessons that had seemed useless at the time had real purpose.

The light had brought the suite's objects into sharper relief. The bed was covered in an ivory satin duvet, filled to maximum fluffiness with down. Creeping over to the living room, I saw that the TV was nice — really nice. Large-screen plasma. It looked brand-new. The couches were nice too, covered in matte green leather. It was an unusual color choice for leather, but it worked. All of the furniture in the place — tables, desk, dresser — was made of a smooth, polished black wood. In a corner of the living room, I saw a small refrigerator. Kneeling down, I opened it up to find bottled water and juice, assorted fruits, and bags of perfectly cut cheeses. On top of the refrigerator was more snack-type food: nuts, crackers, and some type of glazed pastry. My stomach growled at the sight of it, but no way was I going to eat anything in this place.

The bathroom was done in the same style as the rest of the studio. The shower and large Jacuzzi tub were made of black polished marble, and little soaps and shampoos lined the counter. A larger mirror hung over the sink, except . . . it wasn't actually hanging. It was embedded so tightly into the wall that there was absolutely no way it could be removed. The material was strange too. It looked more like reflective metal than glass.

At first I thought that was strange, until I raced back out to the main room and looked around. There was absolutely *nothing* here that could be turned into a weapon. The TV was too big to move or break, short of cracking the screen, which looked like it was made of some high-tech plastic. There was no glass in any of the tables. The shelves were embedded. The bottles in the refrigerator were all plastic. And the window . . .

I ran over to it, feeling along its edges. Like the mirror, it was fitted perfectly into the wall. There were no panes. It was one smooth piece. Squinting again, I finally got a detailed view of my outer surroundings and saw . . . nothing. The land appeared to be rolling plains, with only a few scattered trees. It reminded me of the wilderness I'd traveled while going to Baia. I was no longer in Novosibirsk, apparently. And peering down, I saw that I was fairly high up. Fourth floor, maybe. Whatever it was, it was too high to jump without breaking a limb. Still, I had to take some sort of action. I couldn't just sit here.

I picked up the desk's chair and slammed it into the window — and achieved little effect on either the chair or the glass. "Jesus Christ," I muttered. I tried three more times and still had no luck. It was like they were both made of steel. Maybe the glass was some kind of bulletproof industrial-strength stuff. And the chair . . . well, hell if I knew. It was all one piece of wood and showed no signs of splintering, even after what I'd just put it through. But since I'd spent my whole life doing things that weren't that reasonable, I kept trying to break the glass.

I was on my fifth try when my stomach warned me of a Strigoi's approach. Spinning around, I kept a hold of the chair and charged the door. It opened, and I slammed into the intruder, with the chair's legs pointing out.

It was Dimitri.

Those same conflicted feelings I'd felt on the street returned to me, love mingled with terror. This time, I pushed through the love, not flinching in my attack. Not that it did much good. Hitting him was like hitting the window. He shoved me back, and I staggered, still holding onto the chair. I kept my balance and charged once more. This time, when we collided, he grabbed a hold of the chair and ripped it from my hands. He then tossed it into the wall, like it weighed nothing.

Without that meager weapon, it was back to relying on my own body's strength. I'd been doing it for the last couple of weeks with our Strigoi questioning; this should have been the same. Of course, I'd had four other people then as backup. And none of those Strigoi had been Dimitri. Even as a dhampir, he'd been hard to beat. Now he was just as skilled — only faster and stronger. He also knew all my moves, seeing as he'd taught them to me. It was almost impossible to surprise him.

But just like with the window, I couldn't stay inactive. I was trapped in a room — the fact that it was a big, luxurious room didn't matter — with a Strigoi. A Strigoi. That's what I had to keep telling myself. There was a Strigoi in here. Not Dimitri. Everything I'd told Denis and the others applied here. *Be smart. Be vigilant. Defend yourself.*

"Rose," he said, deflecting one of my kicks effortlessly. "You're wasting time. Stop."

Oh, that voice. Dimitri's voice. The voice I heard when I fell asleep at night, the voice that had once told me he loved me . . .

*No! It's not him. Dimitri is gone. This is a monster.*

Desperately, I tried to think of how I could win here. I even thought of the ghosts I'd summoned on the road. Mark had said I could do that in moments of wild emotion and that they'd fight for me. This was as wild as emotion could get, yet I couldn't seem to call them. I honestly had no clue how I'd done it before, and all the wishing in the world couldn't make it happen now. Damn. What good were terrifying powers if I couldn't use them to my advantage?

Instead, I pulled the DVD player off its shelf, cords ripping from the wall. It wasn't much of a weapon, but I was desperate now. I heard a strange, primal battle scream, and some distant part of me realized I was making it. Again, I ran at Dimitri, swinging the DVD player as hard as I could. It probably would have hurt a little — *if* it had hit him. It didn't. He intercepted it again, taking it from me, and throwing it down. It smashed to pieces on the floor. In the same motion, he grabbed a hold of my arms to stop me

362

from hitting or reaching for something else. His grip was hard, like it could break my bones, but I kept struggling.

He tried reason again. "I'm not going to hurt you. Roza, please stop."

*Roza.* The old nickname. The name he'd first called me when we'd fallen prey to Victor's lust charm, both of us wrapped naked in each other's arms . . .

*This isn't the Dimitri you knew.*

My hands were incapacitated, so I struck out with my legs and feet as best I could. It didn't do much. Without full use of the rest of my body for balance, I had no force to throw into my kicks. For his part, he looked more annoyed than truly concerned or angry. With a loud sigh, he grabbed me by the shoulders and flipped me around, pressing me against the wall and immobilizing me with the full force of his body. I struggled a little but was as pinned as the Strigoi had been when the others and I had gone hunting. The universe had a sick sense of humor.

"Stop fighting me." His breath was warm against my neck, his body right up against mine. I knew his mouth was only a couple inches away. "I'm not going to hurt you."

I gave another fruitless shove. My breath was coming in ragged gasps, and my head injury throbbed. "You'll have to understand if I have a hard time believing that."

"If I wanted you dead, you'd be dead. Now, if you're going to keep fighting, I'll have to tie you up. If you stop, I'll let you stay unrestrained."

"Aren't you afraid I'll escape?"

"No." His voice was perfectly calm, and chills ran down my spine. "I am not."

We stood like that for almost a minute, deadlocked. My mind raced. It was true that he probably would have killed me already if that were his intent, yet that gave me no reason to believe I was even remotely safe. Nonetheless, we were at a draw in this fight. Okay, *draw* wasn't entirely accurate. *I* was at a draw. He was toying with me. My head was throbbing where his blow had landed, and this pointless fighting would only take a further toll. I had to regain my strength in order to find a way to escape — if I lived that long. I also needed to stop thinking about how close our bodies were. After our months of being so careful not to touch, this much contact was heady.

I relaxed in his hold. "Okay."

He hesitated before letting me go, probably wondering if he could trust me. The whole moment reminded me of when we'd been together in the little cabin on the periphery of the Academy's grounds. I'd been raging and upset, brimming with spirit's darkness. Dimitri had held me down then, too, and talked me out of that horrible state. We had kissed, then his hands had lifted my shirt, and — no, no. Not here. I couldn't think about that here.

Dimitri finally eased up, releasing me from the wall. I turned around, and all my instincts wanted to lash out and attack him again. Sternly, I reminded myself to bide my time so that I could gain more strength and information. Even though he'd let me go, he hadn't moved away. We were only a foot apart. Against my better judgment, I found myself taking him in again, like I had on the street. How could he be the same and yet so different? I tried my best not to focus on the similarities — his hair, the difference in our heights, the shape of his face. Instead, I concentrated on the Strigoi features, the red in his eyes and pallor of his skin.

I was so fixated on my task that it took me a moment to realize he wasn't saying anything either. He was studying me intently, like his eyes could look right through me. I shivered. It almost — *almost!* — seemed as though I captivated him the same way he captivated me. That was impossible, though. Strigoi didn't possess those kinds of emotions, and besides, the thought of him still having any affection for me was probably just wishful thinking on my part. His face had always been hard to read, and now it was overlaid with a mask of cunning and coldness that made it truly impossible to know what was on his mind.

"Why did you come here?" he asked at last.

"Because you hit me on the head and dragged me here." If I was going to die, I was going to go in true Rose style.

The old Dimitri would have cracked a smile or given an exasperated sigh. This one remained impassive. "That's not what I meant, and you know it. Why are you *here*?" His voice was low and dangerous. I'd thought Abe was scary, but there was no competition at all. Even Zmey would have backed off.

"In Siberia? I came to find you."

"I came here to get away from you."

I was so shocked that I said something utterly ridiculous.

"Why? Because I might kill you?"

The look he gave me showed that he thought that was indeed a ridiculous thing to say. "No. So we wouldn't be in *this* situation. Now we are, and the choice is inevitable."

I wasn't entirely sure what *this* situation was. "Well, you can let me go if you want to avoid it."

He stepped away and walked toward the living room without looking back at me. I was tempted to try to do a sneak attack on him, but something told me I'd probably only make it about four feet before getting backhanded. He sat down in one of the luxurious leather armchairs, folding his six-foot-seven frame up as gracefully as he'd always done. God, why did he have to be so contradictory? He had the old Dimitri's habits mixed with those of a monster. I stayed where I was, huddled against the wall.

"Not possible anymore. Not after seeing you now . . ." Again, he studied me. It felt strange. Part of me responded with excitement to the intensity of his gaze, loving the way he surveyed my body from head to toe. The other part of me felt dirty, like slime or muck was oozing over my skin as he studied me. "You're still as beautiful as I remember, Roza. Not that I should have expected anything different."

I didn't know what to say to that. I'd never really had a conversation with a Strigoi, short of trading a few insults and threats in the midst of a fight. The nearest I'd come was when I'd been held captive by Isaiah. I actually had been tied up then, and most of the talking had been about him killing me. This . . . well, it wasn't like that, but it was still definitely creepy. I crossed my arms over my chest and backed up against the wall. It was the closest I could come to some semblance of a defense.

He tilted his head, watching me carefully. A shadow fell across his face in such a way that it made the red in his eyes hard to see. Instead, they looked dark. Just like they used to, endless and wonderful, filled with love and bravery . . .

"You can sit down," he said.

"I'm fine over here."

"Is there anything else you want?"

"For you to let me go?"

For a moment, I thought I saw a bit of that old wryness in his face, the kind he'd get when I made jokes. Studying him, I decided I'd imagined it.

"No, Roza. I meant, do you need anything here? Different food? Books? Entertainment?"

I stared incredulously. "You make it sound like some sort of luxury hotel!"

"It is, to a certain extent. I can speak to Galina, and she'll get you anything you wish."

"Galina?"

Dimitri's lips turned up in a smile. Well, kind of. I think his thoughts were fond, but the smile conveyed none of that. It was chilling, dark, and full of secrets. Only my refusal to show weakness before him stopped me from cringing.

"Galina is my old instructor, back from when I was in school."

"She's Strigoi?"

"Yes. She was awakened several years ago, in a fight in Prague. She's relatively young for a Strigoi, but she's risen in power. All of this is hers." Dimitri gestured around us.

"And you live with her?" I asked, curious in spite of myself. I wondered exactly what kind of relationship they had, and to my surprise, I felt . . . jealous. Not that I had reason to. He was a Strigoi, beyond me now. And it wouldn't be the first time a teacher and student had gotten together. . . .

"I work for her. She was another reason I returned here when I was awakened. I knew she was Strigoi, and I wanted her guidance."

"And you wanted to get away from me. That was the other reason, right?"

His only answer was a nod of his head. No elaboration.

"Where are we? We're far from Novosibirsk, right?"

"Yes. Galina's estate is outside the city."

"How far?"

That smile twisted a little. "I know what you're doing, and I'm not going to give you that sort of information."

"Then what *are* you doing?" I demanded, all of my pent-up fear bursting out as anger. "Why are you holding me here? Kill me or let me go. And if you're going to just lock me up and torture me with mind games or whatever, then I really would rather you kill me."

"Brave words." He stood up and began pacing once more. "I almost believe you."

"They're true," I replied defiantly. "I came here to kill you. And if I can't do that, then I'd rather die."

"You failed, you know. On the street."

"Yeah. I kind of figured that out when I woke up here."

Dimitri made an abrupt turn and was suddenly standing in front of me, moving with that lightning-fast Strigoi speed. My Strigoi-nausea had never gone away, but the more time I spent with him, the more it faded to a low-level sort of background noise that I could more or less ignore.

"I'm a little disappointed. You're so good, Rose. So very, very good. You and your friends going around and taking down

Strigoi caused quite a stir, you know. Some Strigoi were even afraid."

"But not you?"

"When I heard it was you . . . hmm." He turned thoughtful, eyes narrowing. "No. I was curious. Wary. If anyone could have killed me, it would have been you. But like I said, you hesitated. It was your ultimate test of my lessons, and you failed."

I kept my face blank. Inside, I was still beating myself up over that moment of weakness on the street. "I won't hesitate next time."

"There won't be a next time. And anyway, as disappointed as I am in you, I'm still glad to be alive, of course."

"You aren't alive," I said through gritted teeth. God, he was so, so close to me again. Even with the changes to his face, the lean and muscled body was the same. "You're dead. Unnatural. You told me a long time ago you'd rather die than be like this. That's why I'm going to kill you."

"You're only saying that because you don't know any better. I didn't either back then."

"Look, I meant what I said. I'm not playing your game. If I can't get out of here, then just kill me, okay?"

Without warning, he reached out and ran his fingers along the side of my face. I gasped. His hand was ice cold, but the way he touched me . . . again, it was the same. Exactly the same as I remembered. How was this possible? So similar . . . yet so different. All of a sudden, another of his lessons came to mind, about how Strigoi could seem so, so like those you'd once known. It was why it was so easy to hesitate.

"Killing you . . . well, it's not that simple," he said. His voice dropped to a low whisper again, like a snake slithering against my skin. "There's a third option. I could awaken you."

I froze and stopped breathing altogether.

"No." It was the only thing I could say. My brain couldn't come up with anything more complex, nothing witty or clever. His words were too terrifying to even begin to ponder. "No."

"You don't know what it's like. It's . . . amazing. Transcendent. All your senses are alive; the world is more alive —"

"Yeah, but you're *dead.*"

"Am I?"

He caught hold of my hand and placed it over his chest. In it, I could feel a steady beating. My eyes widened.

"My heart beats. I'm breathing."

"Yeah, but . . ." I tried desperately to think of everything I'd ever been taught about

Strigoi. "It's not really being alive. It's . . . it's dark magic reanimating you. It's an illusion of life."

"It's better than life." Both of his hands moved up and cupped my face. His heartbeat might have been steady, but mine was racing. "It's like being a god, Rose. Strength. Speed. Able to perceive the world in ways you could never imagine. And . . . immortality. We could be together forever."

Once, that was all I'd ever wanted. And deep inside of me, some part still wished for that, wished desperately to be with him for all time. Yet . . . it wouldn't be the way I wanted it. It wouldn't be like it used to be. This would be something different. Something wrong. I swallowed.

"No . . ." I could barely hear my own voice, barely even form the words with him touching me like that. His fingertips were so light and gentle. "We can't be."

"We could." One of his fingers trailed down the side of my chin and came to rest on the artery in my neck. "I could do it quickly. There'd be no pain. It'd be done before you even knew it." He was probably right. If you were forced to become Strigoi, you had the blood drained from you. Then a Strigoi would usually cut himself and bring that blood to your lips. Somehow, I imagined I'd pass out before I was even half-drained.

*Together forever.*

The world blurred a little. I don't know if it was because of my head trauma or the terror coursing through my body. I had envisioned a hundred scenarios when I set out after Dimitri. Becoming a Strigoi hadn't been one of them. Death — his or mine — had been the only thought consuming me, which had been stupid on my part.

My sluggish thoughts were interrupted when the door suddenly opened. Dimitri turned, shoving me away hard so that he stood protectively in front of me. Two people entered, shutting the door before I could even consider running for it. One of the newcomers was a Strigoi, a guy. The other was a human woman carrying a tray, her head bowed down.

I recognized the Strigoi immediately. It was hard not to; his face haunted my dreams. Blond hair, about the length of Dimitri's, hung over the side of a face that looked like he'd been in his early twenties when he turned. He had apparently seen Lissa and me when we were younger, but I had only seen him twice before. Once had been when I fought him on the Academy's grounds. The other time was when I'd encountered him in the cave that other Strigoi were using as a hangout.

He was the one who had bitten and turned Dimitri.

The guy barely spared me a glance and instead turned the full force of his anger on Dimitri. "What the hell is going on?" I had no trouble understanding him. He was American. "You're keeping some pet up here?"

"It's none of your concern, Nathan." Dimitri's voice was ice. Earlier, I'd thought he conveyed no emotion in his words. Now I realized it was just more difficult to detect. There was a clear challenge in his voice now, a warning for this other guy to back off. "Galina gave me permission."

Nathan's eyes drifted from Dimitri to me. His anger turned to shock. *"Her?"*

Dimitri shifted slightly, putting himself directly in front of me now. Some rebellious part wanted to snap that I didn't need a Strigoi's protection, except . . . well, I kind of did.

"She was at the school in Montana. . . . We fought. . . ." His lips curled back, showing his fangs. "I would have tasted her blood if that fire-using Moroi brat hadn't been around."

"This doesn't have anything to do with

you," replied Dimitri.

Nathan's red eyes were wide and eager. "Are you kidding? She can lead us to the Dragomir girl! If we finish that line off, our names will be legendary. How long are you going to keep her?"

"Get out," growled Dimitri. "That's not a request."

Nathan pointed at me. "She's valuable. If you're going to keep her around as some blood whore plaything, at least share. Then, we'll get the information and finish her."

Dimitri took a step forward. "Get out of here. If you lay a hand on her, I will destroy you. I will rip your head off with my bare hands and watch it burn in the sun."

Nathan's fury grew. "Galina won't allow you to play house with this girl. Even you don't have that much favor."

"Don't make me tell you to leave again. I'm not in a patient mood today."

Nathan said nothing, and the two Strigoi stood there in a staring match. I knew Strigoi strength and power were partially related to age. Nathan had obviously been turned first. I didn't know by how much, but watching them, I got the feeling that Dimitri might be stronger or that it was at least a very, very even match. I could have sworn I saw a glimpse of fear in Nathan's red eyes, but he turned away before I could get a good look.

"This isn't over," he snapped, moving toward the door. "I'm talking to Galina."

He left, and for a moment, nobody moved or spoke. Then Dimitri looked at the human woman and said something in Russian. She'd been standing there, frozen.

Leaning over, she carefully placed her tray on the coffee table by the couch. She lifted a silver lid up, revealing a plate of pepperoni pizza loaded with cheese. Under any other circumstances, someone bringing me pizza in a Strigoi home would have been ludicrous and funny. Now, in the wake of Dimitri's threat to turn me Strigoi and Nathan's desire to use me to get to Lissa, nothing was funny. Even Rose Hathaway had limits when it came to making jokes. Next to the pizza was a huge brownie, thick with frosting. Food I loved, as Dimitri well knew.

"Lunch," he said. "Not poisoned."

Everything on the tray looked amazing, but I shook my head. "I'm not going to eat."

He arched an eyebrow. "Do you want something else?"

"I don't want anything else because I'm not going to eat anything *at all*. If you aren't going to kill me, then I'll do it myself." It was occurring to me that the suite's lack of weapons was probably for my own protection as much as theirs.

"By starving to death?" There was dark amusement in his eyes. "I'll awaken you long before then."

"Why aren't you just doing it now?"

"Because I'd rather wait for you to be willing." Man, he really did sound like Abe, except that breaking one's kneecaps seemed kind of soft-core in comparison.

"You're going to be waiting a long time," I said.

Dimitri laughed out loud then. His laughter had been rare as a dhampir, and hearing it had always thrilled me. Now it no longer had that rich warmth that had wrapped all around me. It was cold and menacing. "We'll see."

And before I could form a reply, he moved in front of me again. His hand snaked behind my neck, shoving me against him, and he tilted my face up, pressing his lips against mine. They were as cold as the rest of his skin . . . and yet there was something warm in there, too. Some voice in me screamed that this was sick and horrible . . . but at the same time, I lost track of the world around me as we kissed and could almost pretend we were back together in the cabin.

He pulled away as quickly as he'd moved in, leaving me gasping and wide-eyed. Casually, like nothing had happened, he gestured to the woman. "This is Inna." She looked up at the sound of her name, and I saw she was no older than me. "She works for Galina too and will check in on you. If you need anything, let her know. She doesn't speak much English, but she'll figure it out." He said something else to her, and she meekly followed him to the door.

"Where are you going?" I asked.

"I have things to do. Besides, you need time to think."

"There's nothing to think about." I forced as much defiance into my words as I could.

It must not have sounded very fierce, though, because all my speech earned me was one mocking smile before he left with Inna, leaving me alone in my luxurious prison.

# NINETEEN

For someone who had preached to Denis about impulse control, I wasn't setting a very good example. Once left alone in the suite, I continued trying everything possible to get out — emphasis on the "try" part.

Nathan had acted like keeping a prisoner was a rare thing, but from what I could tell, this place had been built to hold people in. The door and window remained impassible, no matter how hard I beat at them or threw objects against them. I didn't bother with the chair this time and instead used one of the living room's end tables, hoping it would carry some extra heft. It didn't. When that didn't work, I actually tried entering random codes into the door's keypad. Also useless.

Finally, exhausted, I collapsed onto the leather sofa and tried to assess my options. The process didn't take very long. I was trapped in a house full of Strigoi. Okay, I didn't know that for sure, but I knew there were at least three here, which was far too many for me. Dimitri had referred to this place as an "estate," which I didn't find comforting. Estates were *big.* The fact that I appeared to be on the fourth floor was proof of that. A big place meant that there could be lots of room for lots of vampires.

The one comfort I had was that Strigoi didn't cooperate very well. Finding large groups of them working together was rare. I'd observed it a couple of times — the attack on the Academy being one such occasion. They'd come then because the school's wards had dropped, and that had been a big enough incentive for the Strigoi to unite. Even when they did try to work together, the unions were usually short-lived. The friction I'd observed between Dimitri and Nathan was proof of that.

Dimitri.

I closed my eyes. Dimitri was the reason I was here. I'd come to free him from this state of living death and had promptly failed, just as he'd said. Now, it appeared I might be on the verge of joining him. *Yeah, good job, Rose.* I shivered, trying to imagine myself as one of them. Red rings around my pupils. Tanned skin gone pale. I couldn't picture it, and I supposed I'd never have to actually see myself if it happened. Strigoi cast no reflections. It would make doing my hair a real pain in the ass.

The scariest change of all would be within, the loss of my connection to my soul. Both Dimitri and Nathan had been cruel and antagonistic. Even if I hadn't been around to start the fight, it probably wouldn't have taken long for them to find some other reason to turn on each other. I was combative, but it was always driven by some passion for others. Strigoi fought because they relished the bloodshed. I didn't want to be like that, seeking blood and violence because I enjoyed it.

I didn't want to believe that of Dimitri either, but his actions had already branded him as a Strigoi. I also knew what he had to have been eating this whole time to survive. Strigoi could go longer without blood than Moroi, but it had been over a month since he was turned. There was no question he had fed, and Strigoi almost always killed their victims to eat. I couldn't picture that of Dimitri . . . not the man I'd known.

I opened my eyes. The topic of feeding had brought my lunch to mind. Pizza and brownies. Two of the most perfect foods on the planet. The pizza had long gone cold during my escape efforts, but as I stared at the plate, both it and the brownie looked delicious. If the outside light was any indication, it hadn't been a full twenty-four hours since Dimitri had caught me, but it was getting pretty close. That was a long time to go without food, and I wanted to eat that pizza badly, cold or not. I didn't really want to starve to death.

Of course, I didn't want to become Strigoi either, but this situation was quickly running away from what I wanted. Starvation took a long time, and I suspected Dimitri was right: he'd turn me long before I had a chance to truly starve. I'd have to find some other way to die — God, not that I wanted that at all — and in the meantime, I decided I might as well keep up my strength on the feeble chance I might be able to escape.

Once the decision was made, I gobbled down the food in about three minutes. I had no idea who Strigoi hired to do their cooking — hell, Strigoi couldn't even eat regular food, unlike Moroi — but it was fantastic. Some wry part of me noted that I'd been given food that required no silverware. They really had thought of every possible way I might get my hands on a weapon. My mouth was full of my last giant bite of brownie when the door suddenly opened. Inna slipped deftly inside, the door shutting almost immediately.

"Son of a bitch!" Or at least I tried to say that through my mouthful of food. While I'd been debating whether to eat or not, I should have been staking out the door. Dimitri had said Inna would check in on me. I should have been waiting to overpower her. Instead, she'd gotten in while I wasn't paying attention. Once again, I'd slipped up.

Just like when she was around Dimitri and Nathan, Inna made very little eye contact. She held a pile of clothes in her arms and paused in front of me, holding them out. Uncertain, I took them from her and set them beside me on the couch.

"Um, thanks," I said.

Pointing at the empty tray, she actually glanced up at me shyly, a question in her brown eyes. Seeing her straight on, I was surprised at how pretty she was. She might even have been younger than me, and I wondered how she'd ended up being forced to work here. Understanding her query, I nodded.

"Thanks."

She picked the tray up and waited a moment. I wasn't sure why; then it occurred to me she must be waiting to see if I wanted anything else. I was pretty sure "the combination to the lock" wouldn't translate very well. I shrugged and waved her off, my mind spinning as I watched her approach the door. *I should wait for her to open the door and then jump her,* I thought. Immediately, a gut reaction sprang up in me, hesitation at striking out at an innocent. Another thought squashed that one: *It's me or her.* I tensed.

Inna pressed herself close to the door as she punched in the combination, effectively blocking my view. Judging by how long she was punching in numbers, the code appeared to be pretty long. The door clicked open, and I braced myself to act. Then — I decided against it at the last moment. For all I knew, there could be an army of Strigoi out there. If I was going to use Inna to escape, I probably only had one opportunity. I needed to make it count. So, instead of leaping up, I shifted slightly so that I could see beyond her. She was just as fast as before, slipping out as soon as the door unlocked. But in that moment, I caught a glimpse of a short corridor and what looked like another heavy door.

Interesting. Double doors on my prison. If I did follow her, that would prevent me from making an immediate escape. She could simply wait by the other locked door, holding out until Strigoi backup showed up. That made things more difficult, but understanding the setup at least gave me a spark of hope. I just needed to figure out what to do with this information, provided I hadn't screwed myself by not acting now. For all I knew, Dimitri was about to walk in and turn me into a Strigoi.

I sighed. Dimitri, Dimitri, Dimitri.

Looking down, I took the time to actually see what she'd brought me. My current attire wasn't bothering me, but if I stayed here much longer, my jeans and T-shirt were going to get pretty gross.

Like Tamara, someone wanted to dress me up.

The clothes Inna had brought were all dresses and all in my size. A red silk sheath. A long-sleeved, form-fitting knit dress edged in satin. An empire-waist, ankle-length chiffon gown.

"Oh, great. I'm a doll."

Digging deeper into the stack, I discovered there were a few nightshirts and nightgowns tucked in there — as well as some underwear and bras. All of those were satin and silk. The most casual item in the whole lot was a forest-green sweaterdress, but even it was made of the softest cashmere. I held it up, trying to imagine myself making a daring escape in it. Nope. With a shake of my head, I heedlessly tossed all of the clothes onto the floor. Looked like I'd be wearing grungy clothes for a while.

I paced around after that, turning over futile escape plans that I'd already spun around in my head a million times. In walking, I realized how tired I was. Aside from the blackout when Dimitri had hit me, I hadn't slept in over a day. Deciding how to handle this was like deciding how to deal with the food. Let down my guard or not? I needed strength, but each concession I made put me more at risk.

At last, I gave in, and as I lay down on the massive bed, an idea suddenly occurred to me. I wasn't totally without help. If Adrian came to visit me in my sleep, I could tell him what had happened. True, I'd told him to stay away last time, but he'd never listened to me before. Why should this time be any different? I focused on him as hard as I could while I waited for sleep to come, as though my thoughts might act as some sort of bat signal and summon him.

It didn't work. There was no visit in my dreams, and when I woke up, I was surprised at just how much that hurt me. Despite Adrian's infatuation with Avery, I couldn't help but recall how kind he'd been to Jill the last time I saw them. He was worried about Lissa, too, and he'd displayed none of his usual carefree bravado. He'd been serious and . . . well, sweet. A lump formed in my throat. Even if I had no romantic interest in him, I'd still treated him badly. I'd lost both our friendship and any chance of calling for help through him.

The soft rustling of paper snapped me from my musings and I jerked upright. Someone was in the living room, his back to me as he sat on the couch, and it took me only a moment to recognize who. Dimitri.

"What are you doing here?" I asked, climbing out of bed. In my groggy state, I hadn't even registered the nausea.

"Waiting for you to wake up," he said, not bothering to turn around. He was overly confident in my inability to inflict damage — as well he should have been.

"Sounds kind of boring."

I walked into the living room, moving myself far to the side of him and leaning against the wall. I crossed my arms over my chest, again taking comfort in that meaningless protective posture.

"Not so boring. I had company."

He glanced over at me and held up a book. A western. I think that shocked me almost as much as his altered appearance. There was something so . . . normal about it all. He'd loved western novels when he was a dhampir, and I'd often teased him about wanting to be a cowboy. Somehow, I'd imagined that hobby would go away when he turned. Irrationally hopeful, I studied his face as though I might see some radical change, like maybe he'd turned back to the way he'd been while I slept. Maybe the last month and a half had been a dream.

Nope. Red eyes and a hard expression looked back at me. My hopes shattered.

"You slept for a long time," he added. I dared a quick look at the window. Totally black. It was nighttime. Damn. I'd only wanted a two-hour power nap. "And you ate."

The amusement in his voice grated at me. "Yeah, well, I'm a sucker for pepperoni. What do you want?"

He placed a bookmark in the book and set it on the table. "To see you."

"Really? I thought your only goal was to make me one of the living dead."

He didn't acknowledge that, which was a bit frustrating. I hated feeling like what I had to say was being ignored. Instead, he tried to get me to sit down.

"Aren't you tired of always standing?"

"I just woke up. Besides, if I can spend an hour tossing furniture around, a little standing isn't that big a deal."

I didn't know why I was throwing out my usual witty quips. Honestly, considering the situation, I should have just ignored him. I should have stayed silent instead of playing into this game. I guess I kind of hoped that if I made the jokes I used to, I'd get some kind of response from the old Dimitri. I repressed a sigh. There I was again, forgetting Dimitri's own lessons. Strigoi were not the people they used to be.

"Sitting's not that big a deal either," he replied. "I told you before, I'm not going to hurt you."

" 'Hurt' is kind of a subjective term." Then, in a sudden decision to seem fearless, I walked over and sat in the armchair across from him. "Happy now?"

He tilted his head, and a few pieces of brown hair escaped from where he'd pulled it back in a small ponytail. "You still stay beautiful, even after sleeping and fighting." His eyes flicked down to the clothes I'd tossed on the floor. "You don't like any of them?"

"I'm not here to play dress-up with you. Designer clothes aren't going to suddenly get me on board with joining the Strigoi club."

He gave me a long, penetrating stare.

"Why don't you trust me?"

I stared back, only my stare was one of disbelief. "How can you ask that? You abducted me. You kill innocent people to survive. You aren't the same."

"I'm better, I told you. And as for innocent . . ." He shrugged. "No one's really innocent. Besides, the world is made up of predators and prey. Those who are strong conquer those who are weak. It's part of the natural order. You used to be into that, if I remember correctly."

I looked away. Back at school, my favorite non-guardian class had been biology. I'd loved reading about animal behavior, about the survival of the fittest. Dimitri had been my alpha male, the strongest of all the other competitors.

"It's different," I said.

"But not in the way you think. Why should drinking blood be so strange to you? You've seen Moroi do it. You've *let* Moroi do it."

I flinched, not really wanting to dwell on how I used to let Lissa drink from me while we lived among humans. I certainly didn't want to think about the rush of endorphins that had come with that and how I'd nearly become an addict.

"They don't kill."

"They're missing out. It's incredible," he

breathed. He closed his eyes for a moment, then opened them. "To drink the blood of another . . . to watch the life fade from them and feel it pour into you . . . it's the greatest experience in the world."

Listening to him talk about killing others increased my nausea. "It's sick and wrong."

It happened so fast that I didn't have any time to react. Dimitri leapt out and grabbed me, pulling me to him and spreading me out on the couch. With his arm still wrapped around me, he positioned himself so that he was half beside me and half on top. I was too stunned to move.

"No, it's not. And that's where you have to trust me. You'd love it. I want to be with you, Rose. *Really* be with you. We're free of the rules that others put on us. We can be together now — the strongest of the strong, taking everything we want. We can eventually be as strong as Galina. We could have a place just like this, all our own."

While his bare skin was still cold, the press of the rest of his body against mine was warm. The red in his eyes practically gleamed while this close, and as he spoke, I saw the fangs in his mouth. I was used to seeing fangs on Moroi, but on him . . . it was sickening. I briefly toyed with the idea of trying to break free but promptly dismissed it. If Dimitri wanted to hold me down, I would stay down.

"I don't want any of this," I said.

"Don't you want me?" he asked with a wicked smile. "You wanted me once."

"No," I said, knowing I lied.

"What do you want then? To go back to the Academy? To serve Moroi who will throw you into danger without a second thought? If you wanted that kind of life, why did you come here?"

"I came to free you."

"I *am* free," he responded. "And if you'd really intended to kill me, you would have." He shifted slightly, resting his face close to my neck. "You couldn't."

"I messed up. It won't happen again."

"Suppose that were true. Suppose you were able to kill me now. Suppose you were even able to escape. What then? Will you go back home? Will you return to Lissa and let her continue bleeding spirit's darkness into you?"

"I don't know," I replied stiffly. And it was the truth. My plans had never gone past finding him.

"It will consume you, you know. As long as she continues to use her magic, no matter how far away you go, you'll always feel the side effects. At least as long as she's alive."

I stiffened in his arms and moved my face away. "What's that mean? Are you going to join Nathan and hunt her down?"

"What happens to her is no concern of mine," he said. "You are. If you were awakened, Lissa would no longer be a threat to you. You'd be free. The bond would break."

"And what would happen to her? She'd be left alone."

"Like I said, that's no concern of mine. Being with you is."

"Yeah? Well, I don't want to be with you."

He turned my face toward him so that we were looking at each other again. Once more, I had that weird feeling of being with Dimitri and not with Dimitri. Love and fear.

He narrowed his eyes. "I don't believe you."

"Believe what you want. I don't want you anymore."

His lips quirked into one of those scary, smirking smiles. "You're lying. I can tell. I've always been able to."

"It's the truth. I wanted you before. I don't want you now." If I kept saying it, it would be true.

He moved closer to me, and I froze. If I shifted even half an inch, our lips would touch. "My exterior . . . my power, yes, that's different. Better. But otherwise, I'm the same, Roza. My essence hasn't changed. The connection between us hasn't changed. You just can't see it yet."

"Everything's changed." With his lips so close, all I kept thinking about was that brief, passionate kiss he'd given me the last time he was here. No, no, no. *Don't think about that.*

"If I'm so different, then why don't I force you into an awakening? Why am I giving you the choice?"

A snappy retort was on my lips, but then it died. That was an excellent question. Why *was* he giving me the choice? Strigoi didn't give their victims choices. They killed mercilessly and took what they wanted. If Dimitri truly wanted me to join him, then he should have turned me as soon as he had me. More than a day had passed, and he'd showered me with luxury. Why? If he turned me, I had no doubt that I'd become as twisted as him. It would make everything a lot simpler.

He continued when I remained silent. "And if I'm so different, then why did you kiss me back earlier?"

I still didn't know what to say, and it made his smile grow. "No answer. You know I'm right."

His lips suddenly found mine again. I made a small sound of protest and tried vainly to escape his embrace. He was too strong, and after a moment, I didn't want to escape. That same sensation as before flooded me. His lips were cold, but the kiss burned between us. Fire and ice. And he was right — I *did* kiss him back.

Desperately, that rational part of me screamed that this was wrong. Last time, he'd broken the kiss before too much could happen. Not this time. And as we continued kissing now, that rational voice in me grew smaller and smaller. The part of me that would always love Dimitri took over, exulting in the way his body felt against mine, the way he wound my hair around one of his hands, letting the fingers get tangled up. His other hand slid up the back of my shirt, cold against my warm skin. I pushed myself closer to him and felt the pressure of the kiss increase as his own desire picked up.

Then, in the midst of it all, my tongue lightly brushed against the sharp point of one of his fangs. It was like a bucket of cold water tossed upon me. With as much strength as I could muster, I jerked my head away, pulling out of the kiss. I could only guess that his guard had been momentarily down, allowing me that small escape.

My breathing was heavy, my whole body still wanting him. My mind, however, was the part of me in control — for now, at least. God, what had I been doing? *It's not the Dimitri you knew. It's not him.* I'd been kissing a monster. But my body wasn't so sure.

"No," I murmured, surprised by how pathetic and pleading I sounded. "No. We can't do this."

"Are you sure?" he asked. His hand was still in my hair, and he forcibly turned my head so that I was face-to-face with him again. "You didn't seem to mind. Everything can be just like it was before . . . like it was in the cabin . . . You certainly wanted it then. . . ."

The cabin . . .

"No," I repeated. "I don't want that."

He pressed his lips against my cheek and then made a surprisingly gentle trail of kisses down to my neck. Again, I felt my body's yearning for him, and I hated myself for the weakness.

"What about this?" he asked, his voice barely a whisper. "Do you want this?"

"Wh—"

I felt it. The sharp bite of teeth into my skin as he closed his mouth down on my neck. For half an instant, it was agonizing. Painful and horrible. And then, just like that, the pain disappeared. A rush of bliss and joy poured through me. It was so sweet. I had never felt so wonderful in my life. It reminded me a little of how it had been when Lissa drank from me. That had been amazing, but this . . . this was ten times better. A hundred times better. The rush from a Strigoi bite was greater than that of a Moroi's. It was like being in love for the first time, filled with that all-consuming, joyous feeling.

When he pulled away, it felt like all the happiness and wonder in the world had vanished. He ran a hand over his mouth, and I stared at him wide-eyed. My initial instinct was to ask why he'd stopped, but then, slowly, I reached inside myself to fight past the blissful daze that his bite had sent me into.

"Why . . . what . . ." My words slurred a little. "You said it would be my choice. . . ."

"It still is," he said. His own eyes were wide, his breathing heavy too. He'd been just as affected as me. "I'm not doing this to awaken you, Roza. A bite like this won't turn you. This . . . well, this is just for fun. . . ."

Then, his mouth moved back to my neck to drink again, and I lost track of the world.

# TWENTY

The days after that were like a dream. In fact, I honestly can't say how many days even passed. Maybe it was one. Maybe it was a hundred.

I lost track of day and night too. My time was divided into Dimitri or not-Dimitri. He was my world. When he wasn't there, the moments were agony. I'd pass them as best I could, but they seemed to drag on forever. The TV was my best friend during those times. I'd lie on the couch for hours, only half following what was going on. In keeping with the rest of the suite's luxury, I had access to satellite television, which meant we were actually pulling in some American programming. Half the time, though, I wasn't sure that it really made a difference to me if the language was Russian or English.

Inna continued her periodic checks on me. She brought my meals and did my laundry — I was wearing the dresses now — and waited around in that silent way of hers to see if I needed anything else. I never did — at least not from her. I only needed Dimitri. Each time she left, some distant part of me remembered I was supposed to do something . . . follow her, that was it. I'd had some plan to check out the exit and use her as a way to escape, right? Now, that plan no longer held the appeal. It seemed like a lot of work.

And then, finally, Dimitri would visit, and the monotony would be broken. We'd lie together on my bed, wrapped in each other's arms. We never had sex, but we'd kiss and touch and lose ourselves in the wonder of each other's bodies — sometimes with very little clothing. After a while, I found it hard to believe I'd once been afraid of his new appearance. Sure, the eyes were a bit shocking, but he was still gorgeous . . . still unbelievably sexy. And after we'd talked and made out for a while — for hours, sometimes — I'd let him bite me. Then I'd get that rush . . . that wonderful, exquisite flood of chemicals that lifted me from all my problems. Whatever doubts I'd had about God's existence vanished in those moments because surely, surely I was touching God when I lost myself in that bite. *This* was heaven.

"Let me see your neck," he said one day.

We were lying together as usual. I was on my side, and he was snuggled up against my back, one arm draped around my waist. I rolled over and brushed my hair away from where it had fallen over my neck and cleavage. The dress I wore today was a navy halter sundress, made of some light, clingy material.

"Already?" I asked. He usually didn't bite me until the end of his visits. While part of me longed for that and waited in anticipation to feel that high again, I did kind of enjoy these moments beforehand. It was when the endorphins in my system were at their lowest, so I was able to manage some sort of conversation. We would talk about fights we'd been in or the life he imagined for us when I was Strigoi. Nothing too sentimental — but nice nonetheless.

I braced myself for the bite now, arching up in anticipation. To my surprise, he didn't lean down and sink his teeth into me. He reached into his pocket and produced a necklace. It was either white gold or platinum — I didn't have the skill to tell which — and had three dark blue sapphires the size of quarters. He'd brought me a lot of jewelry this week, and I swore each piece was more beautiful than the last.

I stared in amazement at its beauty, at the way the blue stones glittered in the light. He placed the necklace against my skin and fastened it behind my neck. Running his fingers along the necklace's edges, he nodded in approval.

"Beautiful." His fingers drifted to one of the dress's straps. He slid his hand underneath it, sending a thrill through my skin. "It matches."

I smiled. In the old days, Dimitri had almost never gotten me gifts. He hadn't had the means, and I hadn't wanted them anyway. Now, I was continually dazzled by the presents he seemed to have at each visit.

"Where'd you get it?" I asked. The metal was cool against my flushed skin but nowhere near as cold as his fingers.

He smiled slyly. "I have my sources."

That chastising voice in my head that sometimes managed to penetrate through the haze I lived in noted that I was involved with some sort of vampire gangster. Its warnings were immediately squashed and sank back down into my dreamy cloud of existence. How could I be upset when the necklace was so beautiful? Something suddenly struck me as funny.

"You're just like Abe."

"Who?"

"This guy I met. Abe Mazur. He's some kind of mob boss . . . he kept following me."

Dimitri stiffened. "Abe Mazur was following you?"

I didn't like the dark look that had suddenly fallen over his features. "Yeah. So?"

"Why? What did he want with you?"

"I don't know. He kept wanting to know why I was in Russia but finally gave up and just wanted me to leave. I think somebody from home hired him to find me."

"I don't want you near Abe Mazur. He's dangerous." Dimitri was angry, and I hated that. A moment later, that fury faded, and he ran his fingers along my arm once more, pushing the strap down further. "Of course, people like that won't be an issue when you awaken."

Somewhere, in the back of my head, I wondered if Dimitri had the answers I wanted about Abe — about what Abe did. But talking about Abe had made Dimitri upset, and I cringed at that, hastily wanting to switch topics.

"What have you been doing today?" I asked, impressed at my ability to make normal small talk. Between the endorphins and him touching me, coherence was difficult.

"Errands for Galina. Dinner."

Dinner. A victim. I frowned. The feelings that inspired in me weren't of repulsion so much as . . . jealousy.

"Do you drink from them . . . for fun?"

He ran his lips along my neck, teeth taunting my skin but not biting. I gasped and pressed closer to him.

"No, Roza. They're food; that's all. It's over quickly. You're the only one I take pleasure in."

I felt smug satisfaction in that, and that annoying mental voice pointed out that that was an incredibly sick and twisted view for me to have. I kind of hoped he would bite me soon. That usually shut the rational voice up.

I reached up and touched his face, then ran my hand through that wonderful, silky hair that I'd always loved. "You keep wanting to awaken me . . . but we won't be able to do this anymore. Strigoi don't drink from each other, do they?"

"No," he agreed. "But it'll be worth it. We can do so much more. . . ."

He left the "so much more" to my imagination, and a pleasant shiver ran through me. The kissing and blood taking were intoxicating, but there were some days that I did want, well . . . more. The memories of the one time we'd made love haunted me when we were this close together, and I often longed to do it again. For whatever reason, he never pushed for sex, no matter how passionate things became. I wasn't sure if he was using that as a lure for me to turn or if there was some incompatibility between a Strigoi and a dhampir. Could the living and the dead do that? Once, I would have found the thought of sex with one of them absolutely repulsive. Now . . . I just didn't think about the complications so much.

But although he didn't attempt sex, he would often taunt me with his caresses, touching my thighs and sternum and other dangerous places. Plus, he would remind me of what it had been like that one time, how amazing it had been, how our bodies had felt. . . . His talk of such things was more taunting than affectionate, though.

In my semi-clear moments, I honestly thought it was strange that I hadn't yet consented to becoming Strigoi. The endorphin fog made me agree to almost everything else he wanted. I'd fallen comfortably into dressing up for him, staying in my gilded prison, and accepting that he took a victim every couple days. Yet even in my most incoherent moments, even when I wanted him so badly, I couldn't agree to turning. There was some intrinsic part of me that refused to budge. Most of the time, he would shrug off my refusal, like it was a joke. But every once in a while when I declined, I'd see a spark of anger in his eyes. Those moments scared me.

"Here it comes," I teased. "The sales pitch. Eternal life. Invincible. Nothing to stand in our way."

"It's not a joke," he said. Oops. My flippancy had brought that hardness back to him. The desire and fondness that I'd just seen now fractured into a million pieces and blew away. The hands that had just stroked me suddenly grabbed my wrists and held me in place as he leaned down. "We can't stay like this forever. You can't stay here forever."

*Whoa,* that voice said. *Be careful. That doesn't sound good.* His grip hurt, and I often wondered if that was his intent or if he just couldn't help his violence.

When he finally released me, I wrapped my arm around his neck and tried to kiss him. "Can't we talk about that later?" Our lips met, fire blossoming between us and urgency coursing through my body. I could tell he had a matching desire, but a few seconds later, he broke away. The cold annoyance was still on his face.

"Come on," he said, pulling away from me. "Let's go."

He stood up, and I stared stupidly. "Where are we going?"

"Outside."

I sat up on the bed, dumbfounded. "Out . . . outside? But . . . that's not allowed. We can't."

"We can do anything I want," he snapped.

He extended his hand and helped me up. I followed him to the door. He was as skilled as Inna at blocking me from the keypad, not that it mattered now. There was no way I could ever remember that long of a sequence anymore.

The door clicked open, and he led me out. I stared in wonder, my dazed brain still trying to process this freedom. As I'd noticed that one day, the door led to a short corridor blocked by another door. It too was heavy and bore a keypad lock. Dimitri opened it, and I was willing to bet the two doors had different codes.

Taking my arm, he guided me through that door and into another hallway. Despite his firm hold, I couldn't help but come to a standstill. Maybe I shouldn't have been surprised at the opulence I suddenly faced.

After all, I was living in this place's pent-house suite. But the corridor leading out of my room had been stark and industrial-looking, and somehow I'd imagined the rest of the house to be equally institutional or prisonlike.

It wasn't. Instead, I felt like I was in some old movie, the kind where people took tea in the parlor. The plush carpet was covered by a gold-patterned runner that stretched off in both directions of the hall. Antique-looking paintings dotted the walls, showing people from ages ago in elaborate clothing that made my dresses look cheap and ordinary. The whole place was illuminated by tiny chandeliers that were spaced along the ceiling every six feet or so. The teardrop-shaped crystals caught the light with their facets, scattering small flecks of rainbows on the walls. I stared, enchanted by the glitter and the color, which is probably why I failed to notice one other fixture in the hall.

"What are you doing?"

The harsh sound of Nathan's voice jerked me from my crystal gazing. He'd been leaning against the wall opposite my door and straightened immediately upon seeing us. He had that same cruel expression on his face that was so characteristic of Strigoi, the one I occasionally saw on Dimitri, no matter how charming and kind he seemed sometimes.

Dimitri's posture turned rigid and defensive. "I'm taking her for a walk." He kind of sounded like he was talking about a dog, but my fear of Nathan trumped any offense I might take.

"That's against the rules," said Nathan. "Bad enough you've still got her here. Galina gave orders for you to keep her confined. We don't need some rogue dhampir running around."

Dimitri nodded toward me. "Does she look like she's a threat?"

Nathan's eyes flicked over at me. I wasn't entirely sure what he saw. I didn't think I looked that different, but a small smirk crossed his lips that promptly disappeared when he turned back to Dimitri. "No, but I was ordered to babysit this door, and I'm not going to get in trouble for you taking a field trip."

"I'll deal with Galina. I'll tell her I overpowered you." Dimitri gave a fang-filled grin. "It shouldn't be that hard for her to believe."

The look Nathan gave Dimitri made me unconsciously step back until I hit the wall. "You're so full of yourself. I didn't awaken you so that you could act like you're in

409

charge around here. I did it so that we could use your strength and inside knowledge. You should be answering to *me*."

Dimitri shrugged. Taking my hand, he started to turn away. "Not my fault if you're not strong enough to make me do it."

That was when Nathan lunged at Dimitri. Dimitri responded so quickly to the attack that I think he knew it would happen. He instantly released my hand, turned to catch hold of Nathan, and tossed the other Strigoi against the wall. Nathan immediately got up — it took more than that kind of hit to faze someone like him — but Dimitri was ready. He punched Nathan in the nose — once, twice, and then a third time, all in rapid succession. Nathan fell down, blood covering his face. Dimitri kicked him hard in the stomach and loomed over him.

"Don't try it," said Dimitri. "You'll lose." He wiped Nathan's blood off of his hand and then laced his fingers through mine again. "I told you, I'll deal with Galina. But thanks for your concern."

Dimitri turned away again, apparently feeling there'd be no more attacks. There weren't. But as I started to follow him, I cast a quick glance over my shoulder to where Nathan sat on the floor. His eyes shot daggers at Dimitri, and I was pretty sure I'd never seen a look of such pure hatred — at least until he turned his gaze on me. I felt cold all over and stumbled to keep up with Dimitri.

Nathan's voice rang out behind us. "You're not safe! Neither of you is. She's lunch, Belikov. Lunch."

Dimitri's hand tightened on mine, and he picked up the pace. I could feel the fury radiating off of him and suddenly wasn't sure whom I should be more afraid of: Nathan or Dimitri. Dimitri was a badass, alive or undead. In the past, I'd seen him attack foes without fear or hesitation. He'd always been magnificent, behaving just as bravely as I'd told his family. But in all those times, he'd always had a legitimate reason for fighting — usually self defense. His confrontation with Nathan just then had been about more, though. It had been an assertion of dominance and a chance to draw blood. Dimitri had seemed to enjoy it. What if he decided to turn on me like that? What if my constant refusal pushed him into torture, and he hurt me until I finally agreed?

"Nathan scares me," I said, not wanting Dimitri to know that I feared him too. I felt weak and utterly defenseless, something that didn't happen to me very often. Usually, I was ready to take on any challenge, no matter how desperate.

"He won't touch you," Dimitri said harshly. "You have nothing to worry about."

We reached a set of stairs. After a few steps, it became clear that I wasn't going to be able to handle four flights. Aside from the drugged stupor his bites kept me in, the frequent blood loss was weakening me and taking its toll. Without saying a word, Dimitri swept me up in his arms and carried me downstairs effortlessly, gently setting me down when we reached the staircase's bottom.

The main floor of the estate had the same grand feel as the upstairs hall. The entryway had a huge vaulted ceiling with an elaborate chandelier that dwarfed the little ones I'd seen. Ornate double doors faced us, set with stained-glass windows. What also faced us was another Strigoi, a man sitting in a chair and apparently on guard duty. Near him was a panel set into the wall with buttons and flashing lights. A modern security system set amongst all this old-world charm. His posture stiffened as we approached, and at first, I thought it was a natural bodyguard instinct — until I saw his face. It was the Strigoi I'd tortured that first night in Novosibirsk, the one I'd dispatched to tell Dimitri I was looking for him. His lips curled back slightly as he met my eyes.

"Rose Hathaway," said the Strigoi. "I remember your name — just like you told me."

He said no more than that, but I tightened my grip on Dimitri's hand as we passed. The Strigoi's eyes never left me until we'd stepped outside and shut the door behind us.

"He wants to kill me," I told Dimitri.

"All Strigoi want to kill you," Dimitri returned.

"He really does. . . . I tortured him."

"I know. He's been in disgrace ever since then and lost some of his status here."

"That doesn't make me feel any better."

Dimitri seemed unconcerned. "Marlen is no one you need to worry about. You fighting him only proved to Galina that you're a good addition around here. He's beneath you."

I didn't find that overly reassuring. I was making too many personal Strigoi enemies — but then, it wasn't like I could really expect to be making Strigoi friends.

It was nighttime, of course. Dimitri wouldn't have taken me out otherwise. The foyer had made me think we were at the front of the house, but the extensive gardens that spread out around us made me wonder if we were in the back now. Or maybe the entire house was wrapped in this kind of greenery. We were surrounded in a hedge maze cut with beautiful detail. Within the maze were small courtyards, decorated with fountains or statues. And everywhere were flowers and more flowers. The air was heavy with their scent, and I realized that someone had gone to an awful lot of trouble to find night-blooming ones. The only type I immediately recognized was jasmine, its long, white-flowered vines climbing up trellises and statues in the maze.

We walked in silence for a bit, and I found myself lost in the romance of it all. The whole time Dimitri and I had been together at school, I'd been consumed with the fears of how we would juggle our relationship and our duty. A moment like this, walking in a garden on a spring night lit with stars, had seemed like a fantasy too crazy to even start to consider.

Even without the difficulty of stairs, too much walking grew exhausting in my state. I came to a halt and sighed. "I'm tired," I said.

Dimitri stopped too and helped me sit down. The grass was dry and tickly against my skin. I lay back against it, and a moment later, he joined me. I had an eerie moment of déjà vu, recalling the afternoon we'd made snow angels.

"This is amazing," I said, staring up at the sky. It was clear, no clouds in sight. "What's it like for you?"

"Hmm?"

"There's enough light that I can see pretty clearly, but it's still dim compared to day. Your eyes are better than mine. What do you see?"

"For me, it's as bright as day." When I didn't respond, he added, "It could be like that for you, too."

I tried to picture that. Would the shadows seem as mysterious? Would the moon and stars shine so brightly? "I don't know. I kind of like the darkness."

"Only because you don't know any better."

I sighed. "So you keep telling me."

He turned toward me and pushed the hair away from my face. "Rose, this is driving me crazy. I'm tired of this waiting. I want us to be together. Don't you like this? What we have? It could be even better." His words sounded romantic, but not the tone.

I did like this. I loved the haze I lived in, the haze in which all worries disappeared. I loved being close to him, loved the way he kissed me and told me he wanted me. . . .

"Why?" I asked.

"Why what?" He sounded puzzled, something I hadn't heard yet in a Strigoi.

"Why do you want me?" I had no idea why I even asked that. He apparently didn't know either.

"Why wouldn't I want you?"

He spoke in such an obvious way, like it was the stupidest question in the world. It probably was, I realized, and yet . . . I'd somehow been expecting another answer.

Just then, my stomach twisted. With all the time I'd spent with Dimitri, I really had managed to push the Strigoi nausea off my radar. The presence of other Strigoi increased it, though. I'd felt it around Nathan, and I felt it now. I sat up, and Dimitri did too, almost at the same time. He'd likely been alerted by his superior hearing.

A dark shape loomed over us, blotting out the stars. It was a woman, and Dimitri shot up. I stayed where I was, on the ground.

She was strikingly beautiful, in a hard and terrible way. Her build was similar to mine, indicating she hadn't been a Moroi when turned. Isaiah, the Strigoi who'd captured me, had been very old, and power had radiated from him. This woman hadn't been around nearly so long, but I could sense that she was older than Dimitri and much stronger.

She said something in Russian to him, and her voice was as cold as her beauty. Dimitri answered back, his tone confident yet polite. I heard Nathan's name mentioned a couple of times as they spoke. Dimitri reached down and helped me up, and I felt embarrassed at how often I needed his assistance, when I used to almost be a match for him.

"Rose," he said, "this is Galina. She's the one who has been kind enough to let you stay."

Galina's face didn't look so kind. It was devoid of all emotion, and I felt like my entire soul was exposed to her. While I was uncertain of a lot of things around here, I'd picked up enough to realize that my continual residence here was a rare and fragile thing. I swallowed.

*"Spasibo,"* I said. I didn't know how to tell her it was nice to meet her — and honestly, I wasn't sure if it was — but I figured a simple thank-you was good enough. If she'd been his former instructor and trained at a normal Academy, she probably knew English and was faking it like Yeva. I had no clue why she'd do that, but if you could snap a teen dhampir's neck, you were entitled to do whatever you wanted.

Galina's expression — or lack thereof — didn't change with my thanks, and she turned her attention back to Dimitri. They conversed over me, and Dimitri gestured to me a couple of times. I recognized the word for *strong.*

Finally, Galina issued something that sounded final and left us without any sort of goodbye. Neither Dimitri nor I moved until I felt the nausea dissipate.

"Come on," he said. "We should get back."

We walked back through the maze, though I had no idea how he knew where to go. It was funny. When I'd first arrived, my dream had been to get outside and escape. Now that I was here . . . well, it didn't seem that important. Galina's anger did.

"What did she say?" I asked.

"She doesn't like that you're still here. She wants me to awaken you or kill you."

"Oh. Um, what are you going to do?"

He stayed silent for a few seconds. "I'll wait a little longer and then . . . I will make the choice for you."

He didn't specify which choice he'd be making, and I almost began my earlier pleas to die before becoming Strigoi. But suddenly, instead, I said, "How long?"

"Not long, Roza. You need to choose. And make the right choice."

"Which is?"

He held up his hands. "All of this. A life together."

We'd emerged from the maze. I stared at the house — which was crazy enormous when viewed from the outside — and at the beautiful gardens around us. It was like something from a dream. Beyond that, endless countryside rolled away, eventually becoming lost in the darkness and blending into the black sky — except for one tiny part that had a soft purple glow on the horizon. I frowned, studying it, then turned my attention back to Dimitri.

"And what then? Then I work for Galina too?"

"For a while."

"How long is a while?"

We came to a stop outside the house. Dimitri looked down into my eyes, his face alight with a look that made me take a step back.

"Until we kill her, Rose. Until we kill her and take all of this for ourselves."

# TWENTY-ONE

Dimitri didn't elaborate. I was too startled by his words and the rest of the night's events to even know how to begin to address them. He took me back inside, past the Strigoi on guard duty, and upstairs to my suite. Nathan was no longer outside.

For a few brief moments, that nagging voice in my head spoke loudly enough to break through my addled thoughts. If I had no guard in the hall and Inna returned soon, I had a very good chance of threatening her enough to get out of here. Admittedly, that would mean I'd have to deal with a house of God only knew how many Strigoi, but my escape odds were better in the house than in this room.

Then, almost as soon as those thoughts appeared, they vanished. Dimitri snaked his arm around me and pulled me to him. It had been chilly outside, and even if his body was cold, his clothes and jacket provided some warmth. I snuggled closer to him as his hands ran all over me. I thought he was going to bite me, but it was our mouths that met, hard and furious. I wrapped my fingers in his hair, trying to pull him closer to me. Meanwhile, his fingers were running against my bare leg, pushing my skirt up almost to my hip. Anticipation and eagerness lit every part of my body. I had dreamed about the cabin for so long, remembering it with so much longing. I'd never expected anything like that to happen again, but now it could, and I was astonished at how badly I wanted it.

My hands moved down to his shirt, undoing all the buttons so that I could touch his chest. His skin still felt like ice, a startling contrast to the burning within me. He moved his lips from mine, down to my neck and shoulder, pushing down the dress's strap as he covered my flesh with hungry kisses. His hand was still on the side of my bare hip, and I frantically tried to pull his shirt off altogether.

Suddenly, with a surprising abruptness, he jerked away and shoved me down. At first, I thought it was just more of the foreplay between us, until I realized he was purposely pushing me away.

"No," he said, voice hard. "Not yet. Not

until you're awakened."

"Why?" I asked desperately. I couldn't think of anything except him touching me — and, well, another bite. "Why does it matter? Is there . . . is there a reason we can't?" Until I'd come here, sex with a Strigoi had never occurred to me . . . maybe it just wasn't possible.

He leaned toward me, putting his lips near my ear. "No, but it'll be so much better if you're awakened. Let me do it . . . let me do it, and then we can do anything we want. . . ."

It was a bargaining chip, I realized vaguely. He wanted me — it was written all over him — but he was using the lure of sex to get me to give in. And honestly? I was this close to accepting. My body was overriding my mind — nearly.

"No," I whimpered. "I . . . I'm scared. . . ."

That dangerous look softened, and while he didn't exactly look like the Dimitri from before, there was something a little less Strigoi about him. "Rose, do you think I'd do anything that would hurt you?" Somewhere, hadn't there been a discussion about how my options were to turn or die? The latter seemed like it might hurt, but I didn't mention that just now.

"The bite . . . the turning would hurt. . . ."

"I told you: It'll be just like what we've already done. You'll enjoy it. It won't hurt, I swear it."

I looked away. Damn it. Why couldn't he still be sinister and scary? It was so much easier to put my foot down and resist. Even in the heat of passion, I was able to resist. But somehow . . . seeing him like this, calm and reasonable . . . well, it was too close to the Dimitri I'd loved. And *that* was hard to turn away from. For the first time, it made turning Strigoi seem . . . not so bad.

"I don't know," I said lamely.

He released me and sat up, frustration filling his features. It was almost a relief. "Galina's patience is running out. So is mine."

"You said we still have time. . . . I just need to think more. . . ." How long could I use that excuse? The narrowing of his eyes told me not much longer.

"I have to go," he said harshly. There would be no more touching or kissing, I could tell. "I need to deal with some things."

"I'm sorry," I said, both confused and afraid. I didn't know which Dimitri I wanted. The terrifying one, the sensual one, or the almost — but still not quite — gentle one.

He said nothing. Without any other warning, he leaned down and bit into the tender skin of my throat. Whatever feeble escape strategies I had were gone. I closed my eyes, nearly falling over, and only his arm wrapped firmly around me kept me upright. Just like when we kissed, his mouth was warm against my flesh, and the feel of his tongue and teeth sent electricity through me.

And like that, it was over. He pulled away, licking his lips as he still continued to hold onto me. The fog was back. The world was wonderful and happy and I was without any cares. Whatever he'd been worrying about with Nathan and Galina meant nothing to me. The fear I'd felt moments ago . . . my disappointment over sex . . . my confusion — I didn't have time to worry about any of that, not when life was so beautiful and I loved Dimitri so much. I smiled up at him and tried to hug him again, but he was already leading me to the couch.

"I'll see you later." In a flash, he was at the door, which saddened me. I wanted him to stay. Stay forever. "Remember, I want you — and I would never let anything bad happen to you. I'll protect you. But . . . I can't wait much longer."

With that, he left. His words made me smile more broadly. Dimitri wanted me. Vaguely, I recalled asking him outside *why* he wanted me. Why on earth had I asked? What answer had I wanted? Why did it matter? He wanted me. That was what counted.

That thought and the wonderful endorphin rush enveloped me as I lay on the couch, and I felt drowsiness overtaking me. Walking over to the bed seemed like too much work, so I stayed where I was and just let sleep come.

And, unexpectedly, I found myself in one of Adrian's dreams.

I'd pretty much given up on him. After my first desperate attempts at escape in the suite, I'd finally convinced myself that Adrian wasn't coming back, that I'd sent him away for good. Yet here he was, standing right in front of me — or, well, at least his dream version was. Often we were in the woods or a garden, but today we stood where we'd first met, on the porch of an Idaho ski lodge. Sun shone down, and mountains soared off to the side of us.

I grinned broadly. "Adrian!"

I didn't think I'd ever seen him look as surprised as he did just then. Considering how mean I usually was to him, I could understand his feelings.

"Hello, Rose," he said. His voice sounded uncertain, like he was worried I might be playing a trick on him.

"You look good today," I told him. It was true. He wore dark jeans and a printed button-down shirt in shades of navy and turquoise that looked fantastic with his dark green eyes. Those eyes, however, looked weary. Worn. That was a little odd. In these dreams, he could shape the world and even our appearances to what he wanted, with only a little effort. He could have looked perfect but instead appeared to be reflecting real-world fatigue.

"So do you." His voice was still wary, as he eyed me from head to toe. I was still in the clingy sundress, my hair down and loose, the sapphires around my neck. "That looks like something I'd normally dress you in. Are you asleep in that?"

"Yup." I smoothed down the dress's skirt, thinking how pretty it looked. I wondered if Dimitri had liked it. He hadn't said so specifically, but he had kept telling me I was beautiful. "I didn't think you'd come back."

"I didn't think I would either."

I looked back up at him. He wasn't like his usual self at all. "Are you trying to figure out where I am again?"

"No, I don't care about that anymore." He sighed. "The only thing I care about is that you aren't *here.* You have to come back, Rose."

I crossed my arms and flounced onto the porch's railing. "Adrian, I'm not ready for anything romant—"

"Not for me," he exclaimed. "For her. You have to come back for Lissa. That's why I'm here."

"Lissa . . ."

My waking self was pumped full of endorphins, and it carried over here. I tried to remember why I should be so worried about Lissa.

Adrian took a step forward and studied me carefully. "Yeah, you know, Lissa? Your best friend? The one you're bonded to and sworn to protect?"

I swung my legs back and forth. "I never made any vows."

"What the hell's the matter with you?"

I didn't like his agitated tone. It was ruining my good mood. "What's the matter with *you*?"

"You aren't acting like yourself. Your aura . . ." He frowned, unable to continue.

I laughed. "Oh yes. Here it comes. The magical, mystical aura. Let me guess. It's black, right?"

"No . . . it . . ." He continued scrutinizing me for several heavy seconds. "I can barely get a fix on it. It's all over the place. What's going on, Rose? What's happening in the

427

waking world?"

"Nothing's happening," I said. "Nothing except me being happy for the first time in my life. Why are you acting weird all of a sudden? You used to be fun. Figures the first time I'm finally having a good time, you go all boring and strange."

He knelt down in front of me, no trace of humor anywhere. "There's something wrong with you. I can't tell what —"

"I told you, I'm fine. Why do you have to keep coming and trying to ruin things for me?" True, I'd desperately wanted him to come a little while ago, but now . . . well, that wasn't so important. I had a good thing with Dimitri here, if only I could figure out how to solve all the not-so-good parts.

"I told you, I'm not here for me. I'm here for Lissa." He looked up at me, wide-eyed and earnest. "Rose, I am *begging* you to come home. Lissa needs you. I don't know what's wrong, and I don't know how to help her. No one else does either. I think . . . I think only you can. Maybe being apart is what's hurting her. Maybe that's what's wrong with you now, why you're acting so weird. Come home. Please. We'll heal both of you. We'll all figure it out together. She's acting so strange. She's reckless and doesn't care about anything."

I shook my head. "Being away isn't what's wrong with me. Probably not what's wrong with her, either. If she's really worried about spirit, she should go back on her meds."

"She's *not* worried; that's the problem. Damn it." He stood up and began pacing. "What's wrong with you two? Why can't either of you see there's something the matter?"

"Maybe it's not us," I said. "Maybe it's you imagining things."

Adrian turned back toward me and looked me over again. "No. It's not me."

I didn't like any of this — not his tone, expression, or words. I'd been excited to see him, but now I resented him ruining my good mood. I didn't want to think about any of this. It was too hard.

"Look," I said. "I was happy to see you tonight but not anymore, not if you're going to sit and accuse me and make demands."

"I'm not trying to do that." His voice was gentle — the anger was gone. "The last thing I want is to make you unhappy. I care about you. I care about Lissa, too. I want you both to be happy and live your lives like you want . . . but not when you're both heading down destructive paths."

He almost made sense. Almost seemed

reasonable and sincere. I shook my head.

"Stay out of it. I'm where I want to be, and I'm not coming back. Lissa's on her own." I jumped off the rail. The world swirled a little, and I stumbled. Adrian caught my hand, and I jerked away. "I'm fine."

"You are not. Jesus Christ. I'd swear you're drunk, except . . . the aura's still not right for that. What *is* it?" He ran his hands through his dark hair. It was his typical sign of agitation.

"I'm done here," I said, trying to be as polite as possible. Why on earth had I wanted to see him again? It had seemed so important when I first arrived. "Send me back, please."

He opened his mouth to say something, then froze a few moments. "What's on your neck?"

He reached forward, and addled or no, I managed to dodge pretty efficiently. I had no idea what he saw on my neck, and I had no interest in finding out. "Don't touch me."

"Rose, that looks like —"

"Send me back, Adrian!" So much for my politeness.

"Rose, let me help —"

*"Send. Me. Back!"*

I shouted the words, and then, for the first time, I managed to pull myself out of Adrian's dream. I left sleep altogether and woke up on the couch. The room was still and silent, the only sound my rapid breathing. I felt all tangled up inside. Usually, so fresh from a bite, I would be floating and gleeful. Yet, the encounter with Adrian had left part of me troubled and sad.

Standing up, I managed to make my way to the bathroom. I flicked on the light and winced. It hadn't been very bright in the other room. Once my eyes adjusted, I leaned toward the mirror and pushed my hair out of the way. I gasped at what I saw. There were bruises all over my neck, as well as signs of fresher wounds. Around where Dimitri had just bitten me, I could see dried blood.

I looked . . . like a blood whore.

How had I never noticed this before? I wet a washcloth and scrubbed at my neck, trying to get the blood off. I rubbed and rubbed until the skin turned pink. Was that it? Were there more? That looked like the worst of it. I wondered how much Adrian had seen. My hair had been down, and I was pretty sure most of it had covered my neck.

A rebellious thought came to my head.

What did it matter if Adrian saw or not? He didn't understand. There was no way he could even come close. I was with Dimitri. Yeah, he was different . . . but not *that* much different. And I was sure I could find a way to make this work without becoming a Strigoi. I just didn't know how yet.

I tried to reassure myself over and over, but those bruises kept staring back at me.

I left the bathroom and returned to the couch. I turned on the TV without really watching, and after a while, the happy fog rolled over me again. I soon tuned out the TV and returned to sleep. This time, my dreams were my own.

It took a while for Dimitri to come again. And by "a while," I mean almost an entire day. I was getting twitchy by that point, both because I missed him and because I missed the bite. He usually visited twice a day, so this was the longest I'd gone without the endorphins. Needing something to do, I preoccupied myself with making myself as beautiful as possible.

I sorted through the dresses in my closet, choosing a long ivory silk one that had purple flowers delicately painted into the fabric. It fit like a glove. I wanted to wear my hair up, but after looking at the bruises again, I decided to wear it down. I'd been provided with a curling iron and makeup recently, so I worked my hair over carefully, turning the ends up in perfect little curls. Once made up, I stared happily at my reflection, certain Dimitri would be happy too. All I needed now was to put on some of the exquisite jewelry he'd given me. But when I turned to leave, I caught a glimpse of my back from the side and saw I'd missed fastening a clasp. I reached around to do it but couldn't get a hold of it. It was in that perfect spot just out of my reach.

"Damn," I muttered, still grappling with the hook. The flaw in my perfection.

Just then, I heard the door open in the other room, followed by the telltale sound of a tray being set on the coffee table. A stroke of luck.

"Inna!" I called, walking out of the bathroom. "I need you to —"

Nausea rolled through me, and as I stepped into the living room, I saw that Dimitri wasn't the source. Nathan was.

My jaw dropped open. Inna stood near him, waiting patiently by the tray, eyes downcast as always. I immediately ignored her and then looked back at Nathan. Presumably, he was still on guard duty, but that had never actually included him coming inside. For the first time in a while, some of my battle instincts kicked in, assessing escape options. My fear urged me to back away, but that would trap me in the bathroom. Best to stay where I was. Even if I couldn't leave the room, this gave me the most space to maneuver.

"What are you doing here?" I asked, surprised at how calm I sounded.

"Taking care of a problem."

I didn't really need any pointers to figure out the subtext here. I was the problem.

Again, I fought the urge to back up. "I've never done anything to you." It was faulty logic to a Strigoi. None of their victims *ever* did anything to them.

"You exist," he said. "You're taking up space here, wasting everyone's time. You know how to find her — the Dragomir girl — yet you'll offer nothing remotely useful until Belikov gets off his ass and awakens you. And in the meantime, Galina forces me to waste time watching you and keeps promoting *him* because he's convinced her that you're going to be some amazing asset to us."

It was an interesting set of grievances. "So . . . um, what are you going to do?"

In a flash, he stood in front of me. Seeing him so close triggered that memory in my mind's eye — him biting Dimitri and starting all of this. A spark of anger kindled in me but didn't do much in the way of development. "I'm getting the information one way or another," he hissed. "Tell me where she is."

"You know where she is. She's at the school." There was nothing useful in giving up that news. He knew she was there. He knew where the school was.

The look he gave me showed he was not happy about me providing knowledge he already had. Reaching out, he gripped my hair and jerked my head painfully back. Wearing my hair down maybe hadn't been so useful after all. "Where is she *going?* She won't stay there forever. Is she going to college? The Royal Court? They must have made plans for her."

"I don't know what they are. I've been away for a while."

"I don't believe you," he snarled. "She's too valuable. Her future would have been planned out a while ago."

"If it is, no one's shared it with me. I left too soon."

I shrugged by way of answer. Rage filled his eyes, and I swear, they grew redder.

"You're bonded! You know. Tell me now, and I'll kill you quickly. If you don't, I'll awaken you to get the information, and *then* I'll kill you. I'll light you up like a bonfire."

"You . . . you'd kill me once I was one of you?" Foolish question. Strigoi felt no loyalty to each other.

"Yes. It'll destroy him, and once Galina sees how unhinged he is, *I* will return to my original place by her side — especially after I stamp out the Dragomir line."

"The hell you will."

He smiled and touched my face, running his fingers along my neck and the bruises all over it. "Oh, I will. It really will make things easier if you just tell me now. You'll die in ecstasy rather than being burned alive. We'll both enjoy it." He wrapped his hand delicately around my throat. "You're definitely a problem, but you *are* beautiful — especially your throat. I can see why he wants you. . . ."

Warring emotions played within me. Logically, I knew this was Nathan — Nathan, whom I hated for having turned Dimitri in the first place. Yet my body's need for Strigoi endorphins was raising its head too, and it barely mattered that it was Nathan. What mattered was that his teeth were only a breath away from my neck, promising that sweet, sweet delirium.

And while one hand held my throat, the

other ran down my waist, down to the curve of my hip. There had been a sultry edge to Nathan's voice, like he wanted to do more than just bite me. And after so many sexually charged encounters with Dimitri — encounters that never resulted in anything — my body almost didn't care who touched it. I could close my eyes, and it wouldn't matter whose teeth bit into me or whose hands peeled off my clothes. Only the next fix would matter. I could close my eyes and pretend it was Dimitri, lost in it all as Nathan's lips brushed my skin. . . .

Except, as some small reasonable part of me recalled, Nathan didn't just want sex and blood. He eventually wanted to kill me.

Which was kind of ironic. I'd been dead set — no pun intended — on killing myself when I got here, lest I become a Strigoi. Nathan was offering me that now. Even if he turned me first, he planned on killing me immediately afterward. Either way, I wouldn't have to spend eternity as a Strigoi. I should have welcomed this.

But just then, as my body's addiction screamed for his bite and that bliss, I realized something with startling clarity: *I didn't want to die.* Maybe it was because I'd gone almost a day without a bite, but something small and rebellious woke up in me. I would *not* let him do this to me. I would not let him go after Dimitri. And I sure as hell wasn't going to let him hunt down Lissa.

Pushing through that endorphin cloud that still hung around me, I summoned up as much willpower as I could. I dug deep, remembering my years of training and all the lessons Dimitri had given me. It was hard to access those memories, and I only touched a few. Still, enough came to spur me to action. I lunged forward and punched Nathan.

And accomplished nothing.

He didn't budge. Hell, I don't even know if he felt it. The surprise on his face promptly turned to mirth, and he laughed in that horrible way Strigoi did — cruelly and without any real joy. Then, with the greatest of ease, he slapped me and knocked me across the room. Dimitri had done nearly the same thing when I'd arrived and attacked him. Only I hadn't flown quite as far or had so miniscule an effect on him.

I slammed into the back of the couch, and good God, did it hurt. A wave of dizziness washed over me, and I realized the idiocy of fighting someone vastly stronger than me when I'd been losing blood all week. I managed to straighten up and desperately sought my next course of action. Nathan, for his part, seemed in no hurry to respond to my attack. In fact, he was still laughing.

Glancing around, I latched onto a truly pitiful course of action. Inna stood near me. Moving with a speed that was painfully slow — but better than I expected myself to manage — I reached for her and wrapped my arm around her neck. She yelped in surprise, and I jerked her harder against me.

"Get out of here," I said to Nathan. "Get out of here, or I'll kill her."

He stopped laughing, stared at me for a moment, and then laughed even harder. "Are you serious? Do you honestly think I couldn't stop you if I wanted? And do you honestly think I *care?* Go ahead. Kill her. There are dozens more just like her."

Yeah, that really shouldn't have been a surprise either, but even I was a bit taken aback by how easily he could throw away a faithful servant's life. Okay. Time to go to Plan B. Or maybe it was Plan J? Frankly, I was losing track, and none of them were very good anyway —

"Ow!"

Inna suddenly elbowed me in the stomach. I released her in my surprise. She spun around with a strangled scream and socked me in the face. The blow wasn't as hard as

Nathan's had been, but it still knocked me over. I tried to catch a hold of something — anything — as I fell but failed. I hit the floor, my back slamming against the door. I expected her to come right back at me, but instead, she darted across the room and — God help us all — threw herself into a defensive posture in front of Nathan.

Before I could fully process the weirdness of her trying to protect someone who was willing to let her die, the door suddenly opened. "Ow!" I said again, as it hit me and pushed me aside.

Dimitri swiftly entered. He looked from face to face, and I had no doubt mine showed signs of both Nathan and Inna's attacks. Dimitri's fists clenched, and he turned toward Nathan. It reminded me of their scuffle in the hallway, all rage and malice and bloodlust. I cringed, bracing myself for another horrible confrontation.

"Don't," warned Nathan, face smug. "You know what Galina said. Touch me and you're out of here."

Dimitri strode across the room and came to stand in front of Nathan, knocking Inna aside like a rag doll. "It'll be worth facing her wrath, particularly when I tell her you attacked first. Rose certainly bears the marks of it."

"You wouldn't." He pointed at Inna, who was sitting dazed on the floor from where Dimitri had knocked her over. Despite my own injuries, I began crawling over to her. I had to know if she was all right. "She'll tell the truth."

Now Dimitri looked smug. "You really think Galina will believe a human? No. When I tell her how you attacked me and Rose out of jealousy, she'll let me off. The fact that you'll be so easily defeated will be proof of your weakness. I'll slice your head off and get Rose's stake from the vault. With your last breath, you can watch her drive it through your heart."

Holy crap. That was a little worse than Nathan threatening to burn me — wait.

My stake?

Nathan's face still bore haughty arrogance — at least to me. But I think Dimitri must have seen something that satisfied him, something that made him think he'd gotten the upper hand. He visibly relaxed, his smirk growing larger. "Twice," Dimitri said softly. "Twice I've let you go. Next time . . . next time, you're gone."

I reached Inna and gently held out my hand. "Are you okay?" I murmured.

With a look of hate, she recoiled and scooted away. Nathan's eyes fell on me, and he began backing toward the door.

"No," he said. "Twice I've let her live. Next time *she's* gone. I'm the one in control here, not you."

Nathan opened the door and Inna stood up, stumbling after him. I stared, mouth agape at the events that had just taken place. I didn't know which of them I found more disturbing. Looking up at Dimitri, I grappled with what to ask him first. What were we going to do? Why had Inna defended Nathan? Why had Dimitri let him go? None of those defiant questions came to my lips, though.

Instead, I burst into tears.

# TWENTY-TWO

I didn't cry very often. And I hated it when I did. The last time I'd done it around Dimitri, his arms had immediately encircled me. This time, all I got was a look of coldness and anger.

"This is your fault!" he yelled, fists clenched.

I cringed backward, eyes wide. "But he . . . he attacked me . . ."

"Yes. And Inna. A human! You let a human attack you." He couldn't keep the sneer from his voice. "You are weak. You are incapable of defending yourself — *all because you refuse to be awakened!*"

His voice was terrifying, and the look he gave me . . . well, it scared me almost more than Nathan had. Reaching forward, he jerked me up to my feet.

"If you had just been killed, it would have been your own fault," he said. His fingers dug into my wrist as he shook me. "You have the chance for immortality, for incredible strength! And you're too blind and stubborn to see it."

I swallowed back more tears and rubbed my eyes with the back of my free hand. No doubt I was ruining the makeup I'd so painstakingly put on. My heart was ready to explode out of my chest, I was so afraid. I expected rage and threats from Nathan — but not Dimitri.

*You've forgotten he's a Strigoi,* something whispered in my mind.

I'd gone long enough without a bite and had enough adrenaline kicking me to alertness that my nagging voice was speaking more loudly than it had in a very long time. Dimitri said I was weak because I wasn't Strigoi, but there was more to it than that. I was weak and had been subdued by Nathan and Inna because I was an addict, because I was living a life of blissful ignorance that was taking a toll on my body and my mind. The thought was startling, and I could barely hold onto it. My yearning for vampire endorphins flared up, and the two factions warred in my mind.

I had enough sense not to voice any of those thoughts. I tried for something that would pacify Dimitri instead. "I don't think I'd be stronger than Nathan, even if I was turn — awakened."

He ran a hand over my hair, his cold voice thoughtful. He seemed to be calming down, but his eyes were still angry and impatient. "Perhaps not initially, but your strength of body and will carries over with the change. He's not that much older than either of us — not enough to make a noticeable difference, which is why he keeps backing down when we fight."

"Why do *you* keep backing down?"

I felt his body go rigid, and I realized my question might be read as a slam against his prowess. I swallowed, my fear returning. He hadn't let go of my wrist, and it was starting to hurt.

"Because he's right about one thing," Dimitri said stiffly. "Killing him would bring Galina's wrath down on us. And that's not something I can afford. Yet."

"You said before that you . . . that we . . . had to kill her."

"Yes, and once we do, it'll be easy to seize control of her assets and organization."

"What is her organization exactly?" If I kept distracting him, the anger might go away. The monster might go away.

He shrugged. "All sorts of things. This wealth isn't bought without effort."

"Effort that's illegal and hurts humans?"

"Does it matter?"

I didn't bother with an answer. "But Galina used to be your teacher. Can you really kill her? And I don't mean physically . . . I mean, doesn't it bother you?"

He considered. "I told you before. It's all about strength and weakness. Prey and predator. If we can bring her down — and I have no doubts we can — then she's prey. End of story."

I shivered. It was so harsh, such a stark and scary way of viewing the world. Dimitri released my wrist just then, and a wave of relief ran through me. On shaky legs, I backed up and sat on the couch. For a moment, I feared he'd grab me again, but instead he sat down beside me.

"Why did Inna attack me? Why did she defend Nathan?"

"Because she loves him." Dimitri didn't bother hiding his disgust.

"But how . . . ?"

"Who knows? Part of it is that he's promised to awaken her once she's put in time here." Sydney's warnings came back to me, about why the Alchemists feared that humans would learn about vampires — because humans might want to turn too. "That's what most of the human servants are told."

"Told?"

"Most are unworthy. Or, more often than not, someone gets hungry and finishes the human off."

I was getting sick to my stomach, independent of Dimitri's proximity. "This is all a mess."

"It doesn't have to be." I didn't think he would shake me again, but there was a dangerous glint in his eyes. The monster was only a heartbeat away. "Time's running out. I've been lenient, Roza. Far more lenient than I would be with anyone else."

"Why? Why have you done it?" I wanted — needed — then to hear him say it was because he loved me and that because of that love, he could never force me into anything I didn't want. I needed to hear it so that I could blot out that terrifying, furious creature I'd seen a few minutes ago.

"Because I know how you think. And I know awakening you of your own free will would make you a more important ally. You're independent and strong-minded — that's what makes you valuable."

"An ally, huh?"

Not the woman he loved.

He shifted so that his face hovered over mine. "Didn't I tell you once I'd always be there for you? I'm here. I'll protect you.

We're going to be together. We're meant to be together. You know this." There was more fierceness in his voice than affection.

He kissed my lips, drawing me close. The usual heat flooded me, my body instantly responding to his. But even as my body did one thing, other thoughts were spinning through my mind. I had always thought we were meant to be together. And he had once told me he'd always be there for me. I'd always wanted that too — but I had wanted to be there for him in return. I wanted us to be equals, always watching each other's backs. Today hadn't been like that. I'd been defenseless. Weak. Never, never in my life had I been like that. Even in horrible, out-matched moments, I'd put up a decent fight. At the very least, I'd had the will to fight. Not now. I'd been terrified. I'd been ineffectual. I hadn't been able to do any-thing except sit there pathetically and wait for someone to rescue me. I'd let a *human* get the best of me.

Dimitri said me becoming Strigoi was the solution. For the last week, he'd said that over and over, and while I hadn't agreed to it, I hadn't been as repulsed as I once had been. Lately, it had become a thought float-ing around out there, a far-off way for us to be together. And I did want to be together, especially in moments like this, when we kissed and desire crackled around both of us.

But this time . . . the desire wasn't quite as intense as usual. It was still there, but I couldn't shake the image of how he'd just been. It occurred to me with startling clarity that I was making out with a Strigoi. And that was . . . weird.

Breathing heavy, Dimitri pulled away from my lips for a moment and stared at me. Even with that composed Strigoi expression, I could see that he wanted me — in a lot of ways. It was confusing. He was Dimitri and not Dimitri. Leaning back down, he kissed my cheek, then my chin, and then my neck. His mouth opened wider, and I started to feel the points of his fangs. . . .

"No," I blurted out.

He froze. "What did you say?" My heart started thumping again, as I braced myself for more rage.

"Um . . . no. Not this time."

He pulled back and looked at me, seeming both shocked and annoyed. When he didn't respond, I began to ramble.

"I don't feel good. . . . I'm hurt. I'm afraid to lose the blood, even though I want . . ." Dimitri always said I couldn't lie to him, but I had to try. I put on my best, most passionate and innocent face. "I want it . . . I want to feel the bite . . . but I want to rest first, get stronger . . ."

"Let me awaken you, and you'll be strong again."

"I know," I said, still keeping my voice slightly frantic. I looked away, hoping to increase the façade of confusion. Okay, with my life lately, faking confusion wasn't that hard. "And I'm starting to think . . ."

I heard a sharp intake of breath. "Starting to think what?"

I turned back to him, hoping I could convince him I was seriously considering turning. "I'm starting to think that I don't ever want to be weak again."

I could see it in his face. He believed me. But then, that last part hadn't been a lie. I didn't want to be weak.

"Please . . . I just want to rest. I need to think about it a little more."

There it was, the moment this all weighed on. The truth was, I wasn't just lying to him. I was lying to myself. Because seriously? I wanted that bite. Badly. I'd already gone a long time without one, and my body was screaming for it. I needed the endorphins, needed them more than air or food. And yet, in only one day without them, I'd gained a tiny shard of clarity. The part of me that wanted nothing more than the joy of ignorant ecstasy didn't care about my mind growing clearer, yet I knew, deep inside, that I had to try for a little bit more, even if it meant depriving myself of what I most wanted.

After a lot of thought, Dimitri nodded and stood up. He'd read my words like I'd reached a turning point and was on the verge of accepting. "Rest, then," he said. "And we'll talk later. But Rose . . . we only have two days."

"Two days?"

"Until Galina's deadline. That's how long she gave us. Then I make the decision for you."

"You'll awaken me?" I wasn't entirely sure if death was on the table anymore.

"Yes. It'll be better for all of us if we don't reach that point." He got off the bed and stood up. He paused a moment and reached into his pocket. "Oh. I brought you this."

He handed me a bracelet encrusted with opals and tiny diamonds, almost like it was no big deal. The bracelet was dazzling, and each opal shone with a thousand colors. "Wow. It's . . . it's gorgeous." I slipped it on my wrist, yet somehow, gifts like this didn't mean as much anymore.

With a satisfied look, he leaned down and

kissed me on the forehead. He headed for the door then and left me lying back against the couch, trying desperately to think of anything else except how I wished he would turn around and bite me.

The rest of the day was agonizing.

I'd always read about addicts, about how hard a time people had breaking away from alcohol or illegal drugs. I'd even once witnessed a feeder go kind of crazy when he was removed from service. He'd grown too old, and it was considered hazardous to his health to keep on giving blood to Moroi. I'd watched in amazement as he begged and pleaded to be allowed to stay, how he'd sworn he didn't mind the risk. Even though I'd known he had an addiction, I just couldn't understand why it would be so worth it for him to risk his life like that. Now I did.

In those hours that passed, I would have risked my life to be bitten again. That was actually kind of funny because if I did allow another bite, I *would* be risking my life. I had no doubt more of that cloudy thinking would lead to an acceptance of Dimitri's offer. But with each miserable, bite-deprived second that passed, my thoughts grew incrementally sharper. Oh, I was still a long way away from being free of the dreamy haze of vampire endorphins. When we'd been captured in Spokane, Eddie had been used as a Strigoi blood source, and it had taken him days to recover. Each bit of clarity now made me realize how important it was for me to stay bite free. Not that that knowledge made it any easier on my body.

I had some serious problems here. It seemed like either way, I was destined to become a Strigoi. Dimitri wanted to turn me so that we could reign together as the vampiric equivalent of Bonnie and Clyde. Nathan wanted to turn me in the hopes of hunting down Lissa — and then kill me. Clearly, Dimitri's option was more appealing, but not by much. Not anymore.

Yesterday, I would have said becoming a Strigoi was something I wasn't going to worry about too much. Now, the harsh reality of what it truly meant hit me, and my old feelings returned. Suicide versus existence as a creature of evil. Of course, being a creature of evil meant I could be with Dimitri. . . .

Except it wasn't Dimitri. Was it? It was all so confusing. I again tried to remind myself of what he'd said long ago — that no matter how much a Strigoi seemed like the person I used to know, they weren't. Yet this

Dimitri said he'd been wrong about that.

"It's the endorphins, Rose. They're like drugs . . ." I groaned and buried my face in my hands as I sat on the couch, the TV droning in the background. Lovely. I was talking to myself now.

Supposing I could break this hold Dimitri had over me and this addled state that kept making me think I'd misunderstood Strigoi . . . well, then what? I was back to the original dilemma. No weapons to fight Strigoi with. No weapons with which to kill myself. I was back at their mercy, but at least now I was closer to putting up a good fight. Sure, it would be a losing fight, but I felt that if I stayed off the endorphins a little longer, I'd at least be able to take down Inna. That had to count for something.

And there it was. Off the endorphins. Each time my mind ran through my options and hit a wall, I would spiral back to the physical reality in front of me. I wanted that high back. I wanted that haze of joy back. I needed it back, or surely, I would die. That would be what killed me and freed me from being a Strigoi. . . .

"Damn it!"

I stood up and began pacing around, hoping to distract myself. TV wasn't doing it; that was for sure. If I could just hold out a little longer, I could shake the drug from my system, I could figure out how to save myself and Lissa, and —

Lissa!

Without any debate, I dove into her. If I was in her body and mind, then maybe I wouldn't have to deal with mine for a while. My withdrawal would pass more quickly.

Lissa and her group had returned from the Royal Court a bit more grimly than they arrived. The cold light of morning had made Lissa feel incredibly idiotic about the party's events. Dancing on a table wasn't the worst thing in the world, but looking back over other parties she'd been to that weekend and her social life with Avery made her wonder what had gotten into her. Sometimes, she didn't even feel like herself. And the kiss with Aaron . . . well, that was an entirely different guilt-inducing matter altogether.

"Don't worry about it," Avery told her on the plane. "We all do stupid stuff when we're drunk."

"Not me," groaned Lissa. "This isn't like me." Despite this claim, Lissa had nonetheless agreed to drink mimosas — champagne mixed with orange juice — on the ride back.

Avery smiled. "I don't have anything to compare it to. You seem okay to me. But then, you aren't trying to run off with a human or some non-royal guy."

Lissa smiled back, and her eyes went to Jill, sitting a little ahead of them on the plane. Adrian had spoken to the younger girl earlier, but she was busy with a book now, her biggest concern seeming to be to stay away from Reed. He sat with Simon again, and Lissa was a little surprised to see the guardian eyeing Jill suspiciously. Maybe Reed had told Simon that the younger girl was some kind of threat.

"You're worried about her?" asked Avery, following Lissa's gaze.

"It's not that. . . . I just can't shake the way she looked at me last night."

"She's young. I think she's easily shocked."

Lissa supposed that was true. Yet young or not, there had been something refreshingly clear and honest in the way Jill had called Lissa out. It reminded Lissa of something I might do. And Lissa couldn't rest easy knowing someone like that thought badly of her. Lissa stood up.

"I'll be right back," she told Avery. "I'm going to talk to her."

Jill was obviously astonished when Lissa sat beside her. The younger girl put a bookmark in what she was reading, and whatever she might be feeling, her smile for Lissa was genuine. "Hey."

"Hey," said Lissa. She hadn't had much of the mimosa yet and still controlled enough spirit to see Jill's aura. It was a rich teal blue, interspersed with purple and darker blue. Good, strong colors. "Look, I wanted to apologize for what happened last night . . . what I said . . ."

"Oh," said Jill flushing. "It's okay, really. I mean, things were kind of crazy, and I know you weren't thinking straight. At least, I don't think you were. I don't really know. I've never actually had a drink, so I can't say." Jill's nervousness always seemed to make her oscillate between rambling and silence.

"Yeah, well, I should have been thinking straight *before* I got in that situation. And I'm really sorry for what happened with Reed." Lissa lowered her voice. "No clue what happened there . . . but that wasn't right, what he did and said to you."

Both girls found themselves studying him. He was deep in a book, but suddenly, as though he could sense them watching, his gaze turned toward Jill and Lissa. He glared, and they immediately looked away.

"That definitely wasn't your fault," said Jill. "And, you know, Adrian was there and everything. So it turned out okay."

Lissa worked to keep a straight face. Adrian was sitting out of their view, but if he hadn't been, Lissa had a feeling Jill would have been gazing at him dreamily. Adrian was doing a good deal of gazing of his own at Avery lately, and Lissa could see Jill was never going to leave that little-sister role for him. Yet it seemed clear that Jill was developing a little bit of a crush. It was cute, and even though Lissa knew it was stupid on her part, she couldn't help feeling a bit of relief that Adrian was the object of Jill's affections and not Christian.

"Well, here's hoping for better choices," said Lissa. "And hoping no one thinks too badly of me."

"I don't," said Jill. "And I'm sure Christian won't either."

Lissa frowned, confused for a moment. "Well . . . there's no point in stressing him out over it. It was my stupid mistake; I'll deal with it."

Now Jill frowned. She hesitated before speaking, that old nervousness returning. "But you have to. You have to tell him the truth, right?"

"It's no big deal," said Lissa, surprised at how defensive she suddenly felt. That unpredictable anger started to raise its head.

"But . . . you guys are in a serious relation-ship. . . . You have to always be honest, don't you? I mean, you can't lie to him."

Lissa rolled her eyes. "Jill, you haven't been in a serious relationship either, have you? Have you even gone on one date? I'm not lying to him. I'm just not telling him stuff that's going to freak him out for no reason. It's not the same."

"It is," argued Jill. I could tell how much it killed her to talk back to Lissa, but I admired her boldness. "He has a right to know."

Lissa sighed irritably and stood up. "For-get it. I thought we could have an adult conversation, but apparently not." The withering look she gave Jill made the girl flinch.

Still, back at the Academy, guilt plagued Lissa. Christian greeted her return happily, showering her with kisses and hugs. She firmly believed Jill had overreacted, yet each time Lissa looked at Christian, she kept thinking about that kiss with Aaron. Was it as wrong as Jill had implied? It had been casual and under the influence of alcohol. Lissa knew telling Christian would upset him, though, and she hated to bring that on. Avery, listening as Lissa deliberated, agreed that there was no need to worry about it. Yet, as I looked at her through Lissa's eyes, my impression was that Avery was more worried about what Lissa's emotional reaction would be if she and Christian had a blowout. The morals seemed beside the point; Avery wanted to protect Lissa.

It seemed like it was all going to blow over . . . until later in the day, when Lissa met up with Christian to walk to dinner. His face was a storm cloud as he approached Lissa in her dorm's lobby, his pale blue eyes looking like they could shoot lightning bolts.

"When were you going to tell me?" he demanded. His voice was loud, and several passing people turned in surprise.

Lissa hurried him to a corner, pitching her voice low. "What are you talking about?"

"You *know* what I'm talking about. You using your weekend getaway as a chance to hook up with other guys."

She stared at him for several heavy seconds. Then the truth hit. "Jill told you!"

"Yes. I had to drag it out of her. She showed up to practice with me and was on the verge of tears."

Uncharacteristic anger suddenly burned through Lissa. "She had no right!"

"*You* had no right. Do you honestly think

you could do something like that — without ever letting me know?"

"Christian, it was a stupid drunk kiss, for God's sake. A joke because he saved me from falling off a table. It meant nothing."

Christian's face grew pensive, and Lissa thought for sure he was about to agree with her. "It would have been nothing," he said at last, "if you'd told me yourself. I shouldn't have had to hear it from someone else."

"Jill —"

"— isn't the problem. You are."

Shock stunned Lissa for a moment. "What are you saying?"

"I . . ." Christian suddenly looked weary. He rubbed his eyes. "I don't know. It's just . . . things have been rough lately. I just . . . I'm just not sure if I can deal with all this. You were picking fights with me before you left, and now this?"

"Why won't you listen? It was nothing! Even Avery agreed."

"Oh," said Christian sarcastically, "if Avery agreed, then it must be okay."

Lissa's temper raised its ugly head. "What's that supposed to mean? I thought you liked her."

"I do. But I don't like how you're confiding in her more than me lately."

"You didn't have a problem with me confiding in Rose."

"Avery's not Rose."

"Christian . . ."

He shook his head. "Look, I don't really want to go to dinner anymore. I just need to think."

"When am I going to see you again?" she asked frantically. Her anger had been supplanted by fear.

"I don't know. Later."

He left without another word. Lissa stared after him, aghast as he walked out of the lobby. She wanted to go throw herself at him, beg him to come back and forgive her. There were too many people around, however, and she refused to make a scene — or intrude on his space. Instead, she took off to the only resource she had left: Avery.

"Didn't expect to see you again," Avery said, opening the door to her room. "What are you — Jesus Christ. What's the matter?"

She ushered Lissa in and demanded the story. With a lot of tears and near-hysteric rambling, Lissa related what had happened with Christian. "And I don't know what he meant. Does he want to break up? Will he come talk to me later? Should I go to him?" Lissa buried her face in her hands. "Oh God. You don't think there's anything going

462

on with him and Jill, do you?"

"Jailbait? No," exclaimed Avery. "Of course not. Look, you need to calm down. You're freaking me out. This is going to be okay." Anxiety lined Avery's face, and she went to get Lissa a glass of water. Then, reconsidering, she poured a glass of wine instead.

Sitting alone, Lissa felt her wild emotions torment her. She hated what she'd done. She felt like there was something wrong with her. First she'd alienated me, and now Christian. Why couldn't she keep her friends? What did it take? Was she really going crazy? She felt out of control and desperate. And she —

*Bam!*

Suddenly, and without warning, I was *shoved* out of Lissa's head.

Her thoughts disappeared completely. I'd neither left of my own choice, nor had I been snapped back because of something in my own body. I stood in the room alone, having come to a standstill while pacing and thinking. Never, never had anything like that happened to me. This had been like . . . well, like a physical force. Like a glass wall or force field slamming down in front of me and pushing me back. It had been an outside power. It hadn't come from me.

But what was it? Had it been Lissa? To my knowledge, she'd never been able to feel me in her head. Had that changed? Had she kicked me out? Had her spinning feelings grown so strong that there was no room for me?

I didn't know, and I didn't like any of it. When it had happened, aside from the sensation of being pushed, I'd experienced another strange feeling. It was like a fluttering, as if someone had reached in and tickled my mind. I'd had brief warm and cold flashes, and then it had all stopped once I was out of her head. It had felt invasive.

And it had also felt . . . familiar.

# TWENTY-THREE

Unfortunately, I couldn't remember where I'd felt it before.

Considering everything else that had been happening to me, the fact that I'd even recalled it at all was remarkable. My memories were a little scattered, but I did my best to sift through them, wondering where I had experienced that tickling in my brain. I received no answers, and pondering it all soon became as frustrating as coming up with an escape plan.

And as more time passed, I realized I really did need an escape plan. The endorphin withdrawal was killing me, but I was thinking more and more clearly as the effects left my system. I was astonished at how out of it I'd let myself become. As soon as I'd allowed Dimitri to bite me . . . I'd fallen apart. I'd lost my higher reasoning. I'd lost my strength and skills. I'd become soft and silly and stupid. Well, not entirely. If I'd completely lost it, I'd be a Strigoi now. There was some comfort, at least, in knowing that even while high on bites, some part of me had still fought through and refused to succumb.

Knowing I wasn't as entirely weak as I'd believed helped keep me going. It made it easier to ignore the yearning in my body, to distract myself with bad TV and eating all the food in the little refrigerator. I even stayed awake for a long time in the hopes of exhausting myself. It worked, and I crashed as soon as I hit the pillow, drifting into a dreamless sleep with no withdrawal effects.

I was awakened later when a body slid into bed beside me. I opened my eyes and stared right into Dimitri's red ones. For the first time in days, I looked at him with fear, not love. I kept that off my face, though, and smiled at him. I reached out and touched his face.

"You're back. I missed you."

He caught my hand and kissed my palm. "I had things to do."

The shadows shifted on his face, and I caught the tiniest glimpse of dried blood near his mouth. Grimacing, I rubbed it off with my finger. "So I see."

"It's the natural order, Rose. How are you

feeling?"

"Better. Except . . ."

"What?"

I looked away, conflicted again. The look in his eyes just then was more than simple curiosity. There was concern there — only a little — but it was there. Concern for me. And yet only a moment ago, I'd wiped blood from his face — blood from some poor person whose life had been snuffed out within the last few hours, most likely.

"I was in Lissa's head," I said at last. There was no harm in telling him this. Like Nathan, he knew she was at the Academy. "And . . . I got pushed out."

"Pushed out?"

"Yeah . . . I was seeing through her eyes like I usually do, and then some force . . . I don't know, an invisible hand shoved me out. I've never felt anything like it."

"Maybe it's a new spirit ability."

"Maybe. Except, I've been watching her regularly, and I've never seen her practice or even consider anything like that."

He shrugged slightly and put an arm around me. "Being awakened gives you better senses and accessibility to the world. But it doesn't make you omniscient. I don't know why that happened to you."

"Clearly not omniscient, or else Nathan

wouldn't want information about her so badly. Why is that? Why are the Strigoi fixated on killing the royal lines? We know they've — you've — been doing it, but why? What does it matter? Isn't a victim a victim — especially when plenty of Strigoi used to be royal Moroi?"

"That requires a complicated answer. A large part of hunting Moroi royalty is fear. In your old world, royalty are held above all others. They get the best guardians, the best protection." Yes, that was certainly true. Lissa had discovered that much at Court. "If we can still get to them through that, then what does it say? It means no one is safe. It creates fear, and fear makes people do foolish things. It makes them easier prey."

"That's horrible."

"Prey or —"

"Yeah, yeah, I know. Prey or predator."

His eyes narrowed slightly, apparently not liking the interruption. He let it go. "There's also a benefit to unraveling Moroi leadership. That creates instability, too."

"Or maybe they'd be better off with a change of leadership," I said. He gave me another odd look, and I was a bit startled myself. There I was, thinking like Victor Dashkov again. I realized I should just be quiet. I wasn't behaving like my usual scattered and high self. "What's the rest?"

"The rest . . ." A smile curved up his lips. "The rest is prestige. We do it for the glory of it. For the reputation it gives us and the satisfaction of knowing we're responsible for destroying that which others haven't been able to destroy for centuries."

Simple Strigoi nature. Malice, hunting, and death. There didn't need to be any other reasons.

Dimitri's gaze moved past me to my bedside table. It was where I took off all my jewelry at night and laid it out. All his gifts were there, glittering like some pirate's treasure. Reaching over me, he lifted up the *nazar* on its chain. "You still have this."

"Yup. Not as pretty as your stuff, though." Seeing the blue eye reminded me of my mother. I hadn't thought about her in a very long time. Back in Baia, I'd grown to see Olena as a secondary mother, but now . . . now I kind of wished for my own. Janine Hathaway might not cook and clean, but she was smart and competent. And in some ways, I realized with a start, we thought alike. My traits had come from her, and I knew with certainty that in this situation, she wouldn't have stopped planning escape.

"This I haven't seen before," Dimitri said.

He'd set the *nazar* back down and picked up the plain silver ring Mark had given me. I hadn't worn it since I was last in the Belikov house and had set it on the table next to the *nazar*.

"I got it while I was —" I stopped, realizing I hadn't ever brought up my travels before Novosibirsk.

"While you were what?"

"While I was in your hometown. In Baia."

Dimitri was playing with the ring, moving it from fingertip to fingertip, but he paused and glanced over at me when I said the name. "You were there?" Strangely, we hadn't talked much about that. I'd mentioned Novosibirsk a few times, but that was it.

"I thought that's where you'd be," I explained. "I didn't know that Strigoi did their hunting in cities here. I stayed with your family."

His eyes returned to the ring. He continued playing with it, twirling it and rolling it around. "And?"

"And . . . they were nice. I liked them. I hung out with Viktoria a lot."

"Why wasn't she at school?"

"It was Easter."

"Ah, right. How was she?"

"Fine," I said quickly. I couldn't bring

myself to tell him about that last night with her and Rolan. "Karolina's good too. She reminds me of you. She really laid into some dhampir guys who were causing trouble."

He smiled again, and it was . . . nice. I mean, the fangs still made it creepy, but it didn't have that sinister edge I'd come to expect. There was fondness in his face, true affection that startled me. "I can see Karolina doing that. Did she have her baby yet?"

"Yeah . . ." I was still a little thrown off by that smile. "It was a girl. Zoya."

"Zoya," he repeated, still not looking at me. "Not a bad name. How was Sonya?"

"Okay. I didn't see too much of her. She's a little touchy. . . . Viktoria says it's because of the pregnancy."

"Sonya's pregnant too?"

"Oh. Yeah. Six months, I think."

His smile dimmed a little bit, and he almost seemed concerned. "I suppose it had to happen sooner or later. Her decisions aren't always as wise as Karolina's. Karolina's children were by choice. . . . I'm guessing Sonya's was a surprise."

"Yeah. I kind of got that feeling too."

He ticked off the rest of his family members. "My mother and grandmother?"

"Er, fine. Both of them." This conversation was becoming increasingly strange. Not only was it the first normal one we'd had since I'd arrived, it was also the first time he'd really seemed interested in anything that wasn't Strigoi related or that didn't involve kissing and biting, aside from some reminiscing about our early fights together — and the teasing reminders of sex in the cabin. "Your grandmother scared me a little."

He laughed, and I flinched. It was so, so close to his old laugh. Closer than I'd ever imagined it could be. "Yes, she does that to people."

"And she pretended not to speak English." That was a pretty small detail in the grand scheme of things, but it still kind of pissed me off.

"Yes, she does that too." He continued smiling, voice fond. "Do they all still live together? In that same house?"

"Yup. I saw the books you told me about. The pretty ones — but I couldn't read them."

"That's where I first got into American westerns."

"Man, I loved making fun of you over those."

He chuckled. "Yes, between that, your stereotypes about Eastern European music, and the whole 'comrade' thing, you had plenty of material."

I laughed too. " 'Comrade' and the music were kind of out of line." I'd almost forgotten about my old nickname for him. It didn't fit anymore. "But you brought the cowboy thing on yourself, between the leather duster and —" I stopped. I'd started to mention his duty to help those in need, but that was hardly the case anymore. He didn't notice my lapse.

"And then you left them and came to Novosibirsk?"

"Yeah. I came with those dhampirs I was hunting with . . . those other unpromised ones. I almost didn't, though. Your family wanted me to stay. I thought about doing it."

Dimitri held the ring up to the light, face shadowed with thought. He sighed. "You probably should have."

"They're good people."

"They are," he said softly. "You might have been happy there."

Reaching over, he set the ring back on the table and then turned to me, bringing our mouths together. It was the softest, sweetest kiss he'd given me as a Strigoi, and my already considerable shock increased. The gentleness was fleeting, though, and a few seconds later, our kissing returned to what it usually was, forceful and hungry. I had a feeling he was hungry for more than just kissing, too, despite having fed recently. Pushing aside my confusion over how . . . well, normal and kind he'd seemed while talking about his family, I tried to figure out how I was going to dodge more biting without raising suspicion. My body was still weak and wanting it, but in my head, I felt more like myself than I had in ages.

Dimitri pulled up from the kiss, and I blurted out the first thing that came to mind before he could do anything else. "What's it like?"

"What's what like?"

"Kissing."

He frowned. Score one for me. I'd momentarily baffled an undead creature of the night. Sydney would be proud.

"What do you mean?"

"You said being awakened enhances all the senses. Is kissing different then?"

"Ah." Understanding flashed over his features. "It is, kind of. My sense of smell is stronger than it used to be, so your scent comes through much more intensely . . . your sweat, the shampoo in your hair . . . it's beyond what you can imagine. Intoxicating. And of course, sharper taste and touch make this better." He leaned down and kissed me again, and something about his description made my insides queasy — in a good way. That wasn't supposed to happen. My hope was to distract *him* — not myself.

"When we were outside the other night, the flowers were really strong. If they're strong to me, are they overwhelming to you? I mean, do the scents get to be too much?"

And so it began. I bombarded him with as many questions as I could, asking him about all aspects of Strigoi life. I wanted to know what it was like, how he felt . . . I asked everything with curiosity and enthusiasm, biting my lip and turning thoughtful at all the right places. I could see his interest grow as I spoke, though his attitude was brisk and efficient — in no way resembling our earlier affectionate conversation. He was hoping that I was finally on the verge of agreeing to turn.

As the questioning continued, so also did my outward signs of fatigue. I yawned a lot, lost my train of thought a lot. Finally, I rubbed my eyes with my hands and yawned again. "There's so much I didn't know . . . still don't know. . . ."

"I told you it was amazing."

Honestly, some of it was. Most of it was creepy as hell, but if you got over the whole undead and evil thing, there were definitely some perks to being Strigoi.

"I have more questions," I murmured. I closed my eyes and sighed, then opened them as though forcing myself to stay awake. "But . . . I'm so tired. . . . I still don't feel good. You don't think I have a concussion, do I?"

"No. And once you're awakened, it won't matter anyway."

"But not until you answer the rest of my questions." The words were muffled in a yawn, but he understood. It took him a while to respond.

"Okay. Not until then. But time is running out. I told you that before."

I let my lids drift closed then. "But it's not the second day yet. . . ."

"No," he said quietly. "Not yet."

I lay there, steadying my breathing as much as I could. Would my act work? It was highly possible he would still drink from me even if he thought I was asleep. I was taking a gamble here. One bite, and all my work to fight the withdrawal would be wasted. I'd reset to how I'd been. As it was, I had no clue how I was going to dodge a bite next time . . . but then, I didn't think there'd be a next time. I'd be a Strigoi by then.

Dimitri lay beside me for a few more minutes, and then I felt him move. Inside, I braced myself. Damn. Here it came. The bite. I'd been certain that our kissing was part of the allure of him drinking from me and that if I just fell asleep, the allure would be gone. Apparently not. All my pretending was for nothing. It was all over.

But it wasn't.

He got up and left.

When I heard the door close, I almost thought it was a scam. I thought for sure he was trying to fake me out and still actually stood in the room. Yet when I felt the Strigoi nausea fade, I realized the truth. He really had left me, thinking I needed to sleep. My act had been convincing.

I immediately sat up, turning a few different things over in my mind. In that last bit of his visit, he'd seemed . . . well, he'd reminded me more than ever of the old Dimitri. Sure, he'd still been Strigoi through and through, but there'd been something else. A bit of warmth to his laugh. Sincere interest and affection upon hearing about his family. Had that been it? Had hearing news of his family triggered some piece of his soul buried within the monster? I confess, I felt a little jealous at the thought that *they* might have wrought the change in him that I couldn't. But he'd still had that same warmth in talking about us, just a little. . . .

No, no. I had to stop this. There was no change. No reversal of his state. It was wishful thinking, and the more I regained *my* old self, the more I realized the truth of the situation.

Dimitri's actions had made me recall something. I'd completely forgotten about Oksana's ring. I picked it up from the table and slipped it on my finger. I felt no noticeable change, but if the healing magic was still in it, it might help me. It could expedite my body and mind healing from the withdrawal. If any of Lissa's darkness was bleeding into me, the ring could help dampen that, too.

I sighed. No matter how often I told myself I was free of her, I never would be. She was my best friend. We were connected in a way that few could understand. The denial I'd been living under lifted. I regretted my actions with Adrian now. He'd come to me for help, and I'd thrown his kindness back in his face. Now I was bereft of communication with the outside world.

And thinking of Lissa reminded me again of what had happened earlier when I'd been in her mind. What had pushed me out? I hesitated, pondering my course of action. Lissa was far away and possibly in trouble. Dimitri and the other Strigoi were here.

But . . . I couldn't walk away quite yet. I had to take one more look at her, just a quick one. . . .

I found her in an unexpected place. She was with Deirdre, a counselor on campus. Lissa had been seeing a counselor ever since spirit had begun manifesting, but it had been someone else. Expanding my senses to Lissa's thoughts, I read the story: Her counselor had left shortly after the school's attack. Lissa had been reassigned to Deirdre — who had once counseled me when everyone thought I was going crazy over Mason's death.

Deirdre was a very polished-looking Moroi, always meticulously dressed with her blond hair styled to perfection. She didn't look much older than us, and with me, her counseling method had resembled a police interrogation. With Lissa, she was more gentle. It figured.

"Lissa, we're a little worried about you. Normally, you would have been suspended. I actually stopped that from happening. I keep feeling like there's something going on that you aren't telling me. Some other issue."

Lissa suspended? I again reached in to read the situation and found it. Last night, Lissa and others had been busted for breaking into the library of all places and having an impromptu party complete with alcohol and destruction to some of the property. Good God. My best friend needed to join AA.

Lissa's arms were crossed, her demeanor almost combative. "There's no issue. We were just trying to have fun. I'm sorry for the damage. If you want to suspend me, go ahead."

Deirdre shook her head. "That's not my decision. My concern is the *why* here. I know you used to suffer from depression and other problems because of your, ah, magic. But this feels more like some kind of rebellion."

Rebellion? Oh, it was more than that. Since their fight, Lissa had been unable to find Christian, and it was killing her. She couldn't handle downtime now. All she thought about was him — or me. Partying and risk taking were the only things that could distract her from us.

"Students do this stuff all the time," argued Lissa. "Why is it a big deal for me?"

"Well, because you put yourself in danger. After the library, you were on the verge of breaking into the pool. Swimming while intoxicated is definite cause for alarm."

"Nobody drowned. Even if someone had

started to, I'm sure that between all of us, we could have pulled them out."

"It's just alarming, considering some of the self-destructive behaviors you once exhibited, like the cutting. . . ."

So it went for the next hour, and Lissa did as good a job as I used to in dodging Deirdre's questions. When the session ended, Deirdre said she wasn't going to recommend disciplinary action. She wanted Lissa back for more counseling. Lissa would have actually preferred detention or cleaning boards.

As she stalked furiously across campus, she spotted Christian going in the opposite direction. Hope lit the blackness of her mind like sunshine. "Christian!" she yelled, running up to him.

He stopped, giving her a wary look. "What do you want?"

"What do you mean what do I want?" She wanted to throw herself in his arms and have him tell her everything would be okay. She was upset and overwhelmed and filled with darkness . . . but there was a piece of vulnerability there that desperately needed him. "I haven't been able to find you."

"I've just been . . ." His face darkened. "I don't know. Thinking. Besides, from what I hear, you haven't been too bored." No surprise everyone knew about last night's fiasco. That kind of thing spread like wildfire thanks to the Academy's gossip mill.

"It was nothing," she said. The way he regarded her made her heart ache.

"That's the thing," he said. "Everything's nothing lately. All your partying. Making out with other guys. Lying."

"I haven't been lying!" she exclaimed. "And when are you going to get over Aaron?"

"You aren't telling me the truth. It's the same thing." It was an echo of Jill's sentiment. Lissa barely knew her and was really starting to hate her. "I just can't handle this. I can't be a part of you going back to your days of being a royal girl doing crazy stunts with your other royal friends."

Here's the thing. If Lissa had elaborated on her feelings more, on just how much her guilt and depression were eating her up and making her spin out of control . . . well, I think Christian would have been there for her in an instant. Despite his cynical exterior, he had a good heart — and Lissa owned most of it. Or used to. Now all he could see was her being silly and shallow and returning to a lifestyle he despised.

"I'm not!" she exclaimed. "I'm just . . . I

don't know. It just feels good to sort of let loose."

"I can't do it," he said. "I can't be with you if that's your life now."

Her eyes went wide. "Are you breaking up with me?"

"I'm . . . I don't know. Yeah, I guess." Lissa was so consumed by the shock and horror of this that she didn't really see Christian the way I did, didn't see the agony in his eyes. It destroyed him to have to do this. He was hurting too, and all he saw was the girl he loved changing and becoming someone he couldn't be with. "Things aren't the way they used to be."

"You can't do that," she cried. She didn't see his pain. She saw him as being cruel and unfair. "We need to talk about this — figure it out —"

"The time for talking's past," he argued. "You should have been ready to talk sooner — not now, not when things suddenly aren't going your way."

Lissa didn't know whether she wanted to scream or cry. She just knew she couldn't lose Christian — not after losing me, too. If she lost both of us, there was nothing left for her in the world.

"Please, don't do this," she begged. "I can change."

"I'm sorry," he snapped. "I just don't see any evidence of that."

He turned and abruptly walked away. To her, his departure was harsh and cold. But again, I'd seen the anguish in his eyes. I think he left because he knew if he stayed, he wasn't going to be able to go through with this decision — this decision that hurt but that he felt was right. Lissa started to go after him when a hand suddenly pulled her back. She turned and saw Avery and Adrian standing there. From the looks on their faces, they'd overheard everything.

"Let him go," said Adrian gravely. He'd been the one to grab her. He dropped his hand and laced his fingers through Avery's. "Going after him now's just going to make it worse. Give him his space."

"He can't do this," said Lissa. "He can't do this to me."

"He's upset," said Avery, her concern mirroring Adrian's. "He isn't thinking straight. Wait for him to cool off, and he'll come around."

Lissa stared off after Christian's retreating figure, her heart breaking. "I don't know. I don't know if he will. Oh God. I can't lose him."

My own heart broke. I wanted so badly to go to her, to comfort her and be there for her. She felt so alone, and I felt horrible for leaving her. Something had pushed her into this downward spiral, and I should have been there to help her out of it. That was what best friends did. I needed to be there.

Lissa turned back and looked at Avery. "I'm so confused. . . . I don't know what to do."

Avery met her eyes, but when she did . . . the strangest thing happened. Avery wasn't looking at her. She was looking at *me*.

*Oh jeez. Not you again.*

The voice rang in my head, and *snap!* I was out of Lissa.

There it was, the mental shove, the brush of my mind and waves of hot and cold. I stared around my room, shocked at how abrupt the transition had been. Yet I'd learned something. I knew then that Lissa hadn't been the one to shove me out before or now. Lissa had been too distracted and too distraught. The voice? That hadn't been hers either.

And then, I finally remembered where I'd felt that brushing touch in my head. Oksana. It was the same sensation I'd experienced when she had reached out to my mind, trying to get a feel for my moods and intentions, an action that both she and Mark admitted was invasive and wrong if

485

you weren't bonded to someone.

Carefully, I replayed what had just happened with Lissa. Once again, I saw those last few moments. Blue-gray eyes staring at me — *me,* not Lissa.

Lissa hadn't pushed me out of her head. Avery had.

# TWENTY-FOUR

Avery was a spirit user.

"Oh *shit*."

I sat back down on the bed, my mind reeling. I'd never seen it coming. Hell, no one had. Avery had made a good show of being an air user. Each Moroi had a very low level of control in each element. She'd just barely done enough with air to make it seem like that was her specialization. No one had questioned her further because honestly, who would have ever expected another spirit user around? And since she was out of school, she had no reason to be tested anymore or forced to demonstrate her ability. No one was there to call her on it.

The more I thought about it, the more the little signs were there. The charming personality, the way she could talk people into anything. How many of her interactions were spirit controlled? And was it possible . . . was it possible that Adrian's attraction had been compulsion on her part? I had no reason to feel happy about that, but . . . well, I did.

More to the point, what did Avery want with Lissa? Avery compelling Adrian into liking her wasn't too out there. He was good-looking and came from an important family. He was the queen's great-nephew, and although family members of the current monarch could never inherit the throne immediately afterward, he'd have a good future, one that would always keep him in the highest circles of society.

But Lissa? What was Avery's game there? What did she have to gain? Lissa's behavior all made sense now — the uncharacteristic partying, weird moods, jealousy, fights with Christian . . . Avery was pushing Lissa over the edge, causing her to make horrible choices. Avery was using some sort of compulsion to spin Lissa out of control, alienating her and putting her life in danger. Why? What did Avery want?

It didn't matter. The why wasn't important. The *how* was, as in how I was going to get out of here and back to my best friend.

I looked down at myself, at the delicate silk dress I wore. Suddenly, I hated it. It was a sign of how I'd been, weak and useless. I hastily took it off and ransacked my closet. They'd taken away my jeans and T-shirt, but I'd at least been allowed to keep my hoodie. I put on the green sweaterdress, seeing as it was the sturdiest thing I had, feeling moderately more capable. I slipped the hoodie on over it. It hardly made me feel like a badass warrior, but I *did* feel more competent. Sufficiently dressed for action, I returned to the living room and started that pacing that tended to help me think better — not that I had any reason to believe I was going to come up with new ideas. I'd been trying to for days and days with no luck. *Nothing* was going to change.

"Damn it!" I yelled, feeling better with the outburst. Angry, I flounced into the desk chair, amazed that I hadn't simply thrown it against the wall in my frustration.

The chair wobbled, ever so slightly.

Frowning, I stood up and looked at it. Everything else in this place was state-of-the-art. Odd that I'd have a faulty chair. I knelt down and examined it more closely. There, on one of the legs, was a crack near where the leg joined with the seat. I stared. All of the furniture here was industrial strength, with no obvious joints. I should know, seeing how long I'd beat this chair against the wall when I first arrived. I hadn't even dented it. Where had this crack come from? Slamming it over and over had done nothing.

But I hadn't been the only one to hit it.

That very first day, I'd fought with Dimitri and come after him with the chair. He'd taken it from me and thrown it against the wall. I'd never paid attention to it again, having given up on breaking it. When I'd later tried cracking the window, I'd used an end table because it was heavier. My strength hadn't been able to damage the chair — but his had.

I picked up the chair and immediately slammed it into that diamond-hard window, half-hoping I might kill two birds with one stone. Nope. Both remained intact. So I did it again. And again. I lost track of how many times I slammed that chair into the glass. My hands hurt, and I knew despite my recovery, I still wasn't at full strength. It was infuriating.

Finally, on what felt like my gazillionth try, I looked at the chair and saw the crack had grown bigger. The progress renewed my will and strength. I hit and hit, ignoring the pain as the wood bit into my hands. At long last, I heard a crack, and the leg broke off. I picked it up and stared in amazement. The break hadn't been clean. It was splintered and sharp. Sharp enough to be a stake? I wasn't sure. But I knew for a fact that wood was hard, and if I used enough force, I might be able to hit a Strigoi's heart. It wouldn't kill one, but the blow would stun. I didn't know if it'd be enough to get me out of here, but it was all I had now. And it was a hell of a lot more than I'd had one hour ago.

I sat back on the bed, recovering from my battle with the chair and tossing the make-shift stake back and forth. Okay. I had a weapon now. But what could I do with it? Dimitri's face flashed in my mind's eye. Damn it. There was no question about it. He was the obvious target, the one I'd have to deal with first.

The door suddenly clicked open, and I looked up with alarm. Quickly, I shoved the chair into a dark corner as panic raced through me. No, no. I wasn't ready. I hadn't fully convinced myself to stake him —

It was Inna. She carried a tray but didn't wear her usual subservient expression. The brief look she gave me was filled with hate. I didn't know what she had to be pissed off about. It wasn't like I'd caused her any damage.

Yet.

I strode over like I was going to examine the tray. Lifting the lid, I saw a ham sand-

wich and french fries. It looked good — I
hadn't eaten in a while — but the adrenaline
running through me had shoved any appetite I might have to the background. I
glanced back up at her, smiling sweetly. She
shot me daggers.

*Don't hesitate,* Dimitri had always said.

I didn't.

I jumped at Inna, throwing her so hard
against the floor that her head slammed
back. She looked dazed, but quickly recovered and tried to fight back. I wasn't
drugged up this time — well, not much —
and my years of training and natural
strength finally showed themselves again. I
pressed my body against her, keeping her
firmly in place. Then, I produced the stake
I'd had concealed and pressed those sharp
points against her neck.

It was like being back in the days of pinning Strigoi in alleys. She couldn't see that
my weapon was a chair leg, but the sharp
points got her attention as I dug them into
her throat.

"The code," I said. "What is the code?"

Her only response was a string of obsceni-
ties in Russian. Okay, not a surprise, considering she probably didn't understand me. I
flipped through the meager Russian-English
dictionary in my head. I'd been in the

country long enough to pick up some vocabulary. Admittedly, it was equivalent to a two-year-old's, but even they could communicate.

"Numbers," I said in Russian. "Door." At least, that's what I hoped I said.

She said more impolite things to me, her expression defiant. It really was the Strigoi interrogation all over. My stake bit harder, drawing blood, and I forcibly restrained myself. I might question whether I had the strength to pierce a Strigoi heart with this, but severing a human's vein? Cake. She faltered a little, apparently realizing the same thing.

Again, I attempted my broken Russian. "Kill you. No Nathan. Never . . ." What was the word? The church service came back to me, and I hoped I had it right. "Never eternal life."

It got her attention. Nathan and eternal life. The things most important to her. She bit her lip, still angry, but her tirade had stopped.

"Numbers. Door," I repeated. I pushed the stake in harder, and she cried out in pain.

At last she spoke, rattling off a series of digits. Russian numbers were something I had memorized pretty solidly, at least. They were essential for addresses and phone numbers. She cited seven numbers.

"Again," I said. I made her say it three times and hoped I had it. But there was more. I was pretty sure the outer door had a different code. "Numbers. Door. Two." I felt like a caveman.

Inna stared, not quite getting it.

"Door. Two."

Understanding glinted in her eyes, and she looked mad. I think she'd hoped I wouldn't realize the other door had its own code. More cutting with the stake made her scream seven more numbers. Again, I made her repeat them, realizing I had no way to know if she was telling me the truth — at least until I tried the numbers. For that reason, I decided to keep her around.

I felt guilty about what I did next, but these were desperate times. In guardian training, I'd been taught both to kill and to incapacitate. I did the latter this time, slamming her head back against the floor and rendering her unconscious. Her expression went slack, her eyelids drooping. Damn. I was reduced to hurting teenage humans.

Standing up, I moved to the door and punched in the first set of numbers, hoping I had them right. To my complete and utter astonishment, I did. The electronic lock clicked, but before I could open the door, I just barely made out another click. Someone had unlocked the outer door.

"Shit," I muttered.

I pulled away from the door immediately, picked up Inna's unconscious body, and hurried to the bathroom. I set her in the tub as gently as possible and had just shut the bathroom door when I heard the main door open. I felt the telltale nausea that signaled a Strigoi was nearby. I knew one of the Strigoi could smell a human, and I hoped shutting her away would be enough to mute Inna's scent. I emerged from the hall and found Dimitri in the living room. I grinned at him and ran into his arms.

"You're back," I said happily.

He held me briefly and then stepped back. "Yes." He seemed slightly pleased at the greeting, but soon his face was all business. "Have you made your decision?"

No hello. No *how are you feeling?* My heart sank. This wasn't Dimitri.

"I have more questions."

I went over to the bed and lay down in a casual way, just like we always did. He followed a few moments later and sat on the edge, looking down at me.

"How long will it take?" I asked. "When you awaken me? Is it instantaneous?"

Once more, I launched into an interrogation session. Honestly, I was running out of questions, and at this point, I didn't really want to know the intricacies of becoming Strigoi. I was becoming more and more agitated with each passing moment. I had to act. I had to make use of my fleeting opportunity here.

And yet . . . before I could act, I had to reassure myself that this really wasn't Dimitri. It was stupid. I should know by now. I could see the physical changes. I'd seen his coldness, the brutality. I'd seen him come fresh from a kill. This wasn't the man I'd loved. And yet . . . for that one fleeting moment earlier . . .

With a sigh, Dimitri stretched out beside me. "Rose," he interrupted, "if I didn't know better, I'd say you were stalling for time." Yeah, even as a Strigoi, Dimitri knew how I thought and schemed. I realized if I was going to be convincing, I had to stop playing dumb and remember to be Rose Hathaway.

I put on a look of outrage. "Of course I am! This is a big deal. I came here to kill you, and now you're asking me to join you. You think this is easy for me to do?"

"Do you think it's been easy for me to wait this long?" he asked. "The only ones who get choices are Moroi who willingly kill, like the Ozeras. No one else gets a choice. I didn't get a choice."

"And don't you regret that?"

"No, not now. Now that I'm who I was meant to be." He frowned. "The only thing hurt is my pride — that Nathan forced me and that he acts as though I'm indebted to him. Which is why I'm being kind enough to give you the choice now, for the sake of your pride."

Kind, huh? I looked at him and felt my heart breaking all over again. It was like hearing the news of his death once more. I suddenly grew afraid I might cry. No. No tears. Dimitri always talked about prey and predators. I had to be the predator.

"You're sweating," he said suddenly. "Why?"

*Damn, damn, damn.* Of course I was sweating. I was contemplating staking the man I loved — or thought I'd loved. And along with sweat, I was sure I was giving off pheromones of my agitation. Strigoi could smell all of those things, too.

"Because I'm scared," I whispered. I propped myself up and stroked the edge of his face, trying to memorize all of his features. The eyes. The hair. The shape of his cheekbones. In my imagination, I overlaid the things I remembered. Dark eyes. Tanned skin. Sweet smile. "I . . . I think I'm ready, but it's . . . I don't know. It's such a big thing."

"It'll be the best decision of your life, Roza."

My breathing was growing rapid, and I prayed he'd think it was because of my fear of being turned. "Tell me again. One more time. Why do you want to awaken me so badly?"

A slightly weary look crossed his face. "Because I want you. I've always wanted you."

And that's when I knew. I finally realized the problem. He'd given that same answer over and over, and each time, something about it had bothered me. I'd never been able to pinpoint it, though. Now I could. He wanted me. Wanted me in the way people wanted possessions or collectibles. The Dimitri I'd known . . . the one I'd fallen for and slept with . . . that Dimitri would have said he wanted us to be together because he loved me. There was no love here.

I smiled at him. Leaning down, I kissed him gently. He probably thought I was doing it for the reasons I always did, out of attraction and desire. In truth, it was a goodbye kiss. His mouth answered mine, his lips warm and eager. I held out the kiss a little longer, both to fight back the tears leaking out of my eyes and to lull him into an unsuspecting state. My hand closed around the chair leg, which I'd hidden in my hoodie pocket.

I would never forget Dimitri, not for the rest of my life. And this time, I wouldn't forget his lessons.

With a speed he wasn't ready for, I struck out and plunged the stake through his chest. My strength was there — sliding the stake past the ribs and straight into his heart.

And as I did it, it was like piercing my own heart at the same time.

# TWENTY-FIVE

His eyes widened in shock, lips parting. Even though I knew this wasn't a silver stake, it might as well have been. To run it through his heart, I had had to act as decisively as I would have if delivering a killing blow. I'd had to finally accept *my* Dimitri's death. This one was a Strigoi. There was no future with him. I would not join him.

That still didn't make some part of me want to stop and lie down beside him, though, or at the very least see what happened next. After that initial surprise, his features and breathing had gone still, giving the illusion of death. That's all it was, however — an illusion. I'd seen it before. I probably had five minutes at most before he healed up and shook this off. I had no time to mourn for what was and what might have been. I had to act now. No hesitation.

I ran my hands over him, searching his

clothes for anything that might be of use. I found a set of keys and some cash. I pocketed the keys and started to leave the cash but realized I might actually need it on the off chance I escaped this place. My own money had been taken when I arrived. I also swept up some of the jewelry on the table. Finding buyers for that kind of thing in big Russian cities wasn't too difficult.

*If* I made it to said city. I stood up off the bed and gave Dimitri one last pained look. A few of the tears I'd hidden from him earlier now ran down my face. That was all I could allow myself. If I had a *later*, I'd mourn then. Before leaving, my gaze lingered on the stake. I wanted to take it with me; it was my only weapon. Pulling it out would mean he'd wake up in about a minute. I needed the extra time. With a sigh, I turned my back on him, hoping I'd find a weapon elsewhere.

I sprinted over to the suite's door and punched in the code again. It unlocked, and I stepped into the corridor. Before going to the next door, I examined the one I'd just stepped through. To get into the suite, there was another keypad. Entry also required a code. Backing up a little, I struck and kicked the keypad as hard as I could. I did it twice more, until the tiny red light on it went out.

I didn't know if that would affect the lock on the inside of the suite, but in the movies, damaging electronic locks always seemed to work.

Turning my attention to the next lock, I tried to remember the numbers Inna had told me. They weren't etched as strongly in my head as the first. I punched in seven numbers. The little light stayed red.

"Damn." It was possible she'd lied about this set, but somehow, I suspected my memory was the culprit here. I tried again, knowing the clock was ticking on how long I had until Dimitri came after me. The red light flashed again. What were those numbers? I tried to visualize them in my head and finally decided I wasn't entirely sure about the last two. I reversed their order the next time I put in the code. The light flashed green, and the door unlocked.

Of course, there was a security system of a different sort outside. A Strigoi. And not just any Strigoi: It was Marlen. The one I'd tortured in the alley. The one who hated me because I'd disgraced him in front of Galina. He was clearly on guard duty and looked as though he'd expected a boring night. Me coming out the door was a shock.

That gave me, oh, about a millisecond of surprise. My first thought was to just run at him with as much brute strength as I could. I knew he would do the same to me. In fact . . . that was *exactly* what he'd do.

I stayed where I was, standing so that I could keep the door propped open. He came at me to stop my escape, and I stepped aside, pulling the door open wider. Now, I was neither skilled enough nor was he inept enough to simply get lured in. He stopped in the doorway, trying to get hold of me. This gave me the difficult task of trying to both fend him off and drag him into the corridor behind the door. I stepped back into the doorway, hoping he'd follow. All the while, I had to keep the door open. It was all complicated, and I would have no time to punch in the code again.

We fought in the confined space. The biggest thing I had going for me was that Marlen appeared to be a young Strigoi, which made sense. Galina would want to keep around henchmen she could control. Of course, Strigoi strength and speed compensated for a lack of experience. The fact that he had been a Moroi once also meant he probably had very little training. That also was a bonus for me. Dimitri was a bad-ass Strigoi because he'd trained as a fighter before being turned. This guy had not.

So, Marlen got a couple punches in on

me, one coming dangerously close to my eye. The other caught me in the stomach, knocking the air out of me for half a second. But most of the time, I was able to dodge him pretty well. This seemed to infuriate him. Getting beat up by a teenage girl didn't really score you cool points when you were a Strigoi. At one point, I even faked him out in one direction and came at him with a surprise kick — easier to do than I'd expected in that damned dress — that knocked him back a few steps. I just barely managed to keep my hand in the door when I did it, but that was all I needed. His stumble gave me a few seconds to slip out the door and into the main hall. Unfortunately, when I tried to close it, he was already trying to come through. With my hands, I tried to pull the door shut while kicking him back inside. We struggled this way for a while, and thanks to whatever luck I had left, I got the door closed enough so that only his arm was sticking through. Bracing myself, I pulled the door toward me in one huge, forceful movement. It slammed into Marlen's wrist. I half expected to see his hand detach and pop into the hall, but he'd jerked it back. Even Strigoi had certain instincts to avoid pain.

Gasping — my physical strength still

wasn't all it could be — I backed up. If he knew the code, this had been for nothing. A moment later, the door's handle shook but didn't open. I heard a scream of rage, and then his fists beat on the door.

Score one for me. No, score one for luck. If he'd known the code, I would have been —

*Thud.* Marlen was still beating on the door, and I saw the tiniest dent appear on the metallic surface.

"Oh, crap," I said.

I didn't stick around to see how many hits it'd take him to break it down. I also realized that even if I'd disabled the first lock, Dimitri would just be able to break that one down too. Dimitri . . .

No. I absolutely couldn't think of him now.

As I ran down the hall, heading toward the stairs Dimitri and I traveled before, an unexpected memory suddenly popped into my head. When Dimitri had last threatened Nathan, he'd mentioned getting my stake out of a vault. What vault was that exactly? Was it here on the premises? If so, I certainly didn't have time to look. When weighing the option to search a four-story house full of vampires or run off into the countryside before they found you . . . well, the choice was clear.

And it was in the midst of that thought process that I ran into a human at the top of the stairs. He was older than Inna and carrying a stack of linens that he dropped when we collided. With almost no pause, I grabbed hold of him and swung him against the wall. I had no weapon to threaten him with and wondered how I'd assert my will now. Yet as soon as I had him pinned, he threw up his hands in a defensive gesture and began whimpering in Russian. There'd be no attacks on me here.

Of course, now I had the problem of communicating what I needed. Marlen was still beating on the door, and Dimitri would be up in a couple of minutes. I glared at the human, hoping I looked terrifying. From his expression, I did. I attempted the caveman talk I had with Inna . . . only this time the message was a little harder.

"Stick," I said in Russian. I had no clue what the word for stake was. I pointed at the silver ring I wore and made a slashing motion. "Stick. Where?"

He stared at me in utter confusion and then asked, in perfect English, "Why are you talking like that?"

"Oh for God's sake," I exclaimed. "Where is the vault?"

"Vault?"

"A place they keep weapons?"

He continued staring.

"I'm looking for a silver stake."

"Oh," he said. "That." Uneasily, he cast his eyes in the direction of the pounding.

I pushed him harder against the wall. My heart felt like it would burst out of my chest, but I tried to hide it. I wanted this guy to think I was invincible. "Ignore him. Take me to the vault. Now!"

With a frightened yelp, he nodded eagerly and beckoned me down the stairs. We descended to the second floor and made a sharp turn. The halls here were as twisty as the hedge maze Dimitri had shown me, all decorated in that gold and chandelier style, and I wondered if I'd even be able to get out of the house. Attempting this detour was a risk, but I wasn't sure if I could get outside without being followed. If I was, there'd be a confrontation. I'd need to defend myself.

The human led me down another hall and yet another. Finally, we reached a door that looked like any other. He stopped and peered at me expectantly.

"Open it," I said.

He shook his head. "I don't have the key."

"Well, I certainly don't — wait." I reached

into my pocket and pulled out the keys I'd lifted from Dimitri. There were five keys on the ring. I tried them one at a time, and on the third one, I got a hit. The door opened.

Meanwhile, my guide was casting hasty glances behind him and looked ready to bolt.

"Don't even think about it," I warned. He blanched and stayed put. The room before us wasn't very big, and while its plush white carpet and silver-framed paintings made it look elegant, the room was . . . well, basically, it looked like a junkyard. Boxes and weird objects — a lot of personal items like watches and rings in particular — lay around in no order. "What is this?"

"Magic," he said, still obviously scared out of his mind. "Magic items kept here to fade or be destroyed."

Magic . . . ah. These were items charmed by Moroi magic. Charms always had some kind of effect on Strigoi — usually unpleasant — with stakes being the worst, since they used all four physical elements. It made sense that Strigoi would want to isolate harmful objects and get rid of —

"My stake!"

I ran forward and picked it up, nearly dropping it because my hands were so sweaty. The stake was lying on top of a box with a length of cloth and some weird stones. Studying it, I realized it wasn't actually *my* stake — not that it made a difference for killing Strigoi. This stake was almost identical, save for a small geometric pattern running around its base. It was something guardians did from time to time if they felt particularly attached to their stake: have a design or initials etched into it. Holding this stake, I felt a momentary pang of sadness. This had belonged to someone who'd wielded it proudly once, someone who was now most likely dead. God only knew how many other dozens of stakes were in here, seized from other unfortunate prisoners, but I had no time to search or mourn those who had died.

"Okay, now I want you to take me to . . ." I hesitated. Even with a stake, it'd be a lot better for me if I didn't face any more Strigoi. I had to assume there'd still be a guard at the front door. ". . . Some room on this floor with a window that actually opens. And is far from the stairs."

The guy thought for a moment and then gave a quick nod. "This way."

I followed him through another maze of twisting corridors. "What's your name?"

"Oleg."

"You know," I said. "I'm getting out of

here . . . if you want . . . if you want, I could take you with me." Having someone else — a human, particularly — would definitely slow me down. Yet, my conscience wouldn't let me leave anyone behind in this place.

He gave me an incredulous glance. "Why would I want to do that?" Sydney had definitely been right about humans making great sacrifices for immortality. Oleg and Inna were living proof.

We rounded a corner and came face-to-face with an elaborate set of French doors. Through the etched glass, I could see book-lined shelves, stretching all the way up the walls. A library — a huge one that extended on and on, out of my sight. Better yet, I saw a large bay window opposite me, framed in heavy satin curtains the color of blood.

"Perfect," I said, pushing open the doors.

That was when the nausea hit me. We weren't alone in the room.

Galina sprang up from a chair near the fireplace on the far side of the room. A book dropped from her lap. I had no time to dwell on the oddity of a Strigoi having a fireside read, because she was coming right toward me. I almost might have thought Oleg had set me up, but he was cowering in a corner, his face mirroring the shock I felt. Despite the library's enormous size, she reached me in seconds.

I dodged her initial attack — or tried to, at least. She was *fast*. Aside from Dimitri, the other Strigoi in this house were clearly the B-team, and I had forgotten just how badass a truly skilled Strigoi was. She caught me by my arm and swung me toward her, mouth open and fangs going straight for my neck. I had the stake in my hand and tried awkwardly to at least scratch her with it, but she was holding me too tightly. At last, I managed to duck a little and move my throat out of her range, but all this did was give her the opportunity to grab hold of my hair. She jerked me upright, and I screamed in pain. How she managed to hold onto my hair without ripping it right out was remarkable. Still gripping it, she shoved me into a wall.

When I'd first fought with Dimitri upon my arrival, he'd been rough but hadn't wanted to kill me. Galina did. She'd taken it on faith from Dimitri that I'd be an asset, but it was obvious now that I was a real pain in the ass. Her amnesty had ended, and she was intent on killing me. I at least had the comfort of knowing she probably wouldn't turn me into a Strigoi. I'd be lunch.

A shout suddenly drew my attention to the door. Dimitri stood there, face blazing with anger. Whatever illusions I'd harbored about him being his former self disappeared. That fury radiated around him, his eyes narrowed and fangs showing. The pale skin and red eyes contrasted sharply against each other. He was like a demon sent straight from hell to destroy me. He strode toward us, and the immediate thought in my head was: *Well, at least this'll end things that much faster.*

Except . . . it wasn't me he attacked. It was Galina.

I'm not sure which of us was more surprised, but in that moment, I was totally forgotten. The Strigoi raced toward each other, and I froze, stunned at the terrible beauty of their fight. There was almost a gracefulness to the way they moved, the way they struck out and skillfully dodged each other. I stared a bit longer and then mentally slapped myself into action. This was my chance to get out of here. I couldn't get distracted.

I turned to the bay window, searching frantically for a means to open it. There was none. "Son of a bitch!" Maybe Oleg had set me up after all. Or maybe there was just some mechanism that wasn't apparent to me. Regardless, I felt pretty confident there was one way to get it open.

I ran to the side of the room where Galina had sat and grabbed an ornate wooden chair. It was obvious this window wasn't made of the hard-core glass that had been in my room. This stuff was similar to the library's French doors, delicate and engraved with fanciful designs, even though darkly tinted. It couldn't require that much force to break. After all that fruitless beating in my room, I took a kind of smug satisfaction in slamming the chair into it with as much force as possible. The impact made a huge hole in one side of the window, glass spraying everywhere. A few shards hit my face, but it was nothing to concern me now.

Behind me, the sounds of battle raged on. There were grunts and muffled cries as they fought, as well as the occasional sound of some piece of broken furniture. I yearned to turn around and see what was going on, but I couldn't. I took the chair and swung again, breaking the other half of the window. There was now a huge hole, perfect for me to get out of.

"Rose!"

Dimitri's voice triggered some instinctive response in me. I glanced back and saw him still grappling with Galina. They were both exhausted, but it was clear he was getting the worst of it. But in their fighting, he kept trying to restrain her in a way that exposed her chest to me. His eyes met mine. Back when he'd been a dhampir, we'd rarely needed words to convey our thoughts. This was one of those times. I knew what he wanted me to do. He wanted me to stake her.

I knew I shouldn't. I needed to hop out that window right *now.* I needed to let them keep fighting, even though it seemed obvious Galina was about to win. And yet . . . despite my misgivings, some force drew me across the room, stake poised and ready. Maybe it was because I would never fully lose my pull to Dimitri, no matter what kind of monster he'd become. Maybe it was an unconscious sense of duty, since I knew he'd just saved my life. Or maybe it was because I knew one Strigoi was going to die tonight, and she was the more dangerous.

But she wasn't easy to get hold of. She was fast and strong, and he was having a hard time with her. She kept wriggling around, trying to renew her attack. All she'd need to do was incapacitate him as I had; then it'd just require decapitation or burning to finish him off. I had no doubt she could arrange either.

He managed to turn her slightly, giving

me the best view of her chest I'd had. I moved forward — and then Dimitri slammed into me. I was addled for a moment, wondering why he'd attack me after saving me, until I realized he'd been pushed — by Nathan. Nathan had just entered the library, along with Marlen. It distracted Dimitri but not me. I still had the opening he'd given me on Galina, and I plunged my stake into her chest. It didn't go in as deeply as I would have liked, and she still managed to fight me, bucking hard. I grimaced and pushed forward, knowing the silver had to be affecting her. A moment later, I saw the pain twist her face. She faltered, and I pushed my advantage, shoving the stake in all the way. It took several seconds, but she eventually stopped moving, her body crumpling to the ground.

If the other Strigoi noticed her death, they didn't pay attention. Nathan and Marlen were fixated on Dimitri. Another Strigoi — a female I didn't recognize — soon joined the face-off. I jerked my stake out of Galina and slowly began backing toward the window, hoping I wouldn't attract too much attention. My heart went out to Dimitri. He was outnumbered. I could possibly lend my strength and help him fight. . . .

Of course, my strength was fading. I was

still suffering from days of vampire bites and blood loss. I'd fought two Strigoi tonight and killed a powerful one. That had been my good deed, removing her from the world. The next best thing I could do would be to leave and let these Strigoi finish off Dimitri. The surviving ones would be leaderless and less of a threat. Dimitri would be free of this evil state, his soul finally able to move on to better places. And I would live (hopefully), having helped the world by killing more Strigoi.

I bumped against the windowsill and looked out. Nighttime — not good. The sheer side of the manor was not ideal for climbing, either. It could be done, but it would be time consuming. I didn't have any more time. Directly below the window was a thickly leafed bush of some sort. I couldn't see it clearly and only hoped it wasn't a rosebush or something equally sharp. A second floor drop wouldn't kill me, though. Probably wouldn't even hurt — much.

I climbed over the ledge, briefly meeting Dimitri's gaze as the other Strigoi moved in on him. The words came to me again: *Don't hesitate.* Dimitri's important lesson. But it hadn't been his first one. His first had been about what to do if I was outnumbered and out of options: *Run.*

Time for me to run.
I leapt out the window.

# TWENTY-SIX

I think the profanities that came out of my mouth when I hit the ground would have been understandable in any language. It *hurt.*

The bush was not particularly sharp or pointy, but it wasn't soft by any stretch of the imagination. It broke my fall somewhat, though it didn't save my ankle from twisting underneath me. "Shit!" I said through gritted teeth, climbing to my feet. Russia sure was making me swear a lot. I tested the weight on my ankle and felt a twinge of pain but nothing I couldn't stand on. A sprain, thank God. The ankle wasn't broken, and I'd had worse. Still, it was going to slow down my getaway.

I limped away from the bush, trying to pick up the pace and ignore the pain. Stretching before me was that stupid hedge maze I'd thought was so cool the other night. The sky was cloudy, but I doubted moonlight would have made it easier to navigate. No way was I going to fight that leafy mess. I'd find where it ended and get out through there.

Unfortunately, when I circled the house, I discovered an unhappy truth: The hedge was everywhere. It encircled the estate like some kind of medieval moat. The annoying part was, I doubted Galina had even had it installed for defense. She'd probably done it for the same reason she had crystal chandeliers and antique paintings in the hallways: It was cool.

Well, there was nothing for it, then. I picked an opening to the maze at random and started winding my way through. I had no idea where to go, no strategies for getting out. Shadows lurked everywhere, and I often didn't see dead ends coming until I was right on top of them. The bushes were tall enough that once I was only a little way into the maze, I completely lost sight of the top of the house. If I'd had it as a navigation point, I might have been able to just move in a straight (or nearly straight) line away.

Instead, I wasn't entirely sure if I was going backward or in circles or what. At one point, I was pretty sure I'd passed the same jasmine trellis three times. I tried to think of stories I'd read about people navigating mazes. What did they use? Bread crumbs? Thread? I didn't know, and as more time passed and my ankle grew sorer, I began to get discouraged. I'd killed a Strigoi in my weakened state but couldn't escape some bushes. Embarrassing, really.

"Roza!"

The voice carried distantly on the wind, and I stiffened. No. It couldn't be.

Dimitri. He'd survived.

"Roza, I know you're out there," he called. "I can smell you."

I had a feeling he was bluffing. He wasn't close enough for me to feel sick, and with the cloying perfume of the flowers, I doubted he could scent me yet — even if I was sweating a lot. He was trying to bait me into giving up my location.

With new resolve, I headed down the next twist in the bushes, praying for the exit. *Okay, God,* I thought. *Get me out of this and I'll stop my half-assed churchgoing ways. You got me past a pack of Strigoi tonight. I mean, trapping that one between the doors really shouldn't have worked, so clearly you're on board. Let me get out of here, and I'll . . . I don't know. Donate Adrian's money to the poor. Get baptized. Join a convent. Well, no. Not that last one.*

Dimitri continued his taunting. "I won't kill you, not if you give yourself up. I owe you. You took out Galina for me, and now I'm in charge. Replacing her happened a little ahead of schedule, but that's not a problem. Of course, there aren't many people to control now that Nathan and the others are dead. But that can be fixed."

Unbelievable. He truly had survived those odds. I'd said it before and meant it: Alive or undead, the love of my life was a badass. There was no way he could have defeated those three . . . and yet, well . . . I'd seen him take on crazy odds before. And clearly his being here was proof of his capabilities.

The path ahead of me split, and I randomly chose the right-hand path. It spread off into the darkness, and I breathed a sigh of relief. Score. Despite his breezy commentary, I knew he was also moving through the maze, getting closer and closer. And unlike me, he knew the paths and how to get out of it.

"I'm not upset about you attacking me, either. I would have done it in your place. It's just one more reason why we should be together."

My next turn took me into a dead end filled with climbing moonflowers. I kept my swearing to myself and backtracked.

"You're still dangerous, though. If I find you, I'm probably going to have to kill you. I don't want to, but I'm starting to think there's no way we can both live in this world. Come to me by choice, and I'll awaken you. We'll control Galina's empire together."

I almost laughed. I couldn't have found him if I wanted to in this mess. If I'd had that kind of ability, I'd —

My stomach swirled a little. Oh no. He was getting closer. Did he know it yet? I didn't fully understand how the amount of nausea correlated to distance, but it didn't matter. He was too close, period. How close did he need to be to truly smell me? To hear me walking on the grass? Each second brought him closer to success. Once he had my trail, I was screwed. My heart started racing even more — if that was even possible at this point — and the adrenaline pumping through me numbed my ankle, even though it still slowed me down.

Another dead end spun me around, and I tried to calm myself, knowing panic would make me sloppy. All the while, that nausea grew in increments.

"Even if you get out, where will you go?" he called. "We're in the middle of nowhere." His words were poison, seeping into my skin. If I focused on them, my fear would win, and I'd give up. I'd curl into a ball and let him come for me, and I had no reason to believe he'd let me live. My life could be over in the next few minutes.

A turn to my left led to another wall of glossy green leaves. I sidestepped it quickly and headed in the opposite direction and saw — fields.

Long, vast stretches of grass spread out ahead of me, giving way to trees scattered off in the distance. Against all odds, I'd made it out. Unfortunately, the nausea was strong now. This close, he had to know where I was. I peered around, realizing the truth of his words. We really were in the middle of nowhere. Where could I go? I had no idea where we were.

There. To my left, I saw the faint purple glow on the horizon that I'd noticed the other night. I hadn't realized what it was then, but now I knew. Those were city lights, most likely Novosibirsk, if that was where Galina's gang did most of their deeds. Even if it wasn't Novosibirsk, it was civilization. There would be people there. Safety. I could get help.

I took off at as fast a run as I could manage, feet pounding hard against the ground. Even the adrenaline couldn't block that much impact out, and pain crackled up through my leg with each step. The ankle held, though. I didn't fall or go to a true limp. My breath was hard and ragged, the rest of my muscles still weak from all I'd been through. Even with a goal, I knew that the city was miles away.

And all the while, the nausea grew and grew. Dimitri was close. He had to be out of the maze now, but I couldn't risk looking back. I just kept running toward that purple glow on the horizon, even though it meant I was about to enter a cluster of trees. Maybe, maybe it would provide cover. *You're a fool,* some part of me whispered. *There's nowhere you can hide from him.*

I reached the thin line of trees and slowed just a little, gasping for breath and pressing myself up against a sturdy trunk. I finally dared a look behind me but saw nothing. The house glowed in the distance, surrounded by the darkness of the hedge maze. My sick stomach hadn't grown worse, so it was possible I might have a lead on him. The maze had several exits; he hadn't known where I'd come out.

My moment of respite over, I kept moving, keeping the soft glow of the city lights in sight through the branches. It was only a matter of time before Dimitri found me.

My ankle wasn't going to let me do much more of this. Outrunning him was slowly becoming a fantasy. Leaves left over from last fall crunched as I moved, but I couldn't afford to step around them. I doubted I had to worry anymore about Dimitri sniffing me out. The noise would give me away.

"Rose! I swear it's not too late."

*Shoot.* His voice was close. I looked around frantically. I couldn't see him, but if he was still calling for me, he likely couldn't see me yet either. The city haze was still my guiding star, but there were trees and darkness between me and it. Suddenly, an unexpected person came to mind. Tasha Ozera. She was Christian's aunt, a very formidable lady who was one of the forerunners of teaching Moroi to fight back against Strigoi.

"We can retreat and retreat and let ourselves get backed into corners forever," she'd said once. "Or we can go out and meet the enemy at the time and place *we* choose. Not them."

*Okay, Tasha,* I thought. *Let's see if your advice gets me killed.*

I looked around and located a tree with branches I could reach. Shoving my stake back into my pocket, I grabbed hold of the lowest branch and swung myself up. My ankle complained the whole way, but aside from that, there were enough branches for me to get good hand- and footholds. I kept going until I found a thick, heavy limb that I thought would support my weight. I moved out onto it, staying near the trunk and carefully testing the limb's sturdiness. It held. I took the stake out of my pocket and waited.

A minute or so later, I heard the faint stirring of leaves as Dimitri approached. He was much quieter than I had been. His tall, dark form came into view, a sinister shadow in the night. He moved very slowly, very carefully, eyes roving everywhere and the rest of his senses no doubt working as well.

"Roza . . ." He spoke softly. "I know you're here. You have no chance of running. No chance of hiding."

His gaze was fixed low. He thought I was hiding behind a tree or crouched down. A few more steps. That was all I needed from him. Against the stake, my hand began to sweat, but I couldn't wipe it off. I was frozen, holding so still that I didn't even dare breathe.

"Roza . . ."

The voice caressed my skin, cold and deadly. Still scrutinizing his surroundings, Dimitri took one step forward. Then another. And then another.

I think it occurred to him to look up the instant I jumped. My body slammed into his, knocking him to the ground back-first. He immediately tried to throw me off, just as I tried to drive the stake through his heart. Signs of fatigue and fighting were all over him. Defeating the other Strigoi had taken its toll, though I doubted I was in much better shape. We grappled, and once, I managed to rake the stake against his cheek. He snarled in pain but kept his chest well protected. Over it, I could see where I'd ripped his shirt the first time I'd staked him. The wound had already healed.

"You. Are. Amazing," he said, his words full of both pride and battle fury.

I had no energy for a response. My only goal was his heart. I fought to stay on him, and at last, my stake pierced his chest — but he was too fast. He knocked my hand away before I could fully drive the stake through. In the process, he knocked me off of him. I flew several feet away, mercifully not hitting any trees. I scrambled to my feet, dazed, and saw him coming toward me. He was fast — but not as fast as he'd been in previous fights. We were going to kill ourselves in trying to kill each other.

I'd lost my advantage now, so I ran off

into the trees, knowing he'd be right behind me. I was certain he could outrun me, but if I could accrue just a tiny lead, then maybe I could secure another good attack place and try to —

"Ahhh!"

My scream rang into the night, jarring against the quiet darkness. My foot had gone out from under me, and I was sliding rapidly down a steep hillside, unable to stop myself. There were few trees, but the rocks and my ungainly position made the fall painful, particularly since I was wearing that sweaterdress. How I managed to keep holding the stake was beyond me. I hit the bottom roughly, managed to briefly stand, and then promptly stumbled and fell — into water.

I stared around. On cue, the moon peeked out from the clouds, casting enough light to show me a huge expanse of black, fast-moving water in front of me. I gaped at it, utterly confused, and then I turned in the direction of the city. This was the Ob, the river that ran through Novosibirsk. The river headed right toward it. Glancing behind me, I saw Dimitri standing on top of the ridge. Unlike some of us, he'd apparently been watching where he was going. Either that, or my scream had tipped him off that something was amiss.

It was going to take him less than a minute to come running down after me, though. I looked to either side of me and then in front. Okay. Fast-moving water. Possibly deep. Very wide. It'd take the pressure off my ankle, but I wasn't thrilled about my chances of not drowning. In legends, vampires couldn't cross running water. Man, I wished. That was pure myth.

I did a double take to my left and just barely saw a dark shape over the water. A bridge? It was the best shot I had. I hesitated before going toward it; I needed Dimitri to start coming down here. I was not going to run off and let him pace me up above on the ridge. I needed the time his hill descent would buy me. There. He took one step onto the slope, and I tore off down the shore, not looking back. The bridge grew closer and closer to me, and as it did, I realized just how high it was. I'd misjudged it from where I'd landed. The slopes around the bridge reached farther up the more I ran downriver. I was going to have a hell of a climb.

No problem. I'd worry about that later — by which I meant in about thirty seconds, since that was probably how long it'd take Dimitri to catch up with me. As it was, I could hear his feet splashing through the shallow water on the bank, the sounds growing nearer and nearer. If I could just reach the bridge, if I could just get to high ground and to the other side —

The nausea surged in me. A hand closed around the back of my jacket, jerking me backward. I fell against Dimitri and immediately began fighting him, trying to free myself. But God, I was so, so tired. Every piece of me hurt, and no matter how weary he was, I was worse.

"Stop it!" he yelled, gripping my arms. "Don't you get it? You can't win!"

"Then kill me!" I wriggled, but his hold on my upper arms was too strong, and even holding the stake, I couldn't do anything with it. "You said you would if I didn't surrender myself. Well, guess what? I didn't. I won't. So just get it over with."

That phantom moonlight lit up his face, eradicating the normal shadows and making his skin stark white against the night's backdrop. It was like all the colors in the world had been blanked out. His eyes merely looked dark, but in my mind's eye, they glowed like fire. His expression was cold and calculating.

*Not my Dimitri.*

"It'd take a lot for me to kill you, Rose,"

he said. "This isn't enough."

I wasn't convinced. Still holding onto me with that unbreakable grip, he leaned toward me. He was going to bite me. Those teeth would pierce my skin, and he'd turn me into a monster like him or drink until I was dead. Either way, I'd be too drugged and too stupid to know it. The person who was Rose Hathaway would leave this world without even realizing it.

Pure panic shot through me — even as that part of me that was still in withdrawal cried out for more of those glorious endorphins. No, no. I couldn't allow that. Every nerve I had was set on fire, ramping up for defense, attack, anything . . . anything to stop this. I would not be turned. I *could not* be turned. I wanted so badly to do something to save myself. My whole being was consumed with that urge. I could feel it ready to burst out, ready to —

My hands could touch each other but not Dimitri. With a bit of maneuvering, I used the fingers of my left hand to pry off Oksana's ring. It slipped off and into the mud, just as Dimitri's fangs touched my skin.

It was like a nuclear explosion going off. The ghosts and spirits I'd summoned on the road to Baia burst between us. They were all around, translucent and luminescent in shades of pale green, blue, yellow, and silver. I'd let loose all of my defenses, let myself succumb to my emotions in a way I hadn't been able to when Dimitri first caught me. The ring's healing power had barely kept me in check just now, but it was gone. I had no barriers on my power.

Dimitri sprang back, wide-eyed. Like the Strigoi on the road, he waved his hands around, swatting the spirits as one would mosquitoes. His hands passed right through them, ineffectual. Their attack was more or less ineffectual too. They couldn't physically hurt him, but they could affect the mind, and they were damned distracting. What had Mark said? The dead hate the undead. And from the way these ghosts swarmed Dimitri, it was clear that they did.

I stepped back, scanning the ground below me. There. The ring's silver gleamed up at me from a puddle. I reached down and grabbed it, then ran off and left Dimitri to his fate. He wasn't exactly screaming, but he was making some horrible noises. That tore at me, but I kept going, running toward the bridge. I reached it a minute or so later. It was as high as I'd feared, but it was sturdy and well built, if narrow. It was the kind of country bridge that only one car at a time could cross.

"I've come this far," I muttered, staring up at the bank. It was not only higher than the one I'd fallen down, it was also steeper. I pocketed the ring and stake and then reached out, digging my hands into the ground. I was going to have to half-crawl, half-climb this one. My ankle got a slight reprieve; this was all upper-body strength now. As I climbed, however, I began to notice something. Faint flashes in my periphery. An impression of faces and skulls. And a throbbing pain in the back of my head.

Oh no. This had happened before too. In this panicked state, I couldn't maintain the defenses I usually did to keep the dead away from *myself*. They were now approaching me, more curious than belligerent. But as their numbers grew, it all became as disorienting as what Dimitri was now experiencing.

They couldn't hurt me, but they were freaking me out, and the telltale headache that came with them was starting to make me dizzy. Glancing back toward him, I saw something amazing. Dimitri was *still* coming. He really was a god, a god who brought death closer with each footstep. The ghosts still swarmed him like a cloud, yet he was managing progress, one agonizing step at a time. Turning back, I continued my climb, ignoring my own glowing companions as best I could.

At long last, I reached the top of the bank and stumbled onto the bridge. I could barely stand, my muscles were so weak. I made it a few more steps and then collapsed to my hands and knees. More and more spirits were spinning around, and my head was on the verge of exploding. Dimitri still made his slow progress but was a ways from the bank yet. I tried to stand again, using the bridge's rails for support, and failed. The rough grating on the bridge scraped my bare legs.

"Damn."

I knew what I had to do to save myself, though it could very well end up killing me, too. With trembling hands, I reached into my pocket and pulled out the ring. I shook so badly that I felt certain I'd drop it. Somehow, I held on and managed to slide it onto my finger. A small surge of warmth radiated from it into me, and I felt a tiny bit of control settle into my body. Unfortunately, the ghosts were still there.

The traces of that fear, of dying or turning Strigoi, were still in me, but it had lessened now that I was out of immediate danger. Feeling less unstable, I sought for the barriers and control I usually kept up, desperate to slam them into place and drive my visitors away.

"Go, go, go," I whispered, squeezing my eyes shut. The effort was like pushing on a mountain, an impossible obstacle that no one could have the strength for. This was what Mark had warned about, why I shouldn't do this. The dead were a powerful asset, but once called, they were difficult to get rid of. What had he said? Those who danced on the edge of darkness and insanity shouldn't risk this.

"Go!" I shouted, throwing my last bit of strength into the effort.

One by one, the phantoms around me vanished. I felt my world settle back into its rightful order. Only, when I looked down, I saw that the ghosts had left Dimitri too — as I'd suspected. And just like that, he was on the move again.

"Damn." My word of the night.

I managed to get on my feet this time as he sprinted up the slope. Again, he was slower than usual — but still more than fast enough. I began backing up, never taking my eyes off of him. Getting rid of the ghosts had given me more strength, but not what I needed to get away. Dimitri had won.

"Another shadow-kissed effect?" he asked,

stepping onto the bridge.

"Yeah." I swallowed. "Turns out ghosts don't much like Strigoi."

"You didn't seem to like them much either."

I took another slow step backward. Where could I go? As soon as I turned around to run, he'd be on me.

"So, did I go far enough for you to not want to turn me?" I asked as cheerfully as I could manage.

He gave me a wry, twisted smile. "No. Your shadow-kissed abilities have their uses. . . . Too bad they'll go away when you're awakened." So. That was still his plan. In spite of how much I'd infuriated him, he still wanted to keep me around for eternity.

"You're not going to awaken me," I said.

"Rose, there's no way you can —"

"No."

I climbed up onto the railing of the bridge, swinging one leg over. I knew what had to happen now. He froze.

"What are you doing?"

"I told you. I'll die before I become Strigoi. I won't be like you or the others. I don't want that. You didn't want that, once upon a time." My face felt cold as a night breeze blew over it, the result of stealthy tears on my cheeks.

I swung my other leg over and peered down at the swiftly moving water. We were a lot more than two stories up. I'd hit the water hard, and even if I survived that fall, I didn't have the strength to outswim the current and get to shore. As I stared down, contemplating my death, I thought back to when Dimitri and I sat in the backseat of an SUV once, discussing this very topic.

It was the first time we'd sat near each other, and every place our bodies touched had been warm and wonderful. He'd smelled good — that scent, that scent of being *alive* was gone now, I realized — and he'd been more relaxed than usual, ready to smile. We'd talked about what it meant to be alive and in full control of your soul — and what it meant to become one of the undead, to lose the love and light of life and all those you'd known. We'd looked at each other and agreed death was better than that fate.

Looking at Dimitri now, I had to agree.

"Rose, don't." I heard true panic in his voice. If he lost me over the edge, I was gone. No Strigoi. No awakening. For me to be turned, he needed to kill me by drinking my blood and then feed blood back to me. If I jumped, the water would kill me, not bloodletting. I would be long dead before he found me in the river.

"Please," he begged. There was a plaintive note to his voice, one that startled me. It twisted my heart. It reminded me too much of the living Dimitri, the one who wasn't a monster. The one who'd cared for me and loved me, who'd believed in me and made love to me. This Dimitri, the one who was none of those things, took two careful steps forward, then stopped again. "We need to be together."

"Why?" I asked softly. The word was carried away on the wind, but he heard.

"Because I want you."

I gave him a sad smile, wondering if we'd meet again in the land of the dead. "Wrong answer," I told him.

I let go.

And he was right there, sprinting out to me with that insane Strigoi speed as I started to fall. He reached out and caught one of my arms, dragging me back onto the railing. Well, half-dragging. Only part of me made it over; the rest still hung out over the river.

"Stop fighting me!" he said, trying to pull on the arm he held.

He was in a precarious position himself, straddling the rail as he tried to lean over far enough to get me and actually hold onto me.

"Let go of me!" I yelled back.

But he was too strong and managed to haul most of me over the rail, enough so that I wasn't in total danger of falling again.

See, here's the thing. In that moment before I let go, I really had been contemplating my death. I'd come to terms with it and accepted it. I also, however, had known Dimitri might do something exactly like this. He was just that fast and that good. That was why I was holding my stake in the hand that was dangling free.

I looked him in the eye. "I will always love you."

Then I plunged the stake into his chest.

It wasn't as precise a blow as I would have liked, not with the skilled way he was dodging. I struggled to get the stake in deep enough to his heart, unsure if I could do it from this angle. Then, his struggles stopped. His eyes stared at me, stunned, and his lips parted, almost into a smile, albeit a grisly and pained one.

"That's what I was supposed to say. . . ." he gasped out.

Those were his last words.

His failed attempt to dodge the stake had made him lose his balance on the edge. The stake's magic made the rest easy, stunning him and his reflexes.

Dimitri fell.

He nearly took me with him, and I just barely managed to break free of him and cling to the railing. He dropped down into the darkness — down, down into the blackness of the Ob. A moment later he disappeared from sight.

I stared down after him, wondering if I would see him in the water if I squinted hard enough. But I didn't. The river was too dark and too far away. Clouds moved back over the moon, and darkness fell over everything again. For a moment, staring down and realizing what I'd just done, I wanted to throw myself in after him, because surely there was no way I could go on living now.

*You have to.* My inner voice was much calmer and more confident than it should have been. *The old Dimitri would want you to live. If you really loved him, then you have to go on.*

With a shaking breath, I climbed over the rail and stood back on the bridge, surprisingly grateful for its security. I didn't know how I would go on living, but I knew that I wanted to. I wasn't going to feel fully safe until I was on solid ground, and with my body falling apart, I began to cross the bridge one step at a time. When I was on the other side, I had a choice. Follow the river or the road? They veered off from each other slightly, but both headed roughly in the direction of the city's lights. I opted for the road. I didn't want to be anywhere near the river. I would not think about what had just happened. I *couldn't* think about it. My brain refused. *Worry about staying alive first. Then worry about how you're going to live.*

The road, while clearly rural, was flat and packed and made for easy walking — for anyone else. A light rain began falling, which just added insult to injury. I kept wanting to sit and rest, to curl up in a ball and think of nothing else. *No, no, no.* The light. I had to go toward the light. That almost made me laugh out loud. It was funny, really. Like I was someone having a near-death experience. Then I did laugh. This whole night had been full of near-death experiences. This was the least of them.

It was also the last, and as much as I longed for the city, it was too far away. I'm not sure how long I walked before I finally had to stop and sit. *Just a minute,* I decided. I'd rest for a minute and then keep moving. I *had* to keep moving. If by some crazy chance I'd missed his heart, Dimitri could be climbing out of the river at any moment. Or other surviving Strigoi could be coming after me from the manor.

But I didn't get up in a minute. I think I may have slept, and I honestly don't know how long I'd been sitting there when head-lights suddenly spurred me to alertness. A car slowed down and came to a stop. I man-aged to get to my feet, bracing myself.

No Strigoi got out. Instead, an old human man did. He peered at me and said some-thing in Russian. I shook my head and backed up a step. He leaned into the car and said something, and a moment later, an older woman joined him. She looked at me and her eyes widened, face compassionate. She said something gentle-sounding and held out her hand to me, cautious in the way one would be when approaching a feral animal. I stared at her for several heavy seconds and then pointed at the purple horizon.

"Novosibirsk," I said.

She followed my gesture and nodded. "Novosibirsk." She pointed to me and then to the car. "Novosibirsk."

I hesitated a little longer and then let her lead me into the backseat. She took off her coat and laid it over me, and I noticed then that I was soaked from the rain. I had to be a mess after everything I'd been through tonight. It was a wonder they'd even stopped. The old man began driving again, and it occurred to me I could have just gotten in a car with serial killers. But then, how would that be any different from the rest of my night?

The mental and physical pain were starting to drag me under, and with my last effort, I wet my lips and choked out another gem from my Russian vocabulary.

*"Pazvaneet?"*

The woman looked back at me in surprise. I wasn't sure if I had the word right. I might have just asked for a pay phone instead of a cell phone — or maybe I'd asked for a giraffe — but hopefully the message came through regardless. A moment later, she reached into her purse and handed me a cell phone. Even in Siberia, everyone was wired. With shaking hands, I dialed the number I now had memorized. A female voice answered.

*"Alló."*

"Sydney? This is Rose. . . ."

# TWENTY-SEVEN

I didn't recognize the guy Sydney sent to meet us when we reached Novosibirsk, but he had the same golden tattoo that she did. He was sandy-haired and in his thirties — and human, of course. He looked competent and trustworthy, and as I leaned against the car, he laughed and spoke to the elderly couple like they'd been best friends forever. There was a professional and reassuring air about him, and soon they were smiling too. I'm not sure what he told them, maybe that I was his wayward daughter or something, but they apparently felt good enough to leave me in his hands. I supposed with their jobs, the Alchemist charm in action.

When the old man and woman drove off, his demeanor shifted slightly. He didn't seem as cold as Sydney initially had, but there was no laughing or joking with me. He'd become distinctly businesslike, and I couldn't help but think of the stories of men in black, the people who cleaned up after extraterrestrial encounters in order to keep the world ignorant of the truth.

"Can you walk?" he asked, eyeing me up and down.

"Unclear at this time," I replied.

It turned out I could, just not very well. With his help, I eventually ended up at a town house over in a residential part of the city. I was bleary-eyed and barely able to stay on my feet by that point. There were other people there, but none of them registered. The only thing that mattered was the bedroom someone took me to. I mustered enough strength at that point to break free of the arm supporting me and do a face-plant right in the middle of the bed. I fell asleep instantly.

I awoke to bright sunshine filling my room and voices speaking in hushed tones. Considering everything that I'd been through, I wouldn't have been surprised to see Dimitri, Tatiana, or even Dr. Olendzki from the Academy there. Instead, it was Abe's bearded face that looked down at me, the light making all of his jewelry gleam.

For a moment, his face blurred, and all I saw was dark, dark water — water that threatened to wash me away. Dimitri's last words echoed in my head: *That's what I was supposed to say. . . .* He'd understood that I wanted to hear that he loved me. What would have happened if we'd had a few moments more? Would he have said those words? Would he have meant them? And would it have mattered?

With the same resolve I'd mustered before, I parted the waters swirling in my mind, ordering myself to push aside last night as long as I could. I would drown if I thought about it. Now I had to swim. Abe's face came back into focus.

"Greetings, Zmey," I said weakly. Somehow, him being here didn't surprise me. Sydney would have had to tell her superiors about me, who in turn would have told Abe. "Nice of you to slither on in."

He shook his head, wearing a rueful smile. "I think you've outdone me when it comes to sneaking around dark corners. I thought you were on your way back to Montana."

"Next time, make sure you write a few more details into your bargains. Or just pack me up and send me back to the U.S. for real."

"Oh," he said, "that's exactly what I intend to do." He kept smiling as he said it, but somehow, I had a feeling he wasn't joking. And suddenly, I no longer feared that fate. Going home was starting to sound good.

Mark and Oksana walked over to stand beside him. Their presence was unexpected but welcome. They smiled too, faces melancholy but relieved. I sat up in bed, surprised I could move at all.

"You healed me," I said to Oksana. "I still hurt, but I don't feel like I'm going to die, which I have to think is an improvement."

She nodded. "I did enough to make sure you weren't in immediate danger. I figured I could do the rest when you woke up."

I shook my head. "No, no. I'll recover on my own." I always hated it when Lissa healed me. I didn't want her wasting the strength on me. I also didn't want her inviting spirit's side effects.

*Lissa . . .*

I jerked the covers off of me. "Oh my God! I have to get home. Right now."

Immediately, three pairs of arms blocked my way.

"Hold on," said Mark. "You aren't going anywhere. Oksana only healed you a little. You're a long way from being recovered."

"And you still haven't told us what happened," said Abe, eyes as shrewd as ever. He was someone who needed to know everything, and the mysteries around me probably drove him crazy.

"There's no time! Lissa's in trouble. I have to get back to school." It was all coming back to me. Lissa's erratic behavior and crazy stunts, driven by some kind of compulsion — or super-compulsion, I supposed, seeing as Avery had been able to shove me out of Lissa's head.

"Oh, now you want to go back to Montana?" exclaimed Abe. "Rose, even if there was a plane waiting for you out in the other room, that's a twenty-hour trip, at minimum. And you're in no condition to go anywhere."

I shook my head, still trying to get on my feet. After what I'd faced last night, this group wasn't that much of a threat — well, maybe Mark was — but I could hardly start throwing punches. And yeah, I still wasn't sure what Abe could do.

"You don't get it! Someone's trying to kill Lissa or hurt her or . . ."

Well, I didn't really understand *what* Avery wanted. All I knew was that Avery had somehow been compelling Lissa to do all sorts of reckless things. She had to be amazingly strong in spirit to not only manage those feats but also keep it hidden from Lissa and Adrian. She'd even created a false aura to hide her golden one. I had no idea how that magnitude of power was possible, particularly considering that Avery's fun-loving personality could hardly be called insane. Whatever her scheme, Lissa was at risk. I had to do something.

Removing Abe from the equation, I looked up at Mark and Oksana pleadingly. "It's my bondmate," I explained. "She's in trouble. Someone's trying to hurt her. I have to go to her — you understand why I have to."

And I saw in their faces that they *did* understand. I also knew that in my situation, they'd try exactly the same thing for each other.

Mark sighed. "Rose . . . we'll help you get to her, but we can't do it *now*."

"We'll contact the school," said Abe matter-of-factly. "They'll take care of it."

Right. And how exactly would we do that? Call up Headmaster Lazar and tell him his party-girl daughter was actually corrupting and controlling people with psychic powers and that she needed to be locked up for Lissa's and everyone else's good?

My lack of an answer seemed to make them think they'd convinced me, Abe in particular. "With Oksana's help, you'd probably be in good enough condition to leave tomorrow," he added. "I can book a morning flight the next day."

"Will she be all right until then?" Oksana asked me gently.

"I . . . I don't know . . ." What could Avery do in two days' time? Alienate and embarrass Lissa further? Horrible things, but not permanent or life threatening. Surely, surely . . . she'd be okay that long, right? "Let me see. . . ."

I saw Mark's eyes widen slightly as he realized what I was about to do. Then I saw nothing in the room anymore because I was no longer there. I was in Lissa's head. A new set of sights settled in around me, and for half a second, I thought I stood on the bridge again and was looking down into black waters and a cold death.

Then I gained a grip on what I saw — or rather, what Lissa saw. She was standing on the ledge of a window in some building on campus. It was nighttime. I couldn't tell offhand which building it was, but it didn't matter. Lissa was on what appeared to be the sixth floor, standing there in high heels, laughing about something while the dark ground threatened below. Behind her, I heard Avery's voice.

"Lissa, be careful! You shouldn't be up there."

But it had the same double meaning that permeated everything Avery did. Even as she said those words of caution, I could feel a reckless drive within Lissa, something telling her that it was okay to be where she was and not to worry so much. It was Avery's compulsion. Then, I felt that brushing of my mind, and the annoyed voice.

*You again?*

I was forced back out, back to the bedroom in Novosibirsk. Abe was freaking out, apparently thinking I'd gone into some catatonic fit, and Mark and Oksana were attempting to explain to him what had happened. I blinked and rubbed my head as I gathered myself, and Mark breathed a sigh of relief.

"It's much stranger watching someone do that than it is doing it myself."

"She's in trouble," I said, attempting to get up again. "She's in trouble . . . and I don't know what to do. . . ."

They were right in saying there was no way on earth I could get to Lissa anytime soon. And even if I followed Abe's suggestion and contacted the school . . . I didn't know for sure where Lissa was at or even if anyone there would believe me. I thought about jumping back in and trying to read Lissa's location from her mind, but Avery would likely throw me out again. From what I had briefly felt, Lissa didn't have her cell phone on her — no surprise. There were strict rules about having them in classes, so she usually left hers in her dorm room.

But I knew someone who would have his. And who would believe me.

"Does anyone have a phone?" I asked.

Abe gave me his, and I dialed Adrian's number, surprised I had it memorized. Adrian was mad at me, but he cared about Lissa. He would help her, no matter his grudge toward me. *And* he would believe me when I tried to explain a crazy, spirit-induced plot.

But when the other end of the line picked up, it was his voicemail that answered, not the man himself. "I know how devastated you must be to miss me," his cheery voice said, "but leave a message, and I'll try to ease your agony as soon as possible."

I disconnected, feeling lost. Suddenly, I looked up at Oksana as one of my crazier ideas came to mind.

"You . . . you can do that thing . . . where you actively go in someone's mind and touch their thoughts, right? Like you did to me?"

She grimaced slightly. "Yes, but it's not something I like to do. I don't think it's right."

"Can you compel them once you're in there?"

She looked even more disgusted. "Well, yes, of course . . . the two things are actually very similar. But reaching in someone's mind is one thing and forcing them into some unwanted behavior is an entirely different matter."

"My friend is about to do something dangerous," I said. "It could kill her. She's being compelled, but I can't do anything about it. The bond won't let me actively reach her. I can only watch. If you could reach inside my friend's head and compel her out of danger . . ."

Oksana shook her head. "Supposing morals weren't an issue, I can't reach into someone who's not actually here — let alone someone I've never met."

I raked a hand through my hair, panic setting in. I wished Oksana knew how to walk dreams. That would at least give her the long-distance capability. All of these spirit powers seemed to be one off from each other, each having some additional nuance. Someone who could dream walk might be able to take the next step and visit someone awake.

An even crazier idea came to me. This was a groundbreaking day. "Oksana . . . you can reach into my mind, right?"

"Yes," she reaffirmed.

"If I . . . if I was in my bondmate's head at the time, could you reach into me and *then* reach into her mind? Could I, like, be the link between you guys?"

"I've never heard of anything like that," murmured Mark.

"That's because we've never had this many spirit users and shadow-kissed around before," I pointed out.

Abe, understandably, looked completely lost.

A shadow fell over Oksana's face. "I don't know. . . ."

"Either it works or it doesn't," I said. "If it doesn't, then there's no harm done. But if you can reach her through me . . . you can compel her." She started to speak, and I cut her off. "I know, I know . . . you think it's wrong. But this other spirit user? *She's* the one who's wrong. All you have to do is compel Lissa out of danger. She's ready to jump out a window! Stop her now; then I'll get to her in another day or so and fix things."

And by fix things, I meant ruin Avery's pretty face with a black eye.

In my bizarre life, I'd grown pretty used to people — especially adults — rejecting my outlandish ideas and proclamations. I'd had a hell of a time convincing people that Victor had kidnapped Lissa and an equally hard time making the guardians believe the school was under attack. So when situations like this happened, part of me almost expected resistance. But the thing was, as stable as they were, Oksana and Mark had been fighting with spirit for most of their lives. Crazy was kind of par for the course for them, and after a moment, she didn't argue any further.

"All right," she said. "Give me your hands."

"What's going on?" asked Abe, still totally clueless. I took a small amount of satisfaction in seeing him out of his league for a change.

Mark murmured something to Oksana in Russian and kissed her on the cheek. He was warning her to be careful, not condemning her for her choice. I knew he'd want the same thing if she were in Lissa's place. The love that flashed between them was so deep and so strong that I nearly lost my resolve to do this. That kind of love reminded me of Dimitri, and if I allowed myself to think about him for even a moment more, I was going to relive last night. . . .

I clasped Oksana's hands, a knot of fear

coiling in my stomach. I didn't like the idea of someone being in my head, even though that was a hypocritical sentiment for someone who was constantly traveling into her best friend's mind. Oksana gave me a small smile, though it was obvious she was as nervous as me.

"I'm sorry," she said. "I hate doing this to people. . . ."

And then I felt it, the same thing that had happened when Avery pushed me out. It was like the actual physical sensation of someone touching my brain. I gasped, looking into Oksana's eyes as waves of heat and cold ran through me. Oksana was in my head.

"Now go to your friend," she said.

I did. I focused my thoughts into Lissa and found her still standing on the window's ledge. Better she was there than on the ground, but I still wanted her off and back in the room before something bad happened. That wasn't for me to do, however. I was the taxi, so to speak. Oksana was the one who had to literally talk Lissa off the ledge. Only I had no indication the other woman had come with me. When I'd jumped to Lissa's mind, I'd lost that sense of Oksana. No more tickling of the mind.

*Oksana?* I thought. *Are you there?*

There was no response — not from Oksana, at least. The answer came from a very unexpected source.

*Rose?*

It was Lissa's voice that spoke in my mind. She froze her position in the window and abruptly cut off whatever she'd been laughing about with Avery. I felt Lissa's terror and confusion as she wondered if she was imagining me. She peered around the room, her eyes passing over Avery. Avery recognized something was going on, and her face hardened. I felt the familiar sense of her presence in Lissa's mind and wasn't surprised when Avery tried to shove me out again.

Except — it didn't work.

Avery kicking me out in the past had always felt like an actual shove. I got the impression that when she tried it now, it felt like hitting a brick wall to her. I wasn't so easy to push around anymore. Oksana was with me somehow, lending her strength. Avery was still in Lissa's line of sight, and I saw those adorable blue-gray eyes go wide with shock that she couldn't control me.

*Oh,* I thought. *It's on, bitch!*

*Rose?* Lissa's voice was there again. *Am I going crazy?*

*Not yet. But you have to get down, right*

*now. I think Avery's trying to kill you.*

*Kill me?* I could feel and hear Lissa's incredulity. *She'd never do that.*

*Look, let's not argue it for now. Just get out of the window and call it good.*

I felt the impulse in Lissa, felt her shift and start to put one foot down. Then it was like some core part of her self stopped her. Her foot stayed where it was . . . and slowly began to grow unsteady. . . .

That was Avery at work. I wondered if Oksana, lurking in the background of this bond, could overpower that compulsion. No, Oksana wasn't active here. Her spirit powers had somehow gotten *me* into actively communicating with Lissa, but she was remaining passive. I'd expected to be the bridge and thought Oksana would jump to Lissa's mind and compel her. The situation was reversed, though, and I didn't actually have compulsion powers. All I had was legendary wit and powers of persuasion.

*Lissa, you have to fight Avery,* I said. *She's a spirit user, and she's compelling you. You're one of the strongest compulsion users I know. You should be able to fight her.*

Fear answered me. *I can't . . . I can't compel right now.*

*Why not?*

*Because I've been drinking.*

I mentally groaned. Of course. That was why Avery was always so quick to supply Lissa with alcohol. It numbed spirit, as demonstrated in Adrian's frequent indulgences. Avery had encouraged the drinking so that Lissa's spirit abilities would weaken and give her less resistance. There were a number of times Lissa hadn't been able to gauge exactly how much Avery was drinking; in retrospect, Avery must have been doing a fair amount of faking.

*Then use ordinary willpower,* I told her. *It's possible to resist compulsion.*

It was true. Compulsion wasn't an automatic ticket to world domination. Some people were better at resisting it than others, though a Strigoi or spirit user certainly complicated matters.

I felt Lissa build up her resolve, felt her repeat my words over and over, that she had to be strong and step back off the ledge. She worked to push away that impulse Avery had implanted, and without knowing how, I suddenly found myself pushing on it as well. Lissa and I joined our strength together and started shoving Avery out.

In the physical world, Avery and Lissa's gazes were locked as the psychic struggle continued. Avery's face showed hard concentration that suddenly became overlaid with shock. She'd noticed me fighting her too. Her eyes narrowed, and when she spoke, it was me she addressed and not Lissa.

"Oh," Avery hissed, "you do *not* want to mess with me."

Didn't I?

There was a rush of heat and that feeling of someone reaching into my mind. Only it wasn't Oksana. It was Avery, and she was doing some serious investigation of my thoughts and memories. I understood now what Oksana meant about it being invasive and a violation. It wasn't just looking through someone's eyes; it was spying on their most intimate thoughts.

And then, the world around me dissolved. I stood in a room I didn't recognize. For a moment, I thought I was back in Galina's estate. It certainly had that rich, expensive feel to it. But no. After a moment's examination, I realized this wasn't the same at all. The furnishings were different. Even the vibe was different. Galina's home had been beautiful, but there had been a cold, impersonal feel to it. This place was inviting and clearly well loved. The plush couch had a quilt thrown haphazardly in its corner, as though someone — or maybe two someones — had been cuddling underneath it. And while the room wasn't messy, exactly, there were scattered objects — books, framed photos — that indicated this room was actually used and wasn't just for show.

I walked over to a small bookshelf and picked up one of the framed photos. I nearly dropped it when I saw what it was. It was a picture of Dimitri and me — but I had no memory of it. We stood arm in arm, leaning our faces together to make sure we both got in the shot. I was grinning broadly, and he too wore a joyous smile, one I'd hardly ever seen on him. It softened some of the protective fierceness that usually filled his features and made him look sexier than I'd ever imagined. A piece of that soft brown hair had slipped his ponytail and lay on his cheek. Beyond us was a city that I immediately recognized: Saint Petersburg. I frowned. No, this was definitely a picture that couldn't exist.

I was still studying it when I heard someone walk into the room. When I saw who it was, my heart stopped. I set the photo back on the shelf with shaking hands and took a few steps back.

It was Dimitri.

He wore jeans and a casual red T-shirt that fit the lean muscles of his body perfectly. His hair was down loose and slightly damp, like he'd just gotten out of the shower. He held two mugs and chuckled when he saw me.

"Still not dressed?" he asked, shaking his head. "They're going to be here any minute."

I looked down and saw that I wore plaid flannel pajama bottoms and a tank top. He handed me the mug, and I was too stunned to do anything but take it. I peered into it — hot chocolate — and then looked up at him. There was no red in his eyes, no evil on his face. Only gorgeous warmth and affection. He was my Dimitri, the one who'd loved and protected me. The one with a pure heart and soul..

"Who . . . who's coming?" I asked.

"Lissa and Christian. They're coming for brunch." He gave me a puzzled look. "Are you okay?"

I looked around, again taking in the comforting room. Through a window, I saw a backyard filled with trees and flowers. Sunshine spilled through onto the carpet. I turned back to him and shook my head. "What is this? Where are we?"

His confused expression now turned into a frown. Stepping forward, he took my mug and set his and mine on the shelf. His hands rested on my hips, and I flinched but didn't break away — how could I when he looked so much like my Dimitri?

"This is our house," he said, drawing me near. "In Pennsylvania."

"Pennsylvania . . . are we at the Royal Court?"

He shrugged. "A few miles away."

I slowly shook my head. "No . . . that's not possible. We can't have a home together. And definitely not so close to the others. They'd never let us." If in some crazy world Dimitri and I lived together, we'd have to do it in secret — somewhere remote, like Siberia.

"You insisted," he said with a small smile. "And none of them care. They accept it. Besides, you said we *had* to live near Lissa."

My mind reeled. What was going on? How was this possible? How could I be living with Dimitri — especially so near Moroi? This wasn't right . . . and yet, it felt right. Looking around, I could see how this was my home. I could feel the love in it, feel the connection Dimitri and I had to it. But . . . how could I actually be with Dimitri? Wasn't I supposed to be doing something else? Wasn't I supposed to be *somewhere* else?

"You're a Strigoi," I said at last. "No . . . you're dead. I killed you."

He ran a finger along my cheek, still giving me that rueful smile. "Do I look like I'm dead? Do I look Strigoi?"

No. He looked wonderful and sexy and strong. He was all the things I remembered, all the things I loved. "But you were . . ." I trailed off, still confused. This wasn't right. There was something I had to do, but I still couldn't remember. "What happened?"

His hand returned to my hip, and he pulled me into a tight embrace. "You saved me," he murmured into my ear. "Your love saved me, Roza. You brought me back so that we could be together."

Had I? I had no memory of that, either. But this all seemed so real, and it felt so wonderful. I'd missed his arms around me. He'd held me as a Strigoi, but it had never felt like this. And when he leaned down and kissed me, I knew for sure he wasn't a Strigoi. I didn't know how I could have ever deluded myself back at Galina's. This kiss was alive. It burned within my soul, and as my lips pressed more eagerly into his, I felt that connection, the one that told me there was no one else in the world for me except him.

Only, I couldn't shake the feeling that I wasn't supposed to be here. But where was I supposed to be? Lissa . . . something with Lissa . . .

I broke the kiss but not the embrace. My head rested against his chest. "I really saved you?"

"Your love was too strong. *Our* love was too strong. Not even the undead could keep us apart."

I wanted to believe it. Desperately. But that voice still nagged in my head. . . . Lissa. What about Lissa? Then, it came to me. Lissa and Avery. I had to save Lissa from Avery. I jerked away from Dimitri, and he stared in surprise.

"What are you doing?"

"This isn't real," I said. "This is a trick. You're still Strigoi. We can't be together — not here, not among the Moroi."

"Of course we can." There was hurt in his deep brown eyes, and it tore at my heart. "Don't you want to be with me?"

"I have to go back to Lissa. . . ."

"Let her go," he said, approaching me again. "Let all of it go. Stay here with me — we can have everything we ever wanted, Rose. We can be together every day, wake up together every morning."

"No." I stepped further back. I knew if I didn't, he would kiss me again, and then I'd truly be lost. Lissa needed me. Lissa was trapped. With each passing second, the details about Avery were coming back to me. This was all an illusion.

"Rose?" he asked. There was so much pain in his voice. "What are you doing?"

"I'm sorry," I said, feeling on the verge of tears. Lissa. I had to get to Lissa. "This isn't real. You're gone. You and I can never be together, but I can still help her."

"You love her more than me?"

Lissa had asked me almost the same thing when I'd left to hunt Dimitri. My life was doomed to always be about choosing between them.

"I love you both," I replied.

And with that, I used all of my will to push myself back to Lissa, wherever she was, and tear away from this fantasy. Honestly, I could have spent the rest of my days in that make-believe world, being with Dimitri in that house, waking up with him each morning like he'd said. But it wasn't real. It was too easy, and if I was learning anything, it was that life wasn't easy.

The effort was excruciating, but suddenly, I found myself looking back at the room at St. Vladimir's. I focused on Avery who was staring me and Lissa down. She'd pulled out the memory that tormented me most, attempting to confuse me and tear me from Lissa with a fantasy of what I wanted more than anything else in the world. I'd fought

Avery's mind trap and felt pretty smug about it — despite the ache in my heart. I wished I could communicate directly with her and make a few comments about what I thought of her and her game. That was out of the question, so instead, I threw my will in with Lissa's once more, and together, we stepped down off the ledge and onto the room's floor.

Avery was visibly sweating, and when she realized she'd lost the psychic tug of war, her pretty face turned very ugly. "Fine," she said. "There are easier ways of killing you off."

Reed suddenly entered the room, looking as hostile as ever. I had no idea where he'd come from or how he'd known to show up right then, but he headed straight toward Lissa, hands reaching out. That open window loomed behind her, and it didn't take a genius to guess his intentions. Avery had tried to get Lissa to jump by using compulsion. Reed was just going to push her.

A mental conversation flew between Lissa and me in the space of a heartbeat.

*Okay,* I told her. *Here's the situation. We're going to have to do a little role reversal.*

*What are you talking about?* Fear flooded her, which was understandable, seeing as Reed's hands were seconds away from grabbing her.

*Well,* I said, *I just did the psychic power struggle. Which means you've got to do the fighting. And I'm going to show you how.*

# TWENTY-EIGHT

Lissa didn't have to say anything to express her shock. The feelings of utter astonishment pouring into me said more than any words could have. I, however, had one important word for her:

*Duck!*

I think it was her surprise that made her respond so quickly. She dropped to the floor. The movement was clumsy, but it removed her body from Reed's direct attack and put her (mostly) out of range of the window. He still collided with her shoulder and the side of her head, but it only bumped her and caused a little pain.

Of course, "a little pain" meant totally different things to us. Lissa had been tortured a couple of times, but most of her battles were mental. She'd never been in a one-on-one physical confrontation. Getting thrown against walls was an average occurrence for me, but for her, a small swipe to the head was monumental.

*Crawl away*, I ordered. *Get away from him and the window. Head for the door if possible.*

Lissa started moving on her hands and feet, but she was too slow. Reed caught hold of her hair. I kind of felt like we were playing a game of telephone. With the delay in me giving direction and her figuring out how to respond, I might as well have been passing the message through five people before it got to her. I wished I could control her body like a puppeteer, but I was no spirit user.

*It's going to hurt, but turn around as best you can and hit him.*

Oh, it did hurt. Trying to turn her body meant his hold on her hair tugged that much more painfully. She managed it reasonably well, though, and flailed out at Reed. Her hits weren't that coordinated, but they surprised him enough that he let go of her hair and tried to fend her off. That's when I noticed he wasn't overly coordinated either. He was stronger than her, true, but he obviously had no combat training short of basic hits and throwing his weight around. He hadn't come here for a true fight; he'd come to just push her out the window and be done with it.

*Get away if you can; get away if you can.*

She scrambled across the floor, but unfortunately her escape path didn't give her access to the door. Instead, she backed further into the room until her back hit a rolling desk chair.

*Grab it. Hit him with it.*

Easier said than done. He was right there, still trying to grab her and jerk her to her feet. She caught hold of the chair and tried to roll it into him. I'd wanted her to pick it up and hit him with it, but that wasn't quite so easy for her. She did, however, manage to get to her feet and get the chair between them. I directed her to keep hitting him with it in an effort to get him to retreat. It worked a little, but she didn't quite have the force to truly damage him.

Meanwhile, I half expected Avery to join in the fight. It wouldn't have taken much effort to assist Reed in subduing Lissa. Instead, out of the corner of Lissa's eye, I saw Avery sitting perfectly still, her eyes unfocused and slightly glazed over. Okay. That was weird, but I had no complaints about her being out of the conflict.

As it was, Lissa and Reed were in a stalemate, one I had to get her out of. *You're on the defensive,* I said. *You need to take the attack to him.*

I finally got a direct answer back. *What? I*

*can't do anything like that! I have no clue how!*

*I'll show you. Kick him — preferably between the legs. That'll take down most guys.*

Without words, I tried to send the feelings into her, teaching her the right way to tense muscles and strike out. Steeling herself, she pushed the chair away so that there was nothing between her and Reed. It caught him by surprise, giving her a brief opening. Her leg struck out. It missed the golden spot, but it did hit his knee. That was almost as good. He stumbled back as his leg collapsed underneath him and just managed to grab the chair for support. It tried to roll, which didn't help him any.

Lissa didn't need any urging to sprint for the door at that point — except it was blocked. Simon had just entered. For a moment, both Lissa and I felt relief. A guardian! Guardians were safe. Guardians protected us. The thing was, *this* guardian worked for Avery, and it soon became clear his services went beyond merely keeping Strigoi away from her. He strode in, and with no hesitation grabbed Lissa and dragged her harshly back to the window.

My direction faltered at that moment. I'd been an okay coach at showing her how to fend off a surly teenage boy. But a guardian? And that surly teenage boy had recovered himself and joined Simon to finish the job.

*Compel him!*

It was my last desperate bid. That was Lissa's strength. Unfortunately, while her earlier drinking had metabolized enough to improve her coordination, it was still affecting her control of spirit. She could touch the power — but not very much of it. Her control was clumsy too. Nonetheless, her resolve was strong. She drew as much of the spirit as she could, channeling it into compulsion. Nothing happened. Then, I felt that weird tickling in my head. At first I thought Avery was back on the scene, only rather than someone reaching into me, it was like they reached *through* me.

The power in Lissa surged, and I realized what had happened. Oksana was still there, somewhere in the background, and she was lending her strength again, channeling it through me and into Lissa. Simon froze, and it was almost amusing. He twitched slightly, rocking back and forth as he tried to advance on her and finish the lethal task. It was like he was suspended in Jell-O.

Lissa was hesitant to move, for fear of breaking her control. There was also the issue that Reed was not being compelled, but for the moment, he seemed too confused about what was happening to Simon to react.

"You can't just kill me!" Lissa blurted out. "Don't you think people are going to ask questions when they find my body shoved out a window?

"They won't notice," said Simon stiffly. Even the words required effort. "Not when you're resurrected. And if you can't be, then it was just a tragic accident that befell a troubled girl."

Slowly, slowly, he began breaking out of her compulsion. Her power, while still there, was weakening a little — there was a leak somewhere, and it was dripping out. I suspected it might be Avery's influence or simply Lissa's mental fatigue. Maybe both. A supreme look of satisfaction crossed Simon's features as he lunged forward, and then —

He froze again.

A blazing gold aura lit up in Lissa's periphery. She glanced over just enough to see Adrian in the doorway. The look on his face was comical, but shocked or not, he'd picked up enough to target Simon. It was Adrian's compulsion holding the guardian in place now. Lissa squirmed away, yet again trying to keep out of that damned window's opening.

"Hold him!" Lissa cried.

Adrian grimaced. "I . . . can't. What the hell? It's like there's someone else there. . . ."

"Avery," said Lissa, sparing a brief glance at the other girl. Avery's face had gone pale even for a Moroi. Her breathing was heavy, and her sweating had increased. She was fighting Adrian's compulsion. A few seconds later, Simon broke free yet again. He advanced on Lissa and Adrian, though his movements seemed sluggish.

*Son of a bitch,* I thought.

*Now what?* demanded Lissa.

*Reed. Go for Reed. Get him out of the picture.*

Reed had been frozen during the struggle with Simon, watching with fascination. And like those of the guardian, Reed's actions seemed a little sluggish. Still, he was moving toward Lissa again. Simon had apparently decided Adrian was the immediate threat and was heading that way. Time to see if dividing and conquering would work.

*What about Adrian?* Lissa asked.

*We're going to have to leave him on his own for a minute. Get to Reed. Knock him out.*

*What???*

But she advanced on him anyway, moving with a determination that warmed me with pride. His face curled into a snarl. He was frantic and overconfident, though — not thinking clearly and still moving in an ungainly way. Once more, I attempted to teach Lissa without words. I couldn't make her do anything, but I tried to make her feel what it was like to punch someone. How to draw back her arm, curl her fingers in the proper way, build up the strength. After what I'd seen her do earlier, the best I could hope for was a decent approximation of a punch, enough to keep him off her and create further delay.

And that's when something truly beautiful happened.

Lissa socked him in the nose. And I mean, *socked.* We both heard the impact, heard the nose break. Blood came out. He flew backward, both he and Lissa staring wide-eyed. Never, never would I have thought Lissa capable of something like that. Not sweet, delicate, beautiful Lissa.

I wanted to whoop and dance with joy. But this wasn't over yet.

*Don't stop! Hit him again. You've got to knock him out!*

*I did!* she cried, horrified at what she'd done. Her fist was also in agonizing pain. I hadn't really mentioned that part during my coaching.

*No, you've got to incapacitate him,* I told

her. *I think he and Avery are bonded, and I think she's taking her strength from him.* It made sense now, why he'd frozen when Avery drew power to use compulsion, why he'd known to show up when he had. She'd used their bond to summon him.

And so Lissa went after Reed again. She got in two more punches, one of which knocked his head against the wall. His lips parted and his features went slack. He dropped to the floor, eyes staring vacantly. I wasn't sure if he was entirely unconscious, but he was out of this for the moment. Off to the side, I heard a small cry from Avery.

Lissa turned to Adrian and Simon. Adrian had ceased any attempts at compulsion, because Simon was engaged in a full-on attack. Adrian's face showed he'd taken a few hits of his own, and I figured that, like Lissa, he'd never engaged in this kind of physical combat. Without any need for direction from me, Lissa strode over and turned on her compulsion. Simon jerked in surprise, not stopping his attack, but caught off guard. Lissa was still weak, but the walls around him had dropped a little, just as I'd suspected they would.

"Help me!" cried Lissa.

With the momentary lapse on Simon's part, Adrian tried to wield his spirit too.

Lissa felt and saw the change in his aura as the magic flowed through him. She felt him join her in their psychic attack on Simon, and a moment later, I sensed Oksana joining the fray. I wanted to play general and shout orders, but this wasn't my battle anymore.

Simon's eyes went wide, and he fell to his knees. Lissa could sense the other two spirit users — and was a bit surprised by Oksana's presence — and had the vague impression that they were all doing slightly different things to Simon. Lissa was trying to compel him to stop his attack, to simply sit still. Her brief brush with Adrian's magic told her he was trying to make the guardian sleep, and Oksana was attempting to get Simon to run out of the room.

The conflicting messages and all that power were too much. The last of Simon's defenses fell as all those mixed messages blasted into him, creating a tidal wave of spirit. He collapsed to the floor. With all of their magic combined, the spirit users had knocked him unconscious. Lissa and Adrian turned to Avery, bracing themselves, but there was no need.

As soon as all that spirit had blasted into Simon, Avery had begun screaming. And screaming and screaming. She gripped the sides of her head, the sound of her voice horrible and grating. Lissa and Adrian exchanged glances, unsure how to handle this new development.

"For God's sake," gasped Adrian, exhausted. "How do we shut her up?"

Lissa didn't know. She considered approaching Avery and trying to help her, in spite of all that had happened. But a few seconds later, Avery grew quiet. She didn't pass out like her companions had. She just sat there, staring. Her expression no longer resembled the dazed look she'd had while wielding spirit. It was just . . . blank. Like there was nothing in her at all.

"Wh-what happened?" asked Lissa.

I had the answer. *The spirit flooded from Simon into her. It fried her.*

Lissa was startled. *How could it go from Simon to her?*

*Because they're bonded.*

*You said she was bonded to Reed!*

*She is. She's bonded to both of them.*

Lissa had been too distracted while fighting for her life, but I'd been able to notice everyone's auras through her eyes. Avery — no longer masking hers — had possessed a gold one, just like Adrian and Lissa. Simon and Reed had had nearly identical ones, with ordinary colors — ringed in black.

They were shadow-kissed, both having been brought back from the dead by Avery.

Lissa asked no more questions and simply collapsed into Adrian's arms. There was nothing romantic about it, just a desperate need on both their parts to be close to a friend.

"Why did you come?" she asked him.

"Are you kidding? How could I not? You guys were like a bonfire with all the spirit you were wielding. I felt it all the way across campus." He glanced around. "Man, I have a lot of questions."

"You and me both," she muttered.

*I have to go,* I told Lissa. I felt a little wistful at having to leave them.

*I miss you. When will you be back?*

*Soon.*

*Thank you. Thank you for being there for me.*

*Always.* I suspected I was smiling back in my own body. *Oh, and Lissa? Tell Adrian I'm proud of him.*

The Academy room faded. I was once more sitting on a bed halfway around the world. Abe was looking at me with concern. Mark also was concerned, but he had eyes only for Oksana, who lay down beside me. She looked a little like Avery, pale and sweating. Mark clasped her hand frantically, fear all over him. "Are you okay?"

She smiled. "Just tired. I'll be all right."

I wanted to hug her. "Thank you," I breathed. "Thank you so much."

"I'm glad to have helped," she said. "But I hope I don't have to do it again. It was . . . strange. I'm not sure what role I played there."

"Me either." It had been weird. Sometimes it was like Oksana had actually been there, fighting right along with Lissa and the rest. Other times, I'd felt as though Oksana had merged with me. I shuddered. Too many minds linked together.

"Next time, you have to be by her side," Oksana said. "In the real world."

I looked down at my hands, confused and unsure what to think. The silver ring gleamed up at me. I took it off and handed it to her.

"This ring saved me. Can it heal you even though you made it?"

She held it in her hand for a moment and then gave it back. "No, but like I said, I'll recover. I heal quickly on my own."

It was true. I'd seen Lissa heal remarkably fast in the past. It was part of always having spirit in you. I stared at the ring, and something troubling came to mind. It was a thought that had struck me while riding with the old couple to Novosibirsk, when I'd moved in and out of consciousness.

"Oksana . . . a Strigoi touched this ring. And for a few moments — while he did — it was like . . . well, he was still Strigoi, no question. But while he held it, he was almost like his old self too."

Oksana didn't answer right away. She looked up at Mark, and they held each other's gazes for a long time. He bit his lip and shook his head.

"Don't," he said. "It's a fairy tale."

"What?" I exclaimed. I looked back and forth between him. "If you know something about this — about Strigoi — you have to tell me!"

Mark spoke sharply in Russian, a warning in his voice. Oksana looked equally determined. "It's not our place to withhold information," she replied. She turned to me, face grave. "Mark told you about the Moroi we met long ago . . . the other spirit user?"

I nodded. "Yeah."

"He used to tell a lot of stories — most of which I don't think were true. But one of them . . . well, he claimed he restored a Strigoi to life."

Abe, silent thus far, scoffed. "That *is* a fairy tale."

"What?" My whole world reeled. "How?"

"I don't know. He never elaborated much, and the details often changed. His mind was going, and I think half of what he said was imaginary," she explained.

"He's crazy," said Mark. "It wasn't true. Don't get caught up in an insane man's fantasy. Don't fixate on this. Don't let it become your next vigilante quest. You need to go back to your bondmate."

I swallowed, every emotion in the world churning in my stomach. Was it true? Had a spirit user restored a Strigoi to life? Theoretically . . . well, if spirit users could heal and bring back the dead, why not the undead? And Dimitri . . . Dimitri had definitely seemed altered while holding the ring. Had spirit affected him and touched some piece of his old self? At the time, I'd just assumed it was fond memories of his family affecting him. . . .

"I need to talk to this guy," I murmured.

Not that I knew why. Fairy tale or not, it was too late. I'd done it. I'd killed Dimitri. Nothing would bring him back now, no miracle of spirit. My heart rate increased, and I could hardly breathe. In my mind's eye, I saw him falling, falling . . . falling forever with the stake in his chest. Would he have said he loved me? I would ask myself that for the rest of my life.

Agony and grief flooded me, though at the same time, relief was there too. I had freed Dimitri from a state of evil. I had brought him peace, sending him on to happiness. Maybe he and Mason were together in heaven somewhere, practicing some guardian moves. I had done the right thing. There should be no regret here.

Oblivious to my emotions, Oksana addressed my last statement. "Mark wasn't kidding. This man is crazy — if he's even still alive. The last time we saw him, he could barely hold up a conversation or even use his magic. He ran off into hiding. No one knows where he is — except maybe his brother."

"Enough," warned Mark.

Abe's attention was piqued, however. He leaned forward, shrewd as ever. "What's this man's name?"

"Robert Doru," said Mark after a few hesitant moments.

It was no one I knew, and I realized how pointless this all was. This guy was a lost cause and had likely imagined the whole idea of saving a Strigoi in a fit of insanity. Dimitri was gone. This part of my life was over. I needed to get back to Lissa.

Then I noticed that Abe had gone very still.

"Do you know him?" I asked.

"No. Do *you?*"

"No." I scrutinized Abe's face. "You sure look like you know something, Zmey."

"I know *of* him," Abe clarified. "He's an illegitimate royal. His father had an affair, and Robert was the result. His father actually included him as part of the family. Robert and his half-brother grew quite close, though few knew about it." Of course Abe would know about it, though. "Doru is Robert's mother's last name."

No surprise. Doru wasn't a royal name. "What's his father's last name?"

"Dashkov. Trenton Dashkov."

"That," I told him, "is a name I know."

I had met Trenton Dashkov years ago while accompanying Lissa and her family to a royal holiday party. Trenton had been an old, stooped man then, kind but on the brink of death. Moroi often lived to be over a hundred, but he'd been pushing a hundred and twenty — which was ancient even by their standards. There had been no sign or whisper of him having an illegitimate son, but Trenton's legitimate son had been there. That son had even danced with me, showing a great courtesy to a lowly dhampir girl.

"Trenton is Victor Dashkov's father," I said. "You're saying Robert Doru is Victor

Dashkov's half-brother."

Abe nodded, still watching me closely. Abe, as I'd noted, knew everything. He likely knew my history with Victor.

Oksana frowned. "Victor Dashkov is someone important, isn't he?" Out in their Siberian cottage, she was removed from the turmoil of Moroi politics, unaware that the man who would have been king had been locked away in prison.

I started laughing — but not because I found any humor in the situation. This whole thing was unbelievable, and my hysteria was the only way to let out all the crazy feelings within me. Exasperation. Resignation. Irony.

"What's so funny?" asked Mark, startled.

"Nothing," I said, knowing if I didn't stop laughing, I'd probably start crying. "That's the thing. It's not funny at all."

What a wonderful twist to my life. The only person alive who might know something about saving Strigoi was the half-brother of my greatest living enemy, Victor Dashkov. And the only person who might know where Robert was was Victor himself. Victor had known a lot about spirit, and now I had a good idea where he'd first learned about it.

Not that it mattered. None of this mattered anymore. Victor himself could have been able to convert Strigoi for all the good it would have done me. Dimitri was dead by my hand. He was gone, saved in the only way I knew how. I'd had to choose between him and Lissa once before, and I'd chosen him. Now there could be no question. I'd chosen her. She was real. She was alive. Dimitri was the past.

I'd been staring absentmindedly at the wall, and now I looked up and met Abe squarely in the eyes. "All right, old man," I said. "Pack me up and send me home."

# TWENTY-NINE

The flight was more like thirty hours.

Getting from the middle of Siberia to the middle of Montana wasn't easy. I flew from Novosibirsk to Moscow to Amsterdam to Seattle to Missoula. Four different flights. Five different airports. A lot of running around. It was exhausting, yet when I handed over my passport to get back into the U.S. in Seattle, I felt a strange surge of emotion in me . . . joy and relief.

Before leaving Russia, I had thought Abe might come back with me and finish his task himself, hand-delivering me to whomever had hired him.

"You really are going back now, aren't you?" he asked at the airport. "To the school? You aren't going to get off at one of your stops and disappear?"

I smiled. "No. I'm going back to St. Vladimir's."

"And you'll stay there?" he pressed. He

didn't *quite* look as dangerous as he had in Baia, but I could see a glint of hardness in his eyes.

My smile slipped. "I don't know what's going to happen. I don't have a place there anymore."

"Rose —"

I held up a hand to stop him, surprised at my own determination. "Enough. No after-school specials. You said you were hired to get me back there. It isn't your job to say what I do after that." At least, I hoped not. Whoever wanted me back had to be someone at the Academy. I'd be there soon. They had won. Abe's services were no longer required.

Despite his victory, he didn't look happy about relinquishing me. Glancing up at one of the departure boards, he sighed. "You need to go through security, or you'll miss your flight."

I nodded. "Thanks for . . ." What exactly? His help? ". . . For everything."

I started to turn away, but he touched my shoulder. "Is that all you're wearing?"

Most of my clothing had been scattered around Russia. One of the other Alchemists had located shoes, jeans, and a sweater, but otherwise, I was winging it until I got back to the U.S. "I don't really need anything else," I told him.

Abe arched an eyebrow. Turning to one of his guardians, he made a small gesture toward me. Immediately, the guardian took off his coat and handed it over. The guy was lanky, but the coat was still too big for me.

"No, I don't need —"

"Take it," ordered Abe.

I took it, and then to my further shock, Abe began unwinding the scarf from around his neck. It was one of his nicer ones, too: cashmere, woven with an array of brilliant colors, more suited to the Caribbean than here or Montana. I started to protest this as well, but the look on his face silenced me. I put the scarf around my neck and thanked him, wondering if I'd ever see him again. I didn't bother asking because I had a feeling he wouldn't tell me anyway.

When I finally landed in Missoula thirty hours later, I was pretty sure I didn't want to fly in a plane anytime soon — as in, like, the next five years. Maybe ten. Without any luggage, getting out of the airport was easy. Abe had sent word ahead of my arrival, but I had no idea who they'd send to get me. Alberta, who ran the guardians at St. Vladimir's, seemed a likely choice. Or maybe it would be my mother. I never knew where she was at any given moment, and suddenly,

I really, really wanted to see her. She would be a logical choice too.

So it was with some surprise that I saw that the person waiting for me at the airport's exit was Adrian.

A grin spread over my face, and I picked up the pace. I threw my arms around him, astonishing both of us. "I have never been happier to see you in my life," I said.

He squeezed me tightly and then let me go, regarding me admiringly. "The dreams never do justice to real life, little dhampir. You look amazing." I'd cleaned up after the ordeal with the Strigoi, and Oksana had continued healing me in spite of my protests — even the bruises on my neck, which she had never asked about. I didn't want anyone else to know about those.

"And you look . . ." I studied him. He was dressed as nicely as always, with a three-quarter-length wool coat and green scarf that matched his eyes. His dark brown hair had that crafted messiness he liked, but his face — ah, well. As I'd noted before, Simon had gotten a few good punches on him. One of Adrian's eyes was swollen and ringed with bruises. Nonetheless, thinking about him and everything he'd done . . . well, none of the flaws mattered. ". . . Gorgeous."

"Liar," he said.

"Couldn't Lissa have healed that black eye away?"

"It's a badge of honor. Makes me seem manly. Come on, your carriage awaits."

"Why'd they send you?" I asked as we walked toward the parking lot. "You *are* sober, aren't you?"

Adrian didn't dignify that with an answer. "Well, the school has no official responsibility to you, seeing as you're a dropout and everything. So they weren't really obligated to come get you. None of your other friends can leave campus . . . but me? I'm just a free spirit, hanging out. So I borrowed a car, and here I am."

His words sparked mixed reactions in me. I was touched that he'd taken the trouble to come out here but was bothered by the part about the school having no responsibility to me. Throughout all my travels, I'd gone back and forth in thinking of St. Vladimir's as home . . . yet, in the most technical terms, it truly wasn't anymore. I would just be a visitor.

As we settled into the drive, Adrian caught me up on the aftermath at the school. After the big psychic showdown, I hadn't delved much into Lissa's mind. Oksana had healed my body, but mentally, I was still exhausted and grieving. Even though I'd accomplished what I set out to do, that image of Dimitri falling and falling still haunted me.

"It turns out you were right about Avery bonding Simon and Reed," Adrian said. "From what information we could gather, it sounds like Simon was killed in a fight that Avery witnessed years ago. Everyone thought it was a miracle he survived, not actually realizing the truth."

"She kept her powers hidden like the rest of you," I mused. "And then Reed died later?"

"Well, that's the weird thing," said Adrian, frowning. "No one can really tell when he died. I mean, he's royal. He's been pampered his whole life, right? But based on what we could get out of him — which wasn't much, since they're all pretty messed up now — it sounds like Avery may have intentionally killed him and then brought him back."

"Just like with Lissa," I said, recalling Simon's words during the fight. "Avery wanted to kill her, bring her back, and bond her. But why Lissa of all people?"

"My guess? Because she's a spirit user. Now that spirit's not a secret anymore, it was only a matter of time before Avery heard about Lissa and me. I think Avery thought bonding Lissa would increase her own power. As it was, she was sucking up a lot of energy from those other two." Adrian shook his head. "I wasn't kidding about sensing that spirit all the way across campus. The amounts Avery had to wield to compel so many people, mask her aura, and who knows what else . . . well, it was staggering."

I stared off at the freeway ahead of us, considering the consequences of Avery's actions. "And that's why Reed was so messed up — why he was so angry and ready for a fight. He and Simon were absorbing all that darkness she was producing by using spirit. Just like I do with Lissa."

"Yeah, except you were nothing like these guys. It wasn't so obvious with Simon — he was better at keeping a straight face — but both of them were totally on the edge. And now? They're over the edge. All three of them are."

I recalled Simon staring at nothing and Avery screaming. I shivered. "When you say over the edge . . . ?"

"I mean totally and completely insane. Those three are going to be institutionalized for the rest of their lives."

"From what you . . . we all did?" I asked, aghast.

"Partly," he agreed. "Avery was throwing

all that power at us, and when we threw it back and then some . . . well, I think it was like an overload to their minds. And to be honest, considering how Reed and Simon already were, the stage was probably set for this. With Avery too."

"Mark was right," I murmured.

"Who?"

"The other shadow-kissed guy I met. He was talking about how Lissa and I might be able to heal the darkness away from each other someday. It takes a careful balance of power between the spirit user and the shadow-kissed. I still don't fully get it, but I'm guessing Avery's little circle of three wouldn't have been able to handle that kind of balancing act. I don't think bonding to more than one person is healthy."

"Huh." Adrian didn't say anything for a while and simply pondered all this. Finally, he laughed. "Man, I can't believe you found another spirit user and shadow-kissed person. It's like finding a needle in a haystack, but that kind of thing always happens to you. I can't wait to hear the rest of what you've been doing."

I looked away and rested my cheek against the glass. "It's actually not very interesting."

None of the Academy officials knew about

my role in the showdown with Avery. So it wasn't like anyone questioned me when we got back. They were still doing cleanup and asking Adrian and Lissa a lot of questions. Spirit was still such a new phenomenon that no one knew what to think of what had happened. Avery and her bondmates had been taken away for help, and her father had already gone on a temporary leave of absence.

Adrian signed me in as his guest, which got me a campus pass. Like all visitors, I was also given a list of where I'd stay and what I could and couldn't do. I promptly ignored it.

"I have to go," I told Adrian immediately.

He gave me a knowing smile. "I figured."

"Thank you . . . for coming to get me. I'm sorry I've got to leave you —"

He waved off my worries. "You aren't leaving me. You're back; that's what counts. I've been patient this long — I can hold out a little longer."

I held his eyes for a moment, startled at the warm feelings that suddenly bubbled up within me. I kept them to myself, though, only giving Adrian a quick smile before I set off across campus.

I got a lot of strange looks when I went to Lissa's dorm. It was right after classes had ended, so student traffic was pretty busy with people rushing in or out to get somewhere. Yet, when I passed by, silence fell and people stopped moving and talking. It reminded me of when Lissa and I had been returned to school after running away. We'd been marched through the cafeteria and had received similar treatment from our peers.

Maybe it was just my imagination, but it seemed worse this time. The looks more shocked. The silence heavier. Last time, I think people had believed we'd run off as some sort of prank. This time, no one really knew why I'd left. I'd come out of the school's attack a hero, only to drop out and disappear. I think some of Lissa's dorm mates thought they were seeing a ghost.

Ignoring the gossip and opinions of others was something I had a lot of practice with, and I sprinted past the onlookers without a backward glance, taking the stairs two at a time. I shut myself off to Lissa's feelings as I walked down her hall. It seemed silly, but I wanted to be surprised. I just wanted to open my eyes and see her in person, with no warnings as to how she was feeling or what she was thinking. I knocked on the door.

Adrian had said seeing me in dreams couldn't compare to seeing me in person.

The same was true with Lissa. Being in her head was nothing like being near her in reality. The door opened, and it was like an apparition materializing before me, some sort of heavenly messenger descended from above. I'd never been away from her for this long, and after all this time, part of me wondered if I was imagining this.

Her hand went to her mouth, and she stared at me wide-eyed. I think she felt the same way — and she hadn't even had warning of my visit. She'd just been told I was coming "soon." No doubt I seemed like a phantom to her, too.

And with that reunion . . . it was like I was emerging from a cave — one I'd been in for almost five weeks — into the bright light of day. When Dimitri had turned, I'd felt like I'd lost part of my soul. When I'd left Lissa, another piece had gone. Now, seeing her . . . I began to think maybe my soul might be able to heal. Maybe I could go on after all. I didn't feel 100 percent whole yet, but her presence filled up that missing part of me. I felt more like myself than I had in ages.

A world of questions and confusion hung in the silence between us. In spite of everything we'd been through with Avery, there was still a lot of unresolved business from when I had first left the school. For the first time since I'd set foot on the Academy's grounds, I felt afraid. Afraid that Lissa would reject me or scream at me for what I'd done.

Instead, she drew me into a giant hug. "I knew it," she said. She was already choking on her sobs. "I knew you'd come back."

"Of course," I murmured into her shoulder. "I said I would."

My best friend. I had my best friend back. If I had her, I could recover from what had happened in Siberia. I could go on with my life.

"I'm sorry," she said. "So sorry for what I did."

I pulled away in surprise. Stepping into the room, I shut the door behind us. "Sorry? What do you have to be sorry for?" Despite my joy at seeing her, I'd come here expecting her to still be angry at me for leaving. None of that mess with Avery would have happened if I'd stayed around. I blamed myself.

She sat down on her bed, eyes wet. "For what I said . . . when you left. I had no right to say the things I did. I have no right to control you. And I feel horrible because . . ." She ran a hand over her eyes, trying to dry the worst of the tears. "I feel horrible because I told you I wouldn't bring back Dimitri. I mean, I know it didn't matter, but I should have still offered to —"

"No, no!" I sank down in front of her and grabbed her hands, still awed to be with her again. "Look at me. You have nothing to be sorry for. I said things I shouldn't have, too. It happens when people are upset. Neither of us should beat ourselves up over it. And as for bringing him back . . ." I sighed. "You did the right thing in refusing. Even if we had found him before he'd been turned, it wouldn't have mattered. You can't safely bond more than one person. That's what went wrong with Avery."

Well, that was part of what had gone wrong with Avery. Manipulation and abuse of power had played a huge role too.

Lissa's sobs quieted. "How did you do that, Rose? How were you there at the end when I needed you? How did you know?"

"I was with another spirit user. I met her in Siberia. She can actively reach into people's minds — anyone's, not just those she's bonded to — and communicate. Like Avery could, actually. Oksana reached into me while I connected to you. It's really strange how it all went down." To say the least.

"Another power I don't have," said Lissa

ruefully.

I grinned. "Hey, I have yet to meet any spirit user who can throw a punch like you can. That was poetry in motion, Liss."

She groaned, but I sensed her pleasure at my use of the old nickname. "I hope I don't ever have to do that again. I'm not meant to be a fighter, Rose. You're the one who charges out there. I'm the one who waits with moral support and post-battle healing." She held up her hands and looked at them. "Ugh. No. I definitely don't want to do any more hitting or punching."

"But at least now you know you can. If you ever want to practice . . ."

"No!" She laughed. "I've got too many things to practice with Adrian now — especially after you keep telling me about more and more things that everyone else can do with spirit."

"Fine. Maybe it's best if things go back to how they were."

Her face sobered. "God, I hope so. Rose . . . I did so many stupid things while Avery was around." Through the bond, I felt her greatest regret: Christian. Her heart ached for him, and she'd shed a lot of tears. After having Dimitri ripped away from me, I knew how it felt to lose that kind of love, and I swore to myself that I'd do something to help her. But now wasn't the time. She and I need to reconnect first.

"You couldn't help it, though," I pointed out. "She was too strong with her compulsion — especially when she got you to drink and killed your defenses."

"Yeah, but not everyone knows that or will understand it."

"They'll forget," I said. "They always do."

I understood her angst over her reputation, but I doubted there would be any truly permanent damage — aside from Christian. Adrian and I had analyzed Avery's manipulation and figured things out once we'd paired it with Simon's comment about Lissa having an unfortunate accident. Avery had wanted to make Lissa look unstable in the event Avery somehow didn't have the strength to resurrect her. If Lissa actually died, no one would investigate much. After weeks of crazy, drunken behavior, her losing control and accidentally falling out of a window would be tragic but not completely out of the realm of possibility.

"Spirit's a pain in the ass," Lissa declared. "Everyone wants to take advantage of you — non-users like Victor and users like Avery. I swear, I'd go back on my medication if I wasn't paranoid now about protecting myself from other Avery-type people.

Why'd she want to kill me and not Adrian? Why am I always the target?"

I couldn't help a smile in spite of the grim topic. "Because she wanted you for a minion and him for a boyfriend. She probably wanted a guy who could help escalate her rise in society and couldn't risk killing him in a bonding attempt. Or who knows? Maybe she would have eventually tried him, too. I honestly wouldn't be surprised if she felt threatened by you and wanted to make sure she had the only other known female spirit user under her control. Face it, Liss. We could spend hours trying to figure out how Avery Lazar thinks and get nowhere."

"True, true." She slid off the bed and sat next to me on the floor. "But you know what? I feel like we could talk about anything for hours. You've been here ten minutes, and it's like . . . well, it's like you never left."

"Yeah," I agreed. Before he was a Strigoi, being with Dimitri had always felt natural and right. Being with Lissa also felt natural and right — though it was a different kind of rightness. In my grief over Dimitri, I'd nearly forgotten what I had with her. They were two sides of me.

In that uncanny way she had of guessing thoughts, Lissa said, "I meant what I said earlier. I'm sorry for what I said — about acting like I have some right to dictate your life. I don't. If you decide to stay or guard me, you do that by your choice and your kindness. I want to make sure you live and choose your own life."

"There's nothing 'kind' about it. I've always wanted to protect you. I still do." I sighed. "I just . . . I just had things to take care of. I had to get myself together — and I'm sorry I didn't handle it with you very well." There was a lot of apologizing going on, but I realized that was how it was with people you cared about. You forgave each other and moved on.

Lissa hesitated before asking her next question, but I'd known it was coming. "So . . . what happened? Did you . . . did you find him . . . ?"

At first, I didn't think I wanted to talk about it, but then I realized that I *needed* to. And the thing was, a few different things had gone wrong with Lissa and me before. One had been that she'd taken me for granted. The other had been that I wouldn't tell her the truth — and then I'd resent her for it later. If we were going to patch up this friendship and forgive each other, we had to make sure we didn't repeat the past.

"I did find him," I said at last.

And I launched into the story, telling her everything that had happened to me: my travels, the Belikovs, the Alchemists, Oksana and Mark, the unpromised, and of course, Dimitri. Just as Lissa had joked earlier, we talked for hours. I poured out my heart to her, and she listened without judgment. Her face was compassionate the whole time, and when I reached the end, I was sobbing, all the love and rage and anguish I'd been holding onto since that night on the bridge exploding out of me. I hadn't told anyone else in Novosibirsk exactly where I'd been during my time with Dimitri. I hadn't dared tell anyone I'd been a blood whore for a Strigoi. I had stayed vague, hoping if I didn't talk about it, then maybe it wouldn't be real.

Now, with Lissa, I had to accept the reality of everything and truly *feel* it: I had killed the man I loved.

A knock at the door jolted us out of a world that contained only her and me. I glanced at the clock and was startled to see it was almost curfew time. I wondered if I was being thrown out. But when Lissa opened the door — after I'd hastily dried my eyes — the waiting dorm worker had a message of a different sort.

"Alberta wants to see you," the woman

told me. "She thought you might be here."

Lissa and I exchanged glances. "When? Now?" I asked.

The woman shrugged. "From the way she sounded? Yeah, I'd say now. Or sooner." She shut the door. Alberta was the captain of the guardians on campus, and when she spoke, people acted.

"I wonder what this is about?" asked Lissa.

I stood up, hating to leave. "Any number of things, I imagine. I'll go see her and then head back to guest housing. Not that I'll sleep. I have no clue what time zone I'm in anymore."

Lissa gave me a parting hug, one we both had a hard time letting go of. "Good luck."

I started to turn the door's handle and then thought of something. I slipped the silver ring off of my finger and handed it to Lissa.

"Is this the ring you — oh!" She wrapped her hand around it, her face growing enraptured.

"Can you feel the magic in it?" I asked.

"Yeah . . . it's weak, but it's in there." She held the ring up to the light and stared at it. She probably wasn't going to notice when I left because I had a feeling she'd be studying the ring all night. "It's so strange. I can almost immediately feel how she did this."

"Mark said we probably had a while to go before we could do the healing they do . . . but maybe you could figure out how to make charms while we wait?"

Her jade green eyes were still on the ring. "Yeah . . . I think I might."

I smiled at her excitement and tried to leave again, but she caught my arm. "Hey . . . Rose . . . I know I'll see you tomorrow, but . . ."

"But what?"

"I just wanted to say, after everything that's happened . . . well, I don't want us to ever have this kind of separation again. I mean, I know we can't be together every single second — and that's kind of creepy anyway — but we're bonded for a reason. We're meant to look out for each other and be there for each other."

Her words sent a shiver through me, like we were wrapped in powers greater than ourselves. "We will be."

"No, I mean . . . you're always there for me. Every time, I'm in danger, and you come rushing in to save me. Not anymore."

"You don't want me to save you anymore?"

"That's not what I meant! I want to be there for you too, Rose. If I can throw a punch, I can do anything. Even though that *really* hurt." She exhaled in frustration. "God, I'm not making any sense. Look, the point is, if you ever have to go off alone, take me with you. Don't leave me behind."

"Liss—"

"I'm serious." Her luminous beauty burned with determination and purpose. "Whatever obstacles you have to go against, I'm going to be there for you. Don't go alone. Swear to me that if you ever decide to take off again, you'll bring me. We'll do it together."

I started to protest as a million fears came to my mind. How could I risk her life? Yet looking at her, I knew she was right. For better or worse, we had a bond we couldn't escape. Lissa was indeed tied to that piece of my soul, and we were stronger fighting together than apart.

"Okay," I said, clasping her hand. "I swear it. The next time I go do something stupid that might get me killed, you can come along."

# THIRTY

Alberta was waiting for me in the front office of the guardians' administrative building. Alberta's role as captain here was remarkable considering the lower numbers of women in our ranks. She was in her fifties and one of the toughest women I'd met. Her sandy hair was showing some gray, and years of working outdoors had weathered her skin.

"Welcome back, Rose," she said, standing up at my approach. She certainly didn't hug me, and her manner was businesslike, but the fact that she used my first name was a generous gesture for her. That, and I thought I saw a small spark of relief and happiness in her eyes. "Let's go to my office."

I'd never been there. Any disciplinary issues I had with the guardians were usually addressed in committee. Unsurprisingly, the office was spotless, everything arranged with military efficiency. We sat on opposite sides of her desk, and I braced myself for an interrogation.

"Rose," she said, leaning toward me. "I'm going to be blunt with you. I'm not going to give you lectures or demand any explanations. Honestly, since you aren't my student anymore, I don't have the right to ask or tell you anything."

It was like what Adrian had said. "You can lecture," I told her. "I've always respected you and want to hear what you have to say."

The ghost of a smile flashed on her face. "All right, here it is. You screwed up."

"Wow. You weren't kidding about bluntness."

"The reasons don't matter. You shouldn't have left. You shouldn't have dropped out. Your education and training are too valuable — no matter how much you think you know — and *you* are too talented to risk throwing away your future."

I almost laughed. "To tell you the truth? I'm not sure what my future is anymore."

"Which is why you need to graduate."

"But I dropped out."

She snorted. "Then drop back in!"

"I — what? How?"

"With paperwork. Just like everything else in the world."

To be honest, I hadn't known what I'd do once I got back here. My immediate concern was Lissa — to be with her and make sure she was okay. I knew I couldn't officially be her guardian anymore, but I'd figured once we were together, no one could stop her from hanging out with a friend. I'd be her hired bodyguard, so to speak, kind of like what Abe had. And in the meantime, I'd bum around campus like Adrian.

But to enroll again?

"I . . . I missed a month. Maybe more." My days were scattered. It was the first week of May, and I'd left near the end of March, on my birthday. What was that? Five weeks? Almost six?

"You missed two years and managed to catch up. I have faith in you. And even if you have trouble, graduating with low grades is better than not graduating at all."

I tried to imagine myself back in this world. Had it really only been a little over a month? Classes . . . day-to-day intrigue . . . how could I just go back to that? How could I return to that life after seeing the way Dimitri's family lived, after being with Dimitri and losing him — again.

*Would he have said he loved me?*

"I don't know what to say," I told Alberta. "This is kind of a lot to take in."

"Well, you should decide quickly. The sooner you're back in class, the better."

"They'll really let me?" That was the part I found a little unbelievable.

"*I'll* let you," she said. "No way am I letting someone like you get away. And now that Lazar is gone . . . well, things are crazy around here. No one's going to give me much trouble in filing the paperwork." Her wry smile slipped a little. "And if they do give us any trouble . . . I've been made to understand that you have a benefactor who can pull a few favors to smooth everything over."

"A benefactor," I repeated flatly. "A benefactor who wears flashy scarves and gold jewelry?"

She shrugged. "No one I know. Don't even know his name — only that he'll threaten to withhold a considerable donation to the school if you aren't let back in. *If* you want in."

Yeah. Deals and blackmail. I was pretty sure I knew who my benefactor was. "Give me some time to think about it. I'll decide soon — I promise."

She frowned, thoughtful, and then gave a sharp nod. "All right."

We both stood up, and she walked me toward the building's entrance. I glanced over at her. "Hey, if I do graduate . . . do you think there's ever any way I could be in line to be Lissa's guardian officially again? I know they've already picked out people for her and that I'm in, ah, a bit of disgrace."

We stopped by the outer doors, and Alberta rested a hand on her hip. "I don't know. We can certainly try. The situation's gotten a lot more complicated."

"Yeah, I know," I said sadly, recalling Tatiana's high-handed actions.

"But, like I said, we'll do what we can. What I said about graduating with low grades? You won't. Well, maybe in math and science — but that's out of my control. You'll be the best among the novices, though. I'll work with you myself."

"Okay," I said, realizing what a concession that was on her part. "Thank you."

I had just stepped outside when she called my name. "Rose?"

I caught the door and glanced back. "Yeah?"

Alberta's face was gentle . . . something I'd never seen before. "I'm sorry," she said. "Sorry for everything that happened. And that none of us could do anything about it."

I saw in her eyes then that she knew about Dimitri and me. I wasn't sure how. Maybe she'd heard it after the battle; maybe she'd guessed beforehand. Regardless, there was no chastisement in her face, only sincere sorrow and empathy. I gave her a brief nod of acknowledgment and went outside.

I found Christian the next day, but our conversation was brief. He was on his way to meet with some of his trainees and was running late. But he hugged me and seemed genuinely happy to have me back. It showed how far we'd come, considering the antagonistic relationship we'd had when we first met.

"About time," he said. "Lissa and Adrian get the market share on worrying about you, but they're not the only ones. And someone needs to put Adrian in his place, you know. I can't do it *all* the time."

"Thanks. It kills me to say this, but I missed you too. No one's sarcasm compares to yours in Russia." My amusement faded. "But since you mentioned Lissa —"

"No, no." He held up his hand by way of protest, face hardening. "I *knew* you were going to go there."

"Christian! She loves you. You know that what happened wasn't her fault —"

"I know that," he interrupted. "But it doesn't mean it didn't hurt. Rose, I know it's in your nature to rush in and say what everyone else is afraid to, but please . . . not this time. I need time to figure things out."

I had to bite back a lot of comments. Lissa had mentioned Christian in our talk yesterday. What had happened between them was one of her biggest regrets — probably the thing she hated Avery the most for. Lissa wanted to approach him and make up, but he'd kept his distance. And yes, he was right. It wasn't my place to rush in — yet. But I did need them to fix this.

So I respected his wishes and simply nodded. "Okay. For now."

My last words made his smile twist a little. "Thanks. Look, I've got to head off. If you ever want to show these kids how to kick ass the old-fashioned way, come by sometime. Jill would pass out if she saw you again."

I told him I would and let him go on his way, seeing as I had places to be. No way was I finished with him, though.

I had a dinner date with Adrian and Lissa, up in one of the lounges in guest housing. Talking to Christian had made me late, and I hurried through the building's lobby, barely taking note of my surroundings.

"Always in a rush," a voice said. "It's a wonder anyone can get you to stop moving."

I came to a halt and turned, my eyes wide. "Mom . . ."

She stood leaning against the wall, arms crossed, with her cropped auburn hair as curly and messy as ever. Her face, weathered like Alberta's from being out in the elements, was filled with relief and — love. There was no anger, no condemnation. I had never been so happy to see her in my life. I was in her arms in an instant, resting my head on her chest even though she was shorter than me.

"Rose, Rose," she said into my hair. "Don't ever do this again. Please."

I pulled back and looked at her face, astonished to see tears spilling from her eyes. I had seen my mother tear up in the wake of the attack on the school, but never, never had I seen her outright cry. Certainly not over me. It made me want to cry too, and I uselessly tried to dry her face with Abe's scarf.

"No, no, it's okay. Don't cry," I said, taking on an odd role reversal. "I'm sorry. I won't do it again. I missed you so much."

It was true. I loved Olena Belikova. I thought she was kind and wonderful and would cherish the memories of her comforting me about Dimitri and always going out of her way to feed me. In another life, she could have been my mother-in-law. In this one, I would always regard her as a kind of foster mother.

But she wasn't my *real* mother. Janine Hathaway was. And standing there with her, I was happy — so, so happy — that I was her daughter. She wasn't perfect, but no one was, as I was learning. She was, however, good and brave and fierce and compassionate — and I think she understood me more than I realized sometimes. If I could be half the woman she was, my life would be well spent.

"I was so worried," she told me, recovering herself. "Where did you go — I mean, I know now you were in Russia . . . but why?"

"I thought . . ." I swallowed and again saw Dimitri with my stake in his chest. "Well, there was something I had to do. I thought I had to do it on my own." I wasn't sure about that last part now. True, I had accomplished my goal on my own, but I was realizing now how many people loved me and were with me. Who knew how differently things might have turned out if I'd asked for help? Maybe it would have been easier.

"I have a lot of questions," she warned.

Her voice had toughened, and I smiled in spite of myself. Now she was back to the Janine Hathaway I knew. And I loved her for it. Her eyes flitted to my face and then to my neck, and I saw her stiffen. For a panicked moment, I wondered if Oksana had missed healing one of the bite marks. The thought of my mother seeing what I'd lowered myself to in Siberia made my heart stop.

Instead, she reached out and touched the bright colors of the cashmere scarf, her face filled with wonder as much as shock. "This . . . this is Ibrahim's scarf . . . it's a family heirloom. . . ."

"No, it belongs to this mobster guy named Abe. . . ."

I stopped as soon as the name crossed my lips. Abe. Ibrahim. Hearing them both out loud made me realize how similar they were. Abe . . . Abe was short for Abraham in English. Abraham, Ibrahim. There was only a slight variation in the vowels. Abraham was a common enough name in the U.S., but I'd heard Ibrahim only once before, spoken in scorn by Queen Tatiana when referring to someone my mother had been involved with. . . .

"Mom," I said disbelievingly. "You know Abe."

She was still touching the scarf, eyes filled with emotion once more — but a different kind than she'd had for me. "Yes, Rose. I know him."

"Please don't tell me . . ." Oh, man. Why couldn't I have been an illegitimate half-royal like Robert Doru? Or even the mailman's daughter? "Please don't tell me Abe is my father. . . ."

She didn't have to tell me. It was all over her face, her expression dreamily recalling some other time and place — some time and place that had undoubtedly involved my conception. Ugh.

"Oh God," I said. "I'm Zmey's daughter. Zmey Junior. Zmeyette, even."

That got her attention. She looked up at me. "What on earth are you talking about?"

"Nothing," I said. I was stunned, trying desperately to assimilate this new piece of data into my worldview. I summoned a picture of that sly, bearded face, trying to hunt down family resemblance. Everyone said my facial features were like my mom's when she was younger . . . but my coloring, the dark hair and eyes . . . yes, that was the same as Abe's. I'd always known my father was Turkish. That was Abe's mystery accent, the one not Russian but still foreign to my ears. Ibrahim must be the Turkish version of Abraham.

"How?" I asked. "How in the world did

you get involved with someone like that?"

She looked offended. "Ibrahim is a wonderful man. You don't know him like I do."

"Obviously." I hesitated. "Mom . . . you must know. What is it that Abe does for a living?"

"He's a businessman. And he knows and does favors for a lot of people, which is why he has the influence he does."

"But what kind of business? I've heard it's illegal. It's not . . . oh God. Please tell me he isn't selling blood whores or something."

"What?" She looked shocked. "No. Of course not."

"But he is doing illegal things."

"Who's to say? He's never actually been *caught* for anything illegal."

"I swear, you almost sounded like you were trying to make a joke." I never would have expected her to defend a criminal, but I knew better than most how love could drive us to crazy acts.

"If he wants to tell you, he'll tell you. End of story, Rose. Besides, you certainly keep your share of secrets too. You two have a lot in common."

"Are you kidding? He's arrogant, sarcastic, likes to intimidate people, and — oh." Okay. Maybe she had a point.

A small half-smile played upon her lips. "I

never really expected you to meet this way. I never expected you to meet, period. We both thought it'd be best if he wasn't in your life."

A new thought occurred to me. "It was you, wasn't it? You hired him to find me."

"What? I contacted him when you went missing . . . but I certainly didn't hire him."

"Then who did?" I wondered. "He said he was working for someone."

Her lovestruck, reminiscent smile turned wry. "Rose, Ibrahim Mazur doesn't work for anyone. He's not the kind of person you can hire."

"But he said . . . wait. Why was he following me? Are you saying he was lying?"

"Well," she admitted, "it wouldn't be the first time. If he was following you, it wasn't because anyone was making him or paying him. He did it because he *wanted* to. He wanted to find you and make sure you were okay. He made sure all his contacts knew to look out for you."

I replayed my brief history with Abe. Shadowy, taunting, infuriating. But he'd driven out into the night to get me when I'd been attacked, been adamant in his goal to get me back to school and safety, and had apparently gifted me with an heirloom because he thought I'd get cold on my way

621

home. *He's a wonderful man,* my mother had said.

I supposed there were worse fathers to have.

"Rose, there you are. What's taking so long?" My mom and I turned as Lissa entered the lobby, her face lighting up when she saw me. "Come on — both of you. The food's going to get cold. And you won't believe what Adrian got."

My mom and I exchanged a quick look, neither of us needing to speak. We had a long conversation ahead of us, but it would have to wait.

I have no idea how Adrian had arranged it, but when we got to the lounge, there was Chinese food set up. The Academy almost never served it, and even then, it just never tasted . . . right. But this was the good stuff. Bowls and bowls of sweet-and-sour chicken and egg foo young. In a corner garbage can, I saw some restaurant takeout cartons with an address in Missoula printed on the side.

"How the hell did you get that here?" I demanded. Not only that, it was still warm.

"Don't question these things, Rose," said Adrian, loading up his plate with porkfried rice. He seemed very pleased with himself. "Just roll with it. Once Alberta gets your paperwork settled, we'll eat like this every day."

I stopped mid-bite. "How do you know about that?"

He merely winked. "When you have nothing to do but hang out on campus all the time, you kind of pick things up."

Lissa glanced between the two of us. She'd been in class all day, and we hadn't had much time to talk. "What's this?"

"Alberta wants me to enroll again and graduate," I explained.

Lissa nearly dropped her plate. "Then do it!"

My mother looked equally startled. "She'll let you?"

"That's what she told me," I said.

"Then do it!" my mother exclaimed.

"You know," mused Adrian, "I kind of liked the idea of us going on the road together."

"Whatever," I shot back. "You probably wouldn't let me drive."

"Stop this." My mother was firmly back to her old self, no grief over her daughter's departure or wistfulness for a lost lover. "You need to take this seriously. Your future's at stake." She nodded toward Lissa. "Her future's at stake. Finishing your education here and going on to be a guardian is the —"

"Yes," I said.

"Yes?" she asked, puzzled.

I smiled. "Yes, I agree."

"You agree . . . with me?" I don't think my mom could ever recall that happening. Neither could I, for that matter.

"Yup. I'll take the trials, graduate, and become as respectable a member of society as I can. Not that it sounds like much fun," I teased. I kept my tone light, but inside, I knew I needed this. I needed to be back with people who loved me. I needed a new purpose, or else I would never get over Dimitri. I would never stop seeing his face or hearing his voice.

Beside me, Lissa gasped and clasped her hands together. Her joy flooded into me. Adrian didn't wear his emotions as openly, but I could see he too was pleased at having me around. My mom still looked kind of stunned. I think she was used to me being unreasonable — which, usually, I was.

"You'll really stay?" she asked.

"Good God." I laughed. "How many times do I have to say it? Yes, I'll go back to school."

"And *stay?*" she prompted. "The full two and a half months?"

"Isn't that implied?"

Her face was hard — and very momlike. "I want to know for sure you aren't going to up and run away again. You'll stay and finish school no matter what? Stay until you graduate? Do you promise?"

I met her eyes, surprised at her intensity. "Yes, yes. I promise."

"Excellent," she said. "You'll be glad you did this down the road." Her words were guardian-formal, but in her eyes, I saw love and joy.

We finished dinner and helped stack dishes for the building's cleaning service. While scraping uneaten food into a trash can, I felt Adrian beside me.

"This is very domestic of you," he said. "It's kind of hot, really. Giving me all sorts of fantasies about you in an apron vacuuming my house."

"Oh, Adrian, how I've missed you," I said with an eye roll. "I don't suppose you're helping?"

"Nah. I helped when I ate everything on my plate. No mess that way." He paused. "And yes, you're welcome."

I laughed. "You know, it's a good thing you didn't say much when I promised Mom I'd stay here. I might have decided otherwise."

"Not sure if you could have stood up to

her. Your mom seems like someone who gets her way a lot." He cast a covert look to where Lissa and my mom stood talking across the room. He lowered his voice. "It must run in the family. In fact, maybe I should get her help on something."

"Getting a hold of illegal cigarettes?"

"Asking her daughter out."

I nearly dropped the plate I held. "You've asked me out tons of times."

"Not really. I've made inappropriate suggestions and frequently pushed for nudity. But I've never asked you out on a real date. And, if memory serves, you did say you'd give me a fair chance once I let you clean out my trust fund."

"I didn't clean it out," I scoffed.

But standing there, looking at him, I remembered that I had said that if I survived my quest for Dimitri, I'd give Adrian a shot. I would have said anything to get the money I needed then, but now, I saw Adrian through new eyes. I wasn't ready to marry him by any stretch of the imagination, nor did I fully consider him reliable boyfriend material. I didn't even know if I wanted a boyfriend ever. But he had been a good friend to me and everyone else throughout all of this chaos. He'd been kind and steady, and yeah, I couldn't deny it . . . even with a fading black eye, he was still extraordinarily handsome.

And while it shouldn't have mattered, Lissa had gotten it out from him that a lot of his infatuation with Avery had been compulsion-induced. He'd liked her and hadn't been ruling out a romantic attachment, but her powers had cranked up the intensity more than he actually felt. Or so he claimed. *If I were a guy and all that had happened to me, I'd probably say I'd been under the influence of magic too.*

Yet from the way he looked at me now, I found it hard to believe anyone had taken my place for him in this last month or so.

"Make me an offer," I said at last. "Write it up, and give me a point-by-point outline of why you're a good would-be suitor."

He started to laugh, then saw my face. "Seriously? That's like homework. There's a reason I'm not in college."

I snapped my fingers. "Get to it, Ivashkov. I want to see you put in a good day's work."

I expected a joke or a brush-off until later, but instead, he said, "Okay."

"Okay?" Now I felt like my mom had earlier, when I'd quickly agreed with her.

"Yep. I'm going to go back to my room right now to start drafting my assignment."

I stared incredulously as he reached for

his coat. I had *never* seen Adrian move that fast when any kind of labor was involved. Oh no. What had I gotten myself into?

He suddenly paused and reached into his coat pocket with an exasperated smile. "Actually, I already practically wrote you an essay. Nearly forgot." He produced a piece of folded paper and waved it in the air. "You have got to get your own phone. I'm not going to be your secretary anymore."

"What is that?"

"Some foreign guy called me earlier . . . said my number was in his phone's memory." Again, Adrian eyed Lissa and my mom. They were still deep in conversation. "He said he had a message for you and didn't want me to tell anyone else. He made me write it out and read it back to him. You're the only person I'd do that for, you know. I think I'm going to mention it when I write up my dating proposal."

"Will you just hand it over?"

He gave me the note with a wink, sketched me a bow, and then said goodbye to Lissa and my mom. I kind of wondered if he really was going to go write up a dating proposal. Mostly, my attention was on the note. I had no doubt who had called him. I'd used Abe's phone to dial Adrian in Novosibirsk and had later told Abe about

Adrian's financial involvement in my trip. Apparently, my father — ugh, that was still an unreal thought — had decided that made Adrian trustworthy, though I wondered why my mom couldn't have been used as a messenger.

I unfolded the note, and it took me a few seconds to decipher Adrian's writing. If he did write me a dating proposal, I really hoped he would type it. The note read:

Sent a message to Robert's brother. He told me there was nothing I could offer that would make him reveal Robert's location — and believe me, I have much to offer. But he said as long as he had to spend the rest of his life in there, then the information would die with him. Thought you'd like to know.

It was hardly the essay Adrian had made it out to be. It was also a bit cryptic, but then, Abe wouldn't want its contents easily understandable to Adrian. To me, the meaning was clear. Robert's brother was Victor Dashkov. Abe had somehow gotten a message to Victor in whatever horrible, remote prison he was locked away in. (Somehow, it didn't surprise me that Abe could pull that off.) Abe had no doubt attempted one of his trades with Victor in order to find out where Robert was, but Victor had refused. No surprise there either. Victor wasn't the most helpful of people, and I couldn't entirely blame him now. The guy was locked up for life "in there" — in prison. What could anyone offer a condemned man that would really make a difference in his life?

I sighed and put the note away, somehow touched that Abe had done this for me, as futile as it was. And again, the same argument came to mind. Even if Victor had given up Robert's location, what did it matter? The farther I got from the events in Russia, the more ridiculous it became to even consider turning a Strigoi back to his original form. Only true death could free them, only death . . .

My mom's voice saved me before I could begin reliving the bridge scene once more in my head. She told me she had to leave but promised we'd talk later. As soon as she was gone, Lissa and I made sure everything was set in the lounge before heading off to my room. She and I still had a lot of talking to do too. We went upstairs, and I wondered when they'd move me out of guest housing and back to the dorm. Probably whenever Alberta finished with the red tape. It still seemed impossible to accept that I was going to be able to return to my old life and move on from all that had happened in the last month or so.

"Did Adrian give you a love note?" Lissa asked me. Her voice was teasing, but through the bond, I knew she still worried about me grieving for Dimitri.

"Not yet," I said. "I'll explain later."

Outside my room, one of the building attendants was just about to knock on the door. When she saw me, she held out a thick padded envelope. "I was just bringing this to you. It arrived in today's mail."

"Thanks," I said.

I took it from her and looked at it. My name and St. Vladimir's address were printed in neat writing, which I found odd, since my arrival here had been sudden. There was no return address, but it bore Russian postmarks and delivery through global overnight mail.

"Do you know who it's from?" Lissa asked once the woman was gone.

"I don't know. I met a lot of people in Russia." It could have been from Olena, Mark, or Sydney. Yet . . . something I couldn't quite explain set my senses on high alert.

I tore open one side and reached in. My hand closed around something cold and metallic. I knew before I even pulled it out what it was. It was a silver stake.

"Oh God," I said

I rolled the stake around, running my finger over the engraved geometric pattern at its base. There was no question. One-of-a-kind. This was the stake I'd taken from the vault in Galina's house. The one I'd —

"Why would someone send you a stake?" asked Lissa.

I didn't answer and instead pulled out the envelope's next item: a small note card. There, in handwriting I knew all too well, was:

You forgot another lesson: Never turn your back until you know your enemy is dead. Looks like we'll have to go over the lesson again the next time I see you — which will be soon.

Love, D.

"Oh," I said, nearly dropping the card. "This is not good."

The world spun for a moment, and I closed my eyes, taking a deep breath. For the hundredth time, I ran through the events of the night I'd escaped from Dimitri. Every other time, my emotions and attention were always on the look on his face when I stabbed him, the sight of his body falling into that black water. Now my mind summoned up the details of the struggle. I recalled how his last-minute dodge had interfered with my shot at his heart. For a moment out there, I hadn't thought I'd gotten the stake in hard enough — until I'd seen his face go slack and watched him fall.

But I really *hadn't* gotten the stake in hard enough. My first instinct had been right, but things had happened too fast. He'd fallen . . . and then what? Had the stake been loose enough to fall out on its own? Had he been able to pull it out? Had the river's impact knocked it out?

"All those practice dummies, all for nothing," I muttered, recalling how Dimitri had drilled me over and over to plunge a stake into the chest so it would get past the ribs and into the heart.

"Rose," exclaimed Lissa. I had a feeling this wasn't the first time she'd said my name. "What's going on?"

The most important staking of my life . . . and I had messed it up. What would happen now? *Looks like we'll have to go over the lesson again the next time I see you — which will be soon.*

I didn't know what to feel. Despair that I

hadn't released Dimitri's soul and fulfilled the promise I'd secretly made to him? Relief that I hadn't killed the man I loved? And always, always that question: Would he have said he loved me if we'd had a few moments more?

I still had no answers. My emotions were running crazy, and I needed to put them on hold and analyze what I knew here.

First: two and a half months. I'd promised my mom two and a half months. No action until then.

Meanwhile, Dimitri was still out there, still a Strigoi. As long as he was loose in the world, there would be no peace for me. No closure. Looking at that card again, I realized I would have no peace even if I tried to ignore him. I understood the card's message.

Dimitri was coming for *me* this time. And something told me that I had blown my chance at being turned Strigoi. He was coming to kill me. What had he said when I escaped the manor? That there was no way we could both be alive in the world?

And yet, maybe we could. . . .

When I didn't answer her right away, Lissa's worry grew. "Your face is freaking me out a little. What are you thinking?"

"Do you believe in fairy tales?" I asked,

looking up into her eyes. Even as I said the words, I could imagine Mark's disapproval.

"What . . . what kind of fairy tales?"

"The kind you aren't supposed to waste your life on."

"I don't understand," she said. "I'm totally lost. Tell me what's going on. What can I do?"

Two and a half months. I had to stay here for two and a half months — it seemed like forever. But I'd promised my mom that I would, and I refused to be rash again — particularly with the stakes so high now. Promises. I was drowning in promises. I'd even promised Lissa something.

"Did you mean it before? You want to go with me on my next crazy quest? No matter what?"

"Yes." There was no uncertainty or hesitation in the word, no wavering in her steady green eyes. Of course, I wondered if she'd feel the same way later when she found out what it was we were going to do.

*What could anyone offer a condemned man that would really make a difference in his life?*

I'd pondered that earlier, trying to figure out what could get Victor Dashkov to talk. Victor had told Abe there was nothing anyone could offer that would make him give up the information about his brother's alleged ability to restore Strigoi. Victor was serving a life sentence; no bribe could matter to him anymore. But one thing could, I realized. Freedom. And there was only one way to achieve that.

We were going to have to break Victor Dashkov out of prison.

But I decided not to mention that to Lissa quite yet.

All I knew for now was that I had a fleeting shot at saving Dimitri. Mark had said it was a fairy tale, but I had to take the chance. The question was: how long did I have until Dimitri came to kill me? How long did I have to figure out if the impossible was actually possible? That was the real issue. Because if Dimitri showed up before I had a chance to find the dragon in this story — Victor — things were going to get ugly. Maybe this whole Robert thing was one big lie, but even if it wasn't . . . well, the clock was ticking. If Dimitri came for me before I could get to Victor and Robert, I'd have to fight him again. No question. I couldn't wait for this magical cure. I'd have to kill Dimitri for real this time and lose any chance I might have to bring back my prince. Damn.

It's a good thing I work well under pressure.

Thank you so much to all of the friends and family who have supported me and helped keep me sane while writing this book. You mean the world to me, and I'm grateful to you guys for actually getting me to leave my office once in a while! Special thanks also to Jay for convincing me this was his favorite book (before it was even written); to Jesse McGatha for helping conceive the Alchemists; to my agent, Jim McCarthy, for having my back and making all this possible; to editors Jessica Rothenberg and Ben Schrank for always working to perfect the manuscript; to I. A. Gordon for "Zmey" and other Russian translation; and to publicist Casey McIntyre for her wonderful promo help.

Finally, thank you also to the many readers who have e-mailed and talked to me about their love for the series and the characters! You're the reason I keep writing.

# ABOUT THE AUTHOR

**Richelle Mead** is the author of the *New York Times* and *USA Today* bestselling Vampire Academy series.

A lifelong reader, Richelle has always had a particular fascination with mythology and folklore. When she can actually tear herself away from books (either reading or writing them), she enjoys bad reality TV, traveling, trying interesting cocktails, and shopping for dresses that she then hardly ever wears. She is a self-professed coffee addict, runs on a nocturnal schedule, and has a passion for all things wacky and humorous. Originally from Michigan, Richelle now lives in Seattle, Washington, where she is hard at work on her next novel.

Visit www.RichelleMead.com to find out more.

The employees of Thorndike Press hope you have enjoyed this Large Print book. All our Thorndike, Wheeler, and Kennebec Large Print titles are designed for easy reading, and all our books are made to last. Other Thorndike Press Large Print books are available at your library, through selected bookstores, or directly from us.

For information about titles, please call:
  (800) 223-1244

or visit our Web site at:
  http://gale.cengage.com/thorndike

To share your comments, please write:
Publisher
Thorndike Press
10 Water St., Suite 310
Waterville, ME 04901

dn, ln